Praise for Scott Spencer an

"In Spencer's new novel, an act of murder goes ... like something toxic in the lives of the characters. . . . Harrowing. . . . Spencer takes his model of the modern couple and uses a chance moment of violence to ask what they—and, by extension, we—are made of, to reveal the vagaries of personal conviction, the fragility of faith in ourselves and in a higher power."
— *New York Times Book Review*

"We don't often encounter novels that combine shrewd plotting, strong characters and gorgeous writing, but Scott Spencer's *Man in the Woods* does precisely that. . . . This is a book to savor and read aloud, a book that is variously wise, funny and heartbreaking. . . . The outcome must not be revealed here, except to say that it is as powerful as everything else in the book. *Man in the Woods* is one of three best novels I've read this year . . . and if you pressed me, I'd put it at the top of the list."
— *Washington Post*

"This beautifully written novel is so much more than just a good read."
— *USA Today*

"[Spencer] writes love stories with such beauty that you want to savor every surprising phrase, but his intense, intriguing plots propel you to race along the pages. He does it again in his new book, a complex novel about what happens to a couple when the man, Paul Phillips, impulsively decides to stop a stranger from beating his dog. Spencer maintains his mastery through the book's final pages, where the thrumming tension reaches a conclusion that is—what? Inevitable? Surprising? Hopeful? The choice will depend on the reader's own view of the world, but you should expect to come out of the woods shaken, and satisfied."
— *Cleveland Plain Dealer*

"Spencer's thriller-like plot, beautifully narrated, about an ordinary man in deep trouble, offers the reader vivid characters and believable action doled out in good prose. You might describe it as *Crime and Punishment* in upstate New York."
— National Public Radio, Alan Cheuse's Best Books of Winter 2010

"Spencer has shown a powerful understanding of the price of passion. In this one, he explores the even more treacherous terrain of guilt, expiation, and longed-for salvation."   —*O, the Oprah Magazine*

"This is a book poised to take its place as an American classic."
        —HuffingtonPost.com

"Spencer, a master of piercing insight and letter-perfect prose, tantalizes to the last climactic sentence of this compelling exploration of the wages of guilt."   —*Booklist* (starred review)

"[A] compelling setup and stunning conclusion. . . . The depth of the characters, the questions they ask and the challenge they confront stay with the reader long after the conclusion."   —*Kirkus Reviews* (starred review)

"No one writes more insightfully or more entertainingly about our deepest connections with lovers, family and friends, with our children and communities. But in this brilliant novel, Scott Spencer further expands his range to embrace our relations with animals—with the loyal pets that consent to share our domestic lives, and with the darker, more alarming beasts that lurk within even the most compassionate and conscious human beings."   —Francine Prose

"A smart, haunting thriller with bass reverb and a pounding heart, *Man in the Woods* takes the reader deep inside the ever-widening mystery of human connection and animal need. Always a magician, Scott Spencer transforms an eight-thousand-dollar gambling debt and a dog with two names into an enthralling literary ride, tightening the tension with every dazzling line. Spencer is an American master: *Man in the Woods* holds the lightning-strike power of the past and the sudden confluence of fate and love in its powerful grip."   —Jayne Anne Phillips, author of National Book Award finalist *Lark and Termite*

"*Man in the Woods* reveals the talent and confidence of a master storyteller at the top of his game. Written with surgical precision as well as heartbreaking insights into the dark frailties of human nature, Scott Spencer holds the reader to his terrifying account every step of the way. A page-turner from beginning to end."
        —Rudy Wurlitzer, author of *The Drop Edge of Yonder*

MAN IN THE WOODS

An *Imprint of* HarperCollins*Publishers*

MAN IN THE WOODS

SCOTT SPENCER

HarperCollins books may be purchased for educational, business, or sales promotional use. For information please write: Special Markets Department, HarperCollins Publishers, 10 East 53rd Street, New York, NY 10022.

A hardcover edition of this book was published in 2010 by Ecco, an imprint of HarperCollins Publishers.

Scott Spencer interview courtesy of *Fresh Air with Terry Gross*. *Fresh Air with Terry Gross* is produced at WHYY in Philadelphia, and distributed by NPR.

FIRST ECCO PAPBERBACK EDITION PUBLISHED 2011.

Designed by Suet Yee Chong

Tree photography © iStockphoto.com/Ricardas Jasakas

Library of Congress Cataloging-in-Publication Data has been applied for.

ISBN 978-0-06-146657-1

11 12 13 14 15   OV/RRD   10 9 8 7 6 5 4 3 2 1

PART I

The beast in me is caged by frail and fragile bars.

—Johnny Cash

CHAPTER
ONE

It might be for pity's sake—for surely there must be pity for Will Claff somewhere along the cold curve of the universe—but now and again a woman finds him compelling, and offers him a meal, a caress, a few extra dollars, and a place to stay, and lately that is the main thing keeping him alive. He is thousands of miles away from his home. His income, his job, his professional reputation are all long gone, and now he has been on the run for so long, living out of one suitcase, changing his name once in Minnesota, once in Highland Park, Illinois, and once again in Philadelphia, that it is becoming difficult to remember that just six months ago he had his own office, a closet full of suits, and a nice rental off Ventura Boulevard, which he shared with Madeline Powers, who, like Will, worked as an accountant at Bank of America.

He used to think that women wouldn't pay you any attention unless you were dressed in decent clothes and had some money to spend, but it isn't true. He has been underestimating the kindness of women. Women are so nice, it could make you ashamed to be a man.

Here he was, running for his life, buying his shirts at the dollar store, his shoes at Payless, and getting his hair cut at the Quaker Corner Barber and Beauty College in Philadelphia. Will had a guardian angel there, too, in the form of Dinah Maloney, whom he met while she was jogging with her dog. Dinah, small and bony, with short russet hair, worried eyes, and nervous little hands, was thirty years old, ten years younger than Will, and she happened to take a breather on the same bench he was sitting on, and somewhere in the conversation, when she told him that she owned a catering service called Elkins Park Gourmet, he said, "You should call it Someone's in the Kitchen with Dinah," and saw in her eyes something that gave him a little bump of courage. He invited her to coffee at a place with outdoor seating, and they sat there for an hour with her dog lashed to the leg of a chair. He told her the same story he had already worked a couple of times—it might have been on Doris in Bakersfield, or Soo-Li in Colorado Springs, or Kirsten in Highland Park—about how he had come to town for a job, only to find that the guy who had hired him had hung himself with his own belt the day before. A lot of women didn't believe this story, and some who did couldn't figure out how that would mean he had almost no money and needed a place to stay, but a small, saving percentage took the story at face value, or decided to trust the good feeling they had about him. Dinah has turned out to be one of those.

She was a spiky, truculent sort, wary of customers, suppliers, and competitors, but ready to make Will (she knew him as Robert) the first man ever to spend the night in her house, partly because he seemed to find her attractive and partly on the weight of her dog's apparent trust of him. ("Woody is my emotional barometer," she said.) She was a shy, basically solitary woman, an expert in the culinary arts, a baker, a woman who gave off the scent of butter and vanilla, an arranger of flowers, all of which led Will to assume in her an old-fashioned faithfulness. He saw only her plainness, her lack of makeup, her loose-fitting checkered pants, her perforated tan clogs, the dark circles under her eyes from the late hours working corporate dinners and Main Line birthday parties, and he assumed that she had a lonely woman's lack of resistance to anyone who would choose her. He had no idea that Dinah had another boyfriend, whom she had been seeing for six years, one of the mayor's assistants, a married man whose wife worked in Baltimore on Tuesdays and Thursdays.

Will is grateful to be an American; he doubts there is anywhere else on earth where you can lose yourself like he needs to get lost, where you can just go from state to state, city to city, not like in cowboy times, but, still, no one has to know where you are. You can drive across a state line but it's only a line on the map and the tires of your car don't register the slightest bump. There's no guard, no gate, no border, no one asks you for an ID, because no one cares. First you are here, then you are there, until you're in Tarrytown, New York, and it's time for your afternoon jog. He's still trying to lose the belly fat acquired in the kitchen with Dinah.

The new apartment smells of emptiness, fresh paint, take-out coffee, and the dog, Woody, stolen from Dinah the day she finally came clean with him.

Will parts the blinds with two fingers and peeks out the window. The cars parked on his street are all familiar and he knows by now who owns each one. There's no one unusual walking the street, either. All very routine, all very familiar. He often reminds himself that the great danger is complacency, the way you can get so used to checking things over that the world becomes like wallpaper and you get too used to everything being nothing until one day when there actually is something unusual you don't even notice it. He goes over the compass points, north south east west. "The lion sleeps tonight," he sings, surprising himself. The sudden merriment excites the dog, a brown shepherd mutt, whose thick, graying tail thumps against the bare wooden floor. Will imagines the people in Mi Delicioso, the luncheonette downstairs, looking up from their yellow rice and chicken.

"Easy, Woody Woodpecker," he says. Will feels a rush of affection for the dog, and crouches in front of him, tugs the dog's ears roughly. Woody is large, but his ears look like they belong on a dog half his size. Considering the circumstances of Will's acquiring him, the dog has been a good sport about the whole thing. "You and me, Woody," Will says, taking the leash down from the nail next to the front door. The dog scrambles up, tail wagging, but with a cringing, uncertain quality to his excitement, squirming and bowing.

When the dog lived with Dinah Maloney in that dimly recalled paradise called Philadelphia, his life was markedly different. He had his own feather-filled bed on the floor and spent the coldest nights sleeping in his mistress's bed. Food was plentiful and there were frequent surprises—especially when she came home from work with shopping bags full of leftovers from whatever party she had catered. The inchoate memories the dog holds of the food, and the woman and the smells of the old house, live within him as bewilderment, but his heart and mind have now re-formed around the loss, just as he would compensate for an injured paw by changing his gait.

Will goes back to the window. It sometimes seems that he has been peeking out of windows his whole life, always afraid that someone or something was going to do a lot of harm to him, but everything that has led up to these past few months has been like a puppet show. The old fear was like an afternoon nap compared to what he feels now.

He yanks the cord to raise the blinds and they crookedly cooperate. He puts his hand to the glass. Cool November afternoon, gray as old bathwater. He misses the California sun and wishes he had soaked up more of it. *Oh well.* Best not to think of it. Self-pity dulls the senses.

Yet he does not consider it self-pity to bear in mind that even in his nearly invisible state, he is a target. What tempts him toward the siren song of self-pity is that it is not his fault. Back home in LA, he had a run of bad luck that turned into very bad luck that made a quantum leap to horrendous luck—a last second shot from a third-string forward, undrafted out of college, a heave from the mid-court line that clanged off the back of the rim, popped straight up in the air, and dropped down through the hoop, barely ruffling the net. There was nothing at stake in the late-season game, excepting, of course, the five thousand dollars Will placed on the Portland Trailblazers to beat the Clippers, an aggressive bet on his part, but when he got the morning line and saw the Clippers weren't even being given points, it seemed he was being offered a license to print money He would have bet more, if he could have, but he was already into his guy for three thousand dollars and five more was all the credit he could get. Not having bet more than 5K was the needle of good fortune he could find in the haystack of bad luck.

But this is what he knows: it all happens for a reason.

The thing is, he was a good gambler. He was sensible, cool-headed, and his bets were based on reality, not blue sky—even the bet on the Portland Trailblazers was smart, and he is sure that a lot of people who knew the game, were real students of the NBA, would have said it was a good bet. You *can* make a smart bet that doesn't pay off. Some clown heaving up a shot from half-court, some once-in-a-lifetime buzzer-beater? These things occur outside the arc of probability. It was still a good bet.

Except he couldn't pay it off. The man through whom Will used to place his bets was an old surfer, a Hawaiian named Tommy Butler. Will never quite got it how Butler figured into the scheme of things, if he was high up or peripheral to the organization, or if there even was an organization. When Butler told him Accounts Receivable was going to have to get involved—"This is automatic, man, when you get to a certain size debt and more than five days pass, it's not personal"—Will had no idea who was now in charge of collecting the money. That's what made it so agonizing—it could be anyone! Every car door, every footstep, every ring of the phone: it was a matter of anyone turning into everyone.

Someone is going to come looking for him, but Will doesn't know who. Someone is somewhere or will be sometime soon. So much mystery. But it all happens for a reason. Every detour, every zigzag, every stinking night in a shit-box motel, even this brown mutt—it's all adding up to something. He just doesn't know what, not yet. The trick is to still be around when the game is revealed.

Hiding out and lying low are not unnatural acts for Will. He doesn't need the creature comforts so important to others—the favorite robe, the favorite coffee cup, the favorite chair. What do things like that mean in comparison to survival? Survival is the main course, everything else is carrots and peas. As for hiding—it heightens the senses, like double overtime, or a photo finish.

Three weeks into his escape he had called Madeline, who was still living in his old apartment on Ventura, even though she had her own place. He was in Denver. It was about ten o'clock at night; he was using the phone booth next to a convenience store, two blocks from the motel where he was week by week. Two teenagers were playing a game, tossing a Rockies hat back and forth and trying to get it to land on the other guy's head. It was a thick, murky night, no moon, no stars, the sky just a bucket of black paint someone accidentally kicked over.

"Hey, it's me," he said, as soon as she picked up. He didn't want to use his name.

"My God, where are you?" Madeline had a low, beautiful voice; it used to make him feel pretty good just to hear it.

"Never mind that, I'm just letting you know."

"But where are you, I've been going crazy. How could you just do this?"

"I'm sorry. It was not exactly a planned thing."

"Okay, baby," she said. "I hear you. Okay. Just tell me where you are. Tell me exactly where you are."

It was then that it hit him—she was in on it, a part of it.

"Things cool there?" he asked her.

"Do you have any idea how this feels? Has anyone ever done something like this to you? Three weeks and you don't even call?"

"Well, I'm calling, but I gotta go."

"You gotta go where? This is nuts. Why don't you tell me what's going on? Where are you?"

Will felt his heart harden and shrink to walnut size. This call was a horrible mistake, but not for the reasons he had worried about. He would like to have carried fond memories of Madeline, but there she was, putting snakes in his garden. Who knew? Maybe they offered her a piece of whatever they got out of him.

"You know what?" she said. "Now I really need you to listen to this, baby, okay? Will you at least try and listen?" He had never heard her voice quite like that, like he was her kid and she was going to try to explain life to him.

"Go ahead," he said, daring her.

"Baby, this thing you're going through," she said. "It's all in your head. I know you took some losses and I know you've got debts and I'm pretty sure they're serious debts. But it's all gotten into your mind. You're really not seeing it clearly. I know it's a serious situation, but it's not all you're making it out to be. You don't need to be running and hiding like this. What do you think they're going to do to you? Kill you? How will they ever get their money? Break your arms and legs? How will you be able to work and make money that by the way would otherwise be going right into their pocket?"

"You mind if I ask you a question," he said to her. "Has anyone been by the place looking for me?"

"What are you talking about?" she said. "You want to know who's chasing you? You, you're chasing you!" By now her voice was rising so much that he held the phone away from his ear, wincing.

"Okay," he said, with exaggerated calm. "Let me ask you another question—how did you know I took some losses? I never said that to you. I am not the type of guy who goes around boo-hooing about his losses. How did you even know that?"

"Oh Jesus," she said, like she was crying or something. But why would she cry? She once told him that Paxil or whatever the drug she was on made it impossible for her to cry. So that had to be acting.

He wasn't sure how it all clicked together—it is something he still turns around and around, a Rubik's cube of motives and reasons and possibilities. Why would she do that to him? What would flip her?

He hung up the phone and forced himself to saunter. He walked past the hat punks and into the 7-Eleven, bought some chips and salsa and a bottle of diet grape soda, some local Colorado brand. All around the cash register, hanging down in colorful strips, were shiny lottery tickets printed up in bright comic-book colors—Pick 4, Powerball, sucker bets, pitiful little prayers for some impossible dream to come true, and though he had never bothered with lottery tickets the sight of them closed a door inside of him. With the bottle of grape soda sweating on the checkout counter, and the Mexican kid working the register counting out his change, Will realized he would never place another bet for as long as he lived.

"Okay," he says now to the dog, as he clips the leash to the metal choke collar. "We're going to do five miles, and we're going to go at a pretty good clip, no stopping, no squirrels, just straight ahead." Will pats the pocket of his tracksuit to make sure he's got his car keys and the apartment keys. He gives the choke collar a sharp tug to remind the dog who is in charge, which, he believes, ultimately makes the dog feel better about himself and his place in the scheme of things. The dog makes a little yelp of protest, which Will is quite sure is the dog's way of manipulating him. So as to not give ground, Will yanks the leash again, and the dog yelps again, and sits down, which makes Will feel terrible, though the dog's tail is still more or less wagging, so it still seems possible that the dog is just screwing with him.

CHAPTER
TWO

"Hey there," Kate Ellis calls out, shielding her eyes with a loose, left-handed salute against the askew aim of the spotlight.

"Hi there!" calls back a booming brocade of five hundred voices, their owners seated before her in church pews—this evening's talk was meant to be in a bookstore near Lincoln Center, but the turnout is so massive that the venue needed to be changed at the last minute.

"Ho there," Kate says, completing what has become her signature greeting. Kate thinks, *It's bad enough to copy someone else. What I'm doing is worse—I'm copying myself.*

The book she has been promoting all over the country—*Prays Well with Others*—began as a series of essays for *Wish*, the magazine with which she had forged a relationship during the O. J. Simpson trial. When the trial was over, her self-preservation instinct helped her stop drinking, and it also gave her a new subject—her pilgrim's progress toward a sober, God-loving life. Eventually there were enough essays to be gathered into a volume, and *Prays Well with Others* was published. Its success was not a total surprise—Kate had developed a following while writing the pieces for *Wish*. But the size and duration of the success were beyond anyone's expectations, and now Kate is no longer worried about money. She is sober. She is a good mother. She has learned how to pray without feeling like a faker or a mental case. There is a man in her life who adores her and whom she can love with a wholeheartedness she once thought impossible, a love that she once thought was as mythical as a unicorn. All this happiness! She sometimes feels unstable and afraid, as if standing in front of the chute to a slot machine that sends out a nonstop torrent of gold.

A microphone has been clipped to the nubby knit of Kate's sweater; the electronic transmitter nestles in the deep front pocket on her floor-length skirt. The toes of her boots flick in and out from beneath her hem like lizard tongues as she paces the pulpit between lectern and altar. Kate dresses for public appearances with considerable modesty, despite her handsomeness, as if it were her wish to have her slender build, dancer's grace, and the plain pioneer beauty of her face go somehow unnoticed. But she is unmistakably beautiful, and at no time more than now, radiantly in love.

It is chilly in the church; hot water hammers hollowly in the radiators, but there hasn't been enough time to warm the place for this impromptu gathering. Kate, still unnerved by the enthusiasm of her crowds, takes a deep, steadying breath. There are mainly women here, dressed for the November cold in knit caps, gloves, and overcoats. The scent of all that wet wool gives the place the smell of a stable full of sheep in for the night. Thunder groans from behind the dark blue stained glass, and a flash of lightning illuminates its cobalt universe. To her left is a statue of Saint George armed with an ax and a sword, his face as petulant and superior as an old baby doll's.

"Well thank you all for coming out on such a cruddy night," Kate says. "I'm . . . well, to be honest with you, I'm overwhelmed." This admission of vulnerability elicits applause from the crowd, and Kate colors, hoping that no one will think she is somehow fishing for an extra round of applause, and wondering, because that is her nature, if she might have in fact been doing just that.

A woman's voice, vigorous and clear, calls up from a side pew. "How's Ruby doing?"

Kate brings her hands prayerfully together, in a burlesque of piety that manages to be slightly pious nevertheless. "She's happy, she's beautiful, and guess what—she's reading!" This piece of good news brings forth cheers and applause. "Yes, God bless J. K. Rowling, the only author I'm not jealous of. We were going to bring Ruby down with us tonight, but she has her babysitter bewitched and she has just started in on *Harry Potter and the Prisoner of Azkaban*. She can read to herself but she likes to have someone in a chair nearby *watching her as she reads.*" Kate shakes her head. "I've tried to talk her out of this but she insists on it. I tell her, *Honey I can't just sit there while you read.* And then she tells me, *Mom, you used to sit in that chair for a real long time, not doing anything but sitting.* *Yes, my darling,* I tell her, *but it was easy then because Mommy was dead drunk.*"

There is a strained, uneasy quality to the laughter, which is oddly comforting to Kate. She has learned that people like to hear about her kind of Christianity, one that includes a fair amount of swearing and swagger, left-of-center politics, and all the sex your average heathen would enjoy. They like to hear you can be devout and still be angry, irreverent, a little selfish, even jealous and competitive. Her envy of a few other writers working the spiritual circuit creates surefire laugh lines. But what audiences don't always like to hear about is lax, careless mothering, and they certainly don't like to hear about drunken mothering, even if it is safely sequestered in the past and is part of a recovery narrative. It's just as well to Kate; universal acceptance seems like a sign of mediocrity; causing a little trouble and offending a few people here and there makes her feel more like herself.

"Ah, those were the days," she says. "I think Ruby misses some things about my drinking days. For instance, I used to have no idea they gave homework in her school, even in first grade." Kate scratches her head, looks confused, out of it. "So let me get this clear," she says in a tipsy slur, "they keep you in school all day and then send you home with more work to do at night? Oh honey-bunny, thass terrible, lemme make you a cocktail."

"Oh Kate? Kate darling?" A woman rises from the aisle seat of the front pew. She is not much taller than five feet and comfortably round. Her short brown hair is graying but her face is youthful, un-lined, and cheerful; she looks like someone who has devoted her life to poetry or music or to the welfare of others, and faces age now with a deep serenity. She wears dark glasses and holds a cane, but despite her blindness there is an aura of authority about her. "I want to welcome you here, Kate, and just to let you know how happy all of us are to have you with us tonight." As she speaks, the woman gestures with her white aluminum cane, waving it in an arc above her to indicate the entire audience. "And to commemorate this won-derful occasion," the blind woman says, in her resonant alto, "I want to tell you my poem."

Kate makes a bow in the woman's direction, and then, realizing her error, says, "How nice," but her own voice is a bit faltering be-cause she has been taken by surprise.

The woman taps out a steady beat with her cane against the church's wooden floor, and sways dreamily from side to side as she recites:

> Sing through me of the woman, Muse, the woman of
> wisdom and wit
> Who comes home to us as from a great journey
> Wherein she slew these many monsters
> The beast of doubt and the fiend of disbelief
> The sirens of wine and wantonness

The vampires of loneliness and the werewolves of fear
Her triumphal return is our triumph, too
The cheers for her are hosannas for us
Sing through me, sacred Muse, the story of Kate Ellis
We are but vines needing strong support, and she is
  our trellis

The woman ends with a salute in Kate's direction, and as the audience cheers lustily for her she soaks it up with unabashed delight, waving her cane and her free hand over her head. She blows a huge kiss in Kate's direction and it is not until the applause begins to die down that she takes her seat again.

"Wow," Kate says. "I am completely overwhelmed. Thank you. Thank you so much. May I ask you—what's your name?"

The woman doesn't seem to have heard the question. The fourteen-year-old boy sitting next to her—her son?—nudges her, whispers something to her. She makes a deep nod of understanding and calls out: "Julie, Julie Blackburn McCall."

"Thank you, Julie Blackburn McCall," Kate says, "and let me tell you that Ellis-trellis rhyme is going to stay with me a long while." Kate picks up *Prays Well with Others*, opens it to the bookmarked page. "Okay, people, I'm going to read about six pages, which will take somewhere between fourteen and fifteen minutes. I don't know about you, but I can't stand readings that go on for more than fifteen minutes. Then I can take questions, or comments, and I can ask you guys questions, and we'll just hang out, but when the clock strikes nine we have to wrap it up. Is that all right?" She smoothes the page down and takes a nervous drink from the bottle of water someone has left for her on the lectern.

The past few months of speaking to audiences have given Kate a confidence in her instincts that allows her to suddenly veer from prepared text into improvisation. "I'm obviously here to read from my book, and sign copies, and sell books. That goes without saying. But I just want to tell you . . ." She stops, breathes deeply; she has surprised herself with how emotional it makes her feel to say what she is about to say. "What I am, or what I want to be, is a messenger of hope. Hope, hope," and she says the words as if she were letting balloons slip from her hands and float up into the air. "Hope, what Emily Dickinson called *the thing with feathers.* I am here with a message of hope because I am here to tell you the most unexpected, astonishing things can happen in a life. I am here because whoever tells you that we are stuck in the mud of ourselves is a liar." She lays her hand over her breasts. "Forty years old, one novel that two people read, and a mini-career calling for O. J. Simpson's head on a pike—and now this." She holds up her book. "Forty years old and drunk on my ass, and now sober, one beautiful, way cool day at a time. Forty years old and then one day against all odds and expectations so into Jesus that most of my old friends think I'm ready for the funny farm, especially my liberal-progressive friends who fear that I've gone all pious and Pat Robertson on them. Or is it Pat Boone? Forty years, all of them spent as an emotional moderate—even at my own marriage ceremony, I insisted on saying *I'll try* rather than *I do*—and after I got sober, after I realized I was no longer in charge, after I finished my book, the next miracle arrived, which I do believe the love of Jesus prepared me for, which is the love of—and for!—a wonderful man. So that's my message of hope. If I can have these things, everyone else can, too. Remember this. Our lives make sense. There is a story, a story of creation and sacrifice and love—and we are all a part of that story." She pauses, clears her throat, tears up. This embarrasses her, but what can she do? She waves her hand in front of her eyes, drying them and mocking herself. "Anyhow, I better get to it, because truth be told my boyfriend doesn't like to stay up late." She looks as if she is about to begin reading, but she stops herself. "Here's another thing about my boyfriend," she says. "He's like the most old-fashioned man in the world—and when I say old-fashioned I don't mean Bob Dole or, I don't know, Bobby Short. I mean Daniel Boone or Davy Crockett. He shaves with a straight razor. He doesn't wait for the hot water to come on before he steps into the shower. He makes things with his hands. His beautiful hands. He can cook, he can sew. He can fix anything, and if he needs a tool he doesn't have he actually makes the tool. One other thing. He pays cash and he carries it in his front pocket. Now I see a guy taking his little credit card out of his wallet I find it . . . I don't know. It seems very girly. And writing a check? Forget it. You may as well be twirling a parasol."

In the tenth row, Paul Phillips, the man who came in with Kate, lowers his head and jams his hands into the pockets of his brown leather jacket. The few times Paul has observed Kate in her public life and witnessed the effect she has on people have been entertaining experiences. He is not unfamiliar with successful people, but he has never had a relationship with a woman of large and worldly achievement, and the pleasure it brings him to bask in the reflected glow of her success has been a surprise to Paul, with an unexpectedly erotic component. There is something grand about going home with a woman everybody loves. Heretofore his romantic life has mainly involved women who worked with their hands—potters, gardeners, weavers, carpenters like himself, and one chiropractor— or else winsome idlers living on the dregs of family fortunes. Despite the pleasure Kate's fame brings him, he is not prepared to become a part of her public life, and as those seated near him turn to look at him he feels not only embarrassment but a degree of irritation. The woman next to him, who, judging by her notebook and her tote bag, works for CBS, looks at him with professional curiosity. She is half-Asian and reminds Paul strongly of a woman he once worked for. A woman wearing a serape in a pew across the aisle gives Paul the thumbs-up sign and an elderly couple with cottony hair and merry blue eyes looks at him fondly.

There's nothing to be done about it, but a couple of hours later, in the hotel room Kate's publisher has secured for them, saving them the two-hour drive back upstate, Paul says to Kate, "When you talked about your boyfriend all those people were staring at me."

"No way," she says. She is in bed, trying to corral her ego and, for the most part, succeeding after the evening of adoration. "I was careful not to look in your direction."

"They knew it was me anyhow," Paul says. "There weren't that many men there."

He doesn't want to sound annoyed, especially not after a big night for her, and surely not in bed. A room service cart presents its own reasons for him to be of good cheer: a spray of orchids, a shrimp cocktail, a bowl of cut fruit. Even though this particular place is not really to Paul's taste, he has spent enough nights sleeping in unheated cabins, in tents, or on bed frames without mattresses to be forever mindful of creature comforts others might take for granted. But if you are in bed and you lean your head back, you ought to feel either the wall or wood, but Paul's head rests against the bed's upholstered headboard and though the softness is vaguely pleasant, upholstered headboards are suburban elegance, a cut or two above the padded toilet seat. Simplicity, durability, and reality are what please Paul, and all of these can be expressed by not hiding the materials out of which objects are made.

Most places in the city are ten degrees too warm for him, including this room, the closeness of which brings up bad memories. Now, while Kate is under the covers in her pale orange silk pajamas, and wearing socks to keep her feet warm, Paul is on top of the comforter, in nothing but his boxers.

"Look at you," Kate says, "stretched out like that." She runs her hand over his chest, down to his belly. "I hit the trifecta. Sobriety, faith, and now you." Her finger hooks under the elastic waist. "Off?"

Paul lifts his hips, takes off his shorts. His penis flops over to the left, his pubic hair glistens darkly. His chest is as smooth as a boy's, except for the kinky fringes around his nipples. Kate has a passing fancy to lick him. Instead, she reaches for a piece of mango and eats it. She often has quick, errant bursts of desire, some of them a bit outré, but marvelously so. Sometimes she feels a kind of erotic Tourette's and wants to say things she has never said to a lover, like *It's okay to be rough, if you want to, why don't you slap me on the ass and pull my hair.* She has yet to surrender to the temptation. What generally restrains her is not the imagination of the act itself but the shadow it would surely cast over everything that followed. How do you talk to someone after you have asked them if they would like to do some of the things that occur to her? The conversational pall would be crushing. Who could she be after, if she were to act out these impulses? It would be too much for daily life to bear, it could be neither absorbed nor forgotten.

"I'm feeling all seven of the deadly sins," Kate says, patting her cheeks, in an imitation of a Victorian lady overcome with the vapors. She is calming herself the only way she knows how—by talking. "Lust, naturally," she says, "the first sin you led me to. Wrath at the thought of anyone else ever getting to look at that beautiful penis, including urologists. Sloth—isn't that one?—because I would gladly spend the rest of my life in bed, if it was with you. Greed, because I want to hoard you like gold. Gluttony, because I want you to fill me up in every imaginable and, frankly, unmentionable way."

Paul rolls closer to her, begins to gather her in his arms, but she places her hand on his chest so she can continue speaking. "Pride, because you are so beautiful and I love to watch when people see us together. And—what is that?" She counts silently to herself. "That's only six. What's the seventh?"

"I don't know," Paul says.

"Come on," Kate urges, "you didn't even try. There's seven of them, try to think of the last one."

"Sneezy," Paul says.

"Oh, I know," she says. "Envy's the seventh. I've got that, too. And it's you that I envy. I wish I were half as beautiful as you. So that's the seven, and mama's got them all."

"I love the way you look," Paul says.

"I need to drink more water," says Kate. "I'm really not aging well."

Kate is the oldest woman with whom Paul has ever been intimate. He has never known a woman who paints her toenails, just one of Kate's manifestations of grown-up femininity. She diets, she regularly visits a hairdresser. She chooses her clothes with great care, trying things on and discarding them, especially if she is to make a public appearance. She will pay a hundred dollars for a jar of silky cream to rub into the lilac indentations beneath her eyes, and somehow believe the magic of the stuff will make her appear younger. And it does! It actually works. The previous women in Paul's life have not worried about their age, and they have been casual, confident of their beauty, finding their power at the edge of gender rather than at its center. They were Levi's and T-shirt types, outdoorsy women more at home at a campground than in a manicurist's chair. Being with Kate makes Paul feel pleasantly and proudly older, as though he has at last taken his place in the world of men. It once seemed as if he was going to have one of those lives that have no particular rhyme or reason, the kind in which people appear and disappear and you never know with whom you're going to have Christmas dinner but you don't worry about it because you rarely end up alone. But now there is order to his life and no longer any mystery as to where he will be next week, or next month. At long last, adulthood has begun.

He awakens a couple of hours later, startled into consciousness by a dream, into a room that is still dark, except for a narrow crack of diffuse street light coming in through the curtains, which Kate has parted. She has left the bed and sits now in a chair near the window. He looks at her watching the street. He wants to make certain nothing is the matter. Once, months ago, he was awakened in the middle of the night by the sense that something was wrong and found her in the living room in the downstairs of her house, curled into a chair, weeping into her hands. "I'm lonely," she said, "I feel so lonely." Bewildered, he tried to reassure her. He told her he was right there and he wasn't going anywhere, and he told her that her daughter was right upstairs. He pointed to the ceiling, with its wedding-cake plaster, its hanging chandelier like a hundred dead eyes. "I know, I know," she had said, breathless with unhappiness, gripping her stomach through the cotton of her summer nightgown. "It won't go away," she said.

But tonight Kate sits, her shoulders still, seemingly serene. She has draped her coat over her lap, and her feet are tucked under her. No, Paul thinks, I won't disturb her. He lies there quietly, eyes open. The light from the street reflects on the ceiling, from corner to corner, a stem of brightness with the refracted shine of headlights floating within it like blips on a radar screen. He closes his eyes, and when he awakens again the curtains are outlined by the trembling brightness of the day. Kate has taken him in her mouth and he feels himself swelling in the warmth of her. It is her pleasure to have him while he sleeps, and to maintain the illusion he keeps his eyes closed. She straddles him, he glides in easily, and she very slowly, and as quietly as possible, moves like an inchworm toward her pleasure which, though invisible, is the most real thing to her right now. Paul opens his eyes just enough to get a glimpse of her through the mesh of his lashes. He loves her expression during sex, open and undefended, with a creaturely purity and singularity of purpose. Her hands are on either side of his pillow. Warm breath pours from her open mouth, and stifled sounds of arousal rattle in her throat. How can she imagine that he is sleeping through all this lovely commotion? Yet he behaves as if he is dead to the world, and neither of them will ever make mention of it. He thinks for a moment about all that must go unsaid—for one, it makes him feel ever so slightly belittled when Kate goes on about his physical beauty, partly because he believes her to be more intelligent than he is, and he has heard it so many times from so many others that those particular words have lost their intended meaning to him, and, for another, he would never tell Kate that she is not the first woman to take her pleasure in him while he slept; it would not only make her jealous but it might diminish her sense of transgression.

Maybe that's the secret of love, sometimes it carries you, and other times it's your turn and you've got to carry it.

CHAPTER
THREE

It is unnerving to wake up in the hotel bed, and to look at the dark red numbers of the digital bedside clock and see it is almost noon. Paul raises himself on one elbow, surveys the dim emptiness of the room. He struggles to remember why he is here, why he is alone, and then remembers that Kate has gone back upstate and he has business to take care of here in the city. He tips the hotel's clock over on its side so he can no longer see its digital display, which he feels is a violation of timekeeping's intrinsic beauty, in which the round face and the sweeping hand reminds us that we are on a planet moving through space. He can't remember the last time he's slept until noon—as a teenager?—and waking so late in the day fills him with unease. Midnight to seven are his preferred hours of sleep. Being in bed while nearly everyone else is awake and productive makes Paul think of his mother, who slept ten to twelve hours a day and who, when awake, moved with agonizing slowness, groggily dragging sleep behind her like the hem of a muddy gown.

Kate has left him a note propped against the vase filled with tulips that her publisher had sent to the room. The tulips are months out of season and some unnatural shade of orange, bright as candy. The vase itself is on the little faux secretary that annoyed him last night. Without Kate's presence Paul is able to fully exercise his crotchety scorn for certain aspects of modern life. It is not only that he hates the shoddy and the false, but he experiences commercial incursions into the natural order as a contagion.

> Dear You, Good luck on your stuff today. See you this
> afternoon and hurry hurry hurry. Also don't forget to
> order yourself a big fat breakfast and charge it to the
> room. And don't forget parking's already paid for. Kisses,
> hugs, unmentionable etceteras . . .

Still naked, Paul idly plucks a corner of the table, where the glue holding the mahogany veneer to the particleboard tabletop has dried and become useless. Once the veneer has come loose, he cannot resist peeling it back even further, and before he entirely realizes what he is doing, he has removed several inches of veneer. "Uh-oh," he says, and tries to smooth it down again, but it has risen into a dark, brittle curl, and after once more attempting to correct or at least conceal the damage, he dismisses it with a shrug, and orders breakfast from room service, which comes to thirty dollars, and when the man wheels the breakfast in on a linen-covered cart, Paul writes in a fifty percent tip, generosity coming easily with someone else's money.

He has two stops to make in the city and both are about money. The first stop is the more unpleasant of the two: he must see a client who has owed him eight thousand dollars for more than a year. The errand begins auspiciously. The drive from the hotel to 77th Street goes smoothly, with the traffic heavy but fluid. Adding further to the positive portents is finding a parking spot practically right in front of the building, a spot that, just as Paul drives up, is being vacated by another workman's truck. Up on Fifth Avenue, most of the cars are sleek, black, and expensive, and the contractors and deliverymen in their utilitarian vehicles feel a kinship with one another. They are part of the city's secret life, visible only to each other, the custodians of pipes and plumbing fixtures and floors and carpets, locks and doors, and plate glass, plaster, and paint. As Paul pulls into the space, he gives a friendly wave to the departing driver—a painter, judging by the spattered cap—who gives him a comradely thumbs-up.

Once he is inside the lobby the signs and portents become less promising. The doorman on duty acts as if he were guarding the American embassy in some hostile nation, treating Paul as if he were tracking dog excrement across the colorful compass-point tile work of the lobby. When Paul is allowed to enter the elevator that will take him up to see Gerald Lundeen, the elevator operator, a small man with wisps of white hair, repeats several times: "So you're going to see Lundeen," as if there were something inherently dubious in the enterprise.

Lundeen has been avoiding Paul for months and today he looks as if he has just pulled himself out of his sickbed. His pewter hair is unwashed and mussed, his glasses have thumbprints on the lenses, his long, bare feet seem not to be getting enough blood and are the color of talcum powder. He wears a paisley silk robe over what looks like nothing. His chest hair is moist with perspiration and two fingers on his left hand are splinted and taped together. He reminds Paul of his own father as he careened through his last months on earth, though Paul's father's life had followed a more ominous trajectory, from a secure position in a community college to a brief stint with a third-tier advertising agency to a job in a frame shop on lower Lexington Avenue, all with a great deal of rage and alcohol along the way, so that his death, though premature, was not entirely surprising.

Whatever difficulties Lundeen may be experiencing, there is still enough money in his accounts to afford living in this nine-room apartment on Fifth Avenue. He has agreed to meet Paul to discuss their money matters dating back to a few months ago, when he told Paul that he had mailed him a check, which never arrived. Lundeen had seemed mystified at the time, and said he would make a stop payment, after which he would send Paul a replacement check. Paul waited several weeks and when he called Lundeen to ask again about the money, his calls went unanswered.

Now, at last, Lundeen has agreed to meet. He offers Paul a seat in an original Queen Anne chair, upholstered in custard-yellow damask, and seats himself in a high-backed leather chair behind his desk, which is awash with folders and brochures having to do with the Lundeen family business, which is the manufacture and sale of massage tables.

"So how have you been, Paul?" Lundeen asks, as if this were a social visit.

"Things are okay," Paul says. "How about you?"

Lundeen smiles, cocks his head. "Couldn't be worse." Noticing his chest is exposed, he closes his robe more carefully. "The wonderful world of divorce."

"Well I'm really sorry to hear that," Paul says. Lundeen's eyes flick avidly, and Paul wonders if he has somehow implied that Lundeen now has the right not to pay his bills, and so he adds, "These things happen."

Lundeen folds his hands together and taps them vigorously against his chin. "My finances are in chaos right now, Paul," he says. "I've had to freeze accounts to keep Renee from making off with everything I've worked for. And . . . well it's complicated and I won't bore you with all the grisly financial details. Not really your thing anyhow, is it?"

"It's . . . it's a lot of money," Paul says.

"Is it?" Lundeen asks, and then, catching himself, he says, "Of course it is. I realize that. And you worked, Paul. I know that. And the work you did was beautiful. It's like art, Paul, it really is. I can't tell you how many people have commented upon it. I'm sure some of them have already called you and asked you to do work for them. Am I right about that? So at least I've been helpful in that way."

"The thing about the money, Gerald," Paul says, "is that some of it's for my work and some of it's for materials."

"I know," Lundeen says. "You think I don't know? You think I don't go to bed every blessed night and think about the money I owe?"

Paul clears his throat. He knows it makes him sound uncertain, but if he doesn't cough he won't be able to speak. "So what are we doing here, Gerald? Can you give me some time frame?" Paul feels odd saying *time frame*, it is completely alien to him and it feels as if he were suddenly dropping in a French phrase that was somehow apt, the way one of his clients likes to say *incroyable* when something Paul has made strikes her fancy.

"What I think we're talking about here," Lundeen says, "is a month, at most. But honestly?" He waits for Paul to nod, as if it takes an agreement between the two of them for him to state the simple, unvarnished truth. "Honestly speaking, it's not really in my hands. It's all lawyers and assorted sharks. These people, these absolute fuckers." Lundeen's eyes redden, as if he might cry.

Paul feels suddenly lost and hopeless. What more can he say to this man in order to get the money owed to him? He already feels as if he has compromised and sullied himself by coming here. He has made his wishes clear and he has shown his face to Lundeen. The rest will have to work itself out in its own way, at its own time. Paul runs his hands over the etched mahogany arms of the Queen Anne and rises. "All right," he says. "I've got to get going."

"Okay, Paul, thanks for stopping by."

Paul furrows his brows. *Thanks for stopping by* makes absolutely no sense, except to strongly imply that Lundeen has barely registered the purpose of the visit. "So will you call me when your finances get straightened out?" he forces himself to ask.

"Of course I will," Lundeen says.

"One way or another, I've got to get paid," Paul says.

"That's for sure," Lundeen says, rising. He comes around the desk and places his hand on Paul's shoulder, guiding him toward the door, as the mad roar of a vacuum cleaner starts up from somewhere in the front of the apartment. Lundeen glances nervously in the direction of the invisible housekeeper and his steps quicken as he leads Paul to the front door and out into the hall, where, as chance would have it, the elevator man is there with his car empty and the doors wide open.

Paul can feel the day tipping ever more markedly in the wrong direction, and he has a feeling that is like knowing halfway into the cut on a valuable piece of lumber that the blade of the saw has been miscalibrated. His next appointment is twelve blocks north, and after fifteen minutes, he accepts that he is not going to find another free parking spot and leaves his truck in front of a church like a desperate mother abandoning her child. It is a little past one in the afternoon. The wind is damp and cold and the sun seems to give off no more heat than a lightbulb in a refrigerator. As Paul turns onto Fifth Avenue, five squad cars go yelping by, heading south at a furious clip, their blue and red flashers throwing pebbles of light off the lower windows and the seashell exteriors of the grand apartment buildings. The doormen in full livery don't even show a passing interest.

He has come to look over a job for an actress of whom he has never heard, though Kate tells him she is not only famous but deservedly so. Paul, who never lacks for work, had previously considered this stop mainly a courtesy, but now that it seems he will never see the money Gerald Lundeen owes him he is annoyed with himself for arriving at this second appointment an hour late.

Here, the doorman looks somehow merrier, with his mutton chop sideburns and long blue coat with crimson piping, shiny brass buttons. Paul says the name of the actress and the doorman waves him through, an indication the place must be seething with workmen.

"Ah," the general contractor says, "my favorite carpenter." His name is Haydn Goodwin; he is about fifty, tall and heavy, a Welshman with graying curly hair and the joking, confident manner of someone who is immensely strong. Paul worked for Goodwin two years ago, building a sleigh bed for a pop star.

"I want to show you the kitchen," Goodwin says. They go through the sunken living room, its contents covered by drop cloths. "We're confining ourselves to the south end of her apartment. That way she can at least have some sort of life, and when everything's buttoned up we can tackle the north end." He speaks softly, as if somewhere in this apartment there sleeps a temperamental child who must not be disturbed. Yet in the meanwhile, the sounds of hammers and saws, workingmen in conversation, and the Allman Brothers singing "Whipping Post" make it seem unlikely that anyone within the zip code can sleep or even think clearly.

"She was hoping to be in Rio during construction, but she's come down with grippe." Goodwin's belt is wide and heavy like a razor strop. The pager that hangs from it squawks and he has a terse conversation with someone, which ends with Goodwin saying, "That would be the end of me," and pushing the off button. "Anyhow," he says, returning his attention to Paul, "her daughter was supposed to be here to help out. Nothing massive, just some marketing, taking her to appointments, but the daughter is nowhere to be seen, so things have been rather touch-and-go."

Paul cannot remember ever having seen this guy so on edge, and he feels in himself a growing reluctance to work here. The thought of coming home from his New York errands empty-handed is a little depressing, but Paul has long believed that the secret to a happy life is a willingness to do without, and he is willing to do without the work Goodwin has to offer, or the money it will bring.

He follows along into the kitchen, with its black-and-white tiled floor, modern appliances, and modular built-ins. "She wants a real country kitchen," Goodwin says. "She has wonderful memories of a place she used to visit in Hillsboro, New Hampshire."

"This is an Art Deco building, Haydn."

Goodwin lets out a long, weary sigh, shakes his head. "I know, Paul, I know. But this is what she wants. And you can't argue with her. I mean you can, but it doesn't do any good."

"I don't know, Haydn. That doesn't open a door for me. You understand? It sort of closes a door. If she wants an eighteenth-century country kitchen she should live in an old country house."

"I know, I know." Goodwin roughly claps his hand on Paul's shoulder, gives it a jokey, angry squeeze with his powerful, plaster-dusted hand. "I figured you would say that. But I wanted to give it a shot. So let me ask you this, my friend. Do you remember those flat-plane cabinets you made for Jann Wenner? With all that beautiful old cypress? You have more of it squirreled away up there in the country, am I right? A little birdie told me you've got four thousand feet of northwest cypress and you once told me yourself you've got a massive collection of old bin-pull handles."

"Actually," Paul says, "that wasn't cypress, and it wasn't vintage."

"That wasn't old wood?" Goodwin says, amazed.

"I aged it with gray patina over cream paint."

Goodwin shakes his head. "In the photographs it looks like the real deal."

"It does in real life, too," Paul says.

"So? What about it?"

"I can tell whoever you get how to age the wood. Or you can. It's simple."

"And that's it? How about the old cypress? How about the bin-pulls?"

"I can't do that," Paul says. "I keep my stock for my own projects."

"I can pay you top dollar."

"It could never be worth to you what it's worth to me, Haydn."

"Let me be the judge of that," Goodwin says, his good humor all but vanished. Goodwin continues to work on Paul, beseeching him one moment, berating him the next. Paul keeps his eyes on Goodwin and gives every impression of considering the contractor's arguments, but in fact he's barely listening, until all at once Paul realizes with a jolt of dread that his truck is in a no-parking zone. It would be one thing to get a ticket along with a job, but to get a ticket instead of a job . . .

"I have to get out of here," Paul says. "I'm sorry it didn't work."

"I want that wood and the hardware, too," Goodwin says, pointing at him and smiling falsely. He makes a sudden move, as if to throw his shoulder into Paul or make some insane attempt to tackle him, and Paul feels a spout of adrenaline rising through him.

"Haydn, she wants you," a voice says. It's one of Goodwin's crew, a young, cherub-faced man in his twenties, with his protective eyewear pulled back into his plaster-flecked hair.

"Is anything wrong?" Goodwin anxiously asks.

The young helper shrugs. "She just said get you."

Without another word, Goodwin leaves the kitchen and disappears into the apartment. Paul stands there for a moment; it is only in the wake of Goodwin's absence that Paul realizes how angry he feels. As he finds his way back to the front door he thinks: *I should have clocked him*.

His agitation continues on the walk back to the Episcopal church where he defied both God and Caesar by parking his truck, and even from a distance he can see the parking ticket lodged beneath his windshield wiper, one end shuddering in the dank November breeze, the other stuck to the windshield's condensation. *Oh come on*, Paul says, as if there were something petty and unjust about his getting a parking ticket, though, in fact, he has gotten caught four times this year alone. It's easy for him to forget that, since he hasn't yet paid any of the fines. He pulls the ticket free of the wiper blade and sticks it in his back pocket, where he will keep it before it joins the others shoved into the rear of the glove compartment.

Driving uptown, and getting ready to turn west so he can head back to Leyden, Paul finds that the street he was going to take is closed and he must go east a block and then north before heading west again. But while he is going east he decides, almost without thought, to keep going all the way to First Avenue so he can drive past the apartment building where his father spent the last year of his life.

When Matthew Phillips left his wife, she was in no mood to make it easy for him to see either Paul or his sister, Annabelle. This was agreeable enough to Annabelle but not to Paul, even though he had been the main target of his father's rages, the worst of which being the time he clamped his hand over Paul's nose and mouth and kept it there until Paul lost consciousness. Despite this, and despite other acts of violence both petty and prosecutable, Paul had missed Matthew. He was afraid he would hurt his mother's feelings if he asked her for help in seeing his father, and so he mowed lawns and shoveled snow to make money for train fare from Connecticut to New York. It was his only reprieve from what was otherwise a world of women—mother, sister, teachers, even his customers: all women.

Matthew had rented a railroad apartment, a narrow, shadowy alley of faltering bachelorhood, with soft walls and scarred floorboards, a tub in the kitchen and accordion gates on all the windows. The bedroom was in the back—a mattress on the floor beneath a grimy window—and the front, marginally sunnier half of the apartment was given over to easel and paints. From one end to the other, the paintings were propped against the walls three and four deep in an almost defiant display of nobody's wanting them. Matthew was interested in the color brown, which he said was the most soulful of all the colors, and each canvas was heavily painted in some shade of brown with one stripe of another color bisecting the field. Toward the end of his life, Matthew was placing the stripe on the upper third of the canvas, and in the very last painting he made there were two stripes, one pale green, the other black, and he called that one "Easter." He was like a man possessed by an incommunicable vision, an apprehension of something vast and eternal, a compulsion of the soul's deepest recesses, powerful enough to jolt a man from society but not quite powerful enough to transport him anywhere else.

When Paul had come calling Matthew would be dressed in paint-spattered jeans, huaraches from Mexico, his pale green eyes wet and unfocused, like olives at the bottom of a martini glass. Away from the pressures of family life, Matthew was placid, distant, polite. He had become someone who didn't want anything looked at too closely, someone whose peace of mind depended on things being glossed over. Matthew held forth, speaking in generalizations; in fact, he lived in generalizations. *Soon, one day,* and *not quite yet* were his measurements of time; *some, a bit,* and *not quite enough* were his customary monetary denominations. *A guy I knew, this woman, a fella, a couple of girls, a neighbor,* and *a bunch of folks* were the people in his life.

One warm spring day, Paul had left Connecticut without telling his mother or sister, taking the commuter train to Grand Central, along with the businessmen, office workers, and the well-to-do shoppers. He thought he would surprise his father. He walked the couple of miles from Grand Central; the sun was a hot, oily smudge in a gray sky. Displayed on the buzzer board was one of the return address stickers UNICEF had sent Matthew. Paul pressed the button, waited, tried the door, found it open, and trudged up, feeling some nameless queasy dread, a sense of foreboding he would never again ignore.

His father's door was unlocked. The apartment was a diorama illustrating man left to his own devices. Socks drying on table lamps, curls of dust as dark as steel wool beneath the radiators, the walls thick and soft with paint, stacks of newspapers in the corners, empty bottles, unfinished meals turned into ashtrays, the imploring notes taped strategically to the door, between the locks and the peephole, admonishing himself to Turn Off Lights! Check Stove!

Matthew was dead; alone and undressed in the bedroom. Later, Paul would learn that his father had had a massive heart attack and had probably died instantly. His top half was on the bare mattress, his feet were on the floor. It felt like it was a hundred degrees inside that apartment; the smell was something Paul would never forget. He knew his father was dead, but he didn't know you were supposed to call the police when someone died. He thought this was a family matter and what must be done was to put his father upright, cover his nakedness, and then figure out how to get the body back to Connecticut where he and his mother and sister could bury it. With his hand over his nose and mouth, Paul approached the body, peered into his father's ruined face. He tried to lift Matthew, and, for a moment, he succeeded, but then the worst thing happened. The body slowly came down like a drawbridge, and try as he might Paul could do nothing to stop it until it was on top of him. At first, he couldn't utter a sound, and then he cried out for his mother. He began to shout. The weight, the odor, the great and terrible darkness closing in. He pushed Matthew's lifeless, expressionless face away from his. He must have done it more roughly than he realized, and the push left a mark.

For years after his father's death, Paul walked by the apartment house whenever he came to the city—it seemed disloyal and callous not to, especially since Matthew had been cremated and there was no grave to visit. But by the time he turned twenty, he was making the sad pilgrimage less and less often, and now as the traffic dumps him out onto First Avenue, he realizes he has not seen his father's apartment house in maybe eight years.

Approaching 90th Street, he sees that the little shop where Matthew bought his art supplies has been turned into a Verizon store, and Zurich and Kaufman Quality Shoes has been turned into a coffee boutique, and, worse, the very building in which Matthew lived and died has been razed, along with the buildings on either side. In their place has been built a glass-and-steel apartment building calling itself The Verdi, a twenty-story hive of windowsills and reflecting glass, indistinguishable from hundreds of nearly identical buildings all over town. Paul doesn't even slow down; his thoughts disappear behind an engulfing blankness. *If I hurry*, he thinks, *I can make the light before it turns red*.

On the way out of the city, there is a long, infuriating delay—minutes pass, a quarter hour, half an hour, forty-five minutes. He is surrounded by the rumble of idling engines, heartsick over the wasted day, yet he is in no hurry to get back to Leyden. He would like to see something beautiful that might neutralize the sourness of the day. Halfway up the Saw Mill Parkway, and finally free of the city's gravitational pull, Paul exits the highway on a sudden impulse, and heads toward a two-thousand-acre park he came to know the year before, when he was working in Westchester, building a wine cellar for a French banker. The road follows the shoreline of a man-made lagoon full of Canada geese rocking back and forth like hundreds of little boats, then he turns onto a county blacktop and the approach to Martingham State Park.

The booth at the park's east entrance is boarded up for the winter, and leaves blow this way and that across the stripes of the parking lot. The maple leaves are gaily colored red, orange, and yellow; the oaks are somber brown, like bread crust, though some have a tinge of what looks like dried blood.

Paul parks and walks along a footpath, a quarter of a mile into the woods, past pine, spruce, hemlock, locust, oak, and maple, all permitted by state decree to flourish and age, with time their only natural enemy. The pine rots when it dies, growing softer, more and more fragrant. The maple and the birch, the alder and the black cherry refuse to die. Even if they are cut down, they send up a new crown of leaves as quickly as possible, new growth eager for the sun. The leaves beneath Paul's feet are starting to decompose; the loamy soil beneath them is soft and black.

A small picnic area. Today it is a staging area for some vast squirrel jamboree—big gray ones with thick coats and pom-pom tails, darting little red ones with mad eyes and skinny feet, all working frantically against the oncoming winter. There are eight tables in the clearing, painted green and needing a bit of maintenance. Shitty mass-produced tables. Paul sits at the one closest to the path. He breathes deeply, drawing the sharp, autumnal air into his nose, slowly exhaling it through his mouth. He hears cries above him and he tilts his head back to find the source—an old, peeling white birch's leafless crown has filled with orioles, all of them surely hastening south. The birds are waiting for the rest of the flock, and when the crown is black with feathers and alive with high-pitched screeches, the birds explode into flight again, funnel up into the air, wheeling left, then right, until they are in formation again. The sky is a moody luminous greenish blue. He sees a sparrow perched on the swaying branch of an empty mountain ash and he thinks of a song Kate likes to sing, in her throaty, touching, tuneless way: *His eye is on the sparrow, so I know God is watching over me.* Pretty sentiment, but nothing could be further from the truth, as Paul sees it. The sparrow is alone, and you are alone, too.

He is not entirely sure why he is here but he is glad he has turned off the highway and taken this time to absorb the melancholy solitude of the woods and the poignancy of the autumn. Alone with the silence of these trees, their crowns slowly waving in the wind, their empty branches splayed out like nerves, their roots plunged deep in the earth, extracting nutrients with a gorgeous greed. The watch Kate gave him for his birthday feels heavy and he takes it off, places it on the picnic table, and rubs away the imprint the metal band has left on his wrist. Far above him, a passenger jet streaks across the sky, heading south toward LaGuardia or Kennedy. Paul watches the plane disappear and when he returns his gaze to the world around him, he realizes he is no longer alone—a dark-haired, barrel-chested man in his forties, in a white thermal shirt, black satin workout pants, and running shoes has joined him in this secluded clearing in the woods.

CHAPTER
FOUR

At first Will Claff seems frightened to encounter someone here, but he gains his composure and he glares at Paul. Will sits down at one of the picnic benches, his chest heaving, a shimmering girdle of pain cinched around every breath. With him is the dog, whose leash he loops around the leg of the bench.

Will produces a water bottle and begins to drink from it. The tall, bony, brown-and-gray dog places his paws up on the picnic table and gazes imploringly with his perfectly round eyes. "Down!" Will Claff says, and smacks the dog hard on its snout, causing him to quickly drop back down. Will does this for Paul's sake, wants him to know that Will is no one to be pushed around.

Woody continues to behave as if there is still some hope of getting a drink. He cocks his head to the left and then to the right, and his narrow tail wags enthusiastically, around and around, like a helicopter propeller. "Down," Will says, and this time the dog obeys. Will feels a surge of confidence. Yet as soon as Woody sits, he is up again, freshly agitated.

No respect.

Once upon a time, the brown dog was used to tender treatment, and to this day he cannot completely rid himself of the idea that humans are a friendly, useful species. He misinterprets Will's momentary reverie as a softening and he barks again, and again, his front paw scratching at the ground, his rear half shimmying back and forth.

"What did I tell you?" Will shouts at the dog, so loudly that the animal immediately falls silent. But the cessation of barking isn't enough for Will; stirred by the sound of his own voice, he grabs the dog by his silver choke collar and pulls it close to him, shaking Woody's head back and forth with such force that the dog, clearly afraid for its own life, lets out a yelp that is close to the sound of a human scream.

"Hey, hey," Paul says. "Take it easy." The man squints in Paul's direction, juts out his chin.

"Do I know you?" he asks.

"All I'm saying is don't hit the dog," Paul says, his tone indicating, he thinks, a reasonable nature.

It's happening, Will thinks, *it's happening right now.* He feels a whoosh within, as if he has begun to fall from a great height, and he cuffs the dog, hitting it harder than he has ever hit it before, serving notice to this man who has come to do him harm. Will does a calculation. What does he owe? Eight grand? This guy—well you have to give him credit for one thing, he had found him, right here at the end of his jog. But he doesn't look particularly tough, and what's he going to get for collecting the debt? Thirty percent? Tops. So what is that? Twenty-four hundred bucks?

"Will you stop doing that?" Paul says, moving toward the man, and feeling his own fury, shocking in its intensity: it is like opening a closet door and discovering it is filled with the brightest, most vivid light.

Will Claff stares at Paul, who has just said the word *Will*. That he knows his name tells Will everything he needs to know. For instance, only one of them is walking away from this. He tries to shove the dog aside, but it is on a leash and tethered to the thick leg of the bench.

Paul continues to face the man, with his hands folded monkishly before him, hoping to communicate, to both of them, his intention to do no harm, though he does semiwordlessly say to himself, *I would like to fucking kill this guy.*

He can hear a sparrow, its sharp, tuneless exclamation.

"This is a beautiful part of the state, don't you think?" Paul says. The man doesn't say anything at first, as if this is a statement that needs to be inspected for possible hidden meanings.

"It's f-f-fine," Will Claff manages to say. He lets out his breath.

Paul notes the stammer, wonders if that will make this guy somehow easier to deal with. "I don't know why you'd want to hit him," he says. "Seems like a nice enough dog." He has stopped walking toward the man and stands now, ten, fifteen feet away, too far for the man to take a swing at him, and far enough to react should he make a move.

"Hear that, dog?" Will says. He feels as if he were walking on air, somehow putting one foot in front of the other, a mile high, terrified and omnipotent. "Our friend here wants to know why I want to hit you. Guess he'd rather I use my foot." And with that he lands a swift kick into the dog's rib cage. The dog leaps with fright, yelping again and instinctively baring its teeth and growling menacingly, drawing from its meager arsenal.

"What the fuck?" Will cries, as if betrayed. "You turning on me, is that what you're doing? Biting the hand that feeds you?"

Will feels Paul's eyes upon him, and he understands this and this alone: there is only one way out, and that is more of the same. His next kick lands in the middle of the dog's rib cage and knocks the wind out of the animal; the beast's mouth gapes open, his tongue unfurls, and he drops to his side, whimpering.

Paul puts his hands on either side of his head, as if his skull will otherwise explode. What he had wanted most was to sit somewhere and not deal with another human being. Behind his thoughts is a steady roar of hatred, like the noise of traffic. Now he is only a couple of feet away from the man and all he can think of to say is "How would you like someone to kick you around like that?"

To which Will Claff replies, "You th-think I don't kn-know?"

Paul is no expert in conflict. He hasn't had a fight since he was a teenager, a fight whose origins and purpose are now forgotten, but what is remembered of that afternoon remains unsettling: the five sets of hands dragging Paul off of Marshall Judd, who was bleeding, crying. Instinct tells Paul to stand close to the man, so close that he will be able to react instantly if the guy tries to use something he may be carrying in his pocket—a knife, a gun. Paul is standing now barely six inches away.

"Watch yourself," Paul says, jabbing his finger toward the man, moving his face so close that their noses are almost touching. The dog looks up with interest; his tail thumps against the leaves. "You can't do that to a dog."

"It's m-mine," the man says.

"I don't care," Paul says. "It's not about that."

So it's true, Will thinks. *He has just admitted it.* He feels a wave of grief, as if he had already been killed and is now standing at his own grave, watching as the casket is lowered into the ground.

The dog is looking uneasily at his own side, where the kicks have landed. Paul shoves the man's shoulder, not so hard as to hurt him but hard enough to let him know that physical pain might very well be on the way.

Will steps quickly away and then launches himself at Paul, slamming into him with his considerable weight, grabbing Paul's hair with one hand, while using the other to deliver a series of quick blows to the side of Paul's head.

There is more fury than strength behind the wild punches. Paul shoves Will back, steps out of the chaotic spray of punches, and then, as if to put one toe into the ocean of violence which so much of life springs from and so much of it returns to, he slaps the man across the face. It is meant to insult and demoralize the man, but it's a direct hit, with more force behind it than Paul intended, and the man lets out a howl. "Okay?" Paul says, by which he means *Had enough?*

Will keeps his distance for the moment; torn between the impulse to lay a comforting hand on his own face and to strike back, he seems lost and infirm. His hand trembles, he blinks rapidly, he turns his head to the right and to the left. He is looking for something to throw at Paul.

First comes the water bottle, which he pitches at Paul with surprising accuracy, hitting him in the chin, and though it barely hurts, it is startling. The bottle falls to the ground; the water flows into the leaves, darkening them. The man tries to lift the picnic table, to heave that at Paul, but he forgets he lashed his dog to the leg of it, and as soon as he lifts the table, the dog's choke collar tightens, and the animal scrambles in fear.

"Put it down!" Paul shouts, and he rushes Claff, shoving him in the chest and then watching as the man falls backward.

But already he is scrambling onto his feet again. A sterner lesson will have to be taught, Paul thinks, and he considers kicking the man in the head, but—a kick to the head? No: too much. Instead, Paul drops to one knee, grabs the man by the shirt, and delivers one abrupt, discrete punch—aiming for the nose and landing on the cheekbone. The man's body bucks back and forth. As if doing a sit-up, he is able to elevate the top half of his body and then, momentarily rearing back, he smashes his head into Paul's mouth. Paul's lips go numb and he feels his mouth fill with warm, greasy blood. *Mother-*

fucker, he whispers, or thinks, and he hits the man again, this time with greater accuracy, greater force, and then again, and once more.

The strangest thing about it is that he isn't really all that mad, or at least he is not whirling in some mind-altering vortex of fury. He is coldly angry, and even in his anger he mainly wants to put a stop to the whole fight before the man lands another lucky punch. And even as his anger increases—as the numbness in his lips turns to pain, and he wonders if that head butt has cost him a tooth—it is not the kind of anger that is a portal to madness. No. What is taking place is more like a realignment of inner forces, in which the voice of reason grows fainter and the voice of animal instinct becomes more and more dominant, expressing itself in a long, low, guttural roar. Except for that interior roar, Paul feels strangely calm.

"Go away! P-p-please," Will cries out, sorry now, truly sorry, sorry for kicking the dog, sorry for not having the money to pay his debts, sorry for running, sorry for everything. But he is also flailing, and each time he swings his arms another blow lands on Paul.

"Stop!" Paul cries. His own voice sounds unfamiliar to him. His breath comes in jagged bursts; his heart races. Yet all the while a serene, confident self, a shadow self, remains aloof, silently urging him on. *Fucking punch his ticket*, the voice suggests. Each time the man takes a swing, Paul punishes him with a real blow. There are slaps, just to demoralize the guy and drain his strength, and there are punches, on the side of the head—how many? Paul has lost count—and then on the chin, with the hope of knocking him unconscious and then, as luck would have it, a blow to the throat.

With that final blow, Paul falls forward, practically on top of the man. Will grabs Paul's hair but even as he pulls and twists he seems to be surrendering. "No, no," Will Claff says, his voice soft and thick, a bubble rising in his throat, spit and blood, the mortal lava of him.

No, no are his last words. Whatever pity the universe has shown him has run its course.

Paul does not know this, not quite yet. The violence is still coursing through him; he is like a runner who cannot stop his legs from churning, even after he has snapped through the tape at the finish line. He grips the man's throat. He is not trying to choke him. He is trying to hold him at bay, as you might pin a poisonous snake beneath the crook of a branch.

"All right?" Paul says, in that voice you use when you have fulfilled someone's worst expectations. "All right? All right? Will you stop now?"

The man makes a deep sound of distress, an urgent, guttural cry. Startled, Paul relaxes his grip a little. But the sound persists; it takes a moment for Paul to realize that the sound is not the man choking but the dog barking.

"Uh-oh," Paul says, getting quickly to his feet.

A stain spreads out over the front of the man's workout pants; as his crotch darkens, the color drains from his face, making each of his whiskers appear blacker and more distinct. Paul feels a sharp, wrenching pain in his hand, looks at it and realizes he is gripping the side of his jeans and squeezing the denim with all his might. He lets go and falls to his knees, places his ear on the man's chest, but all he hears is the pounding of his own heart. He shakes the man by the shoulders and places one finger beneath his nostrils, though he already knows there will be no breath to feel.

The trees encircling the clearing seem to have gotten closer, their empty crowns etched against the soft sky like ten thousand cracks in a mirror. Paul turns in a circle, willing his eyes to see someone, anyone, but all is stillness, and, except for the wind and the wooden creaking of the trees, all is silent.

He runs back to the parking area. Once he is there, he leans on the hood of his truck, his head pitched forward, his heart beating so violently that his own death seems to be pounding up the stairs.

What just happened? What have I done?

He knows he must think clearly now. In the chaos of surging, disconnected thoughts, he remembers: call 911. He opens his truck's door, finds his cell phone in the glove compartment, turns it on, waits. *What do I say?*

There is no reception in this dense preserve of forest. He stares at the silent phone and, suddenly, adrenaline begins to course through him. He can feel the blood draining from his face, and his skin growing colder with each heartbeat. A scalding, churning distress of the bowels. He clutches his stomach and thinks *Oh my God I'm going to be sick.* Guided by animal instinct, he hurries into the woods at the very edge of the parking area, unbuckles his jeans, squats. A momentary ecstasy of relief, vile, burning, stinking relief. He closes his eyes, holds his breath, creating an inner silence in which the spatter of his sickness sounds thunderous against the brittle forest floor. Still in a crouch, he staggers forward. He loses his balance, falls to his knees.

Oh God, God, God, he whispers, and the word brings him up short. He shakes his head, as if to dispel it. He grabs a handful of leaves, makes an effort to clean himself, and then, still half-undressed, still on his knees, he kicks leaves, twigs, dirt, and stones on the foulness, and shuffles back to the truck but does not get in. His mind whirs uselessly, an engine that will not turn over.

He will find the proper authorities in Tarrytown, nearby; small towns are laid out with a predictable plan and he will have no trouble finding the police station. Or he can call them from the first house he sees. He can explain and direct them to this spot. Or he can ride with them, sit in the backseat, and explain while they drive. Whatever happens, he should probably contact a lawyer—though the only lawyer he knows is the man who used to live with Kate. Or no, there's Gilbert Silverman, a lawyer Paul worked for last year. Loft. Chambers Street. Bedroom ruined by leaking skylight. But Silverman's practice was taken up with artists and gallery owners. A man lying dead in a park outside of Tarrytown would not be in his area of expertise.

I'm not even innocent. I won't even be able to say it was self-defense, because I was never in danger. I did it. I'm going to be arrested.

But what difference does the possibility of arrest make next to the overriding fact that a man's life has just ended? A man is dead, a heart has stopped, a future has been canceled. A wife. Children. Friends. All of the pleasures of love, sky, music, touch, food, wine have just been taken away forever. A man is dead, no more able to share in the glories of the earth than if he had never been born. Paul clutches his head.

It is so difficult to think. This much he knows. His life is a coin that has been flipped and now against the darkening sky it turns over and over.

From the morass, there rises a question: *How can this be happening?* And he wishes suddenly, fervently, that there *was* a God looking on, with his eye on the sparrow and everything else, knowing what we did, what we meant, what we did not mean, what was deliberate, what was accidental, what was so perplexing and mixed you couldn't with any confidence say what was what.

What if he's wrong? What if that man is alive? What if it's not as bad as it seemed—so many things turn out that way.

Back down the path, the man lies where Paul left him. The night seems to be hurrying in; already half the trees are invisible and, as Paul approaches the man, his legs are missing, eaten by the darkness. The dog, still tethered, is busying himself with a stick, chewing on it diligently, every now and then shaking it back and forth as he would a small animal whose neck he wishes to snap.

In the failing light, Paul scours the ground for something he might have dropped. *Hurry, hurry,* he thinks, but he doesn't know if he means hurry and get help, or hurry and make sure you haven't left something here that can connect you to this place. As he walks in a circle that encompasses where he had been sitting and where the man first appeared, Paul wonders if he ought also to be kicking dirt over his own footprints. But he realizes that he would never be able to remove his every footprint; best to let them take their place with the dozens of other footprints.

It isn't as if feet are on file somewhere. Ditto his fingerprints, and his DNA. Paul in the day-to-day pursuit of his duties and pleasures generally has an agreeable sense of invisibility as he swims through the vast American sea. As far as the state is concerned he may as well be unborn.

During his sixth time around the circumference of the circle he had drawn in his mind, something catches Paul's attention. The watch Kate gave him on his birthday is on the picnic table. The catastrophic potential of leaving it behind is so vast it almost buckles his knees. With terror and relief, he snatches up the watch and slips it back onto his wrist, and as he does, something suddenly settles within him: he is not a criminal. A court of law would certainly find him guilty of manslaughter and sentence him to prison. How stiff a sentence does the charge carry? Three? Seven? More?

But no matter how many months or years Paul spends in prison, the man on the forest floor will not be any less dead.

The dog continues to chew at the stick. "You going to be all right here?" Paul asks the dog, but the animal gives no sign of having heard him, any more than he reacts to the fact that his former master is dead on the ground. If the dog had been motivated to, he could have reached Will's body, but he seems to know that whatever use this man had once been is now a thing of the past. Paul feels the stirrings of panic. He needs to leave. Yet he stands for an extra moment, looking at the dog, this living witness to the thing that has happened.

What do they do with a dog found with a corpse? What if they kill him? It would be asking for trouble to take the dog with him. But what if they put him in a shelter? A middle-aged brown dog with a stick in his mouth. Who would want him? What if by the man dying, the dog dies, too?

"All right," Paul says. "You come with me."

But where? Where will I take him? He approaches the dog slowly, remembering that mistreated dogs often turn mean. When he is close, the dog grips the stick tighter in his jaws and shakes his head back and forth. It seems his primary concern is to keep that stick away from Paul.

"The stick's yours," Paul says, touching the dog behind the ear, ready to jerk his hand away if the dog makes a sudden move. In fact he is ready to leave the dog right where he is if need be. But the dog doesn't mind being touched. He drops the stick and licks the back of Paul's hand, a quick lilac flash, a deep yet cryptic intimacy.

"Oh dog," Paul says, his voice quavering. He unties the black nylon leash. As soon as he is freed, the dog scrambles to his feet, ready to get on to whatever is next. Paul picks up the end of the leash and the dog picks up his stick.

The trees are black against the slate gray sky, tied together by a band of orange that runs like a skein of silk along the horizon.

CHAPTER
FIVE

Paul drives north toward home, checking the stability of his teeth with the tip of his tongue. The truck's headlights are askew. They illuminate the edges of the road but barely touch the center, leaving the middle of Route 100 in darkness. He has taken local roads for the entire drive, adding at least an hour to the journey. He drives slowly, intently looking for a deer, or a turkey, or even a possum that might come darting out into harm's way.

The brown dog sitting next to him, whom Paul has already named Shep, is salivating anxiously and shedding fur at a prodigious rate. The dog is clearly falling apart, but he is trying to keep his dignity. He is like a minor character in a Mafia movie who knows he is being taken for a ride from which he is never going to return, but who has for so long subscribed to the code that ordains his very undoing that it is beneath him, or beyond him, to protest.

Is anybody looking? Paul wonders. He looks up at the rearview mirror and sees only his eyes.

Kate sits in the studio Paul has made for her. He has put in wise old windows that seem to increase and enrich every bit of available light, and even the darkness seems to have a luster as it presses against the wavy glass. Above her is a ceiling fan, salvaged from a plantation-style house in Biloxi, and near her desk is a blue enamel woodstove from Finland, brand-new. The floors are pale pine, the plaster walls conceal modern wonders of insulation—most particularly a hybrid weave of recycled newspaper, wool, and fiberglass, made by a friend of Paul's and gotten in exchange for a cherrywood bedside table, a spindly, coltish piece with frail legs and a sunny finish, which took Paul an entire month to build and which Kate came to love so much that she practically cried when it left the house.

"Every gain comes with a loss," she'd said to Paul, as they stood in the driveway and watched the precious little table bounce around the gritty, straw-flecked bed of Ken Schmidt's old truck.

"Don't worry," he'd said, "I can make a hundred tables like that."

"But you won't."

Schmidt's truck was out of view, but they could still hear it. The funnels of dust kicked up by the back tires rolled lazily in the sun-light.

"I'm glad to get that insulation," Paul said.

Kate shook her head, with the passive, rueful sadness of some-one who realizes a mistake when it's too late to correct it. "We should have just paid for it," she said. "And who the hell even wants insulation?"

"Katey," Paul said, "come on." He put his arm around her, turned her around, walked to the house with her. "Now, if I come out here on a cold winter morning and slip my hands under your shirt, your breasts will be nice and warm."

She stopped, carved a faint line in the gravel with the toe of her shoe. "Don't ever leave me," she said with abandon, not caring what it sounded like or what he might say in response.

Next to the stove, Paul has stacked seasoned, stove-sized pieces of wood, and there is a battered old tin bucket, itself a piece of found art, filled with kindling. All Kate needs to do is strike a match and the studio could be warm in ten minutes, but she has, guiltily, turned on the electric space heater instead. The space heater emits a hot flannel smell, its coils crinkle like cellophane, the heat itself corrugates the air around it. Kate has been at her computer, answering e-mails from readers in the order they have arrived. She writes quickly, as if not really writing but talking. Every now and then she comes up with an idea or a phrase that might be used in her real writing and she records it in a notebook next to her computer. Every little bit helps—now that her career is bringing in money, she has put herself on a serious production schedule, with the understanding that good things don't last forever.

The door to Kate's studio opens and there, framed by bare trees and cold, dark, gray air, is her daughter, home from her after-school program. "Hey there," Kate calls, doing her best to sound thrilled.

"Hi there," Ruby answers, in her powerful voice. Her cheeks are red with cold and wind; her pale green eyes sparkle. She shrugs off her lavender backpack and lets it fall to the pine floor.

"Ho there," Kate says, making a rah-rah gesture, rocking her fist back and forth. "Will you look what somebody sent me?" She goes through the day's mail until she finds it, a delicate little crucifix on an even more delicate chain. She dangles the cross before Ruby as if trying to hypnotize her.

"It's the most beautiful cross in the world," Ruby says, managing to sound both fervent and ironic. She clasps her hands together and places them beneath her chin, posing. She is a nine-year-old trying to be funny, and, to Kate, she actually *is* amusing—there is something sincere in the girl's love of hyperbole. Lately, with Ruby, everything good is the best, everything at all fetching is the most beautiful in the world.

"I know. One of my readers sent it to me. It *is* quite pretty," Kate says, a little tug of instruction in her carefully modulated voice. "So I guess it only makes sense that I would give it to a very pretty girl."

Ruby shakes her head and makes a sweeping gesture, an actress playing to the second balcony. "I'm not pretty," she says, "I'm not, I'm not, I'm not." And her eyes well up.

How is she able to do that? Surely, she is not that upset, she can't be. But she can imitate any of the surface emotions. She can do a credible gaiety, with a tinkling, convincing laugh, she can do fear, and she is particularly expert at remorse. All these thespian wiles are self-taught; though Ruby has frequently asked to be given acting lessons, Kate resists, on the (unspoken) grounds that any more proficiency in manufacturing emotions and her skills will have to be registered with the police, just as professional boxers are said to register their fists. Still, Kate cannot help but be amazed at how realistic Ruby's performance is. Those sea green eyes blurring with tears, the little trembling hand against the heaving chest—it's like double-jointedness, at once astonishing and nauseating.

The phone rings, Kate's recently installed private line to which only Paul has the number. Her pulse quickens. He still has that effect on her. "Are you using your phone!" Kate asks, with unalloyed delight. The snazzy little Nokia was a present to him a few months ago, and since then it has seen little else but the inside of his glove compartment.

"I'm a ways," Paul says, his voice mixed with the hum of the road and the wind. Also, he doesn't seem to be aiming his voice at the phone's little triad of speaker holes. Kate feels a weirdly erotic twist of annoyance. He could very well be doing this on purpose, as a demonstration of the technology's deficiencies. Yet the frequent but fleeting moments of irritation Kate feels around Paul are cool air that only oxygenates the fire.

"Where exactly are you?" Kate says.

"I'll be there in a half hour or an hour, something in there," Paul says. He never really answers the questions she asks. And how can he not know the difference between being thirty and sixty minutes away? It's not as if he needs to make an allowance for traffic. There is no traffic at this hour. Does he intend to make a stop?

"I'm supposed to be at an AA meeting at seven," Kate says. "Will you be here in time for me to go?"

"I don't know," Paul says.

She waits for the explanation or the apology that should follow but it does not come. She's always a little off-rhythm with him; it's how they dance.

"Well, I guess I'll take Ruby with me," Kate says.

"Okay, but I'd like to see her. I've got a surprise for her."

"Really?"

Not a sound from Paul's end. Perhaps he has gone out of range. Kate waits for another few moments, and then, acknowledging the lost connection, hangs up her phone.

Ruby has poured the contents of her backpack onto the floor and now paws through the jumble of books, notebooks, crumpled-up papers, pencils and pens and hair clips, looking for a juice box.

"Paul's coming home soon," Kate says. "And he's got a wonderful surprise for you." She instantly regrets saying this. What if it's not a wonderful surprise, what if it's just a passing everyday surprise, like a toy ring from a vending machine, or a book of puzzles, and now, because it has been overhyped, Ruby will feel let down. Kate feels she has committed an act of social gracelessness reminiscent of what her ex-husband, Ruby's long-absent father, used to do to her at dinner parties. He always managed to step on Kate's best lines; he had an uncanny instinct for coughing or offering to refill someone's wineglass just when Kate was getting to the punch line of a story. And if he wasn't wrong-footing her like that, he was up to some alternate form of sabotage, like announcing to a table of guests, *Oh, you've got to hear this, Kate has just had the most amazing experience of her life*, and all eyes would be on her, and all she could do was tell her story about how the man who came to fix the refrigerator turned out to be an old patient of her father's.

Kate sits on the floor, and commences to put the cross on her daughter. "What are you doing?" Ruby asks, without looking up.

"I'm putting the little cross on you, it looks so pretty." *Why do they have to make the fucking clasp so small?* Kate says to herself. The circle she is trying to get the hook through is tiny, the size of an air bubble exhaled by a goldfish. There: at last.

Ruby feels the cool slither of the chain on her neck, the infinitesimal weight of the cross itself as it drops onto the bib of her overalls, with barely more substance than a shadow.

A couple of towns south of Leyden, Paul stops at a supermarket to get a bag of dog food, and a bowl for Shep to eat out of, in case Kate has views about a dog using her dinnerware. The strip mall is ringed by tall metal lampposts and bathed in enough bright silvery light to illuminate a night baseball game, yet the parking area is nearly bereft of cars—all this electricity and what it takes to make it, the utter mindless waste of it disgusts him.

When Paul opens the door, Shep makes a move to jump out. "No, no, stop," Paul says, grabbing at the dog's collar. But Shep is determined to get out. He twists away from Paul and a moment later the dog is on the asphalt, his tail twirling around in that helicopterish way. "What are you doing, man, get back in the truck," Paul says, hoping to strike a tone that is both commanding and reassuring.

The dog turns its back on Paul and trots over to the nearest lamp pole. He lifts his leg. The light above illuminates the stream of urine that arcs out of him.

"Good boy!" Paul says, "what a good dog you are." Shep looks off into the distance, patiently waiting for his bladder to empty, and when he is finished he turns and trots back toward Paul. Paul gives him a pat on the head and the dog hops back into the truck. It is this that brings back the man in the woods with a stunning all-at-onceness. Because who had trained this dog to be so well-mannered if not that man? Paul stands there coping with this thought, and slowly, steadily, with the patience you need to sand down a slab of walnut until it is perfectly smooth, he applies the purifying abrasion of contrary reasoning: who but a terrorized, brutalized dog would hold its urine for such a long time without so much as a whimper of complaint?

He walks across the parking lot toward the supermarket. It is the first time he has been away from the dog since leaving the woods. A dozen times at least he has told himself he needs to find a place to leave that dog. Even after he drove through Tarrytown and kept going right past the police station, not stopping, not slowing down, keeping his eyes locked on the road in front of him, even then he was thinking, *If I am going to have a chance of really walking away from this, I need to get rid of this dog.* But he could not think it through, he couldn't figure out where he would bring the dog, where the dog would be safe. The dog had suffered enough, that much was clear. That one fact was true north. Paul could not beat a man to death for kicking the dog in the ribs and then just open the door of his truck and let the dog fend for itself.

The dog is his witness, his confessor, he has seen it all and can still sit next to Paul, breathing with him, trusting him, the dog is the reason, the dog is what has been salvaged from the worst moment of Paul's life, the dog is the bridge which Paul walks upon as he inches his way over the abyss, the dog is *God* spelled backward. Paul turns for another look at Shep, but can't see him. The dog has drowned in the darkness of the truck's cabin.

The inside of the supermarket is a bright, throbbing riot of colors, but is nevertheless somewhat desolate. It is an immense store but there are only a half dozen or so shoppers, lonely, bedraggled-looking people in late middle age in no hurry to bring their groceries home. The piped-in music is string arrangements of Rod Stewart hits. Even in the best of circumstances, there is something disquieting about seeing so much food, fruit piled up like cannonballs, slabs of meat seething beneath airtight plastic wrap, whole aisles devoted to potato chips. On his way to the pet food aisle, Paul passes two elderly men whose carts have bumped up against each other. One of them has poet-laureate white hair with a yellowish tinge, like the keys of an old piano; the other is stooped, using his cart as an ad hoc walker. They are sharing a great laugh over something, and when the stooped man picks out an item from his basket—a small jar of tartar sauce—and shows it to his friend, their laughter increases. And the sound of those old men laughing plunges Paul into a sense of despair and remorse greater than anything he has felt since the fight in the woods. Just the sound of their voices makes his hand throb, his heart lurch drunkenly.

"Something we can do for you, young man?" the white-haired fellow says to Paul.

"Not that we will!" his stooped-over friend quips.

Paul carries a fifty-pound sack of dry dog food slung over his shoulder; a month's supply of kibble makes it seem as if life were predictable, that there are things you can plan on and measures you can take. When he pays at the checkout counter, the woman working the cash register looks at him strangely, and when he gives her the money he sees his hand: it is swollen and red. And his face, too, must tell some version of the story of what he has been through.

Something must be done about this. Paul drives out of the parking lot with his left hand on the steering wheel and his right arm slung over the dog's shoulders. He has owned a dog only once before in his life and that was King Richard, a golden retriever Paul's mother bought from a local breeder the first Christmas after Matthew left Connecticut for New York. Paul and his sister were electrified with joy when their mother came home with the fat, honey-colored pup.

"Oh my God, oh my God," Annabelle said, over and over, her hands clasped.

The puppy seemed happy to be with children; it romped and panted and licked their hands—and bit their fingers, too, it couldn't help itself, all that exuberance and passion to connect. But there was something wrong with the dog. When it rested it was unnervingly still and its eyes went dull, like some life-of-the-party drunk who, after regaling the table with his hilarious anecdotes, slumps into a melancholy stupor. Soon, the puppy was coughing, deep, wracking coughs, Paul couldn't believe such an ominous sound could come out of something so soft and small. Like a bicycle horn bleating inside a bowl of oatmeal. By week's end, the dog was dead, its eyes like smashed fuses, the tip of its little pickled tongue protruding from its mouth.

"King!" Paul had called out, as if to rouse the puppy back to life.

"Well that didn't take very long," his mother said, her voice flat, affectless; she had already entered that phase of her life in which misfortune was the norm.

About fifteen miles from Kate's house, Paul makes a series of turns and takes first a two-lane blacktop that leads to Victory Hill, a convalescent home for the aged, and a place Paul knows will suit his purposes. The nursing home, once the summer residence of a spice broker down in the city, who summered there with a series of short-lived wives in the early nineteenth century, is on a perch with a partial view of the river. But Paul's destination is the employee parking lot, which is nearly empty and sheltered from view.

"Okay, Shep, time to get out." The dog has curled up on the seat, with his nose close to his hindquarters, and doesn't wish to be disturbed. When Paul touches his mahogany-colored ear to roust him up, the dog doesn't open his eyes but growls softly. "You've got to be fucking kidding me," Paul says. This for some reason makes Shep's eyes open—they are round as marbles and rimmed with red.

"Wait right there," Paul says and slides out of the driver's side. The night air is dry, blade-sharp. Withered oak leaves, desiccated and crisp, blown by the wind, scurry across the parking lot like rats. *Is anybody looking? Can anybody see?* Paul turns up the collar of his leather jacket and opens the passenger side of the truck. Shep does not seem very interested in getting out but when Paul calls to him, the dog laboriously gets up, section by section, and when he is standing at last he gazes at Paul, as if hoping for some last-minute reprieve. "This is going to be fast," Paul says, and there is something reassuring enough in his voice to induce the dog to hop down out of the truck's warmth and onto the cold asphalt.

Paul leads the dog, with his finger crooked around the dog's metal choke collar. He doesn't want to pull too hard on it and yank back sense memories of the rough treatment this dog has had to endure, but he wants Shep to mind him. He walks with him to where an old abandoned Comet is sitting, its tires flat, its windshield cracked, and commands the dog to sit. "You stay here."

He points at Shep and looks sternly at him, hoping to convey the importance of the order. Shep tilts his head to the left and opens his mouth, letting his long tongue unfurl and giving himself an unaccountably happy-go-lucky expression. Paul backs away, continuing to motion for the dog to stay put, and when he is halfway between the dog and the truck he turns and quickly walks over to his truck, opens the door, gets in, disengages the parking brake, puts it into gear, and runs it with some vigor into the closest large tree, which happens to be a red maple, judging by the diameter of its trunk.

"Sorry," Paul whispers to the tree as the front end of his truck strikes it. He braces himself and, in fact, is barely jostled by the impact, though he forgot to fasten his seat belt. He throws the truck into reverse; his headlights reveal a couple of gouges in the tree's hide, but the red maple is a hardy tree, and Paul is sure it will barely be affected by the sudden laceration of its bark.

What worries him more is if he has done enough damage to his truck to explain the bruises on his face and hands. He climbs out of the cab and checks the damage. Perfect. His spirits lift, unreasonably so, as if he has just solved every one of his problems. There is a large, deep dent along the left side of the front bumper, and the left headlight has a spiderweb of cracks over its entirety. Shep is at his side, leaning his weight against Paul's leg. Paul reaches down and scratches behind the dog's ears. "You see why I wanted you to get out of the truck," Paul says to the dog, opening the passenger door for him.

A half hour later, Paul takes the turn onto Kate's long driveway. Locust trees, tall and bare, many of them dead but still standing, line either side of the curving quarter-mile. The house is an old Colonial farmhouse, built simply and in sections, the earliest part from 1766, with a subsequent addition from 1810, and another from 1890—the Victorian section, with dark pine built-ins, a carved marble mantel, and a wedding-cake ceiling.

When Paul first came to this house he was looking for work. Kate had said, "I hear you're the man to talk to about windows," and ushered him in with a wave of her fingers. An electrical charge passed between them; it was a moment they relived together, months later. "The old owners put these crummy aluminum frames in and I want nice new windows," Kate had said. "Maybe . . ." When she paused for a moment, Paul lowered his eyes, telling himself not to look quite so intently at her. She mentioned a brand of window often advertised in lifestyle magazines, usually with an illustration of a family sprawled out in a living room, husband, wife, daughter, Dalmatian, cozy and carefree, with a view of a winter wonderland through the double-paned glass.

"This is a beautiful house," Paul had said, "and it would be nice to have really great old windows. Those mass-manufactured ones? They're okay, but not like the old ones. The old ones . . ." He closed his eyes, shook his head: there were no words with which he could describe the poignancy of the old glass.

"So old glass," she said. "Where do you find such a thing?"

"Lady, I've got a truckload of just what you're looking for. The problem is you've got new frames and sashes—the people before you didn't care what they put up." Paul had made this aside in a low voice, as if the previous owners might still be within earshot. "What I have to do is make all new frames and put the old glass in them. It'll end up looking as if they're the original windows, here forever, and if you want to save on your heating I could double-pane them, but I have to tell you it's not going to be cheap. You might want to go with whatever they've got at Home Depot."

"No, no, I'd rather go with what you're recommending," Kate said.

Paul smiled. He had a handsome man's absence of vanity—he didn't take very good care of himself. His bottom teeth were crossed, his fingernails were caked with dirt. "I have to tell you," he said, "I'm very glad you're going to do this. I happen to love this building." He walked to the front of the house, patted the plaster near one of the windows he would now replace, as if to reassure the muted white walls that better days were ahead, and these offensive windows were going to be plucked out like thorns from the paw of a mighty lion.

Now, Ruby stands at one of those shimmering windows as

Paul swings his truck around the circular parking area in front of the house. She shields her eyes with her little starfish of a hand. The sight of a child disturbs his fragile equilibrium of remembering and not remembering. Her face, her smallness, her newness, triggers in Paul a sudden chaos of remorse. He begins to talk to the dog because it makes him feel better. "All right, here's the drill. I'm going to go inside for a minute, I'm going to talk to Ruby, and then we're both going to come out here. Okay? Shep?" The dog does not seem to be listening. Something on his paw has captured his full attention and he is alternately licking and nibbling at the webbing between his blunt, black claws.

Paul turns off the truck's engine. Even this small change in reality is upsetting—the engine's hum gone, the headlights extinguished. Everything must be just so for him to tolerate the memory of this afternoon. He is like a man carrying a load that is far heavier than he can manage but who has nevertheless found a way to hoist it up and stagger forward a few steps. If his balance is at all disturbed, the true weight of what he is carrying will assert itself, and the task will prove impossible. He slides out of the truck, feels the familiar crunch of the driveway's stones. When he looks again at the window, Ruby is no longer standing there. A wedge of light falls onto the gravel. Ruby has opened the front door. She is in jeans and a lavender turtleneck.

"Hi Paul," she says. "Your truck looks beat up."

"And you look like a girl who might do very well with a surprise." Paul is calmed by the jolly boom of his own voice. The role of father is a comfort to him, the powerful encompassing mask of it.

"Do you have one?" Ruby says. The cold breeze whips her hair around. The light from the house illuminates the back of her; moonlight glistens on her teeth. *Children should not be in the dark*, Paul thinks. He sees her shiver and he hoists her up, brings her close. Her finger hovers above the bruise on the right side of his forehead. Her knees grip his rib cage.

"All right," he says, "I'll show you." He carries her back to the truck. Shep has come to the window. He has lifted his snout to the little crack of opening Paul has left, and his tail is going around and around. His eyes bulge, but he has stopped drooling.

Ruby's first response is to shrink back. "No, no, it's okay," Paul says. "He's friendly."

"Whose dog is that?" Ruby asks.

"It's a lost dog, is what it is," Paul says. "I found him and I thought this good old dog needs himself a home."

Ruby, still in Paul's arms, leans forward, takes a closer look at Shep, who seems to understand that this is some sort of audition and has pressed his nose through the crack in the window. His nostrils expand and contract. "Where'd you find him?" Ruby asks.

Paul has already rehearsed the answer to any question that anyone is likely to ask about this dog. The commission of his crime may have been completely spontaneous, but the aftermath is already full of intricacy and cunning. "I met a trucker at a rest stop, the one your mom likes to stop at when we go to the city, and he came up to me and he said he found a dog in North Carolina and he was going to bring him home but when he talked to his wife she said if he came home with a dog she would be really really mad at him."

"Why?" Ruby asks.

"Not everyone likes dogs."

Ruby nods, taking in this sad fact of life. "Do we get to keep him?" she asks, her voice vigilant.

"I don't know. I want to talk it over with your mom. A dog's a lot of work. It might not be the best idea. But I wanted you two guys to meet."

Ruby wriggles free of him. Once on the ground, she opens the truck and Shep, used to bounding out of a front seat not quite so high as this one, hesitates for a moment, panting and gathering his courage. Finally, he lowers his head, raises his rump, and jumps out of the truck. He seems interested in neither Ruby nor Paul; rather it is the gravel that commands his attention, and he sniffs at it greedily, snorting, his mahogany cheeks puffing out, his tail revving faster and faster. He half-lifts his leg and marks his spot. *Welcome home*, Paul thinks.

"Can I pet him?" Ruby asks.

"Why don't you put out your hand and see if he comes over and gives it a sniff." Ruby does as she is told and Shep, seeing her hand, makes his peculiar, mincing gait over to her, sniffs her fingertips. Ruby's lips stretch, her eyes widen, she looks like a kid on a roller coaster.

"You see?" Paul says. "He's getting to know you."

Kate emerges from the house, buttoning her heavy coat and looking at them curiously. "I thought I saw a dog," she says. She's still fifty feet away, and she is silhouetted before the steady deep yellow lights of the house, but Paul is sure he can see her smiling. "Did you really bring a dog for us?" Kate asks.

Shep's tongue shyly engages Ruby's hand. "He likes me!" she cries. The sudden sound of her delight makes the dog cower, as if he is going to be beaten.

"What the hell happened to your truck?" Kate asks.

CHAPTER
SIX

Four days after his death, a picture of William Robert Claff runs in the weekly Tarrytown newspaper. When he first sees it, Frank Mazzerelli doesn't realize the man pictured is someone he knows, but when he happens to glance at the picture again while having a solitary meal and hoping to occupy his mind with something other than stale thoughts about the past, it becomes clear to Mazzerelli that this is a picture of his tenant, the man he knows as Alfred Krane. The question is: what ought he to do about it? Having contact with local law enforcement is just about the last thing he wants.

Frank Mazzerelli is a former Yonkers police officer whose entire career in the YPD was shadowed by the fear that one day his secret and infrequent homosexual love life would become public knowledge. In his thirty years on the job, no one with whom he worked ever asked him why he wasn't married or at least with a girlfriend, but Frank did not fail to note that no one ever offered to fix him up, either. His last day at work, at the obligatory retirement party at Bennigan's, after all the tepid toasts and forced joviality from people whom after all these years he felt he barely knew, custom dictated that Frank himself make a toast, preferably one that mixed nostalgia and hard kidding. To his horror, Frank teared up in the middle of it, though he decided later the sentiment was not about saying good-bye to any of the faces in that room but an expression of sheer relief, such as he had felt only once before in his entire life, when he'd been shot at by two teenage bank robbers he was pursuing from a Washington Mutual branch to the southbound Sprain Parkway.

Frank's retirement plan originally had been to move west and buy income properties, maybe in California, or possibly even Hawaii, where his sister and his nephews lived. But somehow he ended up just a few miles from Yonkers, in Tarrytown, because in the end it made sense to him to do business in a place he knew. Muscular, olive-skinned, his salt-and-pepper hair cut Caesar-style, with a taciturn manner and sharp, unfriendly eyes, Mazzerelli now owns two apartment buildings, one with four units, the other with six residential units plus retail space at street level, all of which combine with his YPD pension to make for a comfortable retirement. He's scrupulous in the upkeep of his property. His tenants find him fair if not friendly, and they appreciate the clean hallways, the ample heat and hot water, the shoveled sidewalks, the monthly pest control—the fact is, he *loves* his property—and the renters know not to be late with the rent. Mazzerelli's motto is *The first of the month means the first of the month*, and he has been known to park his black hand-waxed Infiniti across the street from one or the other of his buildings and to eat his lunch slouched behind the steering wheel.

When prospective tenants called looking to rent, Frank met them at the Fonz's Corner, a diner out on South Broadway, where he used to eat occasionally when he was on the job. It is a red-and-silver place, a bastion of manufactured nostalgia for the American 1950s. The benches in the booths look like the backseats of old Impalas and the tables are grooved in bright aluminum. Frank would always be a few minutes early and he'd sit with a view of the parking area, so he could get a look at the applicant's car and the way he walked, which Frank believed told him more than any payroll stub or copy of last year's tax returns. After a brief interview they'd get into Frank's car and drive over to the apartment and as they cruised the streets of Tarrytown Frank allowed his left pant leg to hike up just enough so the new tenant could get a peek at the Glock he carried in a black nylon ankle holster. Two things Frank needed to keep his operation clean and trouble-free: a month's security paid in advance and giving tenants a glimpse of that gun.

Alfred Krane/Will Claff was late for that first meeting at Fonz's Corner, and when he finally walked in Frank realized he had seen Krane/Claff ten minutes before, pacing the parking lot and then getting back into his white Honda, the behavior, surely, of a man on the lookout for enemies. And there was another thing that Frank had seen as a red flag: Claff came to the meeting looking like he'd spent the night in a doorway. His jacket was rumpled, he needed a shave, his hair was mussed, his fingernails were filthy. His tie seemed to have a ladybug tie tack, but it turned out to be an actual ladybug, and when Frank pointed it out Claff crushed it between his thumb and forefinger and flicked the husk to the floor. But Frank was sitting on two empty apartments at the time and was inclined to say yes. On the ride over to the apartment, when Frank hiked up his Dockers and let Claff see the piece, Claff did something none of the other tenants had dared—he mentioned it.

"I would fucking love to have a gun like that," he'd said, pointing down at Frank's left foot.

"You have any guns?" Frank asked him quickly.

Claff shook his head.

"I would need to know that," Frank said. "I would need you to be very honest with me about that, right up front."

"I never owned a gun, Mr. Landlord," Claff said. "I'm a very good boy." He made a small, surrendering smile, which Frank understood to mean *You got me now, but one day maybe it'll be my turn.* Frank didn't begrudge it; most men kept a tally sheet.

The photo in the Tarrytown weekly was taken off Claff's driver's license, which the cops found stuck between the driver's seat and the center console in his car, in the west lot of Martingham State Park. Even with the driver's license the cops couldn't be sure about the dead man's name. The wallet held a blue-and-white card showing a teddy bear holding a toothbrush reminding Alfred Krane about an upcoming dentist appointment in Sleepy Hollow, an Exxon credit card belonging to a Henry Lloyd, a library card from Evanston, Illinois, with the name Ivan Kline on it, a customer-reward card from The Running Emporium also bearing the name Ivan Kline. They found a business card from a place called Happy Valley Massage, with no address and no phone number, and another card from Elkins Park Gourmet, with a Philadelphia number. The police ran the dead man's prints through the system and got no hits, and the state of California seemed to have lost track of William Claff; the last address Motor Vehicles had for him was in an apartment complex that burned to the ground three years ago.

When Frank Mazzerelli sees the picture of Claff in the local paper, his first impulse is to turn the page. He does not wish to have anything to do with the police, the local police, the state police, any police. He has an aversion to cops that would rival that of a career criminal. He is also on guard about having 2C involved in a possible homicide—just having police in there will delay renting it out again. But, finally, something so simple, corny, and dumb as *good citizenship* changes his mind and he decides to step forward.

Before going to the precinct, Mazzerelli goes to Will's apartment and lets himself in. It is not his first time entering a dead man's apartment, but here there is no scatter of mail on the floor, no accumulation of newspapers, no flies droning around a plate of rotting food, no throbbing red light on the answering machine indicating dozens of missed calls.

Frank stands in the front room for a few more moments; there is a quality to the silence, a heaviness, a completeness that feels fatal. He notices the front window is open a few inches. A spray of wet snow is coming into the apartment, flying this way and that like sparks off a grinder. Frank closes the window and walks into the bedroom, opens the closet. There are few things hanging there, and fifty empty hangers, as if in anticipation of better days ahead. The bed is unmade, there are socks on the floor, a bottle of Armani hand lotion on the bedside table, a stale smell in the air. And then the kitchen: fridge filled with water bottles, vitamins, a cooked chicken in its plastic dome. Next to the refrigerator is a bag of dog food, showing a picture of a golden retriever running through tall grass toward a perfect family of four.

That little cocksucker, Frank thinks. *He had a dog. I could fucking kill him myself.*

CHAPTER
SEVEN

Ruby has once again attempted to get the dog to sleep in her bedroom. Though she normally is reluctant to close her door at night, now she shuts it tight, hoping to frustrate the dog's ability to escape. Nevertheless, Shep comes walking down the twenty-step staircase. By day he is full of energy, but at night his steps are cautious, mincing.

"Uh-oh, look who's here," Kate says, as the dog makes his way into the living room, where Paul is crouched in front of the fireplace, jabbing at a couple of hissing locust logs with the fireplace poker in a way that to Kate always seems random and a little angry, but which is generally effective. Sure enough, the flames open into full bloom and the smoke, which had been curling out over the edge of the hearth, is now rushing up the flue and out the chimney.

"Hello there buddy," he says. Instead of rising from his crouch, Paul sits down on the hooked rug in front of the hearth, and Shep, his head bowed in an elaborate show of deference, comes to Paul's side.

"How did you ever exist before you found this dog?" Kate asks.

She has brought a pot of tea and a plate of sliced apples out to the living room. There is an air of discomfort and irony when Kate performs domestic duties. "I forgot sugar," she says.

"Just as well," says Paul. "The apples are sweet." He scrambles to his feet, picks up a thin, nearly translucent apple slice, and holds it up to the firelight. "You cut these so beautifully."

Kate looks at him oddly. "You compliment me about the weirdest little things. You tell me how neat my purse is. You're really reaching, trying to come up with *something*."

Paul continues to inspect the apple. "Beautifully cut, one cut and one cut only. Am I right? No hesitation."

"Yes, I'm really quite amazing," Kate says. "You really lucked out with me." She hands him the tea in a black-and-gold mug bearing the title of her book, just one of the promotional items her publisher and bookstores have made on her book's behalf—T-shirts, water glasses, a vase, a pious silk bookmark, a scarf, posters announcing her appearance at various bookstores, churches, art centers, and colleges, a monogrammed briefcase, pens, pencils, a cell phone holder—she even has a wristwatch, a gift from her publisher, with a picture of Kate on its face, the hour and the minute hands sometimes protruding from the sides of her nose like cat whiskers. She treats all these small souvenirs of success as if they were part of a joke, yet none of them are discarded. She can't help it.

She sees that Paul's eyes have settled on the mug. She shrugs, makes a comical face, and then grimaces. "How do you make tea again?" she says, laughing, putting the mug on the mantelpiece. She is wearing jeans, a turtleneck, and a knit cardigan. She plunges her hand into the sweater's pocket. She occasionally finds a couple of stray candies in her pockets. Since stopping drinking, she craves sweets—in fact, all of her tastes and desires have become more vivid, and more urgent: salt, laughter, sex. She finds two foil-wrapped chocolates: *and some people say there is no God!*

"I feel a little like we're losing touch with each other," she says. She sits on the sofa and pats the cushion next to her, beckoning Paul. He continues to fuss with the dog. "What did your insurance guy say about your truck?" Kate asks.

"I don't know," Paul says.

Kate considers this for a moment. It makes absolutely no sense to her—she knows he *has* auto insurance, and she knows his insurance agent, who is her insurance agent as well, speaks clearly and in English, and she also knows that no repairs have yet been made on Paul's banged-up truck, nor has he seen a doctor about his array of bangs and bruises. She counsels herself: *let it pass*.

"How can you not know?" she asks. "Did you even call?"

"I'm just going to take care of it myself," Paul says. "It was my fault anyhow."

It sounds simple enough, but the mode of living and making decisions at the core of Paul's statement is finally so at odds with Kate's way of being in the world that, despite reminding herself again that here is a perfect example of something she can just as well let alone, something that does not need her participation or commentary, she finds herself saying, "But that's what insurance is for, honey. Why would you make that kind of decision? I don't get it."

Paul takes a breath; even under better circumstances, it is often difficult for him to order his thoughts when it is time to present them. Even when he can bring his thoughts forward he has trouble sequencing them—he often sounds like a child to himself, interrupting himself with salient details he forgot to put in, and further interrupting himself with so many parenthetical thoughts that the implied parentheses burst open like soaking-wet paper sacks. The greater pity of it is that he knows what it is like to imagine himself eloquent, and to imagine his opinions and memories flowing out like a song as he spins out an anecdote about his youthful travels and travails, or about the extreme alpha-males he meets in the course of his work, but these songs remain unsung, buried and entombed beneath an avalanche of you-knows and nervous laughs. He can be articulate with children, with fellow carpenters, and with strangers. Kate is a different story altogether. As much as he loves her and feels confident in her feelings for him, he sometimes finds himself tongue-tied and stammering around her, and sometimes when he does say what he means to his voice is soft, flat, and bears, without his intention, a pattern of discouragement, in the way that parasites beneath the bark of a tree will create swirling designs in the wood.

Kate senses there is a reason Paul has not called the insurance agent about the truck. Her best guess is that he long ago forgot to pay his premium, or maybe he absentmindedly allowed his registration to lapse, and now would rather pay for the repairs himself or leave the truck as it is than face the consequences of his loosey-goosey lifestyle. It's fine with her. There are enough punctual people in the world, enough bankers, and enough computer programmers—the people who might be escorting everyone to the apocalypse when their machines fail to recognize the end of the twentieth century at the end of next month.

No, Kate does not need for Paul to pay keener attention to worldly affairs, and she surely does not need for him to be more clever about money. She is making plenty of money now, and, really, in his own way, Paul seems to always find time for his high-end clients. Yes, every job takes much, much longer than he originally anticipates, but, in the end, he is always handsomely paid. What Kate needs from Paul is what Paul already supplies: his honesty, his beauty, his tenderness toward Ruby, and the passionate attention he pays to her.

She joins him on the floor, nuzzles closer, and gently but insistently pulls him down, so they are both lying in front of the fireplace, with the dozing dog between them and the flames. As she kisses his nose, his closed eyes, she thinks, *Who cares about insurance?* And then: *Wouldn't it make a lot more sense if we were on the same policy?*

"Hey," she says. "You know what? We should get married."

She sees what she hopes is merely surprise on his face. "You're making me a little nervous," she says.

"I'm sorry, I don't mean to."

"I just proposed and you look like I pulled a knife on you."

Paul takes her in his arms, holds her close to comfort her and make her feel loved, and to relieve her from having to study his face for clues. He is bereft, abandoned: how can she not know he is a ruined man?

"My God," Kate says, "your poor heart is pounding."

"I'm fine."

"You know what?" Kate extricates herself from his embrace. She clears her throat. "We don't have to get married. Maybe we'll just have a party, a big old party so everyone in Leyden can see us together and, you know, all the women can just be sick with envy that I've snagged the most desirable man in New York State." She waits for him to say something. "We can do it on New Year's Eve. Everyone needs a place to go on New Year's Eve, especially this one, since the world is supposed to come to an end, and I can invite all my sober friends who need a place to go where there is plenty of seltzer and cranberry juice. We'll have booze, and lots of chocolate. And smoking will be allowed because a few of my AA friends need to smoke—I think their self-image depends on having at least one horrible habit."

She rolls onto her back and tucks her hands behind her head, and looks up at the ceiling. Reflected light from the fireplace dashes across the smooth white plaster. She is still waiting for Paul to say something—not necessarily about the proposal of marriage, or even the proposal of a party. She would just like him to say *something*.

Cold midnight. The moon is parked outside the bedroom window and Kate's breathing buzzes richly, oddly soothing to Paul, though he would love to be asleep himself. He lifts his corner of the comforter and slips out of bed. The wooden wide-board floor is cold on his bare feet.

I did it.

I ended a life.

The night air moves through the room like black water. Paul steps back, stumbles on Shep, who has still not found a stable sleeping spot. The dog's tail thumps on the floor. "Shhh, Sheppie, shhh," Paul says, but the sound of Paul's voice makes him wag his tail with more vigor and intensity. "All right, come on, let's go," Paul whispers, and the dog scrambles up noisily.

Kate and Paul's bedroom is on the second floor; the house's other substantial bedroom, Ruby's, is at the other end of the landing. Between the bedrooms are three smaller rooms, including the garretlike one, with faded rose wallpaper, described once by the real estate saleswoman as the sewing room, and used by Kate as her office before Paul built her a real studio. Paul has now made it his own, where he stores his tool and fixtures catalogs, issues of architecture and home-decorating magazines in which his work has been featured, and where, with a sleek little computer Kate gave him a few months ago, he searches the Internet for materials. Whereas he was once confined to a hundred-mile radius to find old windows, barn boards, salvaged mantels, and old-growth lumber, now he has a nation-spanning network of contractors, carpenters, lumber brokers, hardware collectors, salvagers, rural archaeologists willing to sell anything from a steeple to a stall. He had even recently succumbed to an impulse buy of six 125-year-old ladders rescued from an abandoned apple orchard in Yakima, Washington, the wood as smooth and gray as fog, the length and taper so beautiful and so perfect and so deeply redolent of the past that it moved Paul practically to tears when he dismantled them to incorporate their parts in new construction.

He appreciates the sleek design of his computer, its compactness, its waste-free functionality, but, aside from the action of the keyboard and the hinges of the case, how his laptop actually *works* is mysterious to him. In his personal life, what brings him joy are animal pleasures—eating, drinking, sex, air, freedom. Most of what the world offers at the push of a button or the flick of a switch does not appeal to him.

The computer sits on a table his assistant, Evangeline Durand, gave him for his birthday two months ago, a trim four-by-three piece of white oak she had somehow planed and burnished without his noticing. Her card informed him that his birthday was once known in England as Royal Oak Day. She had fastened a sprig of oak to the card, and in her own calligraphy she copied a poem by John Evelyn, linking the oak tree to kingliness:

> A rugged Seat of Wood became a Throne
> Th' obsequious Boughs his Canopy of State
> With bowing Tops the Tree their King did own
> And silently ador'd him as he sate.

"Are you sure she's a lesbian?" Kate had said, when he showed her Evangeline's present. She ran her palm over the smooth, waxed wood, and furrowed her brow. "I think you're so used to women having crushes on you, you don't even see it when it's right in front of you."

"She lives with a woman," Paul said. "Who she calls her husband."

"I don't know," Kate had persisted. "She wears that little pearl necklace to work."

"Maybe from her husband," Paul replied.

The computer has already taught him the difference between murder and manslaughter and that his crime, if he were to be tried for it and found guilty, as he surely would be, carries a sentence of somewhere between three and ten years, though by now he would probably be given the harshest sentence allowable—the law seems to hold a particular loathing for runners and hiders. Tonight Paul wants to find out anything he can about the man who died in the woods. He turns the computer on and cringes at the heartless chord it plays when it is powered up. Shep is next to him on the bare floor, sighing and snoring in an almost human way, snout resting on his front paws. The dog, this seventy-five pounds of consciousness, is the only part of the universe, except for the trees and the sky, that has seen what Paul can do when fury and instinct take the place of thought, and yet this dog seems to have bestowed his fealty upon him, totally and unshakably.

Thank you, Shep, old buddy, Paul thinks as he goes to the AOL site and types in Recent Deaths Westchester. An innumerable list of options presents itself, most of them months old. Not only are the entries outdated but he has seen them all himself, though in slightly different order, on previous nights. Suddenly, he sees a new one: "Recent University Study on Westchester Deaths."

Paul clicks on the story, and waits nervously while it simmers up to the surface.

> If you are found dead or go missing in Westchester County, there is a 1 in 22 chance that local law enforcement authorities will do little or nothing to determine the cause of your death. Even in cases where it is clear that a crime has been committed, Westchester leads New York State counties in police inaction. This is the conclusion come to by Dr. Mansfield Trumbull, a law professor at the University of Connecticut.

"Given the number of local and state police we have in Westchester," Dr. Trumbull said, "the number of unexplained and uninvestigated deaths and disappearances is remarkable. The only area in the U.S. we found with a comparable number of unexplained deaths and disappearances is in the Native American reservations in North Dakota, where law enforcement has been almost nonexistent. Westchester, with its numerous police forces and adequate funding, is not going to be the next North Dakota, but nevertheless the pattern emerging of official inaction is, quite frankly, disturbing."

Paul reads, shaking his head with worry. This voice from the mysterious regions of his computer, this blather of opinion that may have been written five years ago and has perhaps gone unread since then, these pixelated paragraphs floating around the Internet like garbage in outer space . . . *Shut the fuck up, professor*, Paul thinks.

Stumbling around the Internet, slowly going from one site to the next, Paul happens upon a page that is more than he can bear. The site is called *They Are Missed* and basically it is a bulletin board for posting pictures of and rudimentary information about missing persons. Page after page of pictures—smiling faces from high school yearbooks, serious stares taken off driver's licenses, or employee IDs, young men in tuxedos, young women in bridal gowns, suggesting lives in which no one had bothered to take their photograph except on their wedding day, missing men and women, boys and girls, with their heads cocked, brows furrowed, flirty, furious, fucked up on booze or drugs, an astonishing number of them last seen going out to a convenience store at some forsaken hour, a likewise astonishing number coming from either Texas or Maryland, black, white, Asian, Latino, all of them citizens of a vast underground archipelago of suffering, whose inhabitants include not only the murdered and the missing but all those who loved them and who wait for some final word. And also: those who were responsible for their violent ends, they were condemned to the archipelago, too.

Paul looks at each of the missing people and does not find one of them who looks like the man in the woods. Next he must look at the pages containing images of bodies the police have yet to identify, but before the site will allow him access to these images there is a warning: *Some of the content profiled in the Unidentified section may be disturbing and contains postmortem photographs that are not suitable for children. Do you wish to continue?* Paul has no choice but to click Yes and, through a frightened squint, as if his eyelashes can soften the blow of those thumbnail pictures, he looks for the evidence of what he has done in the photos of the horribly decomposed faces, or, in some cases, the graphite renderings of the suspiciously deceased, when the body, once discovered (most often by hunters, joggers, or dog walkers) has been pulled too deeply into the vortex of decomposition to photograph.

There is a tap at his door and Paul quickly closes his computer.

"Paul? Are you in there?" Kate says in a dry, cracked whisper. She opens the door and gives him a quizzical look. "I rolled over and you weren't there."

"Well you found me," Paul says, rising from his chair, taking her in his arms. She smells of the bed, and the lingering lilac scent of her evening bath. Even as he holds her he feels as if he is remembering her. "Thank you for finding me," he whispers.

CHAPTER
EIGHT

Walking through the woods, it's step by step, one foot in front of the other. What could be more fundamental? It's like breathing—inhale through the nostrils, exhale through the mouth, the taste and tickle of your own mortality coursing over your lips like running water over stones. We are under a sea of air, to which we have adapted just as fish have adapted to their life underwater.

A walk in the woods is like wading through a river; you can't walk in the same woods twice, no matter how you may try. You can tread the same path and at the same pace and at the same time of day, you can measure your steps so that Tuesday's walk matches Monday's as closely as possible, but no matter what, the walk will be singular and unique. Leaves will have fallen since your last time here, pinecones, acorns, berries, shit, a beer can, a candy wrapper. Procreation will have taken place, pursuit, death, shoots will have been eaten, brush will have been trampled, bark will have peeled, roots will have grown deeper. Decay and regeneration are a wheel that will not stop turning, even now, autumn by the calendar, winter by the bone, the gray wash-water sky, the liquefying leaves underfoot, even now the wheel turns, slower than in the warmer months but with a bleak grandeur.

"My soul," Paul says, "there's steam coming off this pile of deer shit." *My soul, my soul*, he repeats to himself. It was his mother's phrase, a verbal keepsake now. She used to deliver it full of irony, just as she did *Land's sake*, and *Lamb's sake*, too, because both seemed right to her, she just wasn't sure which was which, and it didn't entirely matter either because it was all a part of an act, the part she liked to play of a good country woman hanging on to her Christian principles in an evil, crazy world, a pose among many and no less or more true than her other assumed identities—the antimaterialist wild child, the fallen American aristocrat full of frontier virtue, the self-sacrificing mother hen, the natural artist, the woman with a surfeit of common sense.

Shep is hovering over the fresh scat, his bristly muzzle less than a quarter inch from the soft pile, which looks like a mound of plump raisins. "Don't do that, boy," Paul says, but the dog only half-listens—he hasn't put any deer shit in his mouth yet but his nostrils dilate and contract as he takes in the full sensual delight of his find. His thin black lips part, his tongue emerges to taste nature's bounty. "Shep, that's no good," Paul says, this time pressing two fingers on the back of the dog's neck.

"Something to bear in mind the next time you give that dog a big old smooch on the lips," says Todd Lawson, with whom Paul is walking.

Lawson, like many in Leyden, is hard to place occupationally, or socioeconomically. He is loosely but not profitably related to various local big shots, politicians, ministers, and the owners of riverfront estates, but whatever local pedigree he may claim, none of it is of much material use. Right now, Lawson has five jobs, which altogether generate enough income to support his modest, solitary life, including spending the coldest part of the New York winter in Mexico, which might strike some as a luxury for a man who is often in arrears on his rent, but the urge to head south for the winter is a trait Lawson has inherited from his flush forebears. The original makers of the family's fortune were industrious, driven men, but there followed generations of idlers, ending with Lawson's father, Harley, who worked two days a week at a brokerage off Maiden Lane managing to lose so much money that his family was grateful he didn't work full-time.

Idleness is not an option for Todd. Part of his income comes from Marlowe College, whose tennis team he coaches. He also works at a horse farm on the edge of Leyden, where he gives riding lessons. He makes two hundred dollars a month touring visitors through one of the most spectacular of the river estates, a Victorian monstrosity painted black and gray, whose exterior has been used by the makers of several horror films, and whose interior, full of dark wood and clashing wallpapers and overall sense of foreboding, leaves most visitors feeling quite content not to have been born into nineteenth-century wealth. He also makes deliveries for Of the Manor, his brother's antiques store, and he has yet another source of occasional income, which is choosing the wines for three local restaurants owned by a woman named Indigo Blue, who is drawn to Lawson but reluctant to get involved with him, and for whom keeping him around as a part-time employee is an ideal solution.

Paul and Lawson are walking on posted land. They come to a small cluster of fallen hemlocks and then to a couple of large granite boulders, with open seams of glistening mica running through them. Lawson has picked up a long, bare branch and is using it as a walking stick.

"It's as tall as you," Paul says.

"You know," says Lawson, "Daniel Boone was about an inch taller than his gun and it weighed almost ten pounds, plus the buffalo horn full of powder and a bag full of shot. It must have really gotten old after a while, carrying all that. I think that's why he was so fond of buffalo jerky and johnnycakes. They weighed next to nothing and he was always looking to lessen his load."

It is their habit, Paul's and Lawson's, to speak of Daniel Boone when they meet for their walks in the woods. They have been conducting this informal seminar for over a year, but today Paul is finding it difficult to enter into the spirit of it. Waking this morning and remembering he was going to see Lawson, he felt, and still feels, that here is a chance for him to spend time with someone he can show his worst side, or if not the whole freak show, with all the human monsters in their unkempt cages, then at least he can momentarily pull the curtain to one side, giving Todd a glimpse. No, he does not think he will ever tell Todd about what happened in those Westchester woods, but there might be words he can say that will relieve the silent fever.

They hear a distant rustling. Shep lifts his head, tenses, and Lawson whirls toward the sound, holding his walking stick like a rifle.

"Deer," Paul says.

"Boone was a good shot, but you had to be," Lawson says. "If you missed it took almost a minute to get your musket ready for a second shot. And by that time it was often too late."

Paul stops, listens to the invisible birds cawing and squawking in the treetops. These are the hardy ones, willing to brave the oncoming winter. "It's so beautiful here," Paul says, in a whisper. "Hey, by the way, do you ever check out Martingham State Park, down near Tarrytown?"

Either the question doesn't interest Lawson, or he hasn't heard it. "Let's sit," he says, fishing a cigarette out of his denim jacket. He has an olive complexion, long black hair; he looks like he might be part American Indian. Yet for all his vigorous looks, it is always Lawson who needs to rest when they walk together. His body has accumulated the many mishaps he has endured in the course of making a living. The horse barn has taken its toll, and so has moving furniture—the weight of some of those pieces squeezes the life out of him. Last year he got his pant cuff snagged in a tractor's PTO and for months after that he dragged his right leg around like a useless thirty pounds of meat. That's finally healed, but he is always nursing something, always banged up, and he's not sure but he may be dependent on painkillers.

The men sit on the boulder and the dog sits on the ground with his back to them, looking out through the woods, at the dim world beyond, divided into strips by the intersection of countless trees.

"Back in the day," Lawson says, "this is where the preachers told everyone you had to go to find God. No Jesus in the parlor, that's what they said."

"I'll tell that one to Kate," Paul says.

"So," Lawson says, leaning back on his elbows, stretching out his legs. "How are things at the place?"

Paul has noticed that Lawson doesn't ever call where Paul lives his home. Or house. He will say the place, even your place, he will say crib, pad, domicile, abode, residence, residencia, he has called it a tent, he will even go so far as to refer to it as your corner of the zip code. But he evades ever calling it Paul's home, and this can have only one meaning: Lawson does not believe that Paul belongs in Kate's house. Does he think Paul is somehow too good to allow himself to be installed in a position that might call into question his independence? Does he worry that Paul has become one of those men who manage to saw and hammer their way into a period of cohabitation with the lady of the house, a period that, at least in Windsor County, is always short-lived and always ends with the bourgeois lady coming to her bourgeois senses and the carpenter out on his proletarian ear? Or is it that Todd Lawson believes Paul Phillips is not worthy of that house? Is there in Lawson's view something incongruous about Paul's inhabiting those prim and proper rooms, and that to see him there is to witness a display that is inherently absurd, upsetting, and distasteful, like a chimp in a tux?

"Since when did you start smoking?" Paul asks.

"A while ago," Lawson says. "You want one? They're chemical-free." He exhales a long trail of smoke, the same color as the autumn air. "So things are okay?" Lawson asks.

Paul is silent for a moment, seeing his chance to say something, and trying to gauge what his life would be like were he to actually tell his secret. When he feels as though the silence cannot be extended further, he says, "Kate's annoyed with me, I think."

"You think?" Lawson says. "That's the problem right there. You can't be guessing what she feels, you've got to know."

"I brought this dog into our life, and I didn't exactly have the green light on that one."

"You just walked in with it?" Lawson's tone conveys that he is impressed.

Paul senses another opening, a place where he can imply more of the truth. It is like being lost in the darkest heart of the woods and seeing a flash of light that suggests a way out. But for now he remains in darkness.

"That's a whole other story," Paul says. "But Shep's a stray."

"Well not anymore he isn't," Lawson says, with a laugh. Lawson snaps his fingers, beckoning the dog to come. Shep turns toward the sound but doesn't move.

"He's actually sort of practical," Paul says. "You haven't done anything for him so he doesn't figure to owe you anything."

Lawson shrugs. "I can relate," he says. He pats Paul's knee and looks at him curiously. "You look sort of tired."

"Up late," says Paul. "Three o'clock in the morning, not good."

Lawson smiles. "Maybe that's what we should be talking about, my friend. What would a fine hardworking man such as yourself be doing up and around at three in the morning? Why would you abandon the bed of your lovely consort? Why would you expose yourself to the demons who rule the earth at that ungodly time?" Lawson wets his fingertips with saliva and pinches out his cigarette, drops the twisted butt of it into his jacket's pocket.

"I've got a lot on my mind," Paul says, looking away. Shep has seen or heard or picked up the scent of something—not enough to bring him to his feet, but his spine straightens, his ears go back, and he raises his muzzle.

"Anything you feel like putting out there?" Todd asks, and when Paul shakes his head Lawson looks somewhat relieved. He gets off the boulder, and Paul readies himself to resume walking, too. They walk beneath an old spruce. Lawson lifts the lowest bough so he can pass under it, and lifts it a little higher as Paul passes under, followed by Shep.

"All right, here's the Todd Lawson diagnostic test for good relationships. Do you guys still laugh together? I mean, is it still fun?"

What would be funny, Paul thinks, *is if I right now just said, "Hey I killed a guy a couple of weeks ago."* But instead he says, "No problems there."

"Well, if you guys are still laughing. And I'm assuming the other more unmentionable things are all copacetic."

"Very much so," says Paul.

"Well then," says Todd.

Paul is quite sure that this is as far as the inquiry will go. Women have told him that among female friends all sorts of sexual confidences are exchanged, often quite graphically, but in Paul's experience this is not the case with men. Men protect the details of their intimate lives like poker players holding their cards close, and for very similar reasons, too—they either want to give the impression of holding aces or they want to be able to quietly fold without showing their hand. Knowledge is power and men don't want to give it away.

"Well if you're still laughing, and the night life is still cooking, who knows? This one might be a keeper."

"My keeping Kate isn't really the issue," Paul says. "I'm more worried about her keeping me."

"You? A fine strapping young specimen such as yourself?"

"When was the last time you hit someone?" Paul asks. "I mean really fucking whacked them in anger?"

"Oh man, I have no idea," Lawson says. "Years, many years. Not since I was a kid." He rubs the stubble on his chin with his palm. "You didn't hit her, did you?" Paul shakes his head. "Then what? The dog? The kid?"

"Nothing like that," Paul says. "Just thinking, that's all. There's something inside of me that scares the shit out of me."

"Is that all?" Lawson says. He puts his arm over Paul's shoulders. "Welcome to the world. And, by the way, welcome to America. I was just last night reading this story by D. H. Lawrence where he says the typical American is private, independent, and sort of a killer, in his heart." Lawson delivers a thump to his chest, as if to correct an irregularity. "I'll give you the book sometime, if you want."

Paul shoves his hands into his pants pockets. His hands feel suddenly cold, stiff. Fallen leaves cover the ground in gold, yellow, brown, and orange, and make walking slippery and difficult, though not for Shep, whose tongue is lolling out the side of his mouth and whose eyes sparkle, as though remembering some droll incident from his past. The woods are filled with birds who are staying put for the long winter—woodpeckers and blue jays, cardinals and chickadees. A hefty crow lights upon the tip of a nearby spruce, and sits there swaying back and forth like a black star on top of a Christmas tree. The temperature seems to be dropping, but there is a sudden presence of light coming from the west, as the sinking sun is making the last ten degrees of its journey toward the horizon free of the cloud cover. Traces of brilliant orange and red sky show through the spaces between the trees. The light, the light. Yet what Paul is thinking is: *Every step I take I go deeper into the darkness.*

CHAPTER
NINE

"Don't touch nothing more in the apartment," Jerry Caltagirone says to Frank Mazzerelli. "I'm going to send someone over there and matter of fact I'm going over myself. As far as I'm concerned, you touch anything in there you're tampering with evidence. But you know what? I still don't understand why you waited this long to come in."

On Mazzerelli's request, they have left the station and are sitting across from each other at a sticky little table at a nearby Wendy's. "Some reason for that?" Caltagirone persists. "You'd think you'd know better." He is recovering from the walk over, having gained nearly fifty pounds in the past couple of years. His heart is still not used to the increased work, and it is always a bit exhausted and a little bit behind, or so it seems to Caltagirone: there is always some part of his body where the heart has failed to send the proper amount of blood and he feels cold and clammy either around his feet or his hands, and sometimes between his shoulder blades, assuming they are still in there, somewhere.

Mazzerelli shakes his head, extends his lower lip. He feels monstrously unlucky. True, he chose this place because he didn't want to talk to Caltagirone or anyone else at the station—just smelling that cop smell of aftershave and shoe polish and onions and tobacco-tinged collars, seeing that bleak cop light falling from the fluorescents, those metal desks with the family pictures four years out of date, just five minutes in that place was more than he could take. But what were the odds, what were the *fucking odds* against walking away from Depot Plaza and ending up in this Wendy's and the first thing he sees is the one man he's been with in the past year and a half? The guy's name is Lester Ortiz, at least that's the name he gave, and he doesn't give the slightest flicker when Frank walks in. Maybe he feels shitty being seen working behind the counter in this place like some kid. As Frank remembers it, Ortiz said he taught in the high school. Frank looks at his watch. It's after four, so maybe this is Ortiz's after-school gig, though even thinking this way is dumb since what reason is there to believe a thing Ortiz said, up to and including his name, even though Frank himself had been more or less honest, saying his right name, his right first name anyhow, he didn't say his family name, and also saying Yonkers when Ortiz asked him, though Frank wasn't living in Yonkers anymore, and probably never would again, in fact he more or less held his breath when he passed the sign for the Yonkers exit when he drove into the city, but still it was where he was from, it was the place he worked, spent all those years, it was, as a friend used to say, the place where the deal was done.

"I don't follow the news except in baseball season," Frank says. He can feel Ortiz's eyes on him. "But I saw the picture, and here I am."

"And you say this guy, you knew him to be Alfred Krane, with a K."

"That's right," Frank says. "Which I gather is not his real name."

"Who the fuck knows at this point," says Caltagirone. "We ran his prints, we got no hits. And we got three different kinds of ID, with another name on each one. We figured our best bet is the driver's license, but the address on it doesn't exist and the California DMV doesn't even have him in their system, which is not too unusual from what I can tell. And now you—what'd you call him?"

"Klein," Frank says. "Alfred Klein."

"Klein or Krane?" Caltagirone says.

"Krane," says Frank.

"Yeah, but you said Klein," Caltagirone presses.

"It was just a mistake. I meant Krane."

Caltagirone looks at Frank for an extra couple of moments and then lets it go. "Yeah, well whatever name he gave you—" Caltagirone waves his fingers through the air, indicating nothingness, powerlessness, a world of false leads and blind alleys, the tedium of things not adding up. "Did you ask him for any proof when you rented to him?"

"What kind of proof?" Frank says.

"Of identity," Caltagirone says. His tray holds a milkshake, three hamburgers, a large order of fries, and some sort of pie. He had ordered freely, but now, suddenly, he is doing his best to resist what appetite has put before him. "Proof of employment, bank account, references. This guy comes to you, you don't know him, he could be wanted in six states. I think you'd want a little reassurance."

"That's not how I do it," Frank says. He holds a French fry between his thumb and forefinger, shakes off some of the salt. Ortiz is working hard behind the counter; he seems to be managing the place, barking orders at the four teenagers running the counter and six more of them back in the kitchen, but he also seems to be doing the same work as everybody else. "I got my own method," Frank adds, which he immediately regrets. Years on the job taught him that the road to hell is paved with extra words. People who know how the world works say as little as possible.

"Yeah," Caltagirone says. "I got that. Well your *method*"—Caltagirone says the word as if it were in itself suspect—"is what maybe put this whole mess in my vestibule." He hurriedly, angrily unwraps one of the hamburgers, pokes it with his forefinger, looks at it as if it were an uninvited guest. He starts to wrap it up again but reverses himself and picks it up, takes a large bite, and drops it back onto the tray.

Frank folds his arms over his chest. He wants to ask Caltagirone how renting out an apartment without running a credit check on the tenant has anything to do with anything, but he holds it back.

"This guy's three days away from potter's field, you know?" Caltagirone says. "I got prints going nowhere, I got no witnesses, and I got no motive because I don't know who the fuck this guy even was so how am I supposed to know who wants to beat the shit out of him? And speaking of shit, someone took himself a dump about a hundred yards away from the crime. You know what they're calling me down at the station? I come in it's like Hey Bag of Shit, How you doin', Bag of Shit, Good night, Bag of Shit."

"Is everything okay here, gentlemen?" It's Ortiz, he's standing there like the table's covered by a white tablecloth and he's holding the cork from the wine bottle for them to sniff. "Is there anything else we can help you with?" He's saying this with a straight face and mostly looking at Caltagirone. Frank feels like someone's tossed a bucket of horse piss in his face.

"We're good," says Caltagirone, acting like there's nothing out of the way about some guy in a Wendy's coming to your table.

"Okay," says Ortiz. "Just making sure. Customer satisfaction is job number one."

But he just stands there, in his Wendy's apron and a kind of shower cap, with the headset that connects him to all the important goings-on behind the counter and in the kitchen. Ortiz seems to have fallen into a trance and by now Frank has fixed his own gaze so powerfully on his own hands that his fingers look like they're melding together. At last, Ortiz snaps out of it and comes to his senses. "Okay, enjoy," he says, and heads back to the counter, where by now there's got to be at least fifteen people waiting for their orders, which tells Frank that headset or no headset, Ortiz's responsibility is no different from any seventeen-year-old kid's working the counter, because if he was the manager his stepping away from the counter for a couple of minutes wouldn't have caused a logjam.

"I'll tell you another thing," Frank says to Caltagirone, feeling suddenly expansive from the relief of Ortiz's leaving. He takes a deep breath. "Another lie that guy told me." He taps the side of his head, by which he means he is just now thinking of it. "He had a dog."

"He had a dog," Caltagirone repeats.

"Yeah, he had a dog," says Frank.

"And what? He told you he didn't have a dog?"

"No, he never said nothing about it. Nothing about a dog one way or the other. It was a lie of o-mission."

"All right," says Caltagirone, "he had a dog. That could be something."

"He definitely had a dog," Frank says. "I went into his apartment and there was a bag of dog food, and a bowl, plus dog hair on the floor, a lot of it."

"I don't want you going in that apartment," Caltagirone says.

"Got it," says Frank. "Next forty-eight hours it's all yours. But after that . . ." Frank shrugs, as if his right to clean that place out and get it rented again is an immutable law of nature.

"So the dog ain't there, right?" Caltagirone says.

"No, no dog."

"I'm thinking that sometimes dogs get microchipped," Caltagirone says. "We get the dog, we check out the microchip, that could be the thing. If he put a microchip in that dog it's because he don't want it going lost, in which case I'll bet you anything he gives the vet his real information, name, telephone number. Some guy going to the trouble plus expense having his dog microchipped, it would pretty much defeat the whole purpose if he puts down a bunch of bullshit on the forms."

"Yeah, but I don't have the dog," Frank says.

"I'm saying if you did," says Caltagirone.

Suddenly, practically tearing the tissue paper, Caltagirone unwraps another of his hamburgers and eats it. He chews the bun and the meat, moving it around his mouth in a circle; Frank imagines the food tumbling around like laundry in a dryer. Barely giving himself time to swallow, Caltagirone begins on the third hamburger. It's as if he knows he has perhaps a minute in which he can slip the collar of cause and effect, a minute of waking dream in which he can eat the way he bitterly imagines other people eating—freely, lustily, and without consequence. He believes that the massive coat of calories he wears is a special curse he bears, a piece of metabolic misfortune. He has several ways of consuming food that come down to magical eating—eating very very quickly is one way, breaking the food into pieces is another, as are eating while standing up, eating after midnight, and eating in the car. Yet, for the most part, he knows he will one day collapse at his desk or keel over in the street face-first and end up with a mouth full of blood and porcelain or black out dead in the car and run it right through a plate-glass window and every last person who knows him—even his own wife and kids—will think, *What the fuck, Jerry? What did you think was going to happen?*

"My thing is," Caltagirone says to Frank, "someone's waiting for this guy." As he speaks, he rewraps what is left of his third hamburger, and then his hand suddenly manages to dump the order of fries onto the tray. "Maybe he was a piece of shit," Caltagirone says, staring at the oily heap of fried potatoes, "and maybe at the end of the day we're going to figure this for a misdemeanor homicide, but right now there's someone out there waiting for him and maybe worrying themselves sick, maybe his mother, or his sister, maybe he's married, and I'm going to put it to rest for them because knowing someone is dead is better than just not knowing and waiting and waiting for something that don't ever happen."

"Nothing in Missing Persons?" Frank asks. A little tremor of nostalgia for the job goes through him. The thing about the job, whatever bad you could say about it—and Frank hated it, hated the way people looked at him, hated the way people hated him, he hated the precinct and just about every last person in it—but the thing about the job was you were always up to something, you were always doing or maybe you were about to do or you just got through doing something that mattered.

"I keep checking," Caltagirone says. "Maybe someone's waiting for a little more time to pass. Or maybe they haven't figured out he's missing yet." Detective Caltagirone pries the plastic cover off his cup of Coke and tips it a little, spilling soda on all his fries and the remains of his hamburgers, like he's putting out a fire.

CHAPTER
TEN

Kate has been invited to speak before a group in Harrisburg, Pennsylvania—a gathering that she calls The Convocation of Extremely Liberal Ministers and Their Life Partners, by which Paul takes her to mean they are either gay or offbeat in some other way that makes them worthy of Kate's barbed, teasing affection. The ministers have sent a driver from a nearby car service, and at eight forty-five on a cold Tuesday morning Shep is barking urgently at the window as a blue Ford Taurus pulls in. The back bumper bears a silver-and-purple bumper sticker that reads ALL MEN ARE IDIOTS AND MY HUSBAND IS THEIR KING, but the person driving the car is a man with a Nashville pompadour and black-framed glasses, the collar of his peacoat turned up against the wind. He is looking skeptically at the house and then goes back to the car and consults a piece of paper.

"They didn't send a limo or even a town car," Kate says, turning away from the window. "My career's in free fall!" She puts her arms around Paul and whispers into his ear, "I feel you dripping out of me."

His smile has a frozen quality. Ordinarily, he enjoys this benignly smutty side of Kate, and has even, with an inward boastfulness, taken some credit for it himself, believing her when she tells him that she used to be entirely circumspect in her conjugal utterances, and that if the Old Her would somehow be able to overhear the New Her, the Old Her's face would scald with embarrassment. But today does not feel ordinary, and Kate's dirty talk seems oddly lacking in its usual charm—it may come down to this: he does not wish to be reminded of this morning's pleasure. It is not as if all the rituals and joys of his former life have come to a halt, but it seems as if his self, this inchoate "I" whom he pictured as the initiator and the judge of his daily actions, has now been joined by its long-lost, never before acknowledged, heretofore lingering in the shadows twin, a twin whose very existence is dependent on its negative capacity, who will say no to every yes.

"Hey," Kate says, touching his face. She wonders for a moment if she should stay home.

"Don't forget to tip the driver," he says.

"Don't you worry your pretty little head about it," Kate says. She rises on her toes and kisses his forehead.

Paul watches out the window, while filling the kettle at the kitchen sink. The driver opens the door for her and glances at her ass as she climbs into the backseat. The water drums into the kettle. Shep is sitting close to him now, his tail swishing back and forth on the kitchen floor. Shep is looking particularly jolly. He seems to be thinking, Oh good, she's gone, let's grill a couple of steaks and take naps, side by side. The Taurus backs up, begins its three-point turn. Paul sees his own reflection in the tarnished convex of the teakettle, and he thinks, *He will never watch anyone from the window, he won't ever hear the sound of water. He doesn't exist.*

Paul follows the dog onto the flagstone patio, off the kitchen. The sound of the band saw is coming from the workshop, where Evangeline has been since eight o'clock. She always brings a thermos filled with espresso generously sweetened with raw sugar; it's a pleasure to drink coffee with her in the morning, maybe bum an American Spirit off her. But he has promised Kate—and Ruby—that he will go to Windsor Day School this morning to see the school assembly, the theme of which is "Countdown to the New Millennium," in which Ruby has an undisclosed role. He must shower, but first he goes back to his computer and rather than typing Recent Deaths Westchester he types Murder Westchester and when he can find nothing like that he types in Dead Body Martingham State Park, though it feels almost as if he is confessing to the police by doing so. Yet even with so forward a question he comes up with nothing and he wonders how this man's death can go unnoted. He tries to tell himself this is good news, he even wonders for a moment, piercingly, punishingly, if the man actually died. Maybe. Maybe he had just lost consciousness and Paul, overwhelmed by adrenaline, had missed the pulse, assumed the worst, and fifteen minutes later the man had crawled out of the woods. Yet what is far more likely, Paul thinks, is that he is phrasing the question wrong. He searches the Internet for the names of the local newspapers in or near Tarrytown but he comes up with none and can't imagine what they'd be called—the *Tarrytown Tribune*? The *Westchester Times*?—and of course there is no one he can ask. He wanders the Internet feeling not only lost but *followed*, remembering that everything you type and everywhere you "go" is retrievable, that the disk inside of the computer keeps an indelible record of your activities, and sometimes the police can simply yank the disk out of its casing and use it as evidence.

His time at the computer is brought to a sudden conclusion by someone calling his name. It takes him a moment to realize it's Evangeline, calling out from downstairs. Every surprise feels as if the bottom has just dropped out of life.

"I'm up here," Paul says, his voice sounding far too intense.

There is a moment's silence before he hears Evangeline's footsteps coming up the stairs, rising up toward him with an ever-increasing sound—she has a heavy gait; her slender legs are not made to move the freight of her steel-toed work boots.

She has a mild, open face, with dark eyebrows and preternaturally blue eyes, and wears her hair pulled back in a Jeffersonian ponytail. Today she's wearing wide-wale corduroy pants and a fleece vest over a brown-and-red Carhartt shirt, with pearl studs in her ears. The studs are new, probably a gift from her parents in New Orleans, who are trying to lure her back to the kind of life they had once envisioned for her by sending her jewelry, cashmere sweaters, gift certificates to Leisure Time, Leyden's day spa, things they hope might lead her away from her life of lesbianism and carpentry.

"Are you okay?" she asks.

"Yeah, I'm good," Paul says. "I'm sort of late."

"Really? Late for what?"

"Oh, there's a thing at Ruby's school. Kate's giving a talk so I'm going to go instead."

Evangeline takes a deep breath, nods. "You're so good," she says. It sounds as if she might be poking a bit of fun at him, but her eyes radiate tenderness. "Anyhow," she goes on, "we're getting a delivery. George is here. I'm assuming it's the teak, which is very exciting, yes?"

Paul thinks for a moment. George? Oh yes, George. The UPS driver. Evangeline knows everyone's name, every trucker, every supplier, every parts salesman. She believes everyone is connected, and we're all in it together. "Is he waiting for me to sign for it?" Paul asks.

"I can do it," says Evangeline.

He watches as she turns, walks down the steps. She rolls her shoulders as she walks; she has a broad, flat bottom. Paul lowers his eyes, annoyed with himself for invading her privacy.

Suddenly, Evangeline stops, halfway down the stairs, and turns.

"Do you want me to keep Sheppy with me?" she says. "He's getting used to the noise."

"Sure, that would be nice," says Paul.

Shep is downstairs, near the steps. He has found a spot where he can have the heat of the radiator, see two and a half rooms of the first floor, and keep an eye on the staircase. Though he lies flat on the bare wood, his eyes are alert.

"You hear that, Sheppy?" Evangeline says. "You're going to the shop with me. And mostly I'll be checking the new wood and organizing stuff so you won't even have to listen to that nasty old saw."

Having heard his name again, Shep slowly rises—he seems headed for arthritis further down the road—and when Evangeline has descended the stairs he stands next to her, as if guarding her.

"What an awesome dog," Evangeline says. "You were so lucky to find him. It's so great how things can work out." She locks her fingers together, illustrating a universe in which the pieces fit together beautifully.

Windsor Day School is housed in a nineteenth-century Georgian mansion, surrounded by locust trees. For a century and a half the house was the property of a stern mercantile family named Norris, and it was large enough to contain the school's limited enrollment. But now that the number of people with money has increased in Windsor County, the eighteen-room house is no longer sufficient. A new, modern building is under construction, next to the old building, which will be, once construction is complete, demoted to administrative use.

Everyone involved in Windsor Day's expansion is supposedly making an effort to preserve some of the school's former grandeur, protecting as many trees as possible and roping off the locally famous peony garden from the backhoe's blade. The faux-Roman statuary have been cordoned off with yellow tape, as if they were part of a crime scene, and the school's governing body has agreed to absorb untold extra expense so that the new parking area will not disturb the grave of Caroline Norris, Windsor Day's original benefactress and its first headmistress. Still, the nature of the place has been forever altered, and the presence of a huge excavation drains not only the beauty but the meaning from the property in a way that seems irrevocable to Paul. Now, those trees, the statuary, even the house itself are like animals in a zoo, silent testaments to their own subjugation.

Paul knows this property from when he first came to Windsor County as a twenty-year-old, after a summer working on a fishing boat in Alaska. He had come to Leyden ostensibly in pursuit of a girl named Roberta McNulty, whom he had met in Seward, where she was sunning herself on a warm Alaska afternoon on the shores of Resurrection Bay. She was a high school senior, traveling with her parents and her younger brother, but she and Paul managed to steal time and privacy, and Paul felt for her everything from admiration to lust. *Come see me*, she whispered in his ear during their final good-bye, with her entire family standing twenty feet away, her father's foot resting on his suitcase, her mother with her oddly short arms folded over her fulsome chest. *I will*, he whispered back. *I promise.*

When Paul collected his final week's check from his boss he immediately set off for her hometown of Leyden, New York. It was good to have someplace he needed to be, and good to think there was someone who might be waiting for him, someone to whom, however tangentially, he was obligated. He had never broken a promise, never, and he never intended to. He made his way, slowly, forwarded like a piece of mail with the minimum postage, traveling on boats, buses, trains, and in the backseats of those passing motorists he could entice with his thumb and good looks. He figured the journey would take, at most, two weeks, but certain distractions presented themselves on the way. He ran out of money, he helped to put out a forest fire, he joined in a frantic, futile search for an insurance claims adjustor who absconded with a neighbor's five-year-old son, he dislocated his shoulder in a school-yard basketball game, he ended up staying three weeks in Colorado Springs with two brothers who picked him up on the highway one evening when he was running a fever of a hundred and two, he met a guy who made mandolins who patiently taught him a lot about woodworking and wood itself, he fell under the spell of a slender, sad-faced girl who worked in a bakery in Lima, Ohio, and spent a week kissing her and listening to her dream of becoming a songwriter, all the while trying to keep his heart fastened to the image of Roberta McNulty. The memory of her was starting to cloud over. He imagined arriving in Leyden, going to her high school as it was letting out for the afternoon, with the idea of surprising her, and then failing to pick her out from the rush of students leaving the building. It wasn't as if he no longer remembered her, but there was no one thing he remembered about her as vividly as he remembered the barely audible gasp of breath she took before speaking, and the smell of chocolate on her fingers as she stroked the side of his face.

When he finally arrived in Leyden, it was winter. There was no snow, only sheets of cold rain. The village reminded him of Connecticut, the people in a stupor of comfort, the little shops, the penny-candy mentality of the place, nothing like the bare-knuckled beauty of Alaska. On his first night he went to a bar, with just enough money left for a beer, and met Walter Seifert, an elderly radio and TV repairman from Prague whose wife had died a few months ago, and Seifert told Paul he could stay at his house on Belmont Street for thirty dollars a week. Living next door to Seifert was a boisterous drunk named Dave Markay, who, with his longtime buddy named Butch Kirkwood, also a steady drinker but not nearly so boisterous, had a house-painting company called True Colors. Dave saw Paul scraping the ice off Seifert's front walk and asked him if he wanted to work as a painter for seven dollars an hour, and Paul, who had always been in the habit of letting things happen to him, said it sounded like a fine idea, and the next day he was at the Norris house, which was already Windsor Day School, painting side by side on the second floor with Dave and Butch to the strains of the Allman Brothers while the teachers and the students did their best to work around them.

Weeks went by. There was always some reason to delay getting in touch with Roberta. He had lost her phone number, he couldn't recall her address, he was dead tired at night, he was waiting to save a little money so he could come to her as a grown-up rather than just some pathetic kid—if she'd wanted a little boy there were plenty of those to chose from at her high school. But as bad luck would have it, Roberta's father owned an office-supply shop, and he appeared one morning at Windsor Day, delivering an electric typewriter. McNulty took a moment to place Paul but once he did he wasted no time letting him know that the distant good manners he had shown Paul in Alaska would not prevail here on McNulty's home ground.

"Would you mind telling me what in the hell you are doing here?" he asked, and when Paul, not trusting himself to give a calm, masterful answer, remained silent, McNulty muttered, shook his head, and walked away.

Now, whatever chance the reunion had of rekindling the attraction they'd felt for each other on the chilly, rocky shore of Resurrection Bay would be wrecked by misunderstanding and resentment. But by the time Paul went to bed he was, in truth, giving more thought to the recurring pain in his shoulder than to the botched reunion with Roberta. Dave had given him a book called *Heal It Yourself,* which had a whole section about shoulder injuries, and Paul had fallen asleep with that book on his chest and the interrogating glare of his bedside lamp not six inches from his face.

Though Leyden was a small town, with fewer than five thousand full-time residents, he never once ran into Roberta, not at the super-market with the sawdust on the floor and the smell of freezer burn in the air, nor the post office with its WPA mural of Indians and settlers sharing sheaves of wheat and bushels of corn, not at the gas stop nor the little park. He thought it was possible that Roberta at one time or another had caught a glimpse of him and quickly changed course, to spare them both the embarrassment. Yet even this much thought about Roberta, and where she might be and what she might do, was infrequent.

Paul knew how to stave off an unwanted thought, how to de-prive it of attention so that it died of neglect. Back then, for instance, he hadn't thought of finding his father in that walk-up railroad flat in over a year, and when it did come back to him again it was as if the whole thing had happened to someone else, except that it hadn't, but nevertheless it perplexed and fascinated him, how things you thought would kick your ass forever and ever can over time lose their power.

Beautiful girls, lost to time.

Men lost to their own violence, or the violence of others.

Today, walking quickly from his truck to the school, Paul has an inkling that he has arrived late for today's assembly, and when he mounts the whitewashed stone steps to the front entrance and sees no one milling about he feels a sour twist of self-reproach. He had had every intention of being there a few minutes before the hour so that he could sit close to the front where Ruby could see him, especially since she had already voiced her disappointment over her mother's not being able to come today. But, alas, it wasn't to be. A combination of not looking at the clock, talking to Evangeline, and getting lost in his computer had all conspired to make it so he was walking into the school a full half hour after the assembly had begun.

In the entrance foyer, where once the Norrises' butler admitted visitors, a store-bought maple desk has been set up in the sloping space between the two main stairways—one that curves off to the east side of the house, the other to the west. A gaudy chandelier, some of its flame-shaped bulbs burned out, creaks back and forth in the breeze Paul brings in with him. A male teacher sits at the desk, British in his features, with blue eyes, soft sandy hair. He puts down the *New York Times*. "May I help you?" he asks. Paul doesn't have the mild, tidy appearance of most of the Windsor Day parents, who are for the most part lawyers and doctors, landowners, drivers of expensive automobiles—in other words, Paul's clients.

"I'm here for the assembly," he explains. The teacher cocks his head curiously, not wishing to be impolite by asking any further questions but clearly waiting for some clarification. "Ruby Ellis?" Paul says.

The teacher brightens, rises from his chair. "Oh, yes, well I think you're in luck. Ruby's class hasn't had their turn yet. Come, I'll show you in." The teacher leads Paul through the corridor, every few steps looking back at him over his shoulder and smiling encouragingly. What had once been the main floor of the Norris house has been divided up into classrooms, a science lab, a language lab, a music room, an art room.

"Here we are," the teacher says, in his kind voice, opening the doors to what was once the Norrises' ballroom, a cavernous French-windowed room that many years ago Paul had helped to paint, and though the slate-blue walls are sorely in need of freshening up and the eggshell ceiling is water-stained, he is glad to see his old work still exists—nineteen gallons of Benjamin Moore Shaker Afternoon, straight out of the can.

The ballroom/auditorium has a stage built out of indifferent material, the plywood of it peeking out from where the gray indoor/outdoor carpeting has worn away. A huge handmade calendar hangs in the middle of the stage, and the rest of the wall is decorated with clocks, watches, sundials, egg timers, hourglasses, and above that is a blue-and-white banner that says WINDSOR DAY COUNTDOWN TO Y2K! Facing the stage are a hundred or so folding chairs, nearly all of them occupied. Paul's memories of school are of a world of women, but there are quite a few men with white or gray hair, men on their second families, determined, this time, not to miss events in the lives of their children. Right now a small boy with shoulder-length hair plays a guitar that is almost as large as he is and sings "Stairway to Heaven" in a plaintive, unstable voice.

Paul takes an empty seat next to a woman named Joyce Drazen, here with her husband, Leonard Fahey, with whom she runs a mail-order business in antique maps and globes. Their daughter, Nina, is a junior, and Joyce has already tried to enlist Kate in the plan to help Nina get into Harvard, Yale, or Princeton, though *help* might not be the correct word, since Nina herself has said she would rather attend a nearby state university, where her best friend has already been accepted. Joyce, convinced that Nina's talent as a writer will be her ticket to the college of her mother's choice, and convinced as well that all Kate has to do is read Nina's work and she will write a glowing letter of recommendation, has recently appeared without warning, bearing some of Nina's schoolwork—an essay about the *Dred Scott* decision, another about penguins.

Paul has his own relationship with Joyce and Leonard, dating back several years to when they hired him to repair a maple globe, thirty inches in diameter, made in Vietnam and consisting of over a thousand pieces. The oceans alone were made of nearly seven hundred wedges of wafer-thin wood, all fitted together in a jigsaw pattern, the continents a rainbow variety of bright colors, the lettering in gold, as were the longitude and latitude lines. Joyce and Leonard had bought the globe from a library in the Adirondacks, and it had arrived with a piece of France missing and severe cracks in Australia. Other dealers in wooden works of art and antiquities had told them that Paul Phillips was the man to see about putting the globe into saleable condition, and though there were some hard feelings when Paul completed the job in three months rather than the agreed-upon three weeks, his restoration was clearly impeccable. He had, in fact, done more work than the agreement called for, discovering that half of Alaska was made of mahogany rather than maple and replacing the discordant piece without ever mentioning it to Joyce or Leonard.

Now they want a screened porch, they want to replace their windows, they want to rescue an old barn at the back of their property, which is slowly collapsing in a long, splintery sigh of defeat, but so far Paul has not been able to schedule them in. Joyce makes a comic frown and wags her finger at him as he takes the seat next to her.

Normally, Paul reacts to her jokey scolding with a smiling sheepishness, but today he feels an impulse to grab her finger and tell her—tell them both—that if they ever want him to work on their house again they had best back off and wait their turn, and this sudden sour spurt of temper is so unexpected and yet so stark and clear that he feels bewildered. It is like catching a glimpse of yourself in a mirror you didn't know was there.

"Our junior class is full of amazingly talented young men and women," Sam Robbins, the eleventh-grade English teacher, says. He has a cap of gray curls, a cardigan and bow tie, and, judging by the cheers that greet his appearance onstage, he's a great favorite among the students. "We have a magician and juggler in our midst, some fantastic musicians, visual artists who I predict will be showing in the great museums of the world within ten years, and some amazing writers. One of our writers—Nina Drazen-Fahey—is going to read a poem. She tells me it's about what will happen in our world when our computers all have nervous breakdowns. On a personal note, I'd like to add that if the computers break down it will be all right with me. As Picasso once said, 'Computers are completely uninteresting—all they can do is give answers.' "

Robbins raises his chin, as if to stem a surge of outrage, but there is only a bit of laughter, and a general shifting of weight and shuffling of papers. "Well, as I said, this is just my minority opinion. And so let's bring up Nina, okay? Nina?"

Joyce and Leonard's sturdy-looking daughter mounts the steps to the stage with the dignity of a martyr, accompanied by only a light sprinkling of applause. Her parents beam proudly, though their love seems to include some apprehensiveness, as if they fear Nina's life will not be easy. Joyce applauds emphatically, while Leonard, who is holding a video camera to his eye now, must content himself with clapping his left hand against his thigh.

Paul looks at his hands resting in his lap, and then covers them with his jacket, as if they were shameful things.

Nina takes a few moments to adjust the microphone to a comfortable height, and gently clears her throat and begins, holding the page upon which her poem is written down at her side. Her voice is unexpectedly forceful.

> *Hey, hey Y2K*
> *How many lives have you ruined today?*
> *Town and village, crossroads and junction*
> *All laid low by computer malfunction*
> *IBM and Gateway*
> *Apple and Dell*
> *All flashing and crashing*
> *A cyberspace hell*
> *Who would have guessed it?*
> *Who would have known?*
> *My knees are knocking*
> *My mind is blown.*

Leonard extends his free hand in Joyce's direction and she rubs her palm over his, in a silent celebration of their daughter.

> *If you're thinking of flying*
> *I beg you: hesitate*
> *Without computers*
> *How will your plane navigate?*
> *If you're thinking of money*
> *Well I don't want to cause you stress*
> *But since the banks will be broken*
> *I recommend a good mattress.*

As the poem trots toward its conclusion, Paul finds something in it oddly soothing, and he sinks into a waking dream of universal anarchy, a world of chaos, not only ungoverned by God but immune to the entreaties of humankind as well, swept over by an all-destroying mania brought on by every computer's being abandoned by its internal clock and therefore sinking into a lobotomized state, unable to monitor the worldwide transit of money, the takeoffs and landings of jets, the traffic of the shipping lanes, the flow of electricity, the phones, the schools, the mail, the hospitals, that final zero in the year 2000 exploding in civilization's brain, a ruptured blood vessel of data that brings us to our knees.

Last night, Paul had walked through the front room, where Kate was watching TV, and they listened to a senator from Utah going on about what was going to happen to all of us when the twentieth century's end crippled our computers. The senator was in a gray suit, a red tie, oval glasses, he had an ingratiating but invincible smile. Even as he delivered his apocalyptic message, the smile endured—he probably meant it to be reassuring, but it was unnerving.

The senator placed his hands on his radiant desk. "When people say to me, 'Is the world going to come to an end?' I say, 'I don't know.'

I don't know whether this will be a bump in the road—that's the most optimistic assessment of what we've got, a fairly serious bump in the road—or whether this will, in fact, trigger a major worldwide recession with absolutely devastating economic consequences in some parts of the world . . . We must coldly, calculatingly divide up the next weeks to determine what we can do, what we can't do, do what we can, and then provide for contingency plans for that which we cannot."

"What the fuck?" Kate had said. "For the first time in my life I'm making money and now the monetary system has to collapse? Where's the justice in that?"

Yet now Paul sees a glimmer of hope in the impending chaos of Y2K, a rough, approximate justice in, of all things, his escape from justice. If this impending doomsday for accountants is real, or even half-real, so much will be lost, so much data will disappear, it will be like the world will have to start from scratch, a universal amnesty.

In the meanwhile, Ruby and four children from her third-grade class have mounted the stage. All of them are wearing black pants and black T-shirts, except for Ruby, who must have forgotten about the agreed-upon costume and is wearing blue jeans and a red-and-tan cowgirl shirt, though it's conceivable she simply saw herself as the lead singer in this quintet with the others in black taking on the doo-wop duties.

The third-graders are singing the old Cyndi Lauper song "Time After Time." An unseen piano is accompanying them and the five children seem ardent and uncertain. Ruby is the largest of them, and a full head taller than the child next to her, a wiry little red-haired boy with bony arms and a freckle-splattered face. Ruby seems to be in her own world. She is looking off to the side, possibly for help.

Has she practiced this song? Does she know the words to it? When the children sing, "Sometimes you picture me/I'm walking too far ahead," Ruby touches her head, unconsciously. She appears lost and not completely functional, and though, as the tallest of the quintet, she has been placed in the center, the other children have subtly moved away from her and re-formed as a quartet, with Ruby vaguely behind them, where she now looks out at the audience, wide-eyed and alarmed, as if she has just awakened from a dream.

Paul feels nauseated on Ruby's behalf. Normally, Paul thinks she is extraordinarily fortunate to have Kate as her mother, lucky for the safety of a home where the next month's mortgage is not an issue, lucky for the humor, lucky to be taught through example that women can achieve extraordinary success. His own sister, Annabelle, had no such luck, being raised by their depressive mother, with raccoon circles around her eyes and the smell of medicine on her breath. "She was my role model," Annabelle has said. "Everything I know about pajamas I learned from Mom."

Similarly, what great life lessons could Paul have learned from his father? The choreography of running away from a family? The egomaniacal stubbornness of giving your life to painting when the paintings themselves could barely be given away? The wisdom of keeping your door unlocked so as to not make it overly difficult for someone—preferably someone young and impressionable—to find your body?

No, Ruby was a lucky child, lucky to be healthy, lucky to be loved—yet now, making clownish, outsized gestures one moment and slipping into a catatonic stillness the next, she looked neither healthy nor loved, and she seemed to have no idea of how she was appearing to others.

But how can we ever see ourselves, let alone see ourselves as others see us, when the person seeing is the same as the person seen? And when our senses are clouded by wishes and fears and preexisting images, what chance do we have to glimpse ourselves as others see us?

Joyce nudges Leonard, rather emphatically, and he lifts his camcorder again, capturing Ruby and her classmates as they trudge through the song. Ruby is fading further back—*what has happened to that poor girl?*—her face all but obscured by the suddenly raised arms of her classmates as they sway back and forth in a ticktock motion and chant "time after time" over and over. Paul feels a lurch of pure, pulverizing terror.

When the millennium assembly is over, a platoon of older students efficiently moves the chairs to one side and the old Norris ballroom is the reception area for the parents and children who mill around, drinking punch out of paper cups and eating pastries off of paper plates. It takes Paul a while to wind his way through the crowd and find Ruby, and when he does, she is sitting on the three-step staircase leading to the stage, along with a small, angry-looking boy in a White Zombie T-shirt and gelled blue hair.

She looks at Paul as if surprised to see him here. There is no theatrical widening of the eyes. All expression leaves her small, smooth face, and what remains is the plain prettiness of a powerless little girl. "Were you here?" she asks.

"Sure. I was sitting in the back row." He points, but there are no more rows, just adults and children in a milling mass, with the flash of strobe lights going off steadily—all those wonderful children and jolly parents and everyone happier than they are.

"I gotta go," the blue-haired boy says, Ruby's partner in misfitness. She doesn't say anything back to him and doesn't even glance in his direction as he heads aimlessly into the center of the room, craning his neck as if on the lookout for someone.

"I've always liked that song," Paul says. "Cyndi Lauper, right?"

Ruby shrugs. Her face is blotchy and her eyes sparkle; she looks as if she has been slapped. Paul has never tried to be a father to her—he would rather assume an avuncular role. But even an uncle needs to be a protector, and in the months in which he has lived in the same house with Ruby, driven her here and there, shared meals with her, read to her at night, he has never seen her look so meek, so crushed. The brash, blaring little girl, so brimming with personality, so full of drama and poses, may have tried his patience now and then, but this tender, wounded, undefended girl is almost more than he can bear.

"Did you have lunch yet?"

"Sort of," she says.

"I'm pretty hungry," Paul says. "Why don't we go and have a big Y2K lunch at the George Washington Inn? They make these amazing hamburgers."

"I have school," Ruby says forlornly.

"That's okay," Paul says. "I heard on the radio that the public schools are on half-day. We could get in on that." He extends his hand to her and pulls her out of her sitting position. "Where's your teacher?"

An hour later they've had their lunch and are walking around Leyden. There are a few children around this afternoon but they are for the most part unknown to Ruby, kids who attend the public school. A couple of ten-year-olds clatter past them on skateboards and Ruby gives what seems to Paul a longing look at them over her shoulder. It occurs to Paul that Ruby might be happier going to Leyden Central School, and as he has the thought she unexpectedly takes his hand.

As the afternoon wears on, the air seems to soften; it is nearly winter but the air is warm, and the sky is dark blue with masses of white clouds. Paul and Ruby go to the candle and incense shop, the ice cream parlor, the boutique selling South American sweaters, the diner where the old guard still likes to congregate over hamburgers and fried eggs, and the health food counter where the new people eat dandelion greens and drink special teas from Africa. When there are no more shops to go into, and the sky is suddenly darkening, returning to its stern autumn hue, they drive home and collect Shep for a walk in the woods.

"Look at him wagging," Evangeline says, as the dog greets Paul. "He wouldn't give me even a courtesy wag."

Paul takes Ruby for a walk in her own woods, trees and stones and dirt she may one day come to own herself. He wants her to love it here, and to know there's a place where she belongs. "Can I tell you something, a secret?" he says to her. Despite the warmth of the early afternoon, a brief damp snow has fallen; the gold and red leaves blanketed on the ground now bear a sheen of translucent ice. He holds on to the child's hand as they walk. Twice she has stumbled, first over a tangle of vines, then over the pulpy remains of a log. The trees are black and silver against the sky.

"I won't tell anyone," Ruby says. She swings their arms back and forth, as if his holding her is part of a game, but her grip is adamant. She is wearing a parka with a hood, jeans, hiking shoes. Her clothes seem tight.

Paul stops, gestures at the numberless trees around them. "I think you should pick a tree, some tree you really like, and then I'm going to take that tree down and use the wood to make you something."

"What will you make me?"

"Well that depends on what tree you pick. Different woods are for different things."

"But what if I pick the wrong kind?"

"You can't, honey, there is no wrong kind. In nature there is no wrong."

"God says some things are wrong," Ruby says.

"You know that's not your mom's kind of God, honey."

"Well it's mine," Ruby says.

"In nature, it doesn't work that way," Paul says. "In nature there is no right and wrong, there's just life and death." He hears a sound, and it startles him—but it's Shep, who has found an appealing branch half buried in the leaves and is dragging it along.

Ruby looks out at the trees, unnamed and mysterious.

Shep drops the branch and cocks his head, looking at Paul suspiciously. He has somehow become worried that Paul is going to run away from him, and even as the deep, moldering scent of the forest floor urges the dog onward, he continues to throw anxious glances over his shoulder. But something new seizes the brown dog's attention and for a few moments he paws and snuffles at the ground, dislodging bright, crunching leaves, twigs, and black organic matter, moist and stringy like the pulp of a pumpkin.

"What's Shep doing?" Ruby asks.

"He's got something," Paul tells her, to which she nods sagely.

"I wonder if he misses his old family," she muses.

Shep has dug out an inch or two of dirt and has his nose in the small hole, inhaling its information. There is something down there and he would like to kill it.

"Shep!" Ruby cries, if only to break the spell.

He looks up, his eyes glittering, his nose ringed with dirt. "Come here, Shep," Ruby says, clapping her hands. The dog shifts his gaze to Paul and Paul nods curtly, privately, and the dog trots over to the little girl.

"He's starting to listen to me," Ruby says. When the dog is close enough she takes his collar, pulls him the last couple of inches. "You must obey me," she says, her voice deep and tremulous, like a hypnotist up to no good. Shep turns his body so that the middle of his torso presses against Ruby's knees.

"He's guarding you," Paul says. It renders her speechless for a moment—that a beast, a wild thing of nature, would do such a thing.

"Thank you, Shep," she says, in the softest voice Paul has ever heard her speak in. She strokes the dog's ears and he moves even closer, almost toppling her.

"Do you know what I wish?" Ruby says. "I wish we could see him from the beginning. I wish we could rewind him."

Paul laughs, putting his hand lightly on her shoulder. "So do you see a tree you might want? We'll cut it down and then we'll plant a new one where the old one used to be, and we can make you a bookcase."

She cocks her head. "Is this the secret you wanted to say?"

"That's it."

"Why is it a secret? Because they're Mom's trees?"

"I guess it's not really a secret," Paul says. "Except you're going to build it with me."

"I don't know how to do that," Ruby says insistently.

"Well, I'm going to teach you. I'm going to teach you how to cut things straight and true. We're going to be very careful and you're going to be good at it, that's what I think. You're going to be really good at it."

"Okay," Ruby says. She looks suddenly worried.

"Are you all right?" Paul asks. She nods uncertainly and Paul lets it pass.

"Come here," he says, "I'll show you something."

He touches her elbow, guides her toward a couple of old wild cherry trees. Their bark is the color of bright ash, speckled, bent, at the end of their cycle. He places his hand on one of the trees, like holding someone by the back of the neck. "These are probably about forty years old. All the hemlock block out the light so the cherry trees don't get enough sun. Pretty soon they're just going to fall over. But they have nice wood, sort of reddish. It ages well and if we made you a bookcase it would be something you always had. You could take it to college with you, if you wanted."

"I don't think I will go to college," Ruby says.

"Well that'll be up to you," Paul says. "I went for a year and I wish I went longer. It's good to learn things and when I talk to my friends about their college years it sounds like a lot of fun."

"My mother's roommate committed suicide in college," Ruby says.

"That's a terrible thing," Paul says. He pats the tree. "So what do you think? We'll build it together. That way, it will be partly you. It will have the oil from your fingers in it. And even the mistakes you make, because we all make mistakes, even the best carpenters."

Paul sits on a lichen-laced boulder near the cherry trees and Ruby scrambles up to sit next to him. It's nearly four in the afternoon. The moon is already high, small and pale and lacking in dimension. "You know what makes me laugh sometimes," he says to Ruby. He has never known her to be so calm and quiet; she looks searchingly into his face.

"What?" she all but whispers.

"These people, the well off ones, who take their friends around and show them their new kitchen or their porch and they say *Oh I built this last year*, but they didn't build it, they just paid for it. But to them, writing a check and bringing the carpenter a pitcher of ice water is the same as building it."

"That's funny," Ruby says. "Mom can't even cook rice."

"Rice can be a real beat to make," Paul says.

"But you can, you cook the best rice."

"Rice is one of my specialties," Paul says. "I've eaten a lot of rice in my day." He taps his finger on the child's knee. "You have a fantastic mother. I think you know that. Talk about making things! The stuff I make, the tree does half the work, the tree and its roots and the leaves and the water and the sun, and the people who cut the tree down, and the people who bring it to the mill, and the people who work in the mill, and I even have an assistant. But your mother is all by herself making something out of absolutely nothing. She takes a piece of paper, there's nothing there, and she fills it with words, and then one day there's a book. It blows my mind. She's like a gladiator, it's all up to her, every step of the way, and if she makes a mistake everyone can see it. One day when you read her books you'll be so amazed and proud."

"I don't like reading," Ruby says. "I like music."

"Music is wonderful," Paul agrees. "Where would we be without music?"

It's less than three weeks until the solstice. The sky is suddenly bereft of light, it just drops it like something too heavy to hold, and what remains is a dark, troubling green, like the light flung across the treetops in Tarrytown. Paul slides off the boulder, lifts Ruby up, and sets her on the ground.

"I have to tell you something," she says.

"Talk while we walk," Paul says, taking her hand. "Come on, Shep, whatever it is you're digging for, it's already escaped."

"That thing I said about rewinding Shep?" Her voice is befogged, uncertain. "I didn't make that up," she says. Like someone learning to walk, she watches her feet traverse the forest floor. "This kid in my class? Noah? He said it and I was just copying it."

"It's fine," Paul says. "Noah could have heard it from someone else, too."

The woods are behind them. Now there are just ferns and vines, a little trickle of stream, and the beginnings of the lawn in back of Kate's house. Shep's muzzle touches the moving water as he drinks. When he sees the house it reminds him it is time to eat. He takes a last few excited laps at the stream and begins his rocking-horse lope across the grass. Each time his front paws hit the grass he steals a glance over his shoulder to make sure Paul and Ruby are following. Kate is home and the windows are ablaze with light and the long, low house looks like a ship sailing through the uncertain seas of night.

CHAPTER
ELEVEN

No thanks to anyone but himself, things are starting to fall into place on the William Claff case, and Detective Jerry Caltagirone is starting to get that old feeling, the sense he once had, maybe ten years and seventy-five pounds ago, that not only is he doing a job that made a difference in this world, but that he is good at it. He sees his job as holy housekeeping—he straightens out the world's mess, he brings the world slowly back to order even as it totters on the edge of chaos, because you would have to be half-crazy to want to live in a world in which things happened for no particular reason, a world without predictability, without justice. Piece by piece he is making sense of the case. He is sure of the dead man's name, and all the other forms of identification can be ignored. The last place he lived before coming to New York was Philadelphia, where he shacked up with a woman named Dinah Maloney—her business card was in his wallet. He left her all of a sudden and stole her dog for good measure, which might be reason for Maloney to beat him to death, except she weighs about the same as a suit of clothes, can account for every second of her time the day of the killing, and is still looking for the dog.

More than that, Caltagirone knows Claff was exactly forty-one years and nineteen weeks old when he died. He knows he was born in a town called Phillips, California, a snowy, mountainous place. When Caltagirone poked around to see if there might be a few Claff relatives still around he came up empty, but he didn't mind, that meant he wouldn't have to tell Claff's mother or father or anyone else that their loved one was found beaten to death in the woods. When you are on an investigation, mostly things don't work out. You need to trust the method, you have to believe the evidence will lead you out of the dark and into the light. And you must be patient. Patience is Caltagirone's strong suit. He doesn't get discouraged and he doesn't jump to conclusions.

He has written what he knows for sure in a three-by-five root-beer-colored notebook, name, age, height, weight, distinguishing marks, and he adds every day to the list of known things, until, at last, Caltagirone finds where Claff was last living in LA, the change of address he failed to give to the DMV, and that missing piece is a beauty, because not only does it lead Caltagirone to where Claff had been working (Bank of America, in the accounting department) but it gives him sudden access to another accountant at BOA, Madeline Powers, with whom Claff had had a relationship, and who, though she had her own apartment, shared with him a four-room rental off Ventura Boulevard. Going over his notes with his wife, Caltagirone poked his finger at this line of his notations, and said, "Now all I got to do is figure out a way to talk to her without going out there myself," which reminded Stephanie that the two of them had had a nice time in Fort Myers with a vacationing LA homicide detective named Rudolf Sanchez, and furthermore she never threw anything away and she was sure she could get her hands on Sanchez's card, which he had handed to her while the Caltagirones sunned themselves by the swimming pool, hot and wet in their snow-white chaises while Sanchez stood between them in his dark suit, already checked out of the hotel and on his way to the airport. "Go get the card if you can find it," Caltagirone said, "but first things first." He opened his arms wide for her, though she is small and wiry and with her hair cut short and that eager, sort of hopped-up look she gets when they talk about his career, she looks like a very cute jockey. "Jerry loves Stephanie," he said, careful not to squeeze too hard.

A week later, Caltagirone has one more day to find someone to claim Claff's body. Most of the graves in potter's field are filled with nameless men and women, but there are a few whom they've managed to get a positive ID on and William Claff is on his way to being one of them. Sitting at his desk at the precinct, his head down, his hand cupped over the phone, and talking low, like a man who desperately does not want to be overheard, which is what he is, Caltagirone has Madeline Powers on the line, and he is giving her a minute to collect herself after she hears he is calling about Claff's death, even though Sanchez has already broken the news to her. Caltagirone knows how that can happen, how you can hear about something from one person and then when you hear it from someone else it's like a confirmation that the terrible thing is really true, or maybe your mind just turns its back on the terrible thing the first time through and the information comes again from a different direction and it's a kill shot, right through your mind's heart.

When she gathers herself again, Caltagirone asks the standard question. "Do you know of anyone who might want to harm Mr. Claff, Ms. Powers?" What you usually hear is Oh no, he was the nicest person, people loved him, he didn't have an enemy in the world. Caltagirone thinks Albert Anastasia's old lady would have said as much: such a nice man—and so clean-shaven.

But Madeline Powers surprises him. "I just didn't take it overly serious," she says, her voice racked with sorrow and self-recrimination. Caltagirone sits a bit straighter in his creaking swivel chair. This much he knows from years on the job: people often know a lot less than they want you to think they know, and people often know a lot more, and the art of the job is playing your hunches about which is which.

"What was it you didn't take serious?" Caltagirone says, as casually as possible but in a voice he calls Cop Casual, which means that the question sounds like there's not too much behind it but you've got to answer it anyhow.

"Why do you think he was running around the whole country like a crazy person?" she says, a hint of accusation in her voice. "For his health?"

Caltagirone doesn't take it personally. He knows unhappiness burns like a candle in people and a whiff of it's always in the air.

"What I need is for you to tell me what you know," Caltagirone says, as if he's got a long list of facts he wants to cross-reference. "And we'll take it from there."

"Will was a gambler," Madeline says. "I mean he had gambling *issues*. He never told me about it, but I sort of got the idea anyhow. My father was really into betting. We lived in Bakersfield and Dad ran a very successful dry-cleaning business. He worked hard, really hard, but sometimes he'd get up from the dinner table and say, 'I gotta get going,' and that meant he was going to get back in his car and drive all the way to Vegas. It's a pretty straight shot and you can really book it, but, still and all, it *is* over two hundred miles, each way. But when he was jonesing to gamble there was nothing he could do about it. His game was blackjack, but he wasn't above a bit of keno, and sometimes when he snapped out of it and realized he better get back on the interstate if he was ever going to be on time to open up the shop, he'd get hung up on the slots. You had to walk through a million slot machines between the blackjack tables and the exit doors, and sometimes he just couldn't make it . . ."

She is drifting far away now, but Caltagirone lets her tiptoe through the tulips. He makes little sounds, like it is all valuable information and he is writing it down, and before long she is talking about Claff again. "I don't think Will knew who he was dealing with," Powers says.

"Who was he dealing with?" Caltagirone asks.

"In terms of me, I mean. Like I'm going to judge him for putting down bets? Dynamite man like that, taking such good care of his body, good job—there's going to be some dings, or else he'd already be with somebody else. Anyhow, I'd never in a million years criticize someone for putting some money down on a bet. It's something I'm used to already, and anyhow I'm more like 'If you've got something sure tell me and maybe I'll put a couple of bucks down on it, too.' But Will . . ." The mention of his name sends ripples through her voice. Caltagirone hears her swallow and breathe herself back into composure. Maybe he was worried about me losing money. Whatever. He kept me in the dark. I knew he bet, but I didn't know how often, or how much. I didn't realize what it was doing to him." The weight of this last remark is more than her already fragile voice can bear.

"So he was on the run because of gambling debts, is that what you're saying?"

"That's what I'm saying."

This is all starting to make such perfect sense; Caltagirone can barely believe his own luck.

"Any idea who he placed his bets with?" Caltagirone asks. "I mean, put it this way, what kind of bets? Sports?"

"I don't know. He liked sports. He watched a lot of sports on the TV. But he wasn't jumping up and down or anything, he didn't act like he was doing anything but chilling out and watching TV. Look, I want to get out there. I want to collect his body. He doesn't have any family, and we weren't officially married. But I don't want him just dumped somewhere like he was nobody."

"We can make arrangements, don't worry about that, Madeline." Caltagirone forgets to keep his hand cupped over the phone's mouthpiece and his voice has carried over to the next desk, where Joe Pierpont sits tilted back in his chair, with his size-thirteen shoes up on the desk. All Pierpont has heard is Caltagirone reassuring someone named Madeline and he gives Caltagirone a wink, as if he's up to something, which is invariably Pierpont's pleasure to imagine at the slightest provocation.

"So the gambling thing," Caltagirone says.

"My father ended up broke, you know," Madeline says. "We had to sell everything, the business, the house. I had to work two jobs to put myself through school and even with all that I ran up so many loans, I'm still paying them off."

"But you did it, you made it," Caltagirone says.

"Yeah, I guess. It just doesn't feel like it."

"Never does, no matter what. Everybody thinks they're coming up short."

"I guess."

"So names? He never mentioned anyone?"

"Who we talking about here?"

"Will," Caltagirone says, going for the first name to make her feel it.

"Shit. He ran all that way."

"So who'd he mention?"

"One guy," Madeline says. "I could tell Willy was afraid of him."

"One guy?"

"Yeah, but he didn't really have a name. Willy never called him anything, not that I remember."

Caltagirone stays on the phone with Madeline for a few more minutes, while she worries about getting out to New York and then goes off on a few more tangents about her father, whom it seems she can't stop talking about for more than a minute. When he eventually allows himself to get her off the phone, he stands up, pats his pockets as if he's about to go out for a smoke, though his intentions are to step outside and call his wife on his cell phone. She's been curious about the man in the woods and he wants to give her an update.

Stephanie teaches fourth grade and it would take an emergency for him to call her during class, but Caltagirone knows her schedule by heart and at twelve twenty on a Thursday she's in the teachers' lounge, and it's her habit to reach in her big leather handbag and turn on her phone just in case anyone in her family needs to get hold of her.

He tells her he's gotten in touch with Claff's girlfriend, and she's flying out Saturday morning, to ID the body and to have it cremated so she can bring the ashes back to California. But what he mainly wants to talk to Stephanie about is this thing he's noticed, the way people have of changing the subject when you give them bad news, as if one part of the mind needs to occupy itself while another part comes to terms with the information.

"The thing she wanted to talk about was her father and his gambling, all this shit about him running off to Vegas. It's like she was there, way back." Caltagirone is in the precinct parking lot, leaning on his own car. It's about ten degrees outside. The knit of his sports jacket stiffens and darkens from the cold air. He blows the exhaust out of his mouth as if it were smoke from a Parliament.

"And let me guess," Stephanie says. "You just let her go on and on."

"Yeah. Of course I let her. Why not?"

"I could name some reasons," Stephanie says.

"People do it, I've seen it before. What's happening now is too much, so their mind runs back to the past. The past no matter what, it's already happened and you lived through it so it's not so bad."

"There's no one like you, you know that, Jerry, don't you? Not one police in that whole precinct. You take in their pain. They pour it in you, and you take it in."

Caltagirone doesn't say anything. He is overwhelmed with gratitude for Stephanie. He starts to pace the parking lot but suddenly the cell phone connection is washed over by a wave of static and he traces his steps backward until it is clear again.

"It's just that I worry about you, Jer," Stephanie is saying. He has been hearing the drone of the other teachers in the lounge, but now they are growing fainter as Stephanie walks away from them. He hears the creak of the door and now he can tell she has walked out into the hallway—he hears little kids' voices and the bang of a locker. "You want to know why you're over the weight you're supposed to be?" Stephanie says. Her lips are right on top of the speaker holes on her phone and she pours her voice into him as if it were tea and his ear was a cup. "You need look no further. You're there for the whole wide world, Jerry, they shovel their problems into you and you just eat it up."

"I do like a nice hamburger," Caltagirone says.

"I'm serious, Jerry."

"You want to know what it really is for me?" Caltagirone says. "I don't accept the idea that things don't make sense. There's something out there, something that says this is okay and this is not okay, and I want to catch the people who do what's not okay. It's like being a priest, except you actually fucking go out there and do it."

CHAPTER
TWELVE

The next night Paul's sister, Annabelle, comes to dinner with her Lebanese-Iranian husband, Bernard Maby, who has, in addition to ongoing immigration problems, the distinction of being twenty years her senior. But the age difference between his sister and her husband does not surprise Paul. Lovesick as a teenager, full of temper and desire, Annabelle was disdainful of the boys her own age, finding them superficial, untrustworthy. She listened to Tony Bennett records, she nursed feverish crushes on male teachers—it was only luck that none of them were vain or unkind enough to take her up on her advances. In her caramel-colored bedroom, the pinups were not rock stars or peace symbols or big-eyed giraffes in the wild, but manly old movie idols such as Clark Gable and Jimmy Stewart and even Telly Savalas. In their shared childhood, Paul was more closely connected to their father, for all the good it did him, and Annabelle was fused to their mother, which might have been even more unlucky than pinning your affections to the lapel of someone out the door. Like her pajama-clad mother, Annabelle was far from secretive about her own unhappiness, but the actual manifestations of her moroseness were her own. She was furiously pedantic, correcting your grammar, assuming the role as the arbiter of personal conduct and matters of honor as they were played out in a Connecticut high school. She felt the rules governing personal behavior had reached their apotheosis during the reign of Queen Victoria.

After high school, Annabelle had managed to leave Kent for Mitchell College, in New London, where she spent two years before debilitating migraine headaches—convulsive, vertiginous, and terrifying—ended college for her. By then, their mother was dying of bladder cancer and Annabelle returned home to spend half of each day taking care of her mother, and the other half in a darkened bedroom with a washcloth over her eyes. Paul was already gone, on his way by then to New Mexico, to California, and on to Alaska, and it seemed to Annabelle that he had lost all interest in her. She did her best to track his movements and when their mother died—at home, as was her wish—Annabelle scraped together money to send to Paul so he could come home to Kent for the funeral. He had arrived windswept and whippet-thin, with hair past his shoulders, a beard of sorts. There was a visitation the day before the burial but over the years their mother had isolated herself so completely that fewer than a dozen people signed the visitor's book at the Hammer-Dooley Funeral Home, and five of them were from Annabelle's migraine sufferers' support group.

Paul shaved clean for the visitation. He had creditably cut his own hair and even somehow found a blue suit and a crisp white shirt to wear. Sitting on a folding chair next to their mother's closed coffin, he openly wept, and he wept the next day as well, when they placed her in the ground.

"Well, we're the family now," Annabelle said to him, as they walked away from the cemetery through a cool, stinging mist.

His physical transformation, the openness of his sorrow, the tender way he placed his arm around her shoulders had led her to believe that the two of them were going to experience an emotional renaissance, a new closeness that would make them a team, a unit such as they had never been before, but that very evening, in the quiet, sad-smelling house on Wycoop Lane, as they ate the cold cuts they had purchased for those who might come to the house after the funeral but which had been untouched, because Annabelle and Paul had forgotten to extend the invitations, Paul, suddenly done with weeping and mourning and Connecticut in general, announced that he had to get back to Alaska the next day, and Annabelle, who felt as if she had been slapped across the face, said, "I'll take you to the airport."

Eventually, she had gone to work for the U.S. Postal Service, first as a mail sorter, then a carrier, and eventually in the human resources department, helping to develop an employee training program, which led to her relocation to Los Angeles, where she met Bernard Maby, an accountant for Continental Airlines. But the dull, glaring light of LA had a way of triggering migraines for Annabelle, and Bernard had stormy relations with the Iranian expatriate community, most of them far richer than he, many of them thinking of him as more Lebanese than Persian, and some of them remembering him from his days as a nightclub owner on Rue Monot in Beirut, a place called Cessez-Feu, which had a shadowy reputation, rumored to be a money-laundering operation, though nothing was ever proven.

One day, Annabelle called Paul and announced that she could no longer tolerate her job in HR, and that she and Bernard were unhappy in Los Angeles, and, further, that she had put in for a newly open position delivering the mail back east. Paul said that all sounded good, to which Annabelle replied, "Well you might not think so when I tell you where the opening is." She waited for him to ask where it was but Paul rarely asked direct questions so she just told him her new job was in Leyden. He said that sounded great to him, and she said, "Oh you say, you say. But maybe you better think about it, okay?

I don't want us to come all the way to be treated like strangers."

Annabelle and Bernard have been in Leyden for two months now, and Paul sometimes forgets they are here, not because he isn't glad to have his sister back in his life but because he is so used to living away from her, and his mind, as it makes its way around the parameters of his life, is not used to taking her into account. Nonetheless, he has seen Annabelle a number of times and, somewhat to his relief, twice he has attempted to see her only to be told she is tired, or busy. Tonight, however, is the first time he has seen her since what happened in the woods and he has spent part of the day wondering if the secret sitting in the pit of his stomach gives off a smell that only Annabelle can detect.

Dinner has been planned for six o'clock, out of deference to Annabelle, who rises early for her job. Nevertheless, she and Bernard are nearly an hour late and when they come in they are distracted, private. To Kate, they show the signs of a couple who have quarreled in the car. Annabelle barely apologizes for their lateness, and while she is effusive in her greeting of Paul she is cool toward Kate and barely glances at Ruby. Paul's sister is tall, with an athletic build, and she is pretty when she smiles, but her expression is usually that of someone who suspects she might be entering a room in which unkind remarks have recently been made about her. Paul has told her that Kate doesn't drink and she and Bernard have brought wine, which is served in the living room, with a fire going in the hearth, and a bowl of olives and a platter of cheese and crackers, all contributing to an air of conviviality—all that is missing is the conviviality itself.

When they go into the dining room, Annabelle is absorbed by Bernard, who sits at the dining table with his small hands folded, looking down at his empty plate. He looks forlorn in his brown suit, with his droopy mustache and melancholy eyes. He is bald, except for two strips of dark hair on either side of his head, smooth and shining like the fenders of a hearse.

"Bernard was worried about leaving his job and coming east,"

Annabelle is saying, "but he made so many contacts while he was at Continental and now he can work at home and he's got more clients than he knows what to do with." She reaches over, pats her husband's arm.

Paul's seat at the table—his table, built with his best oak, hand-sanded, hand-stained, not a nail or a screw in the entire thing—is empty. He has rushed the chicken back into the kitchen after having begun to carve it at the table and discovering its moist, translucent joints leaking blood.

"Sorry everyone," Paul calls out from the kitchen. "I got sort of a late start on this."

Kate smiles at Bernard. She is stimulated by his presence, excited to engage with a Muslim. "Does it seem odd to have a man in the kitchen?" she asks.

"Chicken must be cooked," Bernard says.

"Now somewhere in my mind," Kate says, "I have this notion that in Lebanon raw lamb is a delicacy."

Bernard shrugs his narrow shoulders, keeps his eyes on his plate. "Kibbe nayah," he all but whispers.

"Raw lamb?" Ruby trumpets, slapping her forehead in case anyone has failed to notice her astonishment.

"It's fine, Ruby, you just don't understand," says Annabelle, who has taken it upon herself to give the child a sense of boundaries that the girl's mother seems not to be providing.

"We eat it with mint and olive oil," Bernard murmurs.

"Fascinating," Kate says. "I'm sort of curious about another thing," she adds. "I know there are synagogues in Windsor County, but are there any mosques?"

"I certainly hope not," Bernard says.

In the kitchen, Paul slides the chicken out of the oven, hoping for some sudden onslaught of good luck that will in quick order transform the stiff, bloody bird into a succulent golden dinner, but one waggle of the drumstick tells him that the chicken still has a ways to go. He looks at his hands, flecked with blood. He shoves the pan back in, flips the oven door shut, and goes to the sink to wash his hands. The salted and peppered blood is oddly resistant. The red grit of it has lodged beneath his fingernails, the grooves between the palm side of his finger joints remain red, and he stands at the sink trying to scrub them clean.

"You've really civilized my brother," Annabelle is saying, as they hear the slam of the oven door from the kitchen.

"How do you mean?" Kate asks.

"He's just so different," Annabelle says to Kate. "He was always sort of wild. You never knew where he was. He never did anything the usual way. He might give you a bracelet, just out of nowhere, but then your birthday would come around and he'd have no idea that this was the day, this was when you were *supposed* to give someone a present."

A few minutes later, Paul returns from the kitchen. The chicken has been hacked into pieces to hasten its cooking, but it is arranged nicely on the platter and he serves it formally, standing by each of their chairs in turn.

When he gets to Kate with the platter, she notices his hand. It is a bright, translucent red, and a blister has risen, plump and round as a soap bubble. "You burned yourself, baby," she says to him, and he smiles at her in a way that strikes her as nonsensical, as if he is pleased.

Outside, wintry winds keen, rattling the windows. The sky is dotted with stars and the moon is icy-white and full.

"Hey, by the way," Kate says. "Did Paul tell you guys about our New Year's Eve party?"

"Of course not," Annabelle says.

"Well you have to come."

"It will be our pleasure," Bernard says.

"Did you forget?" Annabelle asks her brother.

"Sort of," he says.

"Paul's got a lot on his mind," Kate says. She means it protectively, and she's startled by the look he gives her.

"Aren't we going to say grace?" Ruby says.

"Oh, it's okay, honey," Kate says. "We have guests."

"Come on, Mom, you say the best graces."

Kate looks around the table and says, "I really don't. She's just used to things a certain way."

"By all means," Bernard says with a wave.

"I think it would be lovely if you said grace, Bernard," Kate says.

"I think it would be lovely just to eat," says Annabelle. "This chicken, Paul. It smells so good."

"I'm sorry I brought it out undercooked," he says.

"So, what about it, Bernard?" Kate says. There is a certain truculence in her tone—she hears it herself, and she wonders for a moment why she would want to needle her guest. There is no time to think about it, not now, though it does occur to her that she was in the city seven years ago when a group of Muslims from Brooklyn and New Jersey drove cars packed with explosives into the parking garage of the World Trade Center, and that night she had been out with her boyfriend, a lawyer, and an old pal of his, a self-consciously bizarre writer of children's books, and she found herself unexpectedly eloquent on the subject of Islam and its followers, their self-righteousness, their belief in vengeance, their appalling treatment of women, and her boyfriend started talking about how he would go about defending them in court, as if justice were a game, and then the children's book author said that Muslim extremists were more like Christian extremists than they were like other Muslims, and Kate called the waiter over and asked for the check, mainly because neither of the men she was with seemed to take what she was feeling very seriously.

"Do Muslims say grace?" Kate asks Bernard.

"Muslims say *bismillahi*," Bernard says, "which means I begin in Allah's name."

"Very pretty," says Kate. "How do you pronounce it again?"

"You have this idea that Bernard is a Muslim," Annabelle says. "And he's not." The last word expands emphatically and Annabelle colors, hearing the insistence in her own voice. "And anyway," she says, "who cares what religion anyone is? It's all pretty dubious anyhow, isn't it, and it just gives people another reason to clobber each other over the head. Paul and I never gave a hoot about all that junk."

Ruby's jaw drops, as if she has just heard a confession to the most mind-boggling depravity.

"Is that true?" Ruby asks Paul.

Before he can answer, Bernard is speaking. "In my home, which was a very traditional Maronite household, our grandmother required us to bow our heads before eating so that our foreheads touched the table. This I always did, with blind obedience, until one day I decided it was time to make a rebellion, and I only pretended to bow my head. I looked around the table and there we all were, twelve of us. The family lived in two adjoining houses and we took our evening meal together, without exception. And there was my grandmother, with her little white head bowed, and her eyes tightly shut, and my mother with her head bowed, and my uncle Fady, too, but every other person, my grandfather, my sister, my two other uncles, even my little brother, were simply staring ahead, eyes wide open, heads unbowed, and I realized all those nights, all those prayers, only three out of twelve of us were participating, and the rest were just being quiet for the sake of my grandmother."

"And in the meanwhile," Annabelle says, "my brother's chicken is getting cold." She cuts into her meat, brings it to her mouth, chews. "Oh, Paul, this is brill." She feels color creeping up her neck like an army of ants: *brill* was one of the put-on words she and Paul used to share when they made fun of the Kent, Connecticut, swells who fancied themselves somehow British. "By the way, Kate," she says, "I have your book, and I plan to read it."

"Oh," Kate says, with a wave. "You don't have to do that."

"I love reading. I've always loved reading." Annabelle puts her knife and fork down, dabs at her lips with the corner of her napkin. "I had to leave my college for health reasons. You can ask Paul, if you want."

"I don't need to verify your statements," Kate says. "And anyhow Paul always talks about you and he already told me how upset he was when you had to quit college. He totally admires you." Nothing of what she says is particularly true; she has composed it as a Valentine's Day card to Paul.

"I think some people—I'm not saying you—believe that if you work for the postal service you're automatically dumb," Annabelle says, struggling to control her voice.

"You're a mailman," Ruby declares, though she means it as a question.

"That's right," Annabelle says, "a mail carrier. A mail carrier with two hundred and sixteen stops on my route. Dodging deer all the way. I used to be so excited seeing deer—well that took about a week to get over. But the really scary part is pulling my car over to the side of the road and putting the mail in somebody's mailbox."

"Because something might be in the mailbox?" Ruby says.

"No, no. Not at all. Because I am really scared that some blankety-blank idiot is going to fail to see my hazard lights flashing and come ramming into me full speed ahead. Or maybe some nut job will do it on purpose."

"Why would they do that?" Ruby asks.

"They wouldn't," Kate hastens to say.

"They would," Annabelle says. "There are bad people out there and some of them hate anything to do with the government, and around here there aren't too many symbols of the Fed besides their letter carrier." She turns her gaze away from Ruby and addresses Paul. "I can almost see it happening sometimes. I can almost hear the sound of being rammed from behind."

"I have a good-luck thing," Ruby says, capturing no one's attention.

"So where's this dog of yours?" Annabelle says, fixing her eyes on Paul.

"On my foot!" Ruby proclaims.

"He's under the table," says Paul.

"It's his happy hunting ground," Kate says.

"Hey, I've got a good-luck thing," Ruby says. "I'll give it to you."

"You've really come a long way, Paul," Annabelle says. She gestures with her fork. "This house. A family. The cooking. And now a dog? I think it's great."

Bernard has lifted the tablecloth and peers beneath the table, with a look of grave concern. "There *is* a dog," he says. He resumes his upright position.

"His name is Shep," says Ruby. "We found him."

"Do you remember our dog?" Annabelle asks Paul.

"It's probably better not to even talk about it," says Paul.

"I wasn't going to talk about him, about King," says Annabelle. "I was just asking."

"Who's King?" Ruby directs the question to her mother.

Bernard has lifted the tablecloth again, and asks, "Does he want food?"

"King Richard was a puppy," Annabelle says to Ruby. "A Christmas dog. He was really, really cute. He used to suck on my fingertips like he was trying to get milk out of his mother's breast."

Kate looks over at Paul.

"I'm going to come over in the next couple days and see about fixing up those porch steps," Paul says to Annabelle. "We'll get that squared away."

"The landlord is completely irresponsible," says Bernard. "My foot almost went through." He continues to grip the edge of the tablecloth but refrains from taking another look at Shep.

"I think we should get Shep out from under the table," says Kate. "Paul?"

"So where did you find the dog?" Annabelle asks Paul.

"Coming back from the city," says Paul. He hears a deadness in his own voice, clears his throat. "Come on, Shep," he says, getting up. "Let's find a better spot for you."

Shep slinks out from his spot, though there is a certain hopefulness in his expression. He might be keeping open the possibility he has been called because he is about to be given some chicken

"He's got some of King's color in him," says Annabelle. "He was a Christmas present from my mother," Annabelle says, turning toward Ruby. "My mother got him from some lousy pet shop and there was something wrong with him."

"What?" Ruby asks.

"I don't know. I don't know what you call dog diseases. All I know is King Richard was dead in four days." She delivers this last statement in a somewhat melodramatic tone, and raises four fingers of her hand, to further impress Ruby with the small amount of time the little dog lived.

Kate is relieved to see that Ruby is showing no particular reaction to Annabelle's story. Annabelle seems to have noted this as well, and turns to Paul for reinforcement. "Do you remember how you cried?"

"Of course," Paul says, furrowing his brow. "It's only natural."

"You were always so . . ." Annabelle searches for the word. "I think I was more upset about seeing you cry than I was about poor little King."

"Well he was your brother and you knew him a lot more," says Ruby.

Kate feels a rush of love for Ruby. *You are the most wonderful girl.* The insubordination of Ruby's remark doesn't escape Annabelle, but rather than pushing forward, she heaves a sigh.

"My family had a dog, a Great Pyrenees," Bernard says. "I begged for his life when my father announced we were going to eat him."

"Oh, Bernard, please," says Annabelle. "No war stories."

"What was its name?" Ruby asks Bernard, and when he indicates with a raised eyebrow that he doesn't know what she is asking, she adds, "The dog you ate."

"We called him Roger," Bernard says. "Handsome, clever Roger. And we did not eat him. My father said yes, but he was overruled. There was fighting in the streets. And there was no place in the city that was safe. We were trapped in our house, eleven of us, all ages. Nothing to eat. My father loved the dog, but he had responsibility for all of our being well. Life is a struggle for protein. Protein, and the right to reproduce your genes. You understand? To make a family?"

Ruby nods gravely.

"Of course you do," says Bernard. He gestures toward the food on his plate. "Getting enough to eat, the meaning of life, for plants, and the animals, and for little girls and grown-ups, as well."

"I think Jesus," says Ruby.

"Jesus!" cries Annabelle, as if this was a name all of them had promised not to invoke.

"She means God," says Kate, hoping to protect her child from Annabelle and Bernard, who, she now believes, either have no idea how to speak to a child, or are in some other way deranged.

"What do you think they were fighting about in Bernard's city?" Annabelle says. "All the killing? It was for God. Someone says the wrong prayer—good-bye. Someone eats the wrong food—*adios.* Spring comes and this one says Happy Ramadan, and this one says

Happy Passover, and this one says Happy Easter, and then they pick up their swords and try to cut each other's head off."

Ruby's hands are behind her neck until finally she unclasps the chain and little crucifix Kate had given her a couple of weeks ago. She pools it in the palm of her hand, looks at it for a moment, and offers it to Annabelle. "Here is something that will make you safe in your mail car," she says. "You're supposed to hang it from the mirror thing in the front and it keeps you safe."

Oh no no no, this is not going to end well, Kate thinks.

For a moment, it seems that Annabelle is overcome with the kindness of Ruby's gesture, but she quickly recovers herself. "I'll put it on my rearview mirror and we'll see what happens," Annabelle says. "But let's not forget that all over the world people are hurting each other over this thing called religion, which to me is like fighting over fairy tales. Do you understand, Ruby? It's like people going to war because one side believes in Cinderella and the other side believes in the Little Mermaid."

"The Little Mermaid blows," says Ruby.

Paul sits on the edge of the tub and watches as Ruby brushes her teeth with fanatical thoroughness. At last she spits the foam of toothpaste into the sink; after, she rinses her mouth, raising up a golf ball on one cheek and then the other. Annabelle and Bernard have left, and Paul is grateful for the forbearance Kate has shown throughout the course of the evening, and to thank her he says he will put Ruby to bed, and will also clean the kitchen, leaving Kate to relax and watch a show on PBS about the looming threat of Y2K. Putting Ruby to bed is no easy matter; it involves supervising her various hygienic tasks, and taking her into the bedroom, reading to her for at least twenty minutes, singing several soothing songs, and patting her on the back in the dark until she falls asleep.

"See you in the morning," she says to her reflection in the medicine chest. She takes Paul's hand and they walk into her bedroom, which is painted tan and blue, with stars on the ceiling. On the walls are pictures Ruby herself took in an after-school photography class, portraits of other children in her grade, all of whom look cross and unsmiling, mimicking the existential pout of runway models. Even Señorita Spotnose, the black-and-white cat that lives in the cellar of Windsor Day, seems to have gone over to the dark side—her ears lie flat on her head and her eyes have turned blood-red from the camera's flash.

Paul reads to Ruby while she moves her fingers up and down on her blanket's satin border, pretending to type the words as he says them. After the reading comes the singing, and at last Paul turns off the bedside lamp and kisses Ruby on the forehead. As he pulls away from her, Ruby catches his shoulders, holds him fast.

"Not yet," she says.

Her breath smells of toothpaste and body heat, like candy out of the oven. From a distance comes the sound of a car. It is heading toward the house; its headlights plunge into Ruby's room, swelling the shadows of the furniture and teddy bears so that they rush up the walls and halfway across the ceiling. Shep, who has followed Paul up the steps and has been curled waiting for him outside of Ruby's room, scrambles to his feet and rushes down to the first floor, barking his deep baritone warning. Paul, still held by Ruby's beseeching hands, feels a whirl of anxiety going through him. Who could be coming here at this hour?

"You get a great night's sleep," he says to Ruby, in as relaxed a voice as possible. He peels her grip loose, and Ruby falls back flat onto the bed. She seems a good distance from sleep; this whole ritual has been wasted.

"Don't leave until I fall asleep," she says. "With pats."

By now, Shep's barking has taken on a tinge of mania. "I better see what's going on down there," Paul says, standing up. The blood rushes from his head; consciousness ripples like a flag in the wind.

Downstairs, a driver from a courier service is sitting at the kitchen counter. He has taken off his fur cap and his thinning dark hair is wet with perspiration; he mops his brow with the back of his hand. A bulky package clearly marked URGENT is on the counter. Kate, placing a coffee cup in front of the driver, takes the package with her as she resumes her post next to the stove, where she is waiting for the water to boil.

"Hi Paul," she says, over her shoulder, as Paul walks slowly into the kitchen. "This is Casper, he got lost somewhere between LaGuardia and here."

"I'm not overly accustomed to the roads up this way," Casper says. He has a whiskey voice, lurching and apologetic. Kate has found a box cutter in a drawer, with which to cut the envelope open. The teakettle begins to whistle but Kate is absorbed by the envelope's contents—a letter, a few audiotapes, several brochures. Paul turns the burner off, picks up the kettle to see if there's enough water for an extra cup, and glances at the letter in Kate's hands. On the top of the page is an old-fashioned drawing of a radio tower, with concentric ever-expanding circles of broadcasting power emanating from its peak.

"It's from Heartland Radio," Kate says, her eyes moving, her chin sinking, as she scans the page.

"Who's that?" Paul asks.

Kate presses the letter to her breast, takes a deep breath. "We can talk about this," she says. "Casper has to go all the way back to New York."

"Tarrytown," Casper says. He rakes his fingernails through his hair, as if to comb it. He has the ways of a man who no longer spends his time in the company of others.

"They called you in Tarrytown to pick this up at LaGuardia?" Kate asks. "And then to drive it out here?"

"That's okay with me," Casper says. "Tarrytown's right in the middle of everything, and I'm happy for the work."

Paul struggles to maintain a placid composure. *This guy's got nothing to do with it. Sometimes a coincidence is just a coincidence.* But fear and illogic have entered him at the end of a very long day when his defenses are down.

Kate hands Casper his coffee. "Oh that's good, that's good," he says, taking a sip.

"It's so late to be making deliveries," Kate says.

"I picked your thing up at the airport a little past six," Casper says. "I don't mean to be barging in."

"No, no," Kate says. "It's fine."

"You never know what it is," Casper says. "I've been in the courier business since 1979 and I've had some pretty strange things. I picked up a human heart once, locked up in a metal box, sent from Chicago." He takes another sip of coffee and exhales, turning his shoulders, lifting his chin, and for a moment his younger self, handsome and dramatic, shows through. "I swear to God I could hear it beating."

"No life-saving organs for me," Kate says. "Just fame and fortune."

"So I bring glad tidings," Casper says, placing the cup onto the counter and dismounting the stool as if from a horse. "What's the best way back to Tarrytown from here?" he asks.

"Tarrytown," Paul says. "I don't know. I never go there." He looks out the window over the sink to see what the weather is but the hard, moonless night turns the glass into a mirror. His own face is the last thing in the world he wants to see right now.

Casper gives Paul a lingering, questioning look, but then says, "Just point me in the right direction."

"I'll get you to the parkway," Paul says, opening the door.

Paul gives the courier directions to the Taconic Parkway and walks him to the door to the black, icy night. Casper has left the engine of his Honda running; chalk-white exhaust rushes out of the tailpipe, and the headlights illuminate dashes and dots of slanting snow.

"Just a second," Paul says, and reaches into his pocket, pulls out what feels like the newest and cleanest of the bills. It's a fifty and it's just as well. He hands it to Casper, who seems surprised, and uncertain about accepting it. He glances down, sees Grant's melancholy, drink-blasted face.

"Much appreciated," he murmurs.

As the taillights of Casper's car swerve slowly up the driveway and out of sight, Paul continues to stand there, taking some comfort in the steady darkness of the cold, cold night. When he walks back to the kitchen, the light seems garishly bright and the sudden heat makes him feel as if he has been submerged in water.

Kate is trying to divert Shep's attention while the dog, emitting a series of whines and warbles, his rump in the air, his tail twirling, claws frantically at the cabinet doors beneath the kitchen sink. "Stop it, Shep," Kate is saying. "You're wrecking the paint."

"Shep," Paul commands, clapping his hands, but the dog continues to worry the cabinet doors and now is lying flat on his underside and plucking at the doors with his claws, hoping to open them.

"Why's he doing this?" Kate asks. "Is something in there?"

"I don't know. I don't think he's just goofing around." Paul crouches next to the dog and crooks his finger through the metal circle that tightens the choke collar—the one artifact from the dog's former life. The moment Shep feels the collar tightening, he turns his teeth toward Paul's hand with stunning speed. There is no measurement of time that can describe how sudden this move is, and all that saves Paul from being bitten is Shep's stopping himself.

"Oh my God," Kate says. "Are you all right?" She has backed farther and farther away from the sink.

"What are you doing, buddy?" Paul croons to the dog. "You going a little nuts there?"

Shep is panting, eyes flashing, his avidity masked as merriment. He seems reconciled to Paul's grip on his collar, but when Paul pushes down on his rump and tells him to sit it is as if the dog's skeleton is constructed in such a way as to make that position an impossibility. When Paul pushes harder, Shep's front legs begin to slide on the kitchen floor and a low growl rumbles in the depths of him.

"Paul," Kate says, her voice rising, "that dog's going to bite you."

To demonstrate how much he does not fear this, to show Kate, the dog, and himself, Paul cups his hand over Shep's muzzle. The dog's excited breath is warm and moist against his palm, and Shep's normally peaceful brown eyes show a disquieting amount of white. Though the dog is not going to bite Paul, he is not going to be deterred from rooting out whatever is inside the cabinet beneath the sink, and as soon as Paul relaxes his grip, Shep scrambles to the doors again and begins scratching at them and whimpering.

"What's in there?" Kate asks.

"I don't know. Something. A mouse, a squirrel, maybe a snake."

"A snake?" For Kate, this is the worst-case scenario, far more disturbing than Y2K.

"There are no poisonous snakes around here," Paul says.

"All snakes are poisonous. They poison your mind. You experience such uncontrollable, piercing terror that the fear chemicals released in your brain turn you into a drooling idiot."

"Here," Paul says, "you take Shep and I'll deal with whatever's in there." He leads Shep by the collar, though the dog is unwilling and Paul must virtually drag him across the kitchen to Kate. Just as the transfer is being made, Shep wriggles free and lopes across the room, back to the cabinets, and this time he has instantaneous success in plucking the doors open.

"Oh no!" Kate cries. Her hands fly up to her face.

It's a rat snake, dull muddy gray and eight feet long. It has been enjoying the warmth of the hot water pipe, which the back half of it has been wrapped around. It drops to the floor and slithers slowly toward them. Its flat, rather small head is white on its underside; the black holes of its eyes are ringed in gray several shades lighter than the chain mail covering the rest of it.

Kate is virtually paralyzed with fear. As much as she wants to put distance between her and the rat snake, she is equally afraid to be alone. "What's that bulge?" she manages to say.

"I guess he just ate a mouse," Paul says.

"Oh fuck," whispers Kate, as if there simply could not be worse news. She covers her mouth and nose. "It smells like a horrible cucumber."

Shep, seeing now the bewildering nature of the noise from beneath the sink, has decided the best place for him is at Paul's side. He leans against Paul's leg and watches as the snake slowly makes its way across the kitchen.

"What are you doing?" cries Kate. "You're just standing there!"

"Don't worry," Paul says. "I'm going to get it out of here."

Whatever the snake has swallowed seems still to be alive. It pulsates in the snake's digestive tract, as the nutrients are slowly and inexorably juiced out of it. As it is replenished, the snake is moving toward the kitchen table, and Paul quickly puts himself in its path, and stamps his foot to redirect it. The snake stops, lifts its head, surveys the terrain. With increasing speed, it winds its way toward the door to the cellar, where there is, in fact, a space between the door and the floor that is large enough for the snake to squeeze through and make its way to the bowels of the house, where it may have been wintering all along.

"Get it before it goes down there," Kate says.

"I'm trying," Paul says, his temper rising as his heart sinks: a part of him already knows he is going to kill this snake.

He takes quick strides toward the retreating rat snake and tries to step on its tail to stop it, but it feels as if the tail of the thing actually *shrinks* once it feels the pressure of Paul's shoe, and now, with the snake just a moment or two from the space at the bottom of the cellar door, Paul grabs the thing—it feels as hard and alive as a garden hose through which cold water surges—and flings it, hoping it will land near the back door where he can eventually shove it out into the night. But the snake is heavy, ungainly, and it lands in the middle of the kitchen, where Shep, whose instincts have been reignited by the commotion, lunges upon it and sinks his teeth into its body, roughly midway between head and tail. Kate has her hand over her mouth, hoping her muffled cries will not awaken Ruby. Paul is trying to get Shep to drop the snake, which he is now subjecting to rapid-fire shakes, hoping to snap its neck. The snake, however, is far too pliable to be killed like this; indeed, its head has turned now and even as it is caught between the dog's jaws, its mouth is open and its tongue is flickering. Shep by now has gotten a taste of what he has bitten, and by the look of him he finds it repulsive; he draws himself up to his full height and his mouth slowly opens and the mangled, bleeding snake drops wetly to the floor, though it continues to swerve, this time in the direction of the kitchen cabinets, which still are wide-open. Shep watches the snake, his head cocked to one side, in a pose that might be mistaken for adorable. While he is still tonguing the taste of the snake out of his mouth, the snake's movement makes it irresistible to Shep and he gives every indication of getting ready to attack it again. In the meanwhile, however, Paul has grabbed the teakettle off the burner, and he uses it as a cudgel, slamming the bottom of it hard against the snake's head, stunning it, and then slamming it again, finishing it off.

"Is it dead?" Kate asks.

Paul, looming over the now-inert creature, watches it for signs of life, and Shep, standing between Paul and Kate, looks first at the snake and then at Paul, and Paul, his chest heaving from the exertion and the emotion of the kill, wonders if the dog is remembering what he is remembering.

Paul takes the dead snake outside and throws it in the tall brown grass along the driveway, where crows will find it and pick it to pieces. He stands there for a few extra moments and looks at the moon, his thoughts rapid and indecipherable. At last, he comes back into the house, where Kate has been mopping up the smear left by the snake.

"Well, that was like having two hundred and fifty cups of coffee," she says, throwing away the paper towels and running the base of the teakettle under the hot-water tap.

"Are you okay?" Paul asks.

"Needless to say, I am not a big fan of the snake."

Paul slumps into a kitchen chair, but when Kate is finished cleaning the teakettle, she comes behind him and makes an effort to lift him out of his seat. "Let's go to the dining room," she says. "I need to share something with you. Plus I can't believe I said 'share.' "

They sit across from each other at the dining table. The ring of moisture left by the platter holding tonight's roasted chicken is still visible. Kate is holding the letter from the radio programmers. She moistens her lips with the tip of her tongue, takes a deep, steadying breath.

" 'Dear Ms. Ellis,' " Kate reads. " 'As you know, we here at Heartland Radio are huge fans of you and your work. *Prays Well with Others* has been a company favorite since its publication and we have also followed with keen interest your numerous public appearances, in person, on television, and on radio.' " She suddenly puts the letter down. "Okay, I'm not going to read this letter after all. But long story short? They want me to have my own show. Once a week, it would go out to about two hundred of their stations." She smiles. "I used to think this concentration of ownership and the whole media conglomerates situation was a bad thing for our culture and democracy, but now I have entered the Tour de France of backpedaling and I think it's all good."

Paul rests his chin in his hand, struggling to be a part of this conversation. "It sounds good," he finally says.

Kate gives no indication of finding his response tepid. "I don't know," she says. "They don't mention money, maybe it isn't even worth that much. And I have no idea what it will do to my writing. I don't want it to all fizz out as a bunch of radio talk." She picks the letter up again, glances at it, places it carefully on the table, smoothes it down. "What would you think about that? Me on the radio? Do you think that would be, I mean something you'd be all right with, I mean does it strike you as a good idea?"

"I don't know, I've never thought about being on the radio before. Do they want you to talk about the Bible?"

"I'm not a theologian—and I'm not going to play one on radio. I don't really know the Bible all that well. So many real estate deals and so much revenge."

"So what would you do?"

"Just talk. About . . ." She flutters her eyelashes, places her hand over her heart. " . . . *moi*. The same as my book, the same as every one of my events. All I know is what I know. The story of finding a little bit of grace in a life that is otherwise pretty crazy."

"I'll sure listen."

"This is making me so frightened," Kate says. "I'm used to things being a certain way, and now everything's changing." She reaches across the table, takes his hand. "Everything's so different now—and it's all so much more than I ever expected. Sometimes I don't recognize myself. It's as if I woke up one morning and I had red hair and was six feet tall. I mean it's interesting to be so tall and have red hair—but what happened to *me*? Do you understand?"

"I think so," Paul says. "But we have to be willing to change," he adds, somewhat tentatively.

"I know," she says. "Life on life's terms. Okay, I'm in. Deal the cards. Right? You want to know what I know? I know that our lives are unfolding under God. He's really there, in the most primitive and absolute way. Just the way people thought thousands of years ago, all those people who didn't know shit, they knew that, and they were right."

"But no one can see him," Paul says.

"Of course not," Kate says. "Can you imagine how boring everything would be if you could see God the way you can see Cleveland or a box of paper clips?"

Kate gets out of her chair, walks over to Paul, and leads him out of the dining room, up the staircase, into their bedroom. They are still clothed but she gets on top of him, aligns herself just so. "How much happiness can one woman stand?" she asks. She glances up quickly, to where God might be, and then lowers her eyes gently, covering Paul with her gaze as if it were a soft blanket. "Am I freaking you out? It's too much, isn't it?"

He shakes his head, not daring to speak. Somewhere out in the night, in that vast, cold wilderness between the treetops and eternity, a small plane drones, its engines straining. He imagines the pilot, rigid with fear as the plane loses altitude, and he imagines the plane crashing through the roof, its lethal propellers cutting through the fragile flesh of them. Kate arches her back, presses herself against him, and as she continues to gaze at him she moves her head so the ends of her hair trail lightly over his face.

"All right," she whispers, "I'm through talking, it's a moratorium." She lowers her face to kiss him, and Paul holds her by her hips, to stop her, but she misinterprets his touch and presses her pelvic bone into him. He increases the strength of his grip, holding her fast, an inch or two away from him.

"But one more thing?" Kate says.

"Okay," he says. "You can say as many more things as you want. I love when you talk."

"You really do?"

"Who wouldn't?"

"All right, that settles it," Kate says. "We have to get married. I need to put this whole thing in writing. I need it signed, sealed, and delivered. I need the law on my side."

She kisses him as she speaks, until he turns his head.

"What?" Kate asks.

"I have to tell you something," he says.

She can barely see him in the dim light from the hallway. "That's never good," she says.

He is silent for a few moments. He knows what she cannot know—he is about to change everything. "It's not," he says. "It's not good."

"Oh Paul . . . What is it? Just tell me."

"A couple of weeks ago," he says, and stops. He wants to live for one more moment in a world in which he has not said this. Once it starts it cannot stop; it will be like having taken an ax to a tree.

"What?" she says. "A couple of weeks ago. What?"

"I killed a man," he says. "A couple of weeks ago I killed a man."

The way he was leading up to it, she would have bet anything that he was going to tell her he was involved with somebody else, and in spite of herself her first reaction is a rush of relief. Her second reaction is the rest of her life.

CHAPTER
THIRTEEN

"You seem unusually quiet today," Todd Lawson says.

Paul does not trust himself to speak, and he is doing his best to keep his mind occupied by listening to the moist crunch of his foot-steps through the hardening, thickening loam of the woods, and to the furious territorial squawks of the blue jays, those holdout birds who never leave, a dozen of them circling. The sky is a wrinkled purple-and-gray shawl. Below, rain, melt, and runoff have pooled shallowly and formed a fragile skin of ice. It's difficult to resist apply-ing the rude nudge of a toe to the spun-sugar puddles, turning them into spiderwebs of cracks and fissures.

Now that he has told Kate what he has done, the pressure to say it again and again and again builds daily. Today, Paul, Evangeline, and Shep were at the painter Hunter DeMille's house, a reclaimed lighthouse in the middle of the Hudson. Paul was showing DeMille plans he had drawn up to build a network of wooden walkways, upon which the boggy two acres of land the lighthouse stands might be traversed, and while they spoke Shep effortlessly won the heart of DeMille's seven-year-old son, Cooper, from whom laughter was such an infrequent sound that DeMille immediately put in a bid to buy the dog. As outrageous as it was to think that Paul might spontaneously decide to unload his dog, DeMille carried on in his attempts to buy Shep, and Evangeline looked on, disheartened to see a man whom she had studied in her Marlowe College art history classes behave in such a presumptuous manner. Paul, wishing only to silence the insistent painter, started mentally rehearsing the shocking reveal of why he could never give Shep up, and as DeMille angrily raised the price higher and higher, until he was offering Paul ten thousand dollars for the dog, the urge to simply tell the old guy that he had killed a man over this dog became so strong that the desire to confess to violence became violence in itself. Similarly, he has wanted to tell Evangeline the actual story of how he found Shep, and he has wanted to tell Annabelle, who, last Sunday, when Paul at last got around to repairing the steps on her porch, told him he was being unusually quiet.

The need to talk about what he has done surges behind a dam of common sense, but common sense is not enough to hold such a deep and powerful force and so the dam must be shored up, spackled with words. Yet small talk is impossible for Paul right now and so the words he says are perilously close to the words he is afraid to say.

"Do you think you could make it through if you were ever put in jail?" he asks Lawson.

Lawson has been walking a few paces in front of Paul but stops, turns. "For a night?"

"For a year, or ten years."

"Live free or die, baby, like the license plate says. But why? Thinking of committing a crime?" Lawson plucks a tiny brown and withered pinecone from the end of an icy branch, rubs it between his thumb and forefinger, and lets it fall to the ground. Shep comes seesawing over to check out what has dropped to the ground, sniffs it, and looks up with a cheerful expression, as if to jolly Lawson into dropping something of higher value.

"So do you think you could do it?" Paul persists.

"I don't know. It would be hard. I can't even sit through a movie."

They have been hiking what was once the Leyden Gun Club but which has been recently sold and slated for development: the hundred-unit condo will be called Turkey Hollow, presumably in honor of the many wild turkeys who have met their end on these acres. Suddenly, they are standing on the edge of a winding blacktop road. A couple of joggers come chugging by, two men in their forties and, by the look of them, corporate types, with salt-and-pepper hair, slender legs, sweatshirts announcing their patronage of the Four Seasons Istanbul and a place called Smuggler's Cove, which, by the look of it, with its palm trees and parrots, is somewhere in the Caribbean. The joggers give no indication of having any awareness of either Paul or Todd's presence. A tattered trail of their conversation wafts behind them—the one with the sweatshirt from the Four Seasons is talking about measures his company is taking to back up their data in case worst predictions about Y2K come true.

"That guy in the Istanbul shirt?" Lawson says when the joggers are a safe distance away. "He's married to an old girlfriend of yours."

"Yeah?"

"Lynn Dobkin."

"I thought she moved to London or someplace."

"I think that's where they met, but now they're here. Part of the time, anyhow." Lawson takes a deep breath, the way people do when their thoughts turn to the past. "She was so good-looking she made you good-looking." Todd presents his palm to be slapped, but Paul pretends not to notice.

"That was never going to go anywhere."

"What do you mean?" Todd says. "You were already there, there was nowhere left to go."

"Lynn was very involved with being Jewish," Paul says. "I was the first non-Jew she had ever gone out with."

"And who were you seeing before that?" Todd asks. "The acupuncturist?"

"Pauline. Not an acupuncturist. Shiatsu massage. And you know what? Someone named Paul cannot go out with someone named Pauline."

"Really?" Todd says. "I could deal with a problem like that. She was gorgeous."

Paul shrugs. He hears the distant hum of a car engine and the litfuse hiss of tire treads on wet blacktop; he snaps his fingers and Shep comes to his side, and Paul hooks his finger through the dog's collar. The dog seems wised up to cars, but you never know. An animal is liable to do anything, any animal.

"She was gorgeous and the sex was amazing," Todd says. "Remember?"

Paul frowns. He doubts he said such a thing, but where else would Todd get the idea? Because it was true, truer words were never spoken, there were times when the sense memory of being with Pauline comes back to him, brilliant and unbidden.

"And what about Indigo Albright?" Lawson asks.

"Now you're really reaching into the past," Paul says, but he feels the sweetness of being known. It amazes him that Todd has been so mindful all these years. How long have they actually known each other? He cannot affix a date to the time of their first meeting. Todd is one of those people whom you feel you have always known, even though you have a difficult time imagining where he goes when he is not standing directly in front of you. He seems, both in his remarks and his actions, without motive—but is such a thing possible? Is there any human being without motive? Doesn't motive rule the inner life as commandingly as gravity rules the outer?

"Let me ask you a question," Paul says. They have come to the part of the road that begins the eastern edge of Kate's property; a dying locust tree, its trunk, bulging with cancers, bears a yellow plastic NO HUNTING sign with her name written on it in Magic Marker. The lights of the house are not visible from here, but the glow of them rises through the late-afternoon air like a cool yellowish mist. Paul feels the blind mammalian weight of Shep leaning against his legs. "Did you know the guy Kate was with, before me?"

"Sure. I still do. Daniel Emerson. Why? Need a lawyer?"

"I might," Paul says, and forces himself to smile. "But what happened with him? Something bad, right?"

"Yeah. A fireworks accident. On Ferguson Richmond's property. Thing is, men get into the woods—we go back to our elemental selves, and shit happens. Anyhow, the guy recovered, though it took a while. And in the meanwhile Dan ended up with the guy's wife. Welcome to Leyden."

"He really broke Kate's heart," Paul says.

"I know. Everybody knows."

"She won't even say his name."

"Well now you have her all to yourself."

Paul shakes his head. "What is it with us?"

"With who?"

"You know. Men."

"Men do what men do. We're just part of the scheme of things," Todd says, punching Paul lightly on the arm. "We're just nature."

"Poor Kate," Paul says.

"Well happy ending. She's got you now." Todd reaches down, picks up a rock from the side of the road, and heaves it high into the air, over the trees. Long seconds go by before they hear it come back to earth.

"But what's going on, Paul?" Todd asks softly. "Are you in trouble?

Something you want to tell me? I mean, you don't have to. But if you want to, I'm here."

"I know," Paul says. "And it's much appreciated."

They make the turn around another bend in the road. The northern end of Kate's house is visible here; the lights of the room she has designated as the library burn bright yellow against the sudden deep blue of the evening. If Paul's heart had knees it would fall to them right now.

"I sort of feel like I'm in jail, half the time," Paul says. "I'm living the way you're supposed to when they lock you up, when you just sit there and contemplate your wrongdoing."

"Hey," Todd says. "Listen to me. I don't know what the fuck you're talking about, but I do know this: there is no way on earth that you belong in jail, I don't care what you've done."

Paul laughs. It's unbelievable to him what a lift it gives him to hear those words. "You want to come in?" he asks Todd. "Cup of tea, or we could open a bottle of wine."

"No thanks," Todd says. "I've got señorita plans."

"Well I can't stand in the way of that," Paul says.

"I mean literally señorita," Todd says. "Did you ever meet Vicky Rodriguez? She nannies for the Rosenbergs over at Southwind. My grandfather used to have dinners at that house. The Rosenbergs have no idea what the history of that place is, their own house, I have to tell them all about it. This town is changing so fast."

"It's just different rich people," Paul says. "The new richies will make their own history."

"Not just that. There's five times as many houses. If they put a fast train on the tracks, we're going to be a suburb. No one makes anything, no one fixes anything. Everybody lives by their little rules, everyone's worrying over their retirements and paying their insurance premiums. The adventure's gone. They've cut the balls off this place. It's not for me. And it's not for you either. It's not for us."

They are standing at the beginning of the driveway leading down to Kate's house. Off to the side, a small herd of deer are foraging for what's left of the summer's grass; every now and then one of them lifts its head and its eyes shine like amethyst. From this vantage, the house is not visible, except for its halo of light. Shep has gotten so accustomed to seeing deer and has had so little success chasing them that now he seems to actually *pretend* not to see them. His energies are focused on going back to the house. The back half of his body writhes with excitement; his two favorite parts of a walk are being asked to come along and being allowed to return.

"Well," Paul says, "I'll see you."

"Here's the thing," Todd says. He lays his hand on Paul's shoulder. "If you've done something, you have to trust yourself to deal with it within yourself, on your own terms. It's the do-it-yourself ethic, my friend. Men like us, we don't look to other people to fix things for us. A sink gets stopped up, we don't call a plumber, we snake it out, we change the gaskets, we do whatever it takes, and if a tree gets struck by lightning and falls on our house we get in there with a chainsaw and cut the tree into two-foot lengths and then we repair the roof. Whatever it is that's bothering you, you'll deal with it, I know you will, you always have. You've got something that's so fucking far beyond adherence to the rules—you've got honor."

Todd rocks back on his heels and grins. There's a gap between his right incisor and the next tooth, a dark tunnel leading to the depths of him.

CHAPTER
FOURTEEN

In the silence of the car, he has been composing a letter in his mind, or a speech. *Dear Kate, I love you so deeply and so much.* But he sees her glancing at him and he speaks. "They say that murderers always return to the scene of the crime," Paul says, sinking lower in the passenger seat as Kate steers her car off of the Taconic Parkway and onto the Saw Mill.

"No one's a murderer here, so you can just shut up about that," says Kate. She assumes this will sound affectionate, loyal, and confident, but she sees Paul's uncertain expression and now she reaches for him, rests her hand on his knee, and adds, "I'm sorry."

He looks at her quizzically, as if a world in which Kate has to be sorry is somehow bizarre. *But I don't think I was ever meant to live with another person.*

"Next exit, right?" Kate asks.

Paul's knees ride nervously up and down. He looks like someone in an interrogation room who is starting to realize he won't be able to hold out much longer. He looks like someone who is about to crack.

As they close in on Tarrytown his mind is besieged with irrational fears, fears that began when he acquiesced to Kate's request to see for herself the place where he did it, beat a man to death, and which have intensified the closer they get to Martingham. Yet he maintains his resolve to see it through. Kate is hammering out her own sense of what had happened that November afternoon, what happened to Paul, and what, by extension, and through the intractable bonds of love, has happened to her, and Paul feels he has no right to interfere.

Until today, she did not ask which woods he had stopped in, and Paul never volunteered. Once, maybe the night he told her what he had done, or perhaps it was the day after, he started to tell her in detail where he had turned off the road, where he had parked his truck, but some instinct had made her stop him. Kate, normally curious, and sometimes insatiably so, didn't want to be able to picture Paul's deed too clearly. She had already begun on the path she had chosen, which was to keep him safe, this man, her man, who, except for that one thing, that one terrible thing, did nothing but make life better for everyone around him. Ignorance wasn't bliss but rather a gauzy scarf thrown over the lamp of knowledge, coloring the light, making it less harsh.

Yet it was odd to know so little about what had really happened that November afternoon, and Kate has begun to wonder how the blows had landed, where the body had fallen, what happened first, what happened second, what happened after that. And where? How could Paul and the man find themselves so alone, like two fugitives facing each other in the wilderness, how could this happen in the middle of Westchester County, which was in itself so close to Manhattan, and was really just the hem of the city's long skirt?

Your life was good, really good, when I met you . . . It is eleven in the morning and now that they have turned off the Saw Mill there are no other cars in sight. Kate is aware that Paul hasn't spoken in several minutes, nor has he made eye contact with her. His knees continue to jiggle and he keeps his eyes fixed on the passing landscape. She comes to a stop at a T-junction. "Take a right, and then another right, and then there's the entrance," Paul says.

"I'm sorry," Kate says.

He shakes his head. He will have none of that. *You have your life, your writing, Ruby . . .*

"I just have to do this," Kate says.

"We're here. We're doing it. It's for the best."

"I do think it will be."

Paul shrugs. He turns toward her suddenly, his face lacking in kindness. For a moment she can almost see it happening. "Maybe God wants us to be here. Is that what you're thinking?" he asks.

She feels the words like a blow, and her first response is to say something equally angry, but she is thrown off course by the sheer unfamiliarity of verbal nastiness from Paul, whose infrequent moments of irritation have heretofore been expressed through withdrawal and silence. "Maybe you're right," she says, "maybe that's exactly what God wants."

"Well I'd like to know something about his wishes because this complete silence is a drag. I killed a man and the universe is totally silent."

She turns on the access road leading to Martingham State Park. Blue spruces border the blacktop; the white line dividing the road seems freshly painted. Above, the sky is lumpy and gray, a vast frozen oyster of a sky.

"We're going to be okay," she says. "You're never going to be caught, we're never going to tell anyone. We'll just live with it. What else can we do?"

"I don't know," Paul says. "It might be better if I'd turned myself in. Easier." He slips his hand into his coat; his stomach feels as if he is digesting gravel. *I feel like an infection . . . I think it's time for me to disappear . . .*

"It would be pointless," Kate says, a little sharply. "The thing is, nobody saw you. I used to write about this stuff, Paul, I know what I'm talking about. People who get caught? Most of them are already in the system, with long records of criminal behavior. And most of them are dumb or crazy. Or it's so obvious, like the OJ thing, it's like who else could it have been? Husbands kill their wives, wives kill their husbands, disgruntled employees, impatient heirs, these are the people who get caught."

"I'm already caught," Paul says.

Today there are other vehicles in the park's east lot, six of them, any of which could be an unmarked police car. As Kate noses her car toward the same slot in which Paul had parked his truck, he is suddenly overcome by fear; it feels as if he is inhabited by a thousand small hands, all busily shredding his reason. So fierce, vast, and shaming is his panic that he can barely breathe, and Kate, who last night stayed up late and alone, drinking Snapple and watching an old production of *Macbeth* on PBS, remembers something dear Banquo says in the first act. *Or have we eaten on the insane root/ That takes the reason prisoner?* Good question, Kate thinks, accelerating as she circles the parking lot. Paul is looking into each car as they pass it.

"I think the best thing is to act natural," Kate says.

"There's two people in that black Buick," he whispers. *She's done this to me . . .*

Kate cranes her neck to get a better view. He's right, two people. But they look like teenagers, a kid in a Mets cap, another with pink hair. They've probably come here to smoke pot. But she doesn't want to argue with him. She keeps driving, out of the parking area, back onto the access road. "Now what?" she says.

"I don't know," Paul says. "We're here because of you." He sees the look on her face. He didn't mean to hurt her. *Monster . . .*

"Maybe this was a bad idea," Kate says. "I don't need to see any more. We can go back home."

Home. The word pierces Paul, the idea that there is a place in the world where he belongs, and the ease with which Kate has said it. He reaches for her hand. "No, it's okay. Let's turn around. I'll show you where it happened."

"You don't have to. I get it. I don't even know why I wanted to do this in the first place."

"It was just seeing those cars."

"Those were just a couple of teenage guys in that Buick. I think they were getting high."

"Last time the place was empty. It's weird to see so many cars."

"It's a park. People come and go." She looks over at Paul. His hands are folded in his lap, tightening and loosening their clasp.

"I was at the post office yesterday," Paul says. "A supplier sent me some chips of Louisiana cypress that I had to pick up."

"And?" she asks. His voice sounds hollow, distant. She is starting to miss him and long for him already, as if he has betrayed her and she has not been able to forgive him.

"And there was this guy in front of me, he was already at the window. Buying stamps. But he was very particular about it, he wanted fancy ones. So Gerald shows him some Elvis stamps and those Robert Indiana love stamps, a bunch of stuff, and here's this guy, he's about fifty, he's wearing his earmuffs and mittens inside the post office though it's always insanely hot in there, and he's taking his time making his big decision of the day. I've already been there for quite a while and I've got so much to do back at the shop, and I'm staring at this guy's neck and trying to do a mind control thing to make him hurry up. But he thinks and he thinks and then he finally decides which sheet of stamps he's going to buy and he starts taking nickels and dimes out of his belly bag, ten, twenty, twenty-five, thirty-five, forty, and I'm thinking to myself: I'd like to break this guy's neck." He looks at Kate, pleadingly. "You know what I'm saying. This guy is getting on my nerves and the next thing I know I want to kill him with my bare hands."

"We all think things like that," Kate says.

"But I've actually gone and done it," says Paul. "And it's made me aware of how often I think about it, how often I've always thought about it. Someone's driving too slowly in front of me, or I see some slob throwing garbage out of his truck, or somebody treats me like I'm a servant. I could murder that guy, this one I'd like to kick in the ass, this one I'd like to shake. But when you've actually done it?" He shakes his head. "I hope you never have to wonder about yourself the way I wonder about myself."

They have come to a stop sign. "What do you want me to do, Paul? Shall I turn around, or should we just go back to Leyden?"

"I was just thinking . . . We're going to be having a big party soon? I think that's going to be weird. It doesn't seem right."

"It'll be fine," Kate says. "We need to see people. And we should just act as normally as possible." She means it to be comforting, just old-fashioned common sense, but to her own ears she sounds like someone who has entered into a conspiracy.

"I feel strange around people," Paul says. "I'm not part of them. I'm part of something else."

"People love you, Paul. They really do."

"I'm afraid of myself."

She takes his hand and places it on her throat. "I'm not afraid of you, I don't think you've gone feral or something. I love you and I trust you and my advice, if you're looking for advice, is for you to love and trust yourself, because you deserve it."

"What about—"

"There's nothing we can do about that at this point. It's in God's hands—and the way it seems so far is nobody else cares."

"All right," Paul says. "I'll show you where."

Halfway across the intersecting road, Kate makes a U-turn and they return to Martingham State Park. As they walk from the parking area to the trail, Paul notices a sign informing people of all that is forbidden in the park, including fires, bottles, weapons, and dogs. Dogs. There is a silhouette of a German shepherd, circled in red with a forbidding line drawn through it. Paul wonders if this is new; he has no memory of seeing it last month. He feels something touching him and he is startled for an instant before realizing Kate has taken his hand.

If he was ever to be apprehended for that killing, today would be the day, Paul thinks. He feels both terror and relief at the prospect. He sees something in a nearby white birch—a camera? Maybe that's exactly how the police are proceeding: they are filming everyone who comes to this spot and then checking their footprints against the prints they took on the day of the killing. He grins horribly at the camera. *Film away motherfuckers*. Then he is overcome with remorse: he does not want to get caught. Yes he does. No he doesn't. Yes he does. Doesn't. Does. Does not. Yet when they get closer to the tree the camera turns out to be a cancerous bulge. Still, that doesn't mean anything.

"This is how I walked in. And over there," he says, lowering his voice, because they have come to a turn in the path, and someone—anyone—could be just a few feet away, "that's where the picnic tables are, or were anyhow."

They are still here, and, on this cold winter morning, unoccupied, a coarse sheen of ice on their surface. With the roar of his own surging blood in his ears, Paul shows Kate where he placed his wristwatch, a gift from Kate herself. Though there is no one else near to them, everything he says to her is delivered in a low murmur, and when the wind picks up there are words here and there she cannot make out but she lets it go because even though his voice is flat and seems devoid of emotion, he is continually swallowing, breathing quickly, shallowly, and it seems to her that a sharp noise or a sudden movement would undo him completely. When he walks with her from the picnic table upon which he was sitting to the table where the man was beating Shep, his steps are shaky, uncertain, and when he points to the leg of the picnic table to which the dog had been leashed, his narration of the events of that day suddenly stops and he just stands there in silence, remembering. *I love you Kate . . . You made a home for me I never felt so at home anywhere else . . . I love your body the feel of you your mind your crazy soul . . .*

Kate looks at the trees that encircle this clearing, their branches yearning toward the sky. She is trying to take it in, trying to absorb it and make it indelible, but it all seems like one of those dreams that you know you will forget even as you are dreaming it. "Over here?" she asks. "Is this where he . . ." She points to a spot on the ground, near the table.

"Yes. Maybe a little closer. Like here." His gesture is sweeping, indistinct. *You are holding on to me and I am sinking I need to cut you loose.*

A large, lacy snowflake floats between them, and then another and another. Kate puts her hand out and catches a flake that dissolves on her leather glove. She wraps her arm around Paul's waist as they head back to the car. They are already in a steady snowfall. Blue jays squawk in the distance. The hemlock boughs are catching the snowfall. The sunshine filters through the dark clouds illuminating everything, the trees, the picnic tables, the stones on the ground, and the snowfall itself, an immense swirling softness connecting heaven and earth.

For an instant, they both feel it.

"We're being forgiven," Kate whispers.

"Do you really think so?" Paul wonders if his legs are going to support him. He holds on to Kate for balance.

"Don't ever leave me," Kate says.

I don't have the right to ask you that.

"I won't," Paul says.

Can't.

Jerry Caltagirone steps away from Madeline Powers. Decent manners dictate as much. She is about to look at a dead man in a refrigerated drawer and odds are this man used to be someone she loved. Some kid he's never seen before is working the morning shift at the morgue and Caltagirone feels like slapping him on the back of the head: you do not fucking stand next to someone and chew gum when they are identifying a body.

A cloud of mist forms as the freezing air of the drawer mixes with the merely cold air of the white-tiled room. Caltagirone folds his arms over his chest and respectfully lowers his eyes while Madeline does the dance they all seem to do down here—the leaning forward, the rearing back, the coming forward again, hands up to the face, and then the shaking.

He steps forward, gesturing with his eyes for the kid to close the drawer, though it occurs to him the kid isn't such a kid, and has, in fact, gray in his sideburns. *I'm getting that old*, Caltagirone thinks, as he leads Madeline away.

"Why would God let something like this happen?" she says. There's something about the words and how she says them that strikes Caltagirone as a little stale. If Madeline wants to be taken for the grieving widow, she has dressed for the role: a black skirt with a matching jacket, dark hose, black heels, a simple strand of pearls, sunglasses she's wearing up in her streaked blond hair. She has a flat, not very lively voice, like people have who don't like to argue, the types who will agree to whatever you want, though they won't necessarily *do* anything about it.

"I really appreciate your coming all this way," Caltagirone says to her.

"I'm sorry I couldn't come sooner. Everybody's buying real estate in California these days and my bank's in chaos. They've got half of us in there working Saturdays."

"Important thing is you made it," Caltagirone says. He pushes the door open and they are in the hallway now. Once in a while, for no reason he can figure out, Caltagirone heats up—his face reddens and he can in a minute sweat right through his shirt, right through a jacket, too.

"I guess all these things happen for a reason," Madeline says. She is a tall woman, with strong-looking hands and broad shoulders. The scent of her perfume is flowery and strong. "I really do believe God or whoever doesn't put anything in front of us we can't handle."

Caltagirone nods noncommittally. He hasn't been inside a church since his First Communion, and he and his wife would not put their kids through the horror show of religious education—it's not just mean nuns any longer, at this point it's sex-starved priests, and why would you ever want to put your kids around that? And he doesn't buy it that seven years old is the age of reason, when children know the difference between Good and Evil. What he knows from years on the job is the age of reason is maybe never. And as for God—he's up there, but he leaves it to us to do the dirty work.

"You doing okay, there, Madeline?" he says.

"I'm all right. It's good to have closure."

Yeah, closure, Caltagirone thinks. It's one of the words people use when they're hanging on by their fingernails. The way people start talking about their life as if it were a *journey* when they want to pretend that it is all leading somewhere.

"Why don't we go upstairs," Caltagirone says. "We can sit at my desk, or if you want we can go out to a restaurant."

"I'm not really hungry," Madeline says apologetically.

Shit. You just looked at your dead boyfriend and you don't want any salami and eggs?

"I really appreciate you coming in, all this way, and with everything else."

"It's okay, detective. I've got something else you're really going to appreciate, too."

"What do you mean?"

"I remember the guy, the guy Will was afraid of."

"Just like that?"

"I know who murdered Will."

"Yeah?" He's getting excited but he doesn't want to push.

"I know it as plain as the nose on my face. I know it without any doubts whatsoever."

"How come we're just hearing this right now?"

They are standing in front of the elevator. The chicken-wired diamond window brightens up with the light of the four-person cab, and the dull silver doors open noisily.

"You're looking for a Hawaiian fuck named Tom Butler. I saw him once, he came to the house about a week after my poor Will took off. That's who Will was running from, and eventually he caught him and killed him—and for what?"

She holds up four fingers and a thumb, by which Caltagirone takes her to mean five thousand dollars. He's known plenty of guys who killed men for less.

CHAPTER
FIFTEEN

At the end of the next month, the very last night of the year, the last night of the decade, the last night of the twentieth century, and the last four hours of New York's share of the Second Millennium, silver smoke from the chimneys on either end of Kate's long house streams upward toward the golden moon, the windows blaze with light, and behind the shades silhouettes bow and sway like figures in a shadow play.

Annabelle and Bernard sit in their car on the circular driveway in front of Kate's house. Annabelle turns off the car's engine and the warmth of the interior quickly seeps out, leaving in its wake the scent of damp velour seat covers and Bernard's piney aftershave. She keeps her hands on the steering wheel, and Bernard is next to her with his hands on his knees, but he is all but invisible in the darkness. "How you making out there, buddy?" Annabelle says.

"Time is passing," Bernard says, shaking his head.

"I know," Annabelle says. "And I feel sorry for you, I do. I know it's not easy for you to be away from your old home."

He turns toward her, gratefully. "I worry about my family," he says. "I miss them all. And my city, my home."

"I want to be your home, Bernard," Annabelle says, in the most profound declaration of love she has ever made, which she can barely believe she has spoken in the front seat of the Deathmobile. She pulls her glove off with her teeth, spits it out onto her lap, and touches his cheek with her bare hand. "Maybe one day we can go together and live for a while, back in Beirut."

"My beautiful friend," Bernard says, taking Annabelle's hand and pressing his lips against the cool lines of her face.

Through the windshield, they see Paul walking outside with his dog, a plume of breath flowing over his shoulder like a windblown scarf. He is wearing a leather jacket that he has not bothered to zipper and he walks with his hands folded in front of him, like a monk who prays while he walks.

Annabelle taps the heel of her hand against the side of the steering wheel, blowing the car's horn in a quick, short burst. Paul turns toward the sound, squints to see through the darkness, until he can see his sister's face behind the windshield, floating up through the reflection of upside-down bare treetops.

They meet in the driveway's dappled darkness, the frozen gravel sharp and harsh through the soles of Annabelle's shoes—she has been looking forward to this party for weeks, but she regrets the shoes. Paul kisses his sister, not just on one cheek but on both of them. The gallantry, even in its oddness, lifts her spirits. He shakes Bernard's hand with his right hand and envelops it with the left; the last time she saw a man making that ultra-sincere, hearts-on-fire sort of handshake was someone trying to sell Bernard life insurance.

"You're in a jolly mood," Annabelle says. She hears an odd note of accusation in her voice and smiles broadly to even things out.

"I think I'm a little light-headed."

"At least someone's doing some serious drinking in this house," Annabelle says.

"Actually, I was giving blood. The hospital's expecting a busy night. Anyhow, let's go in where it's warm."

As soon as they open the door, the heat and noise of the party come rushing toward them. Annabelle notes the look of apprehension on Bernard's face. Like other Middle Eastern people she has met, Bernard is often made squeamish by his perception of Americans' lack of hygiene, and for him a crowded room like this is as viral as a day-care center. She links her arm through his, says, "Oh look, Bernard, how happy everything looks."

Twinkling blue lights outline the windows. A Christmas tree, weeping tinsel, stands in the corner. The rugs have been rolled, most of the furniture hauled to the back of the house or pushed against the walls. Music plays from a boom box on the mantel, but no one can hear it over the human noise. There are a few young people in black pants and white shirts, circulating trays of canapés. An oak table has been covered with a white tablecloth and turned into the bar. Two Marlowe College students are pouring the drinks. They are both from Brazil, both stranded in the cold, closed college over the holiday break. Their smiles are broad, bright, and unvarying; they have each taken half tabs of Ecstasy before coming to work.

The two center rooms in the house are filled with people holding plastic wineglasses and small paper plates patterned in exploding confetti, noisemakers, and the numerals of the new year strung together like paper dolls. On nearly every surface throughout the house there are candles and an occasional kerosene lamp, in the event that the electricity is lost and the party is plunged into darkness.

"This is a good place to be," Bernard says to Annabelle, and the generosity and serenity of his remark fills her with happiness and she links her hand in his and presses herself closer to him.

"That's Paul's sister over there," Kate is saying to a semicircle of six people. The man on whose face Kate's eyes neutrally rest is a small, wiry fellow, with a frizzy wedge of copper hair and long, shaggy sideburns, several shades darker. His name is Joseph Van Leuchtenmueller, but he is willing to be called German Joe. He teaches dressage at a large equine facility on the edge of Leyden, and he lives in the damp stone gatehouse on one of the river estates, a vast holding owned by another German, a woman named Ilse Wagner, who is said to be related to Richard Wagner.

Joseph seems to float on waves of goodwill, primarily from the wealthy Leydenites whose children he has taught to ride. His position at Windsor Stables is not well-paying, but he is charged a pittance for his lodgings on the estate, and there is a theatricality and kindness to him that garners invitations to not just picnics and dinners but to European and Caribbean holidays. Kate and German Joe know each other from the AA meeting that convenes in a town called Freedom Trail, eighteen miles south of Leyden. *I am the play toy of our local principessas*, Joseph once declared in a meeting.

"Ilse was going to meet her sisters in Cologne," Joseph says, "but I got her not to go. I said, imagine you are in a jet somewhere and suddenly all the computers everywhere go mad. Is this really where you want to be? Of course Ilse believes that Lufthansa has its own systems entirely independent of all the other computers and so they're immune to any Y2K catastrophes. And you know how persuasive she can be. I found myself half-believing her, until I snapped out of it."

"You should have brought her along," Kate says.

"I tried. But she's furious with me now. She's home all by herself, sitting in her robe, watching television. I'll tell you this much, if there are not a large number of airline catastrophes around midnight, it's going to be a long time before I am welcomed at her table." His laughter is the brave song of a man who has a life based on the good-will of wealthy benefactors, and who knows there are others in the wings who will one day sweep in and take his place.

A number of people have brought their children to the party. Parents with young children have decided to keep the family to-gether, in case even half of the Y2K predictions come true. Most of those with older offspring have not been able to convince their chil-dren to accompany them to the party, but a few of them are here with their teenagers in tow, most of whom have known each other their entire lives. They have gazed at each other from strollers with cereal crumbs in their laps and apple juice–stained smiles, they have stepped on each other's fingers and foreheads as they clambered up and down the monkey bars at the Leyden Rec Center, scrimmaged on soccer and Little League fields, sat together on the school bus with its immemorial redolence of exhaust, anxiety, and milk, and though they have now divided along class lines—those with wealthier par-ents going to one of the county's two private schools, and those with parents of more modest means making do with Leyden High School—this evening there is a fellowship of the stranded among all of them. Like citizens of an occupied country, they cluster together, making comments under their breath and plotting the party's over-throw, a subversion centered on sneaked cigarettes, pilfered liquor, and finding the house's fuse box, with the plan of pulling the master switch at midnight so that they might drag the house into darkness and make all the idiots believe that the infrastructure of the world has gone up in smoke.

Nina Drazen, with wide-set brown eyes, thin, flyaway hair, wear-ing glasses and a long calico dress like those worn by Mormon child brides, stands apart from the others, next to her mother. "All I'm saying," Joyce is telling Nina, in a tone that is at once bossy and put-upon, "is there's nothing wrong with going up to her and asking her if she's had a chance to read your stories. How do you think Kate Ellis became Kate Ellis? Not by sitting on her rear end and hoping someone would come along and discover her. She worked at it. She met the right people and she got to know them, I assure you of that. There's a lot more to success than just doing good work. Sometimes you have to push, Nina, that's all there is to it."

"But Dad said," Nina begins, drawing herself up and then quickly deflating as her mother leaps back in.

"Oh please, don't even go there. Your father is pathologically diffident," Joyce says. "You can't go by what he says." She herself is surprised by how far she is willing to go to make her point. She steals a nervous glance across the room. Her husband is talking with two of his fellow trustees of the Windsor County Hospital, for which he serves as head of capital development, raising three to five million dollars a year, the pathological diffidence his wife perceives notwithstanding. He feels her attention come in his direction, as palpable as a cold draft, and he looks up at Joyce, smiles, and taps his finger against the face of his wristwatch, which might mean that he would like to leave soon, or that it is closing in on the magic hour when the train of civilization will either jump its track and go plunging into the rivers of chaos, or millions of people will shout Happy New Year, twirl their noisemakers, and toot their horns and kiss those they love or wished they loved, just like every other year.

Joyce and Nina are joined by Paul followed by Shep, who walks across the bare floor as if picking his way over ice.

"Hey Joyce," Paul says. "I just wanted to tell you that if the universe survives I am going to stop by and take a look at that kitchen of yours."

"Can I give your dog a piece of cheese?" Nina asks.

"It needs more than you just taking a look at it, Paul," Joyce is saying. "It's a disaster area."

"Sure," Paul says to Nina. "Just be a little careful. He's not too smart about fingers."

Nina takes a couple of moments to choose the right cheese cube and places it on her palm and holds it out for Shep, who nuzzles her hand with his nose and lips.

"He likes me!" Nina exclaims.

"Of course he does," says Paul. "Who wouldn't?"

After carefully picking up the cheese from Nina's outstretched hand, the dog spits it out and sniffs at it suspiciously until, with some reluctance, he picks it back up and slowly chews it, with his shoulders hunched and his gaze fixed on the bare floor.

"He's a little unhappy because we moved the furniture and rolled up the rugs," Paul tells them. "He likes things to pretty much stay the same. I think what I'm going to do is stow him someplace quiet."

As Paul leaves the house again, he wonders if he is acting strangely. His intention is to bring Shep to the shop, stoke up the stove so it will be reasonably warm in there, and then return to the party, yet being inside with all of those people is proving more difficult than he would have imagined. At least fifteen of the guests tonight are people with whom Kate attends AA meetings, hours of the week expressly reserved for confession, during which Friends of Bill W. recall crimes against loved ones or their own livers. Kate herself has joked about how there is an unspoken competition in these meetings, a race to the bottom, in which having suffered the greatest humiliations, the most bewildering blackouts, the most irrevocable losses of love, occupation, position, and self-respect makes you the winner. Would it really be outside the arc of credibility to imagine Kate standing up one evening and saying, *I almost drank today, because my boyfriend killed someone with his bare hands?*

Paul pulls open the door to the workshop, switches on the lights, and the workshop springs into view—the saws, the drafting tables, drills, compressor, the dozens of window frames leaning against the walls, some with glass, some without, the lengths of curing wood stacked one board length on top of the next, with pine wedges between each of them so the air can circulate. The hanging spotlights have rudimentary metal shades, and a protective iron mask covers the face of each bulb. The tangy smell of oil is in the air, mixing with the shop scent of sawdust.

A few months ago, Kate invited Paul to take over this space, and now he cannot imagine working in any other place. Whatever the pleasures of living off the grid, it is a relief to have a place to almost call his own. He spends hours every week putting finishing touches on the workshop, sanding the floorboards, painting the walls, replacing the windows, upgrading the outlets, building shelves and cabinets, bringing in a hot plate, a mini-fridge, and even rescuing a pale, worn Persian carpet from Kate's attic to create a sitting area in the shop's northeast corner, where the stove is perched on a pedestal of old bricks and the firewood is stacked, and where Shep likes to doze, sometimes with one bloodshot eye open, and at other times so deeply asleep it is all Paul can do to stop himself from nudging the dog with the toe of his boot.

Now, Shep sits as Paul crouches to feed a few of the smaller logs into the wood burner—anything larger will extinguish the feeble flame. He watches until the new wood catches fire, and then shuts the door, making sure it is airtight.

"Okay, old buddy," he says to Shep, who turns in a circle a few times, still reliving the ancient instinct to push back the tall grass before collapsing on the carpet.

"Can you fucking believe we've got a party on our hands?" Paul says.

Shep looks up at him with cheerful indifference.

"Do you remember the day we met?" Paul says to the dog. Shep fixes his steady gaze on Paul. "That guy was being awfully rough on you, wasn't he? Why was he doing that to you, Shep? Why would anyone ever do something like that?" Paul runs his forefinger back and forth beneath Shep's chin, over the grizzled, graying fur. The dog raises his head, half-closing his eyes and stretching his thin black lips in an involuntary grimace of pleasure.

"I thought I'd find you here," Todd Lawson says from the workshop's doorway. For a moment, Paul barely recognizes him, dressed as he is in a tuxedo, with a crimson cummerbund, matching bow tie, and patent leather evening slippers. The tux and its accoutrements have an inherited quality to them. The cut of the jacket, the worn-out shine of the fabric, and the approximate fit all suggest that someone has worn these clothes many years ago, someone other than Lawson, perhaps his father. Paul's father's closet held no formal wear. There were a couple of sports jackets, six or seven ties, and a pair of black wing-tips from England, inside of which the cedar shoe trees had resided for so long that they had fused with the leather and were impossible to remove during the hectic, tearful cleanup after Matthew's death.

"So you've come to commune with your dog?" Todd says. His hair falls into his eyes as he leans against the doorway's frame and grins at Paul. He is holding a champagne glass. The champagne, in fact, is being held back and will be uncorked at midnight, but Todd has somehow gotten himself served.

"Not really," says Paul, "it's more making sure he doesn't make a run on the ham."

Todd drains his glass and places it carefully on the floor. He rakes both of his hands through his hair, takes a deep breath. "Hey, Paul, I made a decision this afternoon."

"Yeah?" Paul's heart beats faster. Seeing Lawson now, he realizes he has told him too much during their walks—more than enough, really, for Todd to piece together if not the exact story then at least enough of it to surmise that Paul has stumbled into darkness. As soon as you tell one person it is no longer really a secret and Paul has told two. He thinks, *Oh, I will have to kill both of them now*, which he does not mean, but the thought is still somehow present, like the sharp, rank stink of a decomposing deer wafting up from some unseen spot in the woods.

"I'm getting out of here," Todd says.

Paul searches his friend's face, but all he can find is merriment and self-regard.

"Mexico," Todd says.

"You go to Mexico every winter."

"This time I'm not coming back. This place is fucked. Too much development. Too many new people, too many idiots and cityiots. Everything about Windsor County that I loved is disappearing. I mean, come on, we walk in the woods and we hear the sound of bulldozers and then hedge-fund fuckers come jogging by. Jogging, man. Whatever happened to getting your exercise by actually working?"

"I'll miss you," Paul says. His voice is thin, unconvincing, though he does mean it.

"Too much civilization. They're paving the dirt roads, every little lane has a street sign on it. People like us, Paul, we're just not made for this kind of life. And—by the way—it's not like Mexico is paradise. But you can still get off the grid there. You can still breathe. You can live by your own code."

"What exactly is that code?"

"Do it yourself, baby. DIY. All the way."

"I better get back, Todd. I can't leave Kate there with the party all by herself."

Todd looks at Paul for a moment with a bemused expression, as if Paul has just declared himself on the side of everything Todd has rejected. "Okay," Todd says, "I'll walk you."

Despite the cold, they take an indirect route back to the house, which shines and sings beneath the night sky. They walk left from the workshop and follow the curve of the driveway, passing the pair of hundred-year-old maple trees that now creak and twitter in the cold black wind, well past their prime. Paul expects that in the not-too-distant future, one of those trees is going to fall, and likely both of them together will go. He has already measured the distance from the crowns of the trees to the house and no matter which way they fall the house will be safe—ah, but what a tragedy it will be anyhow. He has pruned them, cabled them, scooped out rot and filled the gaps with cement, but his best hope is that when they go he will not be around to see it, not the mess of their demise nor the eyesore of their absence.

"You don't have to tell me anything you don't want to," Todd says. Their shoes crunch along the gravel; the house and its burning lights seems to rock back and forth behind them. "But let me tell you about what I've been thinking."

Paul gestures, as if to say *Go ahead*.

"I think you stepped over some line. I think you did something, I don't know what, but it's in your eyes. You did something that's really making you wonder." Lawson laughs, but Paul can't tell what the laugh means—is Lawson making a joke or is he uneasy for having said the truth? Sometimes laughter is like sand in your face.

"I hope this isn't why you're moving to Mexico, because you're really really wrong," says Paul. He says it with ease.

"You're one of the good guys, Paul. God loves you. Whatever you did."

Paul shakes his head, as if the matter were too absurd to discuss. But he feels a wave of relief going through him. "My friend," he says, as if amused, putting his arm around Todd's shoulders. "You are truly insane. Or really, really drunk." And after a moment, he adds, "And what if there *is* no God? Then what?"

"Then everything is meaningless and everyone just takes whatever they can get."

"I think we better get back," Paul says.

"I hope I'm not too out of line," Todd says.

"I just don't know where all this is coming from. It's pretty weird, is all."

"Just remember," Todd says, "getting away with it might be easier than *letting* yourself get away with it. Whatever you did."

"I don't think you're drunk," Paul says. "Maybe high? Some of that 'shroom tea you sometimes sip?" *Or have you killed someone, too?*

"And by the way, my old friend," Todd says, "let's not forget that if this Y2K stuff turns out to be true, every slate in the world gets wiped clean. The chaos, man, the chaos. There will be so much shit hitting so many fans, no one's going to know what the hell to do."

Inside, from a temporary perch halfway up the stairs, where she sits with a glass of seltzer and a few seedless red grapes, Kate surveys the party and thinks to herself: *How can this be happening?* As she watches the great human wheel of the party turning slowly in her downstairs rooms, Kate feels her anxiety rising. This is now and will forever be a haunted house. This is a house with a ghost in the attic, or maybe it hovers right this moment above the party, counting down the minutes of the old millennium.

Kate drinks from her glass of seltzer; the fizz of it vibrates against her lips. There are others here sipping carbonated water; the fifteen or so of them are a party within a party—no matter what happens tonight, they will have their sobriety to keep them warm. Yet everyone else here, too, seems to be on their best behavior and whatever grief they carry in their daily lives has been checked at the door, and now, temporarily freed from lugging about their sacks of woe, they are standing up straight, paragons of posture, and moving with a lightness of step, borne by the helium of New Year's Eve. If they believe that the world is about to be plunged into chaos at the stroke of midnight, the hundred unexpected guests have done a sterling job of putting a brave face on it. There, for example, is Sam Holland, who has been working for nearly a decade on a history of anti-Semitism, talking with his son Michael, who Kate guesses is pushing thirty and who drifts about the county doing odd jobs, and Michael's fiancée, Melissa, who is the most elaborately dressed woman here tonight, a second-grade teacher in the public school who has chosen to usher out the millennium in a full-length teal silk and crinoline dress that looks as if it had once belonged to the Countess Anastasia. Melissa feeds a Swedish meatball to her future father-in-law, after which Michael puts his arm possessively around her shoulders. There is Kurt Nelson, the widower playwright, in his maroon felt slippers and paisley smoking jacket, holding court among several attentive young people, and there is the prodigiously versatile young president of Marlowe College with his large head and tiny bow tie, and there is Evangeline with her girlfriend, both dressed in modified tuxedos, and there is Ruby's favorite babysitter, pregnant herself now, here with her baby's father, a jumpy-looking kid with white eyelashes, and here come Annabelle and Bernard, who know few people here and whose expressions are at once removed and inquisitive.

Kate drops a red grape into her seltzer. It displaces a chevron of bubbles, and she marvels at the world, our little wounded, fragile world with its thousands of physical laws, where even our glasses of carbonated water tremble with life. In this, her religious forties, she has sometimes agonized over why people of advanced intelligence often do not believe there is a supreme being, why it is they, and not the high-school dropouts, who are the ones to insist that logic and all the available proof show that religion is a compendium of rumors and fables and outright bullshit strung together by committees of ancient sun-baked men deprived of all scientific knowledge. Kate has sometimes despaired that the average intelligence in the nation of unbelievers is drastically higher than the intelligence in the devout community; surely a convention of atheists would be able to run intellectual circles around the membership of most churches. Yet if Christ and his message are real, then the dumbbells win and the chrome domes lose. Those in the IQ aristocracy have fallen in love with their own minds, which is a dangerous, and foolish, and possibly insane thing to do, and their vanity over their extra IQ points fills them with hubris, and they believe themselves to have no superiors. Not the geniuses, really, it's the valedictorians of the second-rate schools, those are the ones who find the idea of a supreme being so ludicrous, the ones who beat their fists against their empty chests and say, *Prove it. Prove it.* And here is the secret truth about them—it is not God whom they have overcome, not God whom they somehow *see through.* It's the people who do believe in God that are the real target of their atheism . . .

No one seems to notice Kate. She may as well be a ghost. A memory: somewhere near her eighth birthday, seated just like this on the staircase in gray, fragrant Wilmington, gazing sleepily down as her parents and a few of their friends passed around what they said was a peace pipe. They were all trying to remember the words to a Perry Como song—*Catch a falling star/And put it in your pocket/ Save it for a rainy day.* They were finding their mistakes and memory lapses to be matters of the highest hilarity; Kate experienced it all with a mixture of longing and disdain, the laughter, the coughing, the shouts and corrections, and the staggering about. There was her father, with his crisp white shirtsleeves rolled up to reveal dark, virile forearms, who even several hours and several drinks and now several tokes from the office continued to wear his stethoscope around his neck, the chilly silver circle tucked into a pocket. And there was Mother, who would not permit the words *Mommy*, or *Mummy*, or *Mumsie*, or even *Mom*, pinching closed the nostrils of her brief, pointed nose and pursing shut her lips, in Jackie Kennedy pink lipstick, trying to keep from expelling the magical smoke. Who else was there that night? There was Mr. Cunningham, with his military buzz cut and clamshell ears, and his wife, Jan, with her heavy calves and harlequin eyeglasses, and Mr. Stevenson, who made you call him Chip, who wore bell-bottoms and T-shirts with sayings on them, and never worked a day in his life, and his wife, Lulu, who had divorced him and was sick with some bone thing and Chip had remarried her out of kindness, according to Kate's father—or, if Kate's mother was to be believed, it was insanity, Chip's way of telling everyone he was a man capable of throwing his life away as if it were a used Kleenex. Kate will never forget the look her father gave her mother when she said those words, the sour, rueful glance of a man taking pleasure from having his worst suspicions confirmed.

How could she ever have known the sorrows of those six adults? Those six adults capering around and getting stoned on hash; each of them had their own little entry in the encyclopedia of pain. And now her mother, Lulu, and Mr. Cunningham are buried, Chip lives in Thailand and has become a Buddhist, and her father, deaf in one ear, blind in one eye, arthritic, loose-jowled, and cane fat, is on his third wife. How he gets anyone in his bed is a mystery to Kate that even his money cannot quite explain. He has turned into the crybaby of the Western world, sentimental and nostalgic. That caustic walking hard-on of a man is gone; his only existence is in the hell to which Kate has consigned him in her own mind, and it occurs to her tonight that those fires are burning only within her, and she is the only one to feel their vicious heat.

She sees Paul coming in from the outdoors, his hair askew from the wind, his cheeks flushed with cold. His eyes find her immediately; it is as if he is the only person in the house who knows she is sitting on the steps, looking down at all of them. He gives her a little mock salute and points toward the food table, asking her if she would like him to prepare a plate for her. The little gesture of domestic ease fills her with sadness—one day she will lose him, the thing that has happened, the thing he has done, they will never be free of it, they will never outrun it, it will catch up to him, to them, it will destroy everything, and their life will be as dead as that unnamed, indelible man in the woods.

Ruby comes to Paul's side and says something to him with apparent urgency. He points to Kate, and Ruby's eyes widen with relief. And in the brief interval of time between when Ruby has seen her and Ruby is at her side, Kate feels something that she can only describe as a painless stab of light, neither hot nor cold but bright as the summer sun. Everyone here, all these faces, this roomful of secrets, they are here because they cannot suffer being alone. *We need each other.* Sam Holland; Richard and Sonya Martinez; the dreadful Drazens; Jeannie Malkiel, monochromatic in beige; her blind thirty-year-old son, Jonathan; the Colliers; the Trehans; Goldie Evans; the effervescent Kufners; Sonny Reed, who is the world's oldest drunk; arrogant, lonely Kurt Nelson; Evangeline and her partner, Cheryl; the DeMilles; Dodie Pierce; Annabelle; Bernard; Joseph; and, of all people, Ray Pickert (*who the hell invited him?*). They are huddled together with the darkness surrounding them, because it is New Year's Eve. The clock ticks with a peculiar force and fury; the passage of time is suddenly bereft of all gaiety.

"Why are you up here?" Ruby asks, plopping down next to Kate and immediately sticking her finger into Kate's seltzer, trying to capture an elusive floating grape.

"Just looking," Kate says. "Making sure everyone's having a good time."

"It's the best party of all recorded human history," Ruby says, and the diction of this is so inflated and unexpected and so theatrical that it startles a groan out of Kate. "It is, I'm not kidding," Ruby says, and struggles for a moment as Kate puts her arm around her shoulders and pulls her closer. Ruby submits to her mother's embrace, gratefully: she likes being touched.

A sudden and inexplicable silence descends upon the party. It is as if everyone who has been talking has come to the end of their thought at exactly the same instant, and everyone who was about to reply has taken an extra moment to breathe.

"My mother used to say when the room went suddenly quiet, 'An angel just passed over,' " Kate whispers to Ruby, and the girl lifts her eyes, as if she might really see an emissary moving across the rooms. In the two seconds of quiet, Jackson Browne can be heard. *Doctor, my eyes have seen the years. . .*

And in an instant of ice-clear certainty Kate knows that when midnight strikes and all the computers that are responsible for keeping everyone sane and alive fail or don't fail, the end result will be basically nothing. We are not being kept alive by algorithms of 1s and 0s, we are not creatures of some cosmic mainframe. Y2K is going to be a bust, a big letdown posing as a huge relief, a sore disappointment that we will agree to be pleased about. All the precautions, the hard drives copied, the larders filled, the flights postponed, the water stored, the personal information photocopied, the bank accounts emptied into floor safes, wall safes, mattresses, the candles and the kerosene, and the firewood, all those apocalyptic speeches from our leaders—it was all a desperate attempt to find some meaning, a predictable narrative. The hour will come and it will pass, and the only horror of it will be just that—another hour will have passed, and after that another one will, and then another. Y2K will be soon forgotten. The things for which we feverishly prepare aren't generally the things that actually happen. Our undoing comes waltzing in through another door altogether . . .

Kate takes her daughter's hand; it feels warm and sticky, and Kate has a surge of love go through her as powerful as a wave at high tide. "Come on, baby, let's join the others." As they make their way down the steps, her eyes meet Bernard's. He offers a brief, courteous bow in her direction, and lifts his glass of red wine in a silent toast. To her, to the party, to all of them, to the new year, to life.

The dirty dishes and empty glasses and the scuffed floors and the flattened pillows and the tilted picture frames and the cherry-scented pipe tobacco smoke and the finger-smudged windowpanes and the crushed cashews and the slight stink from a piece of punk wood in the fireplace, which will not burn and will not go out, and the listing Christmas tree with its shimmering ganglia of tinsel—the entire archaeology of the late twentieth century still occupies the downstairs of the house, while Paul, Kate, and Ruby and Shep sleep upstairs in the twenty-first.

It is four a.m. on the first day of the new millennium and the computers of the world are working every bit as well as they were the day before. Kate shakes Paul's shoulder and he reaches for her, unconscious but warm, so warm.

"You have to get up," she whispers to him soothingly, and then with considerable urgency when he fails to move. Paul pushes the covers back, stumbles out of bed, rubbing his eyes with the heels of his hands. Unlike the coddled men she has known, Paul knows that sometimes you just do what you are told and there's no time to ask why. He knows that the little creaking sound may well be telling you the ceiling is about to collapse and the snuffing, huffing noise is not your tent-mate's heavy breathing but the sound of a brown bear's hungry approach.

"What's going on?" he asks her, without a trace of sleep in his voice.

"I think we should get rid of your computer."

"Now?"

She nods.

"I need it for work. I'm getting wood from all over the world."

"I'll get you another one. Everyone's asleep. It's a perfect time."

"I was asleep, too," Paul says.

"Who's to say the police haven't been monitoring who goes to certain Internet sites? You keep on asking the Internet to give you information about the thing. And it's all on your hard drive."

"I've erased what's on the hard drive."

"It's all still retrievable."

"But that's not going to happen," Paul pleads.

"Why should we take any chances?"

Not many minutes later, after a whispered back-and-forth, which would have gone on for much longer, and may even have had a different conclusion had not Kate begun to cry, they are in Paul's truck heading to Route 2B (or not 2B, as Kate so often calls it), which winds out to the landfill. Kate holds Paul's computer on her lap, watching as the moon-bright frozen trees and snow-covered roofs of the new millennium flow past.

"What if Ruby wakes up?"

"We'll be home in ten minutes," Kate says.

"That's really not so," says Paul.

"Okay," she says, "fifteen minutes, twenty minutes. I don't care. Shep will keep an eye on her."

Paul sees the greenish iridescent flash of an animal's eyes on the side of the road a few yards in front, and slows, waiting for whatever creature it is to make its move. A house cat, white and brown, with a bushy tail and shaggy ears, clambers over a snowbank and races across the road.

Paul watches the cat streaking across a long expanse of frozen lawn, making its way toward the pale yellow porch light of the house of Magda Tunis, who had appeared at the party on snowshoes, wrapped in homespun scarves, her long, graying hair brittle with frost, full of her upbeat New Age wisdom: she was in the camp that was quite sure Y2K was going to be earthshaking, though hers was not so much a doomsday scenario as a wrenching but ultimately liberating transformation, and when the new millennium began and no one sprouted a third eye and no wave of overwhelming love swept over the guests and, after the pranking teenagers pulled the breaker switch and dunked the house into a bracing moment of darkness, the lamps continued to glow, the stereo continued to play, and the furnace continued to chug, Magda strapped on her snowshoes, rewrapped herself in scarves, put a few crackers in the pockets of her ski parka, and left.

"Sometimes the things we want to stay the same change real quick," Paul says, "and the other stuff we wish would disappear just sort of hangs out forever." He winces. He has never felt self-conscious about speaking, but with Kate he often struggles for words. She is never at a loss for a word, sometimes it seems as if she practices what she is going to say before she says it, maybe saying it to herself, or saying it out loud in front of a mirror. He doesn't mind. It's sort of wonderful, basically. It's making her famous.

It's so wonderful to be with a man who doesn't want to compete with me, she once said, and her face showed immediate regret and the wish to not have said that. But it was fine with him. The idea of competing with her, or begrudging her her success, her following, her large and increasingly frequent paydays was so alien to him that nothing she could say about it would register with him. He would never in a thousand years read as many books as she has, and it would never occur to him to browse the Oxford English Dictionary as a way of relaxing, as he has seen her do with his own eyes.

"Go on," Kate says. "Tell me what you were going to say."

"It's nothing," Paul answers. "I don't even know."

In fact, he was going to recount a long story about his time in Alaska, of returning to a camp on Barter Island and finding a little pool of twenty-weight motor oil in the snow, six months after Ed Bluemink, for whom Paul was working, had accidentally spilled it. But Paul is unsure of the story and what it might illustrate—things hang around for a lot longer than you think?

"Here we are," he says instead, gesturing with his chin as they approach the Leyden Landfill. The days and the hours of operation are posted on a red-and-white sign hammered onto a ten-foot locust pole; the headlights of Paul's truck brush across the letters. Paul stops his truck a foot or two in front of the thick chain that droops across the landfill, a frostbitten, stubborn smile. A few snowflakes dance in the tunnels of light his headlights carve into the darkness.

"This is nuts," Paul says, registering it.

"Just do it for me," Kate says. "Indulge me."

Paul shifts the truck into park, pulls on the emergency brake; this way he can keep the engine running so he'll have someplace warm to return to and the headlights can light the way. He reaches for the laptop. "I'll be back in a minute," he says.

"Oh no, no, I'll come with you." Kate half-turns away from him, shielding the computer.

"I don't really see you as a landfill type of person," Paul says, hoping to cajole her into some sort of compliance, though he has never succeeded in doing so in the past.

"This is my idea," Kate says. "And I don't want to sit all by myself in this truck in the middle of the night."

"Maybe we should just go home," Paul says.

"No, let's get rid of this thing," Kate says. "We have to, Paul. You left footprints in those woods, tire tracks, everything. And what if something else happens?"

"Like what?"

"I don't know. But something. Something to bring them to you. Maybe just to question you. Why would you want to have a computer that they can look at and find out that you've been trying to get information about that guy? Why would we leave a loose end when we both know full well that it's there? It's what the generals call contingency planning."

"Well, we're not generals," Paul says, "and the stuff you plan for isn't always what happens. Look at how everyone was going on about Y2K, and here we are." He gestures at the vast and placid sky, with its scatter of indifferent stars.

"Let's just get this done. Ruby's home all by herself."

They step over the chain and make their way along the snow-packed path to the landfill, with the headlights of the idling truck at their backs and the lit snow fluttering around them like a frenzy of moths. On either side are drooping hemlocks, their boughs heavy with winter. The access road to the landfill is pristine, without tire tracks or footprints, and in an unspoken bit of caution they drag their feet through the snow, hoping to make their prints illegible. Paul relieves Kate of the computer and she links her arm through his. With her free hand she reaches into her parka pocket and pulls out a flashlight.

"You think of everything," Paul says.

"I hope so."

The flashlight bores a hole through a darkness made tumultuous by snow, and they make their way to the edge of the landfill, a three-acre pit covered with snow and dirt. "This is just for the garbage,"

Paul says. "The one back there is for appliances and household items. We may as well do this right."

They pick their way along the edge of the first landfill and approach the second, smaller pit. Here the refuse is uncovered. Kate points the beam of her flashlight down at the tangle of refrigerators, lamps, washing machines, rotisseries, toasters, space heaters, snow shovels, and easy chairs. If there are other computers down there, none are visible as Kate sweeps the light over the tangle of junk. "Okay, here goes," Paul says, and is about to throw his computer down into the pit when Kate stops him.

"Not like that. We should break it."

He doesn't see why, but it will take more effort and time to argue the point than to do as she suggests. He places the laptop onto the ground. "I am so sorry," he says to her.

"It's okay," she says.

"No, it's not. I did a terrible thing and every day is a little bit fucked and I've pulled you into it."

"I want to be where you are," Kate says.

"I'm in the darkness," he says.

"I know. Me, too."

He pulls her close and kisses her. It is as hungry as a first kiss and as solemn as a kiss good-bye. He is kissing every part of her, her happiness and unhappiness, everything that has ever happened to her, he is kissing the day she was born and the day she will die. It is almost unbearable.

Off to the side, whoever has plowed back here has left a long slur of dirty snow, into which are embedded stones and rocks. Paul dislodges a rock about the size of a soccer ball with his ungloved hands and straddles the computer with the rock held over his head. "Maybe step back," he says to Kate, and she does what he asks her to, and it strikes him with all the chaos of conflicting cardinal emotions that the two of them have never before been so deeply in the wrong together and never have they been so close.

He throws the rock down, and it bangs against the hard blue plastic shell of the computer, and to both of their surprise the machine withstands the blow. The plastic cracks but the machine is intact. The blow's energy has fueled the once stationary machine and it spins to the left and begins to slide toward the open pit of the landfill. "Kate," Paul says, and she quickly moves her feet to intercept the laptop and to keep it from flipping end over end into the jumble below. He retrieves it, carries it a safe distance from the pit, and smashes the rock down on it again. This time the destruction is successful. In a primal crouch, Paul hovers over the splintered machine, pulls it further apart, throwing one piece after another into the landfill.

"All right?" Paul says. Kate nods.

There is a strain to her breathing.

"I'm going to tell you something," Paul says. "That time in the woods? I keep on thinking or remembering or maybe just imagining that I wasn't alone."

She stands closer to him. "I'm not surprised," she says, finding her voice.

"You're not?" he asks.

"No," she says. "Because there *was* someone there that day, and he's with us right now, too, in this stinking landfill on the first day of the Second Millennium."

"What do you mean?"

"You know what I mean," Kate says. "Jesus. God. Whatever you want to call the divine beauty of the universe."

"Is that why nobody's caught me? Is that why this whole thing seems to be going away on its own?"

"Don't joke," she says, and then she realizes he's not. He's not joking, he's not teasing, he's not what-if-ing. He means it. And in a spasm of spiritual panic she wishes she had never brought it up. It's one thing to tell someone they are your angel, but it's something else to see that person suddenly begin flapping their arms as if expecting to fly.

PART II

Where is the next one coming from?

—John Hiatt

CHAPTER
SIXTEEN

Could it really be that simple? Could a human being be removed from the ranks of the living with little or no fuss, and no consequences? What about his house? What about his belongings? Was there no one out there to come forward and say, Where's my husband, where is my father, where is my lover, where is the man who worked for me, where is the guy at the next desk, where is my buddy I went to the track with every July, or played cards with, or jogged with, where is that grumpy bastard with the good-looking brown dog, where is my tenant, where is my next-door neighbor? Was no one curious? Was no one making a stink? Wasn't there anyone wanting an answer? Could a man really be plucked from the body of life like a little splinter and just blow away and leave no trace of himself?

But he has left a trace—in Paul. Here he is, carrying a black garbage bag into which he has already placed some broken Coors bottles, an empty bleach container, three crumpled cigarette packs, and a waterlogged paperback edition of *Bonjour Tristesse*, with his animal companion trotting a few feet in front of him. He's walking Shep and cleaning the country road of the winter's debris that spring has exposed, hoping to remove the toxins in his bloodstream through the dialysis of good deeds.

Once a week, Paul goes to the Windsor County SPCA, where he joins the other volunteers who get the dogs out of their cages for a couple of hours. Once a month, he goes to Northern Windsor Hospital and gives plasma, and once a month to the Red Cross and donates blood, and if there is some ridiculous, intrusive law against doing both in the same month he has so far gotten away with it. He feels no loss of vigor, and the various technicians who tap into his veins treat him with good cheer and a soft touch. The hospital gives him fifty dollars for his plasma. He cashes the check immediately and like his sister on her postal rounds he drives the winding road through a nearby mobile-home park, putting ten-dollar bills in random mailboxes. It makes him light-headed to do so.

There are a half dozen elderly people he looks in on. Cal Bowen lives a half mile south of Kate's house and Paul shovels his walkway, and now and again calls on him, usually with a couple of ripe pears or some soft cheese, chosen to complement the dark red wine Cal likes to pour. Cal lives simply but he was once an oenophile and has a cellar filled with old French Bordeaux, and no one to drink them with.

After every snowfall, Paul is sure to stop by and shovel out Margaret Hurley and Dorothy Freeman, both frail and getting apprehensive about strangers, whose little steep cottage is not too far from Bowen's house. They make him ginger tea and honey when he is finished and Margaret, the more outgoing of the two women, invariably says, *Boy oh boy you really like that tea*, as if Paul's showing up is his way of getting a free cup of tea.

To the south of Kate's house lives John Lucy, who until a couple of years ago taught philosophy at nearby Marlowe College and who seems to have gone mad (shaved head, eyeliner). Dr. Lucy, though only fifty-seven, is easily overwhelmed by the details of running his life, and he has come to count on Paul to shore up gutters, repair leaks, and to keep the vermin out of his kitchen by filling in holes in the foundation of his house, whose rapid disintegration seems to mirror Lucy's own.

Farther away, just a mile from the center of Leyden, Bill Veldhuis, the farmer from whom Paul has been getting chicken and duck eggs for the past ten years, is practically crippled from arthritis, and Paul is part of a loosely organized team, consisting mainly of Veldhuis's grandchildren, who make sure that the bossy, scarlet-knuckled old man has what he needs, that there is food in the refrigerator, clean clothes.

When he can, Paul tries to help Liza Moots, a woman he met through Kate—no one mentions it, but Paul assumes that Liza and Kate attend AA meetings together. Liza lives in a four-room apartment over what had once been Forrestal's Soda Shop, and which is now Impulsively Yours, a sundries shop whose name was meant to describe, or perhaps conjure, the spending habits of the rich new comers. Liza is not a newcomer, and she just manages to support herself and her two young children through a sort of Rube Gold berg economic arrangement in which reading astrological charts, housecleaning, pottery making, and wedding photography combine to create an engine that keeps her hovering just an inch above the poverty line. Paul visits her once a week and, upon her request, brings Shep with him because Liza is terrified of dogs and despairs over passing this fear on to her daughters. Her fear of dogs also prevents her from riding her bicycle around Windsor County, and has forced her to quit two of her most lucrative housekeeping jobs, one because of a Rottweiler and the other because of a Jack Russell. Paul has been keeping Shep on a leash while he visits Liza, sometimes staying for an hour while he plays with Maria and Florencia and Shep snoozes peacefully, lashed to a radiator pipe. In the past couple of weeks, Liza has gathered the courage to approach Shep and pat him gravely on top of his head, and Shep, seemingly aware of the momentousness of the occasion, has thumped his tail against the wide-plank oak floor and, with his chin resting on his forepaws, looked mildly up at Liza through the tops of his eyes.

Kate hasn't mentioned that Paul's concentration on good works has cut his workweek in half. Money is, in fact, not an issue. *Prays Well* continues to attract readers, and her radio program's initial syndication has grown from twenty-five "markets" to ninety-eight.

To make up for the decrease in work hours Paul has increased his fees and also the markup on materials. Not entirely to his surprise, this has perversely generated an increased demand for his services, and so the bookkeeping on his charity would have to conclude that it's not only good for the soul but also beneficial to the purse. Paul has been making things out of wood for wealthy clients for over ten years, and this is the first time he has raised the prices on his labor. Over time, the price of materials has risen and he has passed these increases along to his customers, but what Paul himself needs to live on has remained essentially unchanged, and until now it has not really occurred to him that he ought to be putting money aside or making investments or owning property. Even this sudden increase in his prices has left his income essentially undisturbed. He makes about sixty thousand dollars a year, though if he worked faster and ran his business more efficiently he could triple that amount, but money is not important to him. In fact, he has always felt a certain disdain for it, seeing it as an enemy of freedom, and believing that those people who say they need money *in order* to be free are merely taking the society's bait. And everyone knows money won't get you into heaven.

★ ★ ★

Paul and Shep come to a rise in the road and the chimney of Kate's house comes into distant view, emerging from the sea of green like a periscope. Paul stops, shifts the burden of his trash bag from the left shoulder to the right, and reaches down to scratch Shep's head. The day has turned hot, and the trees, still in their delicate spring foliage, look dazed and exhausted, as if it were already mid-August. The industrious, untiring drone of insects is in the air. On the west side of the road, a thirty-acre field and a jumble of slate, sash, and stucco that was once a house, and on the east side a swath of woods gone wild, a thick, boggy tangle of stunted pine, gnarled locust, dying maple, and swirls of thornbushes, as forbidding as barbed wire.

Soon, Paul and the dog are heading down the long driveway leading to Kate's house. It is late morning. Kate is in her writing cabin, preparing her next broadcast. Evangeline's girlfriend's green Subaru is in front of the workshop, and Evangeline is inside sanding down an expensive ten-foot length of black walnut. The double doors to the workshop are open and as Paul approaches he can hear the hoarse whine of the sander.

The sun has been radiating down on the tin roof and even with the doors open it's fiercely hot inside the workshop. It's too early in the season to run the air conditioner, and the sound of the exhaust fans unnerves Evangeline. She is bent over the walnut plank, working the sander around in small circles. Her hair is plastered to her forehead and the sides of her face, and her white T-shirt is dark at the armpits. She is wearing long, baggy shorts and work boots, the tops of which are covered in sawdust. She turns off the handheld sander, holds it shoulder-high as if it were a pistol, and, after licking the palm of her free hand, strokes the section of board she's been working on.

"Should I wait outside?" Paul says.

"Oh hi," she says. "You caught me coming on to the wood."

Paul finds another sander. He squeezes the trigger and the tool comes to life with a pugnacious roar. It's weirdly startling: there seems something violent about striding toward another human being while revving up a power tool. Buried beneath all the things he used to think of as his true and essential nature, his nonconfrontational personality, his live-and-let-live character, beneath the steadily accrued rules of self-government, the limits of what he will do and what he will not do, beneath everything familiar and everything assumed, beneath his style and beneath his ideals, beneath it all he may be a beast.

He notices Evangeline is talking and he turns off the sander, letting it dangle from two fingers.

"Thank you for hiring me, Paul. I just want to tell you that to me you're as much an artist as half the guys in galleries."

"I'm just a carpenter."

"That's like calling Yves Saint Laurent a tailor."

"There's nothing wrong with being a tailor. I'm a carpenter. Anyhow," he says, jerking the reins of the conversation, "how come you drove Cheryl's car to work? Is something wrong with your Honda?"

"Oh the Honda," Evangeline says, in the tone you use to discuss some dear but hopeless friend, some ceaselessly backsliding old comrade whom you love despite the many frustrations. "All these old Hondas need new timing belts when they pass a hundred thousand miles, and it needs a water pump."

"Well that's not going to work," Paul says. "You have to have a car."

"I know," says Evangeline. "But Cheryl's got two cars right now because her brother moved to Brooklyn and he keeps his Rabbit up here."

Evangeline is swaying back and forth as she says this and Paul realizes that her motion mirrors his own, that she is merely following him with her eyes and letting the rest of her come along for the ride.

"Are you all right?" she asks.

"I'm fine."

He used to say I'm good, until Kate pointed out that saying I'm fine is more correct, and to say that you are good refers to moral rather than physical variables. Now, not only is he not good but he doesn't feel fine, either. He's light-headed and though it is hot in the workshop he feels cold.

"You're sort of alabaster," Evangeline says.

"It was a long winter," he says.

"Well," Evangeline says, "at least I got to use the word *alabaster* in a sentence."

Paul drags a chair from the drafting table, turns it around, and sits. It alarms him to feel the relief of it. Once, he saw his father heaving himself exhaustedly into a chair, taking off his shoes, and rubbing his feet, making little murmurs of pleasure, and the gesture seemed so foul and defeated that it has remained something Paul would never do: he sits with his back straight, his feet firmly on the floor.

"I'm worried about this car situation," he says to Evangeline.

"I actually have a plan," Evangeline says. Her voice is scratchy and dry; she sounds like a little girl who has stayed up far past her bedtime. "There's these two dykes up in Lemon Bridge who run an auto repair shop right out of their house? Cheryl is friends with them and I think I can get them to do all the work on my car if I carve them one of those big salad bowls."

"The cherry?" Paul asks.

"Definitely the cherry," says Evangeline.

"You could sell one of those in the city for a thousand dollars," Paul says.

"I don't think so," Evangeline says. "There's a store on Madison called Maison Extraordinaire and they bought one off me for three hundred and fifty bucks and sold it for thirteen hundred."

"That doesn't seem very fair," Paul says.

Evangeline shrugs. "Cheryl and I were going to drive down there and burn the place down, or just fucking stab the guy in the forehead, or something. But what the fuck. It's how the world works."

"You know what," Paul says, placing his hands on his kneecaps, taking a deep breath. It takes a bit of effort for him to stand. It feels for a moment as if an implacable, invisible hand is holding him down. The workshop, the machines, the tools, the boards, the shelves lined up with various types of stains, the new computer still not out of the box in which it was delivered, the stools, the chairs, the drawings of future projects, the snapshots of past work, the rafters, the windows, the sawdust drifting in the sunlight, it all dims, almost to the point of disappearing. But, to his relief, it all comes back and it's as if it never happened, this sudden shrinking of consciousness, this rush to the edge of his own demise.

In its wake, he feels a glowing disorder, as if his sense of the world has for a moment been turned into pure luminescence. And at the shimmering core of this sudden radiance trembles an idea. He walks to the drafting table, dragging the chair behind him, sits, finds paper and pen.

"I'm writing up an agreement," Paul tells Evangeline. "I'm going to make you a partner in this company." He looks over his shoulder so he can see her. "Is that all right with you, Evangeline?"

She opens her mouth to speak, not really sure what she wants to say. At last, her face reddening, her eyes swimming, she says, "You're either a saint or you're crazy."

Kate is pointing out the items on the table one by one.

"The lasagna comes from that new Italian deli—I got it especially for Ruby, but there's enough for everyone. The stuffed peppers come from Streamside Catering, they've got a little take-out counter now. The broccoli and almonds, also from Streamside. The chicken is from the rotisserie place where they have a name that is impossible for me to remember. And the salad, such as it is, I made myself."

She points to a bottle of salad dressing. "Except for that, which Paul Newman takes credit for." Kate hears the defensiveness in her own voice and thinks about adding something to her next broadcast about her need to apologize for serving ready-made food.

Ruby, slouched in her chair, with her chin on her sternum, stares at a manila folder on her lap, while reaching for the bread plate and taking five slices of baguette, each the shape of a small kidney.

"What do you have in your lap?" Paul asks Ruby.

She doesn't reply, except to point to her mouth, into which she has already placed a piece of bread.

"Plate please," says Kate, reaching toward Paul.

"Not too much," he says.

"I know," says Kate, as neutrally as possible. She gives him a small amount of everything. She has chosen it all with him in mind, as though this is the meal that is going to restore his appetite. "Sweetie?" she says, reaching toward Ruby.

"There's a birdy fairy angel on the wall," Ruby says, pointing to a spot directly behind Kate.

"There is?" Kate says, turning around to look. But all that is visible is an eleven-by-fourteen pencil drawing of a bowl filled with eggs, made by a woman in Kate's AA meeting. "Is it pretend?"

Ruby shakes her head no, not emphatically but more as if she were keeping matters straight in her own mind. She looks down at the folder in her lap, for a moment, and then looks up at Kate, her little face full of defiance and fear, like a child looking back at her poor mother as the train pulls away from the station and the mother is thinking, *Why did you leave me?* and the daughter is thinking, *Why did you let me go?*

When all the plates are full, Kate bows her head. "Thank you Lord for this time together." She stops, thinks. There is a vast internal silence. Something she thought was there does not seem to be present after all; it's like thinking you have heard the voices of loved ones coming from another room, but when you open the door and look around all is emptiness. Maybe Jesus does not want to be talked to right now, and that is fine with Kate.

Ruby has folded her hands and bowed her head, awaiting her mother's prayer, but now, in the long silence, she unclasps her fingers and jams her hand past the waistband of her blue jeans. She leans far to one side, putting all her weight on her left buttock while hoisting up the right, which she proceeds to scratch with a single mindedness that seems more animal than human.

"Ruby?" Kate says. The child looks up at her with dark, opaque eyes. "Do you feel itchy?"

"No," says Ruby.

"How about this—stop scratching and let's eat," says Kate.

The meal begins. Moments pass and no one is talking, there is just the busy, arrhythmic clatter of silverware, until Kate speaks up. "So Ruby, school." Ruby looks up from her plate, as if she has just heard the roar of a lion. "Anything interesting?" Kate prompts. "Anything exciting, strange. Delightful? Weird? Anything?"

"I don't know," Ruby says. She puts her eating utensils down, looks pleadingly at her mother. The fingernails on her right hand, the hand with which she had been scratching at herself, are dark.

"Nothing?" Kate asks. "Eight hours of your life and nothing to report?"

Ruby clears her throat. "Maybe Jeremiah's mother came to our class and told us . . ." She sees Paul looking at her fingernails and she quickly tucks her hands beneath her buttocks, and rocks back and forth on them.

"Told you what?" Kate asks.

"I don't know," says Ruby. "Everything." She laughs. The laugh must be nervous, or false, but it sounds uproarious, unhinged. "Birdy Fairy Angel says I need to wash my hands," Ruby declares, jumping up from her seat. The manila folder falls to the carpet, spilling its contents—a crayon profile of a pert young girl, with a button nose, long eyelashes, and a ponytail, another page with nothing but frantic scribbles, as if it was made by an automaton that had sprung a gear.

"You can wash your hands in the downstairs bathroom," Kate calls after her, but Ruby pounds up the stairs, and the next sound is the boom of a slammed door. "Something's not right there," Kate says.

"It's hard work, being a kid," Paul says, pushing his food around his plate. Bad emotional weather is setting in. He has lost his appetite, which is particularly disheartening because this was one meal he thought he would actually eat and enjoy.

"Not happening, huh," Kate says, gesturing with her chin to the food on Paul's plate.

"I don't know," he says. "It's good though."

"Yes," says Kate, "I'm glad the tines of your fork are enjoying it, but I was hoping for a little more." The unintentional sharpness in her voice is an age-old error she doesn't wish to remake, and she reaches across the table to touch Paul's arm. "Do you want me to get your protein drink and vitamins?"

"No, it's okay, I already took them."

"You took them already? You knew you weren't going to eat?"

"No, I thought I was going to eat. I thought for sure."

"Then why did you take your protein drink and the vitamins?" Kate asks.

"Because it was six o'clock, and at six o'clock that's what I do."

Kate shakes her head. "Okay, I know that in the world according to Paul what you just said makes perfect sense, so we'll leave it at that." She reaches for his plate. "Before you give it to the dog," she says.

He hands his plate over, and it feels like turning in his membership card to the club of normal life.

"By the way," Kate says, "I noticed Evangeline leaving this afternoon. She looked quite upset. And I was thinking to myself how strange that is. Because the Evangeline I see, which is, of course, the Evangeline she chooses to show me, is always smiling."

Paul says, "I guess I'm so used to her, I don't even think about things like that. But you know what we should do?" He gestures toward the glazed doors he put into the west wall of the dining room. They are nine feet tall, about sixty-five percent glass, the rest pine, painted white. The doors open up to a bluestone patio and they face in a southwesterly direction; sometimes so much sunlight comes through them that Kate needs to draw the curtains. "We should put transoms over the doors. Right in the space between the tops of the doors and the ceiling molding. That way, when the curtains are closed, light will still come in. And I love transoms. There's something about a transom."

"Which brings us back to Evangeline," Kate says. "What's going on there? Is she a tiny bit falling in love with you?"

"Are you being serious?" Paul asks.

"I don't care how gay she is," Kate says. "Love is love and it tears down walls. You taught me that."

"She's not in love with me. We work together. We like each other."

"So what was going on?" Kate asks. "Was she upset about something or was it just my imagination?"

"I made her a partner in my business," Paul says.

"Seriously?" Kate says, more quickly than she would have liked.

Boom, boom, boom, Ruby is coming down the stairs, as heavy as a conquistador in full armor.

"Yes, she's there every day," Paul says. "And she can't even afford to fix her car."

"Why not give her a raise?" Kate asks. She can feel the falseness of her own smile, the strain of it, its perilous proximity to a grimace.

"I don't know," Paul says. "It didn't feel like the way to go. And I'll say this: it felt good. As soon as I said it, I thought you were right."

"That doesn't even make any sense," Kate says.

"About God, I mean," Paul all but whispers. "I felt it, the energy of . . . of something. It was amazing."

Ruby enters the dining room and makes her way to the table; the dishes and silverware tremble at her approach. "Ruby, please," Kate says. "You just can't walk like that. It's abusive."

The girl's face is piebald, flushed here, cadaver-white there, and her eyes twinkle like Christmas lights. The cuffs of her taupe long-sleeved T-shirt are wet, dark. She bumps the pointer finger of her left hand against the pointer finger of her right hand, over and over, and she sits heavily at her place. She sniffs her food and apparently it is all right because she begins to eat.

"You okay there, Ruby?" Paul asks.

"I don't understand why you'd do that," Kate is saying. "No wonder she looked like that when I saw her after work. She must have been out of her mind with happiness, or something."

"Happy is good," Paul says. "We're all for happy."

"Goddamn it to hell, Paul," Kate says.

"Goddamn it to hell, Paul," adds Ruby, her voice an eerily accurate reproduction of her mother's.

"All right, enough," Kate says to Ruby. "This is serious."

"Okay!" Ruby says brightly, "everybody stand in line and flappy fly."

Kate makes a gesture of small exasperation. "What does that

mean?" she asks, but Ruby mumbles what sounds like *sorry*, and then concentrates on her food, which is just as well for Kate because she wants to pursue the matter of Evangeline with Paul.

"So now you two are partners?" Kate says.

"She's there every day," Paul says. "She does the work, I mean it wouldn't be happening without her. And she's really learned a lot. She believes in what we're doing. So I guess we were partners all along, except we never said it."

Kate feels wild with exasperation, and she struggles to keep herself in check. When it comes to verbal jousting, she knows that Paul is not a true match for her—they both know this. For the most part, Kate uses the knowledge of her prowess as a means of restraint, a way to argue with him less frequently and with less force, even though talking things through, even heatedly, even heedlessly, is ultimately soothing to her. The flow of words has a calming effect, just as boxers say that hitting someone leaves them feeling tranquil.

"You know, Paul," Kate says, her voice so calm she almost sounds drugged, "it is not the same. If she's a partner that means you can't fire her. I'm not saying you should fire her or that you would ever, but it's a very different relationship. Before, you were the boss and she was the employee. Now you're equal."

"I don't want to fire anyone," Paul says. "And I don't want to be *able* to fire anyone. It's inhuman."

"It's inhuman?" Kate asks. Her voice has started to rise but she pulls it back down. "It's not inhuman, it's how people live. It's how people have always lived. It's how work gets done; it's how the world works. Someone is the boss, someone is the worker, there's a chain of command."

She takes a deep breath and does her best to look detached, amused, yet some smaller version of herself that lives within her spits out the words she would never allow herself to say aloud: *I am carrying seven-eighths of the financial burden of this house and our life and you suddenly decide to give away half of your business to a twenty-five-year-old girl who is clearly in love with you?*

"Uh-oh, the birdy angel is back," Ruby says, pointing to the wall. All those outsized, inexplicable, seemingly unsupportable emotions she has been displaying over the past year or two suddenly seem like rehearsals for this moment, because now when her eyes widen and her voice rises in dismay and she shrinks back into her chair as if from the fires of hell, there seems not a jot of play or exaggeration in it. Whatever Ruby has been practicing for is here.

CHAPTER
SEVENTEEN

"Hey Sonny," says Kate, "may I ask you a question?" Though Sonny is her driver, he is also an AA pal. They meet every Wednesday evening in a church basement with about twenty other Leyden-ites ranging from a retired pediatrician to a young shoplifter. It was Kate who, sensing his alcoholism when he first drove her—the smell of that metabolizing booze was unmistakable, as were the sea-creature eyes—teased Sonny into the program, and though there is a bit of Kabuki theater ritual in how they both acknowledge and ignore each other at meetings, Sonny always brings her a cup of coffee before the meeting begins and Kate always gives him a little kiss, which in her case means a foil-wrapped chocolate drop from Hershey. "I'm curious about the bumper sticker on the back of your car. 'All Men Are Idiots and My Husband Is Their King'? Why do you have that?"

"Oh boy," Sonny Briggs says. "I meant to scrape that little son of a gun off it."

Sonny has made an effort to elevate his level of service, which he realizes is more about presentation than it is about driving, though he does, in fact, pride himself on his driving style, which is contained and relaxed, steady in speed, with a minimum of lane changes. So that he may appear more businesslike, his hair, once a monument to hell-raising testosterone, in the style of his father's old favorite, Conway Twitty, is now closely barbered, and he wears what he hopes will pass for a chauffeur's cap but which is, in fact, an Amtrak ticket-taker's hat, given to him by his cousin. The job of driving Kate to New York, waiting the hour and a half it takes her to make her radio broadcast, and then driving her back to Leyden pays Sonny more than half of what he needs to get by every week.

They are nearing the city. They pass a cluster of houses and a large, glassy pond completely overtaken by Canada geese, a thousand of them at least. Kate marvels at the beauty of all those elegant birds with their long necks and pompous waddle and white chin straps, but her view of them is mixed with dread   why would so many geese be gathered here a mile or two outside of Tarrytown? And with that thought the entire landscape seems to tilt   the rambling white houses look suddenly shabby and in need of paint jobs, the green of the grass appears to be too dark and maybe it's more goose shit than grass, the trees seem pitched at odd angles and unstable, and the sky, which moments ago was a bright, goofy blue like a pair of golfing trousers, now has darkened to purple, the color of a funereal sash worn by a minister standing next to an open grave. *Get me out of here*, Kate thinks.

"So Sonny," Kate says, "talk to me." She sees his questioning eyes appear in the rearview mirror and just as quickly they disappear. "How's business?"

Sonny can never decide if it's better to tell people you're doing well, or if you should accentuate the negative and perhaps put them on your side. He has plenty of problems he could talk about. Insurance rates are going up. His back feels like the vertebrae are getting compressed by all the sitting. Yet his wife, Chantal, gives him massages at night and when they go out together she insists on driving because she says it's his turn to relax and let someone else do the work. And as boring as this job is and as uncertain, it's still better than roofing, which he did for eight years, with the wind in his face, the doomy stench of tar in his lungs, and his legs shaking from fear because not a day went by when he didn't have a premonition of sliding off the roof and landing on some flagstone patio, and his head exploding like a jar of jelly.

They are closing in on the city now and the traffic, negligible on the Taconic Parkway, is getting heavy on the Saw Mill. Open space, which turned into single-family houses, has become apartment buildings now, modest brick five-story dwellings, close to the road, interspersed with industrial yards, small offices, a parking lot for trash-collecting trucks.

"The thing I love about driving people," Sonny says, "is the people. All sorts of people. I figured I'd be driving bankers and the cream of the puff, but half the people I drive around are poor folks. I'll bet you didn't know that."

"You're right," Kate says, her voice almost giddy with her relief over having something to talk about. "What are poor people doing with a car service?"

"Poor people sometimes don't have cars. And up where we live, you got to have transportation. Can't take a bus because there ain't no bus, and you can't walk it because most things are too far. So this one lady, every Monday at one in the afternoon I pick her up and I take her to the Grand Union and she does her shopping for the week, and then I drive her home."

"That must cost more than her groceries," Kate says.

"It ain't cheap," Sonny agrees. "I got another customer who needs me to pick him up for doctor appointments, and I drive one guy in to see his parole officer. I guess back in the day you used to have neighbor helping neighbor, but now it's pretty much everyone for themselves." He shrugs, realizes how good that feels, how it relieves the tension in his shoulders and his neck, and he shrugs a few more times, just for the pleasure of it, and the pleasure somehow emboldens him. "That's one thing I think a new president might bring back," Sonny says. "Neighbor helping neighbor, and not everyone looking up to some powerful government bureaucrat to fix everything."

"Like what new president?" Kate asks, fearing the worst.

"I don't know, just not what we've got right now," says Sonny. "I was pretty much behind that Senator McCain, mostly because of what he went through. But you know that Governor Bush out of Texas is one of us."

"George Bush?" exclaims Kate. "You've got to be kidding me. That little spoiled brat?"

Sonny smiles. You've got to be a damned fool to argue politics with a customer. "I guess so," he says, "but doesn't it sort of make you sick the way Clinton was cheating on everyone like that?"

"I don't care, Sonny," Kate says, leaning back, adjusting her legs. "All men are idiots and my president is their king."

Kate's eyes come to rest on her black silk and linen pants, and she sees a couple of long, curled brown dog hairs pressed into the fabric, like veins in a leaf. Shep. The hairs are oddly resistant to her efforts to pluck them free. At last, using her thumbnail and fingernail as tweezers, she lifts them off her pants, but when she drops them to the floor of the car, rather than fall they outwit gravity and rise and drift right back to her leg.

She is not now nor has she ever been particularly fond of dogs, or cats, or any other four-legged creatures, and a lifetime spent listening to various friends prattle on about their pets has been an ongoing marathon of false smiles and empty nods. Their anagrammatic relationship to God notwithstanding, it has always struck Kate that something fundamentally foul is at the root of every dog. Anus, tongue, cascading fur, farts and meaty breath, black claws, icy teeth, and ostensibly adoring eyes, eyes that Kate perceived as primarily *watchful*, the eyes of a hunter mated with a scavenger. In high school Kate had a boyfriend named Rick Laval, a half-Cajun son of a local lawyer, and a boy of delicate bone structure and limited interests. Rick spoke on very few subjects, but one of them was Dolly, his family's water dog, and it was from Rick that Kate learned the immutable law governing men and their dogs, which is you don't want to stand between them. Rick, who seemed tongue-tied when it came to making an apology or stating his feelings or even making a plan, never ran out of things to say about Dolly, even going so far as to touch on her dream life, which, according to Rick, was full of cross-country chases and heart-pounding pond crossings. Kate did not mind Dolly's company, nor did she begrudge the ferocious affection she inspired in Rick; all Kate asked was to be spared having to join in the hysteria surrounding the dog and to be likewise spared having to pretend that the dog had complex feelings that were not appreciably different from Joni Mitchell's or Vanessa Redgrave's.

Paul is *not* that sort of man, his adoration of Shep notwithstanding. His affection is cleaner, more reasonable. The very thought of him makes Kate want to pull her cell phone out of her purse and call him. She won't, though, because he maintains a mid-century attitude toward telephones, believing that they're for the transmission of important, brief messages. The idea of talking on the phone aimlessly and at length because you miss someone makes as much sense to him as looking at pictures of food because you are hungry.

Yet she would love to hear his voice right now, even its tinny approximation through the ear holes of her mobile phone. Memories of his many kindnesses swarm within her. Holy is the silence he affords her when he sees she is thinking, holy are the windows he has placed in her house, in her life, and her soul, holy is the smell of wood, holy is the carpenter, holy is his gaze when she is speaking, holy is the catch in his breath when she kisses him, holy is his come, holy are his balls, holy is the weight of him, holy is the sweet attention he pays to Ruby, holy is his love of trees, holy are the steps he takes upon the face of the earth, holy is his driving fast behind her car and catching up with her to give her the notebook she has forgotten, holy are the stacks of firewood beside her stove, holy are his folded hands as he listens intently to what she reads aloud, holy are the hands that gently pat her to sleep when it's one of those nights, holy holy holy is the touch of his fingertips as he passes her chair, holy are his tears when he thinks of the harm he has done, holy is his sudden thirst for absolution, holy is his stumbling circular path to God . . .

In front of them, the George Washington Bridge is so vividly reflected in the Hudson's still waters that it looks like the top and bottom of a playing card. The sky is a soiled metropolitan blue, and beneath it, all along the curve of Manhattan, the buildings line up to display their wealth and accomplishment, from the Parisian placidity of Riverside Drive to the clunky exclamation points of the World Trade towers on the island's southern tip.

Her show is not a live feed but is taped, and Todd Hoffman, the show's producer, will wait for her, but nevertheless Kate's stomach churns nervously at the prospect of a long delay. She doesn't want to inconvenience anyone, and she doesn't want to be perceived as someone who makes others wait for her. Beyond that, if she can get into the station by one, be out of there by two-thirty, she will miss the afternoon rush out of the city, which sometimes begins as early as three, and be home again not much later than four o'clock. If Kate misses her opportunity to get out of the city before the commuter exodus she is faced with postponing her return trip until eight in the evening. Sonny doesn't mind crawling along, but her own psychic metabolism is thrown into a tumbler by rush hour's frequent, inexplicable stops followed by little forward bursts of ten or fifteen seconds' duration. So far, she has been caught in the city only once, and it is not something that she wants to put herself or Sonny through again.

Her impatience to get back to Leyden is about having time with Paul, before Ruby needs to be picked up at Children First, where she sees a learning specialist—if, that is, Paul is willing to end his workday and Evangeline can pick up on the conjugal vibe and go home.

Most of the planning and machinations that are necessarily a part of their love life are done by Kate. It is not that Paul is indifferent to their life in bed together, but he is in this matter as in every other matter maddeningly ad hoc. He does not seem to understand that if they are both awake at seven in the morning they have exactly thirty minutes before the duck-shaped alarm clock starts quacking on Ruby's bedside table, nor does it seem to occur to him that if he has an appointment to give blood on Wednesday, that makes Tuesday a good time to have sex because they have both learned—at least she has, and he ought to have—that exhaustion follows his biweekly pint. Also on the subject of blood: Paul remains thoroughly unaware of her menstrual cycle, letting the precious days before her bleeding begins go by without any particular sexual interest and then approaching her with urgent, open kisses while she is all plugged up and cannot bear to be touched.

There have been times when she has wondered if his failure to ride herd over time and to force it to yield as many moments as possible for them to be together is not so much a function of his wild-child, creature-of-the-woods spontaneity and his lifelong aversion to structures and schedules, but is really some passive-aggressive tactic to keep their sexual contact down to a minimum, or to have their lovemaking coincide with the ebb and flow of *his* desires. Or it could be—and this is the most disquieting possibility—a way to make *her* responsible for their sexual and emotional health, turning her in effect into a human metronome who maintains the rhythm of their intimate life.

She doesn't mind doing the work, because of the reward. The slow fill of him as he notches his hips inch by inch closer to her, she enjoys the anticipation of the bright delirium sex unleashes in her, an extremity of emotion and abandon that she has never before experienced and never actually believed other people experienced, either, and she enjoys moving things around in her schedule so there is more time for them to be together. It's like clearing brush so the flowers can be seen. But there is no question in her mind that if Paul were in her position right now he would not be thinking of how to get out of the city in time to be home so that there was a chance to lie next to her.

Paul in the city is subject to a thousand and one diversions. He might stumble on a Korean restaurant that strikes his fancy, he might run into an old buddy who needs his help unloading a truck, or he might spend an extra hour wandering Central Park trying to find a sycamore tree that he loved as a teenager. These are all lovely traits, part of his casual charisma, but there is one minuscule problem, barely worth a mention: sometimes she wants to wring his neck. After all, not so long ago, he was in the city checking out a job, and if he had turned around immediately and gone back home to her they would have had a whole afternoon to themselves. But what did he do instead? He drove to the East Side and looked for the apartment house where he had found his father's corpse. And of course he further delayed his journey to Leyden by stopping in

Martingham State Park to clear his thoughts, whereas Kate, had she been at the wheel, with Paul up in Leyden, would have been pushing the speed limit trying to get home, and to think of him flicking on his turn signal—no, forget it, he wouldn't even do that—to think of him suddenly pulling off the Saw Mill and heading for some cathedral of trees where he could make his solitary and inchoate prayers to nature, and to think of all that could be at this very moment so profoundly different in their lives had he not done so, fills Kate with rage, by the way, total, hideous rage, hardly worth mentioning . . .

They arrive with Kate's customary half hour to spare, time she needs to stretch her legs, organize her notes, pee, hydrate, pee again, and chatter amiably with the studio's staff, seven men and women who seem to Kate to be part of some underground species, highly intelligent denizens of a world in which people make no visual impression on one another. A couple of weeks into her show, Kate took her sartorial cue from the station staff and came to work in sweatpants and one of Paul's green-and-black checkered shirts, but it was the worst show she had ever done and now she dresses for each broadcast as if it were a public event, believing that taking some care in her wardrobe has an invigorating effect on her mental processes, a theory that was borne out in a television show about some legendary basketball coach who preached the importance of putting your socks on and lacing up your shoes just so.

"Maybe you can park the car and come in," she says to Sonny, as she slides across the seat and opens the back door.

"Nah, I'm good," he says.

"They have a fabulous water cooler," Kate says. "And a state-of-the-art Naugahyde sofa."

"I'm good," Sonny repeats, gripping the steering wheel more tightly.

"Okay then, sir," Kate says. "I shall see you . . ." She checks her watch, a Cartier tank watch and a gift from a particularly devoted fan. "In exactly ninety minutes, which would be two-thirty, I will come racing and we will get the fuck on the road, okay?" Kate realizes that her profanity is mildly offensive to Sonny, but she likes to swear, especially on the day of her broadcast, when it serves as an inoculation against the occupational hazard of piety.

Heartland Radio, with broadcasting facilities in Burbank, Phoenix, Chicago, Orlando, Richmond, and now in New York, has secured a spot in the low numbers of the FM dial, where the frequency is strong. On the air from five a.m. to midnight—people awake later than that are presumably beyond salvation—Heartland features several hours of good-natured Christian rock, distinguishable from the music on the secular stations only by the lyrics that, to the boom-boom rhythm of pelvic thrusts, extol the virtues of virginity. Its programs include *Live from the Alliance Tabernacle*, *Ask the Experts*, *God and Country*, *Faith and Family*, *The Eleventh Commandment*, and Kate's show, the highest-rated. Just as her book's sales and the crowds at her personal appearances indicated, there are a lot of people like her out there in the whole vast confused, tragic, mysterious country: single mothers, recovering drunks, good old-fashioned Christian do-gooders, and, of course, people simply interested in Kate Ellis—her self-doubts about her mothering, her memories of her past as a child beauty queen, her faith as it is tested in AA meetings when boredom threatens to overcome empathy, her wondering if Jesus thinks any less of her when she prays for a good haircut or the loss of ten pounds.

The New York studio is Heartland's most recent acquisition and it reflects their origins as a regional, cost-conscious company, whose officers make modest salaries and live in a style more befitting dentists or high school principals than media executives. The furnishings were purchased en masse from the previous tenants and the spectral outlines of the various framed bits of memorabilia are still on the dingy walls. A Black Crowes promotional sticker still adheres to Studio 1's glass wall, and Studio 2, despite innumerable cleanings, still holds the skunky aroma of marijuana.

The very best thing about the studio is its vintage microphones, big, tarnished things the size of hair dryers, which have been painstakingly cared for over the years, the way some watches or sports cars can find mechanical immortality in the hands of certain devotees. Radio luminaries from Winchell to Cousin Brucie have used these microphones and a few Heartland techies are in a constant archival flutter over the old mics. Kate, who knows as little about audio technology as she does about Thai kickboxing, is herself surprised by the quality of the sound that comes out of this studio. Hearing the reproduction of her voice, as filtered through the diaphragm and back plate of those old Neumann omnidirectionals and further honeyed by the wizards working the mixing board, has caused in Kate the auditory version of Narcissus's experience at the side of the pond. She has been turned from a kazoo into clarinet; God bless the Christian nerds and their refurbished toys.

In Studio 2, someone has splurged on a new swivel chair, this one with a high back that makes Kate feel more secure than the old one, which seemed ready to tip at any moment. The chief engineer, Tony Smithson, comes in, bringing her a couple of bottles of water, though in the months she has been broadcasting from this studio she has yet to open one of them. Tony is thin and English, with dark, furry legs that are almost fully exposed—he is wearing either bicycling shorts or a bathing suit.

Tony's assistant, Alison Kadar, is on the other side of the glass, leaning over the mixing board. With its little blinking transistors and rows of switches, the board looks like a perfect little town viewed from the window of an airplane. Alison wears a linty blue cardigan over a white blouse that has been scorched by an iron. Her hair looks as if she has cut it herself after a furious fallout with her family.

The intro to Kate's hour is the same every week and was taped a few months back by a famously devout young actor. His kind of piety gives Kate the creeps and she thinks it's bad for Christianity in general and quite possibly personally annoying to Jesus, consisting, as it does, of a rather rabid championing of traditional family structures that seems disapproving of how Kate herself has lived and continues to live.

"And now," the actor is concluding, "unscripted and unedited, Kate Ellis and *Prays Well with Others*."

It's actually untrue—if she flubs a word or goes blank, she can always have another go at it—and Kate cannot hear that intro without wondering why her hour has to begin with a moronic little fib.

Tony, standing now next to Alison, points through the glass to Kate.

Oh, do I ever need a faith lift, Kate begins.

Oh, right, I forgot to say hello. Hello from the mentally ill me. On my way down here from my home in the country, I was thinking about the broadcasters who went crazy right on the air. There's Howard Beale, the great Peter Finch character in Network, *the guy screaming "I'm mad as hell and I'm not going to take it anymore." But there are plenty of real-life episodes of people flipping out on the air and I finally understood it while I was driving the hundred or so miles from my house to here. By the way, I want to urge all of you to write Heartland and urge them please to buy some furniture and hire a decorator because I swear these studios look like the Dallas Book Depository.*

I understood the breaking point the Howard Beales of the world reach, because even on a show like this one, which is about as far as you can be from so-called hard news, you are always dealing with people in the great

Out There—which is how the people with microphones think of the rest of the world without microphones. And the thing about you all—and you sure don't need me to tell you this—is that your lives are hard, and full of suffering, and full of shame, even the so-called fortunate ones among you. That's why you're listening, right? That's why you're not off somewhere eating ambrosia and laughing your heads off and doing little victory dances. You have come to understand that your lives are essentially unmanageable without God. You're not looking for God because you feel like doing him a favor; you're looking for him because you need him to do something for you. You need him to give you courage, and patience, and to help you love one another. And you don't just need it a little, you need it a lot, and let's face it, you need it pretty much right away.

Kate stops for a moment. She feels suddenly and unnervingly surprised to be sitting in this studio. What has she just said? What is she meant to say next? There is a band of numbness around the top of her head, her hands cold and wet, her heart swelling to the bursting point, and then her own confusion flies past her like a frantic flutter of birds, a whoosh and then silence. She moves her lips and inches closer to the microphone, drops her voice a half octave.

You know, when you get sober and you feel Jesus there with you every step of the way, it's like you two have been in a war. You've been in a foxhole together and someone threw a hand grenade in—life is full of these grenades, sometimes it's a person and sometimes it's just a feeling, like jealousy or loneliness, and sometimes it's the smell of wine—and Jesus fell on top of the grenade and absorbed the blast with his own body, and you're alive, you're actually alive and unharmed, and you say to him, What can I do, how can I ever repay you? And you know Jesus, he's like the Godfather, he sort of scratches his chin and says, Well one day I may come to you and ask you to do something for me. And you figure uh-oh, now what have I gotten myself into, and sure enough the very next day the Godfather Jesus says, Hey remember when I fell on that hand grenade and stopped you from getting blown to pieces? And remember wondering if you could ever repay me? And now you're really scared and your mind—which, as you know, is NOT your best feature, it's actually worse than your thighs—your mind is coming up with a lot of very upsetting scenarios, some of them from the Old Testament, some of them from the six o'clock news—and then he tells you what he would like you to do to repay the debt—and you know what he wants? He wants you to treat the people around you with love, and make life on earth a little bit better. He wants you to plant a tree or feed a hungry child, or you can visit someone in the hospital, you can hang out with a lonely person and treat that person with kindness and respect, even if that lonely person happens to be y-o-u.

Kate stops. Her throat is not dry, nor is she confused. She is not tired. But the thing she reaches for—her next sentence—is not there, and its absence is immense. It's like walking into a familiar room and realizing, without precisely knowing why, that intruders have been here and you've been robbed.

Kate feels the icy drip of sweat on her spine. Just to have something to do beyond experiencing her own bewilderment, she opens a bottle of water and takes a small, steadying sip from it. She glances down at the sheet of paper on which the few notes she has brought with her opaquely swim. "Give me a couple of seconds, Tony," she murmurs.

Tony is at the console, wearing an enormous pair of earphones.

"You take your time, love, and when you're ready we can take it from . . ." He looks back at Alison, who gives him the line. "That y-o-u thing," Tony says.

Once, nearly five years ago, sitting on a bridge chair in the cinder-block fluorescent-lit basement of a Methodist church in Leyden, and trying to think of what humanist generalization she could plug in to stand for her Higher Power, Kate had cast her thoughts this way and that, wondering if her writing was her higher power, or if it was Ruby. And then one of the AA people, a girl named Joy W., gone now, maybe drinking again, maybe off to California to zigzag after her dream of becoming a recording star, had her guitar with her, and she had this sneaky way of performing, which was to pretend she was just strumming and humming privately, and the rest of the room was simply overhearing her. Joy, the pain in the ass, sang "I Don't Want to Get Adjusted to the World," in a lovely, clear, kind voice, and the song itself, so simple and so plaintive, forced Kate to look away. And there it was, a simple wooden cross on the basement's wall, and really out of no impulse more elevated than curiosity, and even with a degree of irony and self-mocking, Kate thought the words *Thank you Jesus*, and she whispered them aloud and felt, actually and unmistakably *felt* a presence. This sensation of being entered, filled, radiantly occupied did not make her feel larger but instead made her feel smaller, practically dismantled past the point of self-recognition, and so it was no wonder that like millions before her, she wept. For the cross, for the words to that old church song, for the Father and for the Son, for the suffering, for the sacrifice, for the love, she wept because she was no longer alone, she wept because she knew she was going to stop drinking, she wept because she was—she could barely say this word, even to herself— she was saved.

And now it is gone, just as suddenly as those feelings came they have disappeared.

They are gone.

It is gone.

Gone.

I once could see and now I'm blind / I once was found and now I'm lost . . .

She has five or ten more seconds to decide what she is going to do about it. The Man who has escorted her to the prom has ditched her in the middle of a dance and she is just swaying on her own now, keeping time to the inaudible music, trying to pretend that everything is as it was. There are no tears in her eyes and none seem to be on their way—conversion is convulsive, but reversion is strictly stiff upper lip.

She has a momentary notion simply to stand up, give T&A, as she sometimes thinks of them, a little valedictory salute, bidding them and the entire Christian nation a fond farewell. Not only the Christian nation—but adios to the Jews, the Hindus, and the Muslims, and to all the New Agers with their brains like banana bread, and anyone else out there who likes to pretend that there is some overarching shape and meaning to life on earth, benign or otherwise, that there is someone to turn to in times of trouble and someone to honor with our gratitude, that we are not now and forever on our own, making it up as we go along.

When Kate went from being a garden-variety liberal agnostic to someone who wanted to tell the world about Jesus, one of the things she worried about was her old friends and the people with whom she worked laughing at her. Now, as this great love seems to have burst like a soap bubble, leaving only a barely detectable filminess in its wake, her concern is just as worldly: how will she make a living wage?

"All set, Kate?" Tony's voice, booming as it is over the speakers, nevertheless holds within it a tremor of uncertainty. And without another moment's contemplation, Kate not only nods but gives him a double thumbs-up, as if the cool box of Studio 2 were a module inside of which she is about to be launched into space. Too much is on the line. She has mouths to feed, a mortgage to pay. And who knows? Faith, like some errant demon lover, might decide to come back as suddenly as it departed. In the meanwhile, the show must go on.

* * *

Kate is in the back of Sonny's car and her phone rings from the muf-
fling depths of her pocketbook. Chewing gum, lipstick, compact,
keys, notebook, wallet, coin from her second anniversary, and, finally, the phone. "Hello?" she says.

"Mom!"

"Ruby, what's going on?"

"Mom, come home, please."

"I'm in the car right now. Tell me what's going on."

"Paul's sister." She says something after that but it is buried beneath an avalanche of sobs.

"Ruby, please. Take a breath. Okay? Can you do that?"

Sonny recklessly passes a station wagon and starts to drive faster.

Ruby takes a deep breath; something in the back of her throat
creaks like a door.

"Tell me what happened, baby. Can you do that? Tell me—Paul's
sister."

"I gave her the cross," Ruby says. "The most beautiful cross."

"I know you did."

"A car hit her, Mom."

"Hit her? A car hit her?"

"When she was putting the mail."

"Did she get hit, or did her car get hit?"

"She was IN her car, Mom!"

"Okay, baby, please, please try to stay calm. Can you put Paul on
the phone for me?"

"He's not here. He's going to the hospital."

"You're alone?" Annoyance whirrs within Kate.

"Hello? Kate?" It's Evangeline's voice now at the other end of
the line. Apparently, Ruby has just handed the phone over to her.
"Paul just left for Northern Windsor Hospital. Annabelle's car got
hit while she was making her deliveries. And I'm here, I'm staying
with Ruby."

"Is Annabelle . . ."

"She's alive. We don't know how bad, but it looks like she's going to make it. Cheryl called her brother. He's at Mount Sinai in New York but he's getting in touch with the doctors up here, so we're sort of waiting on that."

This makes very little sense to Kate, though she has noticed that people in Leyden feel better when they can personalize their experiences with the outside world, feeling that knowing somebody's name, or knowing somebody who knows somebody else, will somehow guarantee them better treatment, whether it's at the bank or the post office or the farmer's market or the emergency room. If anyone thinks that any good will come from having someone's brother call the ER—a brother who is basically *a med student*—Kate doesn't know why she begrudges them their little networking fantasy, but she does, she can't help herself: she does. And the irritation generalizes itself to instantly include all the other people in Leyden who refer to the bank tellers by name, who bring something from Buttercrust Bakery and insist on saying *The poppy seed muffins were baked by Charles*, who say their morning eggs come from Bill's farm, and that George, who turns out to be a UPS driver, delivered their new lamp with a dent in the shade. Everything so fucking personal.

Kate takes a deep breath; she is aware of her soul's sudden sourness. Where is the grace, the pity, where is the warmth? They have all fled, along with God . . . Were they all just the tail tied to the kite that was her faith, and now that the string has snapped, have they all disappeared into the wild blue?

"Um . . . Kate?" Evangeline's voice is low, confidential. "I'm out on the patio. Ruby keeps on talking about how she gave Annabelle her cross and it was supposed to be good luck."

Kate hears Ruby's voice calling for Evangeline in the background.

"I'm out here," she calls back.

"Evangeline?" Ruby shrieks. It is the voice of a terrified child in a universe where nothing is guaranteed and nothing can stop bad things from happening, not prayers, not candles, not sermons, not holy water, not songs, nor dances, not crosses.

CHAPTER
EIGHTEEN

Sergeant Lee Tarwater stands in front of Jerry Caltagirone, wringing his long white hands as he speaks. Caltagirone used to think Tarwater was a very worried man, maybe too worried to be police, until he learned Tarwater had eczema and was rubbing lotion into his skin. "We got two people up front," Tarwater says, "father-daughter, and they want to talk to someone about that homicide in Martingham last November. That's you, right?"

And with no more preparation than that, a nice break in the case, which might seem like luck to some but Caltagirone believes you make your own luck when you are police, you make it by working the case, stirring the pot until stuff starts to surface.

Tarwater comes back from the front with the father and daughter in tow. They are both on the small side and Tarwater looms over them. He dumps them on Caltagirone, but not before giving the daughter a look-over, bottom to top, and back to bottom. She's sixteen years old and she may as well be holding a sign that says I AM HERE AGAINST MY WILL. She's maybe five feet tall, tan, dark hair, skinny enough to race at Belmont, with a stubborn expression that Caltagirone knows is mainly bluff—if she really knew how to get her own way she wouldn't be here. Her father is dressed to look rich, which Caltagirone is willing to grant him. He's not much taller than his daughter, but with a *D* and a *G* on his sunglasses, a sporty little sweater, and a Rolex. His name is Alan Slouka and her name is Marmont.

Caltagirone gets them a couple of chairs and the father looks at the daughter, telling her with his eyes that he wants her to speak up. She looks right back at him; she might be afraid of some things, but her father isn't one of them. "All right," Slouka says, "I'll start the ball rolling. My daughter here—I'm single-parenting—"

"Right," Marmont says.

"Well, I am," he says. "You may not like it, but I am. Anyhow, Marmont and I moved to Purchase a little over two years ago, and, without my being aware of it, Marmont developed an attachment to one of the young men who work on our property."

Caltagirone shifts his weight on his new ergonomic chair, paid for by himself, with a thickly padded back and inflatable lumbar support. "And this is about the homicide last November," he says, raising his pneumatic contour coccyx-cut seat an inch or two. He's already so much larger than the Sloukas, he figures he may as well go all the way.

"Yes, it is," the father says. He looks at his daughter. "You want me to go on?"

"You like telling it," she says.

"No," he says, the anger coming up through his voice, "I like telling the truth. In fact, I am addicted to telling the truth." Turning to Caltagirone, he smiles, shrugs. "My daughter and this individual were in the park"—he says the word *park* as if it were the moral equivalent of a by-the-hour motel—"and they were hiding, and . . ." He takes a breath. "Let's say they were not in their Sunday best, when they saw a man being attacked."

Caltagirone looks at the girl. Suddenly, Marmont is all he is interested in. As far as he is concerned, the father has ceased to exist, and he wants her to feel it, too, feel her own importance.

"You saw this?"

She nods.

"And now . . ." He looks at his watch. It's June 3. "Seven months later, you're here?"

She shrugs. And then says, "Sorry," in a whisper.

Even this modicum of mental anguish is hard for her father to witness and he puts a reassuring hand on her shoulder. "She had reasons to remain silent. They were afraid I would be angry about the fact that one of my employees was committing an act of statutory rape against my daughter. They were afraid I would fire him, or perhaps call the police, and because he is an illegal, they were afraid he would be deported, even without the sex charges."

"Fear's a bitch," Caltagirone says to Marmont. She smiles distantly, and she's as far from believing he is sympathetic to her as she is from finding him attractive, and he knows it. It might be best to work her through the father, after all.

"Look here," Caltagirone says. "Withholding material information from the police during the investigation of a felony is a crime. I'm sure your father has already explained that to you."

"I was going to come down here with my lawyer," Slouka says. "Maybe I should have."

The daughter gives him a look; she thinks maybe he should have, too.

Caltagirone opens the bottom drawer of his desk, which squeals like an anguished pig. "Jesus, Jerry, grease that thing!" one of the cops shouts from across the room. Caltagirone rifles through thirty or forty hanging folders, all of them unlabeled. "Here we go," he says, breathing audibly. He opens the folder and pulls out a photograph of a man and a woman on a pier, taken in the evening, with a Ferris wheel in the background, bejeweled like a crown with red, yellow, white, and blue lights. The woman is blond, with broad, masculine shoulders, a wide smile, dressed as if to go sailing, and the man, dark-haired, barrel-chested, is pointing at the camera with his mouth half-open, maybe clowning around and pretending to sing, maybe telling whoever was taking the picture to stop.

"That's William Claff, beaten to death, and you saw it happen," Caltagirone says, tapping his finger on Will's face. "Nobody deserves that. You understand?"

"Sure," Marmont says. "I'm here aren't I?"

"No one, not on my watch." Caltagirone realizes the girl has already agreed it shouldn't happen and there's no need to continue emphasizing the fact. "And this lady here? It's killing her, too. She had to fly across the country to identify the body, all by herself. She's got no family. This man was all she had in the whole world. You understand me? You need to tell me what you saw."

"It was pretty hard to see," Marmont says.

"You told me you saw," her father says.

"All right," Caltagirone says. "Let's start with the easy stuff. When you pulled into the parking lot, did you see another car? Do you remember that?"

"The person I was with doesn't own a car, *he doesn't make enough money*. And my car was in the shop. We rode our bikes and just stowed them in the woods and walked it."

"So you were never in the parking lot?"

"No. But it doesn't matter. I saw him."

"Who?"

"Him." Marmont juts her chin toward the photo in Caltagirone's hand. "He was in a track suit."

"This man here's with God," Caltagirone says. "But we're here, we're here right now, right now. It's the other guy that matters."

Marmont looks as if she's trying to find a way to disagree, but she nods yes. "The other guy was wearing a leather jacket."

"Here we go," says Caltagirone.

"He was younger," she says. "I sort of suck at telling how old adults are. I think everybody's sort of forty."

Her father smiles, and says to Caltagirone, "I'm forty," as if there might be something just a little bit endearing about that.

"What else?" Caltagirone asks. "Clothes? Anything at all."

"He had brown hair, cut sort of long, like folk rock. And boots."

"Boots? Cowboy boots?"

"No. Work shoes. Athletic. No beard, no mustache, nothing to stand out. He just seemed regular, until the fight."

"What did he seem like?"

"Really mad. Hey, I gotta go to the bathroom."

"Can it wait?" Caltagirone asks.

"I've been waiting."

Caltagirone sends her back to the waiting room and when she's gone her father suddenly starts acting as if he regrets ever bringing her to the station in the first place. Caltagirone's guess is that for whatever reason she finally told him what she had seen and told him about the guy she was screwing and Dad blew up and threw her in the Lexus and brought her in to teach her a lesson. Now he wants to tell him what a good kid Marmont is, and what a tough time the both of them have had since her mother died. The way he puts it it seems as if the mother's body isn't cold yet but it turns out she's been dead since Marmont was four years old. Then Slouka announces he's in the rock business, which Caltagirone first takes to mean he builds driveways or has a masonry contracting company, but what it really means is he does concert promotion and he's letting Caltagirone know that if he ever wants tickets to, say, a Neil Diamond show at the Garden or maybe Springsteen at the Meadowlands, Slouka would be more than glad to hook him up. Leaning halfway across the desk, he asks Caltagirone, "How do you think we ought to handle the boy? Of course he's fired, but I don't know if we need to make any more trouble for him than that." As if this was something the two of them were going to decide together.

"We gotta bring him in, too."

"Easier said than done," Slouka says.

Just then Marmont returns, flicking tap water off her fingertips as she walks. "There was some lady crying in there," she announces, as if she had seen a woodpecker.

"I want you to look at another picture for me," Caltagirone tells her. He reaches into his folder, produces a five-by-seven color photo of a round-faced, jowly guy with swept-back hair and sunken eyes. He's wearing a colorful Hawaiian shirt, a riot of pineapples and parrots. His expression is blank but somehow menacing—you'd know that if you knew anything about menace, if you knew that when a man puts on a blank mask it usually means there's going to be hell to pay.

Marmont reaches for the picture but stops herself. "Can I hold it?"

"Be my guest," Caltagirone says.

The overheads put a glare on the glossy finish and Marmont tilts the photograph to get a better look. "Is this the guy?" she asks.

"You tell me."

"His hair's different."

"Hair'll do that."

"Not the eyes though," she says.

"Be careful here, honey," Slouka says.

"You don't need to worry about this guy," Caltagirone says.

"Well it's totally him," Marmont says.

"Totally who?" Caltagirone says, narrowing his eyes.

"The guy we saw." She puts up her fists. Her father must have told her to go easy on the jewelry; there are pale circles on her fingers where the rings used to be.

"You sure?" Caltagirone says. Marmont nods and then Caltagirone says, "You're positive."

"Yeah," Marmont says.

"Who is this man?" Slouka asks.

Caltagirone turns slowly toward him, as if he's momentarily forgotten his existence. "He collects for bookies out in Los Angeles." Caltagirone opens the middle drawer of his desk and pulls out his tape recorder. He peers through the smudgy, postage-stamp-size window on the recorder's side, to make sure there is a microcassette loaded in, and then presses the play button to make sure there is still juice in the triple A's.

"What about the dog?" Marmont says.

"The dog?" Caltagirone asks.

"They were fighting about a dog," Marmont says. "The runner guy was kicking the dog and . . ." Marmont flutters the picture; it looks for a moment as if the Hawaiian is nodding his head in agreement. "This guy was trying to stop him. That's why we were for him. I mean, before we knew how far it was going to go."

Caltagirone writes the word *dog* on the corner of his desk pad, and circles it. Then he remembers talking to the landlord about the dog and the lady from Philadelphia who knew Claff as Robert King, who said that Claff stole her dog, and he's already deduced that the dog leads nowhere, the dog, wherever it is, is collateral damage, and Caltagirone crosses the word out, first with a line, then with another line, and then he rubs the point of his Rollerball over and over the word until it is invisible.

CHAPTER
NINETEEN

Summer arrives early, full of temper—scorching blue-gray days, brooding starless evenings, and stormy, astonishing nights, with the sheets of rain falling with a furious rattle. In the middle of the workday, Shep sleeps in the cool air beneath Paul's truck, with nothing of him showing but his paws. Next to the truck is Evangeline's newly purchased Subaru Legacy, which, according to her, is the car of choice for gay women. Parked closer to the house, and somehow in more direct contact with the sun, is Kate's Lexus, its chrome bumpers and door handles blazing with light, its tinted windshield a fiery greenish mirror in which an upside-down tree holds the white sun in its black leaves.

Inside the house, Ruby sleeps in her bed, after having been up most of the night, sick to her stomach, and full of manic energy after that, dispensing disquieting observations, such as *The floor is happy* or *Now it's the stairs' turn to walk up me* or *My fingers don't want to be fingers anymore.*

While Ruby naps, Kate calls a woman named Dr. Joan Montgomery, who is the only child psychologist in the area. "I actually happen to have an opening for one thirty this afternoon—I just got a cancellation," Montgomery says. Kate isn't sure she believes her, but Montgomery has a pleasant, elegant voice and Kate is relieved there is someone in the area who can take a look at poor Ruby.

Kate sits now in the front of the house, ostensibly reading a thriller, but after half an hour with the book in her lap, she has read only the first paragraph and she had read it four or five times, gathering the words again and again with her eyes and attempting to thrust them into her mind. She has already crept up the stairs a number of times, once to more widely open Ruby's bedroom door so any alarming noises would be easily audible down on the sofa, and a few times after that just to peek in, not that much can ever be gleaned by watching somebody sleep: they will look either ridiculous in their waxy seriousness or darling and vulnerable, but either way their bodies look like the shells left behind after their souls have been taken.

Now, an hour later, taking Ruby to the psychologist, Kate almost collides with the truck from the courier service as she is speeding up her own driveway. The driver, in shorts and a white straw pith helmet, as if he is going on safari, stops next to Kate's car, hands her an envelope, and reverses out of the driveway so fast he looks as if he is on a strip of film running backward. Kate tosses the envelope into the backseat—it's from her agent and she's pretty sure what it is. A proposal from Heartland, renewing her contract.

It is not until she pulls into the parking area of the Windsor Counseling Center that Kate realizes this is the place where she and the last man in her life uselessly went for couples' therapy after he fell in love with another woman. He never had any intentions of breaking it off with his new beloved, and the hour was a humiliating waste of time and money—even the therapist, a Dr. Fox, knew this and didn't bother to ask them if they wanted to make a second appointment as he nervously escorted them out of his office. *Oh my Lord,* she thinks, *I was in a relationship so hopeless I was booted out of couples' therapy!*

That time she could at least vent her displeasure. Now, when she talks to this Dr. Montgomery she can only hint about the subterranean pressures Ruby might be absorbing back home. Her own frequent absences can be mentioned, but not that the new man of the house has killed someone.

Ruby has been essentially silent since her nap and now looks as if she might doze off again. Her eyes are heavy, and she leans her head against the side window. She is wearing yellow shorts and a white tank top, both of which are too small for her, but she won't part with them. Her bare feet are squeezed into a pair of salmon-colored flip-flops, also too small. Kate is not certain what Ruby knows or understands about the nature of their appointment this afternoon.

"There's someone in town who's an expert at talking to kids and helping them with stuff that's bothering them," Kate had said, and Ruby shrugged as if it meant next to nothing to her. "Anyhow, I made an appointment," Kate had said.

All Ruby had wanted to know was if Kate was going to come along, too, and when Kate said she was Ruby changed the subject.

"Well, here we are," Kate says. She reaches over, releases Ruby from her seat belt.

"So this is a psychiatrist?" Ruby asks.

"I don't think so," Kate says, hiding behind a little hedge of pedantry—Dr. probably means PhD. Not MD, and so, technically, she is not a psychiatrist. "Anyhow, the important thing is the rules. Just about every place has rules—like no running in the halls when you're in school, and no talking in the movie theater. Do you want me to tell you what the rules are here?"

"Probably bird rules."

Kate furrows her brow, pretends to consider this, though these increasingly frequent non sequiturs from Ruby are making her frantic. Sometimes Kate is certain that the eruptions of nonsense are deliberate, a continuation of the child's long infatuation with exaggeration and attention grabbing and a primitive sort of theatricality. And there are other times when she believes the nonsense is deliberate and involuntary both, that Ruby knows there are no bird rules yet she feels nevertheless compelled to say there are. And there are other times—and this third way is becoming dominant—when Kate believes her daughter is being slowly stolen away, seduced, perhaps, by an alternate reality that poor Ruby (the prefix is becoming permanent) has created because the one she has been living in is unsustainable. Or poor Ruby may be turning into a different person on the most basic cellular level, transformed into this sleepless, feverish creature by the drip drip drip of bad chemicals. If it is a chemical imbalance, a chemical solution must be found, in which case this Dr. Montgomery, whom Kate already imagines as a font of New Age drool, will not be of much use—she may be able to write a haiku but Ruby will need someone to write a prescription.

"The rule here," Kate says, "is you"—she touches Ruby's nose—"are allowed to say whatever you want, there's no secrets, nothing to be afraid of, nothing to hide."

The asphalt parking area is sticky beneath their footsteps, stinking of pitch, and hellishly hot in the sun. Ruby makes a move as if to scratch herself and Kate takes her hand. In the parking lot Kate reads the bumper stickers with dismay: COMMIT IRRATIONAL ACTS OF KINDNESS and PSYCHOLOGISTS DO IT WITH UNDERSTANDING. Poor Ruby, poor poor Ruby. She gathers the child closer to her. *Why are we here?* she wonders. *Why not a church, a minister, what about God? When was the last time I prayed for this child? When was the last time I prayed?*

Kate pulls open the counseling center door to a blast of air-conditioning. There's a reception desk but no one is at it, a waiting room with nobody in it, a couple of low tables with magazines, a couple of small sofas, and a white-noise machine whooshing away in the corner. The wall clock chimes the half hour and Dr. Montgomery emerges, a compact, conventionally pretty woman, vaguely familiar to Kate, with boyishly cut frosted hair and freckly arms. After a glance at Kate, she directs her attention to Ruby.

"Hello, Ruby, it's nice to meet you." She offers her hand and Ruby shakes it. "You can follow me, if you like."

"Should I come, too?" Kate asks.

"We can all talk together, to begin with," Montgomery says.

"Me want bathroom!" Ruby proclaims.

As Montgomery gives Ruby directions to the toilet, it strikes Kate where she has seen her before—many Wednesday nights ago, at the Leyden AA meeting. She attended only once, maybe twice, and Kate can remember she sat silently, her trembling hands and overwhelmed eyes her only eloquence. Kate follows her into her office, a large space with two child-sized chairs, a small trampoline, and a table upon which is a tray filled with sand and an array of figures made of painted rubber—a man on horseback, a woman holding a wand, a mummy, a groom, a king. Montgomery takes her seat in a stuffed armchair and Kate sits in the other adult-size chair.

"We can take this time and you can tell me what your concerns are," Montgomery says, blushing deeply as she speaks.

"Basically what I told you over the phone. Agitation, sleeplessness, blurring the line between fantasy and reality, and reverting to infant behavior, especially in terms of hygiene." Kate scans the walls, looking for diplomas, but all she sees is a picture of Einstein with his tongue out, and a photo of a huge, quivering sun setting at the seashore, the ocean a vast watery Wurlitzer of bright colors.

"She has a nice firm handshake," Montgomery says.

"Then I guess we're all set."

Montgomery smiles. "I have to tell you something, Kate. I read *Prays Well with Others* a few months ago and it's one of my important books. I haven't heard your show on the radio yet, but that book is really something."

"Thank you."

"I just love your little mishaps. They're quite funny, but there is always the moment, the lightbulb moment, when you get it. You're inspiring—do you know that?"

"I'm not inspiring, or inspired, I'm just broken. But thanks, I am glad I wrote something you could use."

"And I thank you. Most spiritual writers sort of stick in my craw. But you're so honest and so human and so . . . you. I feel as if I know you."

"I don't really think of myself as a spiritual writer," Kate says.

"You don't?"

"Just more like a writer, a regular writer."

"Mom?" Ruby's voice, troubled and confused, comes from outside.

Kate clambers out of her chair. "Just very quickly?" she says to Montgomery. "I gave her a little cross, and she gave it to my boyfriend's sister, for luck, and a while after that the sister had a pretty bad accident and Ruby is sort of blaming herself."

Poor Ruby is three doors down, and when she sees her mother she drops down to the carpeting and scuttles toward her using both hands and feet, with her rump high in the air and her face red from exertion. *Sure,* Kate thinks, *let's go for the full monty.*

Ruby crabwalks into Montgomery's office, with Kate behind her. "Sorry about that," Montgomery says. "That hall can be confusing." She is standing at the sand tray, smoothing the sand down with an index card.

"What are you doing?" Ruby asks, still on all fours, looking up at the psychologist through the tops of her eyes.

"This is my sand tray. I use it to help kids."

"Really?"

"I know," Montgomery says to Kate. "I was once skeptical, too. But it works. The thing about sand, it's been the essence of everything we've built, throughout history. Glass, brick, concrete—it's all sand. The infrastructure of physical life is made of sand—and our inner world has an infrastructure, too."

"Made of sand?" Kate asks.

Montgomery laughs. "Who's to say? Anyhow, if you'd like to relax in front or run an errand in town for the next forty minutes or so, maybe Ruby and I can get to know each other."

Ruby doesn't seem concerned about her mother's leaving her with a virtual stranger; in fact, as Kate departs, Ruby seems detached—Shep reacts with more emotion when Paul leaves the room. As Kate makes her way down the corridor to the front of the building she has vivid and unwelcome memories of walking this same narrow passageway with her treacherous boyfriend half a decade ago—coming in, she was in front; exiting, he was in the lead, so anxious to be on to whatever was next for him.

Kate sits in the otherwise empty waiting room but lasts there only a minute before she springs up, heads for the exit. She has a passing thought: go to the cool, cavernous Episcopalian church in the center of town, not because she favors that denomination but because she knows its doors are never locked, and she can sit there in the blue-stained shadows while her heart beats approximately twenty-eight hundred times and wait for grace to come to her and wait for wisdom, as if she were some sad woman in a trench coat sitting on a park bench waiting for the perfect man. She gets as far as her car, but then she realizes: she once *had* the Perfect Man, the Ideal Husband who could guide and comfort her in a time just like this, and now He has left her, or she has left Him, or they just gave up on each other, or the whole so-called relationship was nothing but a crock of shit in the first place. It's difficult to say; they never really had parting words. Jesus went out for a pack of smokes and never came back. Was that it? Or did she just get sick of His friends? Or did someone come between them?

Yes, that was it. Of course. Someone came between them.

The car is so hot her ears begin to ring, and beads of moisture dot the down above her lip, yet she sits there for nearly a minute with her hands on the steering wheel before it occurs to her to start the engine and the air-conditioning.

As the car cools, Kate reaches in back for the envelope delivered by the courier service. She tears away the plastic wrap and unzips the paper zipper along the envelope's side. The note, folded over a smaller envelope, is from her agent.

> Dear K. We've been trying to get you on the phone.
> Enclosed is the royalty check from the second half of
> last year. T. says that the next check, reflecting Jan–June
> of this year, will be even better. I think the time to
> discuss another book and another contract couldn't be
> more opportune. Maybe it's time to cut down on the
> radio, which I fear is standing in the way of a sequel to
> PRAYS. I'm out of the office for the next couple of days
> but let's talk next week. Promise? In the meanwhile,
> congratulations.

Kate opens the second envelope and looks at her royalty statement, which is essentially indecipherable. She very slowly and stealthily looks at the check. It is for $1,068,395. She holds it in her hands and stares at the numbers, and then she quickly opens the glove compartment and shoves it in with the maps, her insurance card, and the Lexus owner's manual, pushing it to the back of the compartment with a frantic poking motion as if she were hiding contraband.

* * *

Later that afternoon, with a list from Dr. Montgomery, Kate goes to Healthy Valley, Leyden's health food store, to purchase vitamins, supplements, and organic juices and vegetables, while Paul takes Ruby with him to visit his sister, which is part two of Montgomery's plan.

Annabelle is recuperating at home, sleeping on the sofa so she won't have to mount the steps to the bedroom. "We're going to get some food for them," Paul tells Ruby. "Now the thing is, Annabelle's going to be all right, she's going to be completely okay. But right now she looks a little beat up. It's weird at first, but you get used to it. And she's really happy you're coming to visit her."

Ruby gives no indication of listening to a word of this. She sits with him in the cab of his truck and Shep, after a great deal of preparation—pawing at the ground, whimpering and growling—hops into the bed, and finds his spot in a jumble of rags and old shirts Paul has left there for him.

Paul drives slowly up the driveway, in case Ruby has second thoughts and wants to return home. "Just remember," he says, "my sister's going to be all right."

Ruby's lower lip trembles guilelessly. This girl, a former virtuoso of emotional artifice, has lost her taste for illusion. "Are you sure?" she asks.

"I am very, very sure. I talked to her doctors."

"Tell me what they said." Ruby furrows her brows. "But tell me for real."

"This is exactly what the doctor said. Annabelle had multiple fractures in her neck, in vertebrae four, five, and six. You know what that means? That's what they call the bones in the neck. They made an incision in the front of her neck and removed the disk between four and five, and then they did the same thing for the disk between five and six, and they replaced them with bone from a bone bank. Isn't that something? A bone bank? I didn't even know there was a bone bank."

"Is it where people save bones?" Ruby asks.

"It's like a blood bank," Paul says.

"That's where you go," Ruby says.

"Now. Maybe someday I can go to the bone bank. I'm sure glad there is one."

"So they put a new bone in her?"

"Pretty much."

Ruby thinks for a moment. "How do they keep it in?"

"Doctor stuff. They file down Annabelle's own bone and make it so it bleeds and that way when it grows together again it can fuse with the new bone and everything sticks together. Then they put a plate on it, you know, a piece of metal, to hold it all together while it's fusing, it sort of knits itself together. Once everything is stabilized and the fractures heal, my sister will be good as new."

The first stop is the supermarket to pick up the few things Bernard has asked for, and while he fills his shopping cart with crackers, club soda, ice cream, chocolate syrup, pita, and chickpeas, Paul's attention drifts away from Ruby. When he looks around for her she is missing. He can still recall when, no matter what the initial indications were, he always thought that essentially everything was going to be all right. Finding his father dead on First Avenue, being stranded for days in the wilderness, having no money, fighting through a fever with no place to live—none of these things ultimately disturbed his innate certainty that he and what he cared about would always survive. That confidence is gone, yet another thing left in the woods in Tarrytown, New York, along with his footprints, his tire tracks, and who knows how much DNA. He is now a man who is always prepared for the worst possible outcome. He pushes his shopping cart quickly up and down the aisles, with the idea that once he has covered the store he will report the missing child to the store manager and then call the police. He's been wanting to call the police for quite some time.

But he finds Ruby quickly, standing by a large bin of Bosc pears and staring as if transfixed at what looks like an avalanche of copper-coated teardrops. She's safe! The magician who orders our fate, after showing the card signifying catastrophe, has placed it back into the deck, and the slow shuffle of unseen cards has begun again.

"Do you want some pears?" he asks her, and she shakes her head no.

"I didn't know where you went, Ruby. You shouldn't do that."

"I was here." She turns toward him, slowly. "I was going to die."

"You're not going to die."

"Yes I am. Don't be stupid."

Paul pretends not to notice the insult. "Well not for a very, very long time."

"Because I'm ugly," Ruby says.

"You're not ugly. You're a beautiful little kid. Don't you even know that? You're beautiful, like your mother."

"I've got a face like penis vomit," Ruby says. "You want to call that *beautiful*?" She stiffens her arms at her sides and widens her eyes; she looks somehow mechanical.

"Shhhh," he says. "Don't say things like that. You are very, very loved." His words sound a little hollow to him, but when someone is drowning, don't we throw them lifesavers, and aren't the lifesavers hollow, too?

"Penis vomit penis vomit penis vomit penis vomit penis vomit penis vomit penis vomit," Ruby whispers to herself, running the words together so they sound like Latin. A prayer fervently muttered.

Bernard and Annabelle's house is on Guilford Drive, a cul-de-sac not far from the center of Leyden—an easy walk to the post office, for those who can walk. There are fourteen houses on Guilford, all built in 1970, by the same builder, using the same plans and the same materials, and Paul must drive slowly and peer at each one in order to pick out which house is his sister's. He makes his best guess and pulls into an empty driveway. "Here we are," he tells Ruby. If Ruby holds any fear about visiting someone who has been badly injured, or dreads having to confront some putrid odor or gaping wound or gurgling digestive noise, or if she believes that she herself is somehow going to be blamed for what has befallen Annabelle, she gives no evidence of it. She seems drowsy, and when Paul puts his hand on her shoulder she lets out a long sigh, as if he is rousing her from a summer afternoon nap.

Bernard is waiting for them, in shorts, a tank top, and flip-flops. He is dressed similarly to Ruby, though the effect is considerably less sporty in a stocky fifty-year-old man, especially in Bernard's haggard, unshaven, badly rested state. He relieves Paul of the grocery sack and presses two twenty-dollar bills into his hand. Paul doesn't want any money and forty dollars is more than he spent anyhow, but it seems too complicated to refuse payment.

"Wait here while I put these things in their place," Bernard says, in a voice just more than a whisper. "She's sleeping in the front room."

"The hell I am," Annabelle calls out.

"She's been looking forward to your visit," Bernard says to Paul. "And yours, too, Ruby."

"Remember when you said we were going to chop down a cherry tree and make a bookcase?" Ruby says to Paul.

Paul thinks for a moment. "Yeah, I do."

"I think you forgot," Ruby says.

"Well are you coming in or not?" Annabelle's voice is an octave lower than usual, dragged down by the pain medication.

"It's okay," Ruby says to Paul.

"I didn't forget," Paul says. "We'll do it."

They find Annabelle sitting on the sofa in her gray cotton nightgown. A pink-and-blue crocheted blanket covers her lower half; her bare feet, long and narrow, are on the coffee table. The TV is on without the sound; a black bear rakes its paw through a rushing stream, presumably hoping for salmon. Annabelle's right arm is in a soft cast; three fingers of her left hand are taped and splinted. Her head has been partially shaved, and though she has brushed her hair over the exposed area, alarming patches of redness and blackness are still visible, as well as a seemingly random scatter of staples. Flutters of squeamishness make their way through Paul's stomach.

Annabelle reaches for what looks like a bright white bedpan resting next to her on the sofa, but it turns out to be a cervical collar. "I'm supposed to wear this night and day," she says, "but it's really itchy and hot." She holds it up for Paul and Ruby to see; it's pearl and bright white, with bright chrome hardware on the sides. "It's called exo-static," Anabelle says, "which is pretty close to ecstatic, which is a pretty big lie. When I put it on, I look like Queen Elizabeth I, but if I cover it up and you only see the top then it looks like a priest collar, so either way it's pretty cool."

Ruby has made it only halfway into the room and stands where she is, staring at Annabelle and breathing shallowly through her mouth. Life seems to be presenting itself to Ruby as a series of images projected onto a sheet, some of them lurid, some of them inexplicable, which she looks at with the presumption of complete privacy.

"I'm bored out of my mind," Annabelle says, "which is probably a good sign. I know I look horrible, and I totally don't care, which is probably not a good sign, but I think I always sort of wanted to be this person, the person who sits on the sofa and doesn't give an Irish jig what she looks like. It feels right to me. It's my appointment in Samara. Plus, the Vicodin."

"You look a million times better than two days ago," Paul says.

Annabelle adjusts her neck. "What do you think, Ruby? Do I look like a priest to you?"

Ruby doesn't say anything, but she looks unnerved.

Bernard comes in, carrying a teapot, three cups and saucers, and a glass of chocolate milk, all on an ornate brass tray, which rings hollowly from the movement of the crockery.

"Oh Bernard, Bernard, Bernard," Annabelle fairly sings. Then, to Paul, "It turns out I *do* know how to pick them."

"Doing what is normal," Bernard says, setting the tray down onto the coffee table and giving Annabelle's big toe an affectionate little pinch. "I very much liked chocolate milk when I was your age," he says to Ruby.

Slowly, as if against her better judgment, Ruby approaches the tray and very carefully picks up the chocolate milk. Streaks of partially stirred chocolate syrup marbleize the sides of the glass.

"Sit next to me with that," Annabelle says, patting the sofa. "Paul? Will you pour me a cup of tea, and maybe put a little milk in it?"

Paul understands that he is being asked to vacate the couch, and he does so with some trepidation. Yet as uncertain as he is about what his sister has in store for Ruby, when Ruby gives him a questioning look he nods his head and encourages the girl to sit next to Annabelle.

"You know," Annabelle says, "I knew this was going to happen. It was an accident waiting to happen. I just totally knew it."

"It's not your fault," Paul says. "Anyhow, the things we think are going to happen don't usually happen."

"We're not completely in the dark," Annabelle says. "Things don't just *happen*. There are patterns, warnings. How many times did I envision some idiot hitting me from behind? I think I imagined it happening at the very mailbox it happened at. I really do. What went down in Bernard's country? Do you think God just threw down a thunderbolt because the people were drinking too much champagne?

Come on. People saw it coming long before it arrived. Or Dad, what happened to him. God, there was a slow-motion train wreck that anyone could have seen coming."

"I didn't," says Paul.

"You were a child," Annabelle says. Turning from Paul and looking at Ruby, she asks, "Do I look pretty scary?"

Ruby has quickly drunk nearly half her chocolate milk, and now her tongue is crawling down the side of the glass in pursuit of the smears of chocolate syrup.

"Well it looks worse than it really is," Annabelle says. "But I've been wanting to tell you something."

Ruby looks questioningly at Paul, and Paul shrugs, extends his lower lip, as if to say Your guess is as good as mine.

"Do you want some cookies or something like that?" Annabelle asks Ruby. "Actually, I don't think we have any cookies. Do we, Bernard?"

"We have real English water biscuits," Bernard says. "Why not Paul comes with me and we'll look around and see what we have?"

"Me?" says Paul. First removed from the sofa and now from the room. What next? Sent to the truck to wait with Shep?

"Yes. It's too long since I've shared a house with a child. I trust your knowledge of what a little girl will like."

As soon as Paul and Bernard have left the room, Annabelle leans over and grasps her legs beneath their calves and slowly lowers her feet to the floor. "Oh, that feels nice," she says. She eyes the peach plastic bottle of Vicodin planted on the edge of the coffee table and then looks at her watch. She is thinking it might be time for her next dose, but if she's going to do this by the book she has to wait another two hours, or, in other words, sixty minutes. Which can be rounded down to forty-five.

Annabelle points to a vase on the television set, filled with two dozen white roses. "Aren't they pretty? Your mom sent them."

Ruby nods but only pretends to look at the roses. Sometimes she has to be careful about what she sees. Sometimes seeing something new is like being shoved off the top step of a long staircase, especially something new when the knowledge of the thing feels like hands on the small of her back. She knows ways to make her eyes into shields off which the arrows of the outside world merely bounce, and, on the occasions when the shield fails, Ruby can redirect the images before they reach her brain. They are sent down to some wasteland within her, where the unseen things accumulate with all the things she pretends she hasn't heard and all the things she has resolved to forget, until her body gets rid of them.

"I want to tell you something, Ruby," Annabelle is saying. "Paul said you are feeling a little weird because you gave me something to keep me safe and now you think maybe it didn't do the job. And maybe I'm mad at you or something?"

Ruby has listened to only a few words of this, but enough to glean the sense of it. "I guess," she says.

"Well I want to show you something," Annabelle says. She slips her hand beneath the afghan and gropes around her lap for a moment and pulls out the gold cross Ruby gave her, wrapping the delicate chain around her finger and lifting it slowly, and then enveloping the entire thing in her palm. "I think having this saved my life, Ruby. The car that hit me? It was going over sixty miles an hour, really fast. Everyone says I was just unbelievably lucky to survive."

Ruby's eyes widen. Her lips part and then close; she lowers her chin and looks at Annabelle through the tops of her eyes.

The sound of Shep barking comes from outside; he's had it with being in the truck.

"I don't know if it's something about this cross or because you gave it to me," Annabelle says. "Who knows what or why? But this thing?" She opens her hand, moves it back and forth so the crucifix and its chain slither left to right. "This thing saved my life."

"Really?" Ruby asks.

"Really," says Annabelle. "Really and really. So can you come here?"

Ruby starts to slide over but thinks better of it because it messes up the couch. She stands up and then sits down again, directly next to Annabelle, and when Annabelle gives her a small kiss on the top of her head Ruby leans her head on Annabelle's shoulder and closes her eyes. A birdy angel fairy man is there to greet her in the darkness, all eyes and smiles and flashing wings, but she tells him to go away and for once he does.

Paul goes outside to tend to Shep. Bernard has said it's all right to bring the dog in the house, but when Paul unties him Shep seems reluctant to jump down from the back of the truck. Paul has lowered the tailgate and thumps it encouragingly, but Shep will venture only a few feet. Paul could make a quick grab for the dog, take his collar, and more or less drag him to the edge, at which point Shep would probably have no choice but to hop down. But there is something in the way the dog stands that warns Paul away from any sudden moves. The dog has stiffened his legs and his claws are extended, as he tries to gain a firmer purchase on the corrugated floor. He lowers his head and trains his eyes on Paul, and Paul stops trying to reason with the dog and just stares back. Man and beast stand there and regard each other silently, neither of them able to fathom what the other is thinking.

"Paul! Paul!" Ruby has come running out of the house. She is carrying her flip-flops pressed to her chest and her feet are bare. Her hair, the color of weak tea, rises and falls, rises and falls.

Paul turns toward her, with every possible feeling eclipsed by dread. "What's wrong?" he asks.

"Were you going?"

"No, no. Of course not. Just looking in on this idiot." He jabs his thumb toward Shep.

"Oh, I got scared." Ruby throws her arms around Paul's waist and presses her ear against his midsection. He feels the strength of her, the childish, unharnessed power of her biological self. It is like standing in the center of a moving stream and feeling the throbbing pulse of the water as it shakes your bones.

Using his forearm, Tom Butler pushes the dishes of dried toast and the unfinished cups of coffee and the sour wince of half grapefruit in its snug little bowl over to the far side of his kitchen table. Using a paper towel, he dries the area and places fifty sleeping pills and his notebook in front of him. He creaks back in the wooden chair and folds his arms over his chest. He is in his underwear and his Hawaiian shirt is unbuttoned. This bottle of pills, this blue spiral notebook, they are all that is left of the kingdom of his life. Even the dishes and cups have receded into the darkness, the clock ticking on the wall is invisible, the exhaust fan over the cookstove is running, just in case it takes them a while to find his body. As for the rest of his place (four rooms down and two rooms up in a stucco house near Griffith Park) it may as well have ceased to exist, the bed, the sofa, the TV, the Bowflex, the free weights, the safe in the wall, and the world beyond these walls, the houses, the stunned palm trees, the pale yellow sky, the ponies, the gamers, the oohs and the odds, the favorites, the long shots, the spreads, the people and the money, the money that is owed them and the money they owe. A dream, a dream, a dream, a dream you can't remember.

He empties the pills, ovoid and arctic white, and they sound a rattlesnake's warning as they puddle onto the table. He spreads them out with an open hand, as if before a game of Scrabble, yet here, of course, every letter is the same, or would be if *adios* were a letter. Oops. He almost forgot. He needs something to wash these bad boys down.

He gets up a little too quickly and his chair tips over, hits the blue-and-tan linoleum with a mighty bang. *Well bang bang right back at you*, Butler thinks, righting the chair. He opens the refrigerator. He and Tori never eat at home and it shows. There are a few packets of soy sauce, the liquid brown of old blood, an economy-size jar of yeast powder, and twenty or so bottles of various vitamins and supplements, which he glares at with fury. The vegetable drawer has been turned into a nest for beer bottles and he grabs a longneck and takes it back to the table with him. He has certain misgivings about washing the Ambien down with beer—his greatest fear is choking on his own spew—but taking these pills with tap water or even Fuji water is more depressing than suicide.

He opens the beer and takes one pill, just to get the ball rolling. Life was better when you needed a church key to get into a fucking beer. He flips his notebook open, it's first-day-of-school clean and crisp, and he uncaps his pen and writes:

To: Tori Oliver
From: Thomas V. Butler
Subject: You are to Blame

YOU are making me do this. YOUR loveless cruel
cheating whoring sluttishly fucked-up unforgivable
behavior is making me kill myself and you should be
tried for murder. I will see you in Hell but you are so
lucky lucky there probably is no Hell. Like Lennon said,

no Hell below us, above us only Sky. I know there's nothing more, it's ashes to ashes dust to dust. I'll tell you one thing Tori and that's being in the gaming business all these years you really learn to hate all the bullshit people believe. The lucky tie, the lucky shirt, the lucky socks, how it's good luck to dial the phone with your left hand and hold the receiver with your right when you're placing a bet on an NFL game, best if you're sitting down if you're placing an AFC bet, or hockey, and a lizard skin belt is good luck if you're betting baseball but reams you out good if you're betting hoops.

Butler stops to take another pill, swallowing it with barely any beer because the last thing he wants is a full bladder. What he wants her to find is a body, not a puddle.

He has never before taken a sleeping pill; he shook these down from Sonia Dropkin, whose apartment he ransacked two nights ago. Sonia is fifty, with the birthmarked, splotchy skinniness and flyaway orange hair of a recluse slowly going mad. Family money, but not enough for her gambling. For someone who places as many bets as Sonia, she knows remarkably little about cards and next to nothing about sports. In Vegas, she plays blackjack and waits for the dealer to either sweep away her chips or match them with a pile of his own. The bets she places with Butler's organization are invariably on underdogs—they all call her Dog Lady, in fact. She gives no evidence of interest in team histories, match-ups, and she seems utterly without sentiment. Her focus is entirely on long odds or fistfuls of points. She might actually believe that these odds are figured and handicaps granted somehow at random, or the whole operation is in the hands of imbeciles. She doesn't realize there's a science to all of this and she also doesn't realize that in gambling as in life itself the favorites generally win. Sonia, therefore, usually is running about two grand in the red. But she always comes up with it, until recently when the two turned into four and suddenly she was carrying almost 9K in debt, that stuff can get away from you: wildfire indebtedness is what Butler himself used to call it, wildfire stoked by the Santa Ana winds of bad decision making.

Butler visited Sonia on the assumption that she was going to be making a significant payoff—at least four grand—and when Sonia gave him an envelope with six twenty-dollar bills and three tens in it, he patrolled her airless and askew apartment looking for something of value to take, and also wanting to scare a little sense into her: without fear, the whole system broke down. If she'd ever had anything of value it was probably in the pawnshop. She wanted him to take her watch. She slipped it off and handed it to him, but the point of grabbing her stuff was to make her miserable, not to collect the bric-a-brac of her slipping-down life. It wasn't even a watch, it was a Swatch. Come on!

He settled on taking her meds—sleeping pills, a couple of asthma inhalers, and a blood thinner. He told her he was coming back in three days and she'd better have at least four thousand dollars to give him, and then he yanked her hair, hard, like starting a lawn mower. He half-expected that orange mop to come right off her head, but it was rooted and she screamed in pain and called him a dick. This is what I do for a living, he shouted at her. His own passion surprised him; usually, he was on automatic pilot. They don't get paid, I don't get paid, he said to her. You place a bunch of idiotic bets? Find a fucking Bingo parlor somewhere and leave us alone. Sonia was massaging her scalp; her arcade eyes were wet with tears. She asked him to give her back her pills and when he said no she asked for the inhalers and he said no to that, too. And then she said she'd be in trouble without the blood thinners, she was a candidate for an embolism. Well good luck on that, he said. She caught on that she wasn't going to get any breaks and she spit on the floor, her own floor, right in her own house. Do me a favor, she said. Take those sleeping pills, take them all. Put them in your filthy mouth and swallow them. You're a worthless human being and we don't want you here with us anymore.

The idea stuck. It went around and around in his mind like a horrible jingle you can't stop hearing, a little tune that somehow has a purchase on your consciousness and there's nothing you can do to dislodge it. You can't stop it and you can't even trump it with another ditty, even one equally inane.

He takes one more pill and promises himself that next time he will take ten then ten and then ten again. But for now he needs to hold on to consciousness, which comes slanting into the darkened room of his mind like light through venetian blinds.

> It makes me sick that you are the closest thing to
> family. But I guess if mom and dad were still around or
> I had a sister or brother I'd have to feel Oh shit this is
> going to make them feel bad. But you're the only one
> who is going to feel bad and maybe it's because when
> you finally get your cruel little body out of bed you're
> going to find me and it's going to be too bad for you
> because you're going to have to call the fire department
> and the police and wait here with my CORPSE until
> they come. Too bad for you you whore. Too bad for
> you you destroyer. And I fucking loved you, I gave you
> my heart.

Butler stops to read what he has written. The page looks as if it were floating in water. At first he thinks the pills have already started taking effect, but he realizes he is crying. He tears the sheet off its spiral spine and rips it in half and then in half again and then again.

He takes two more pills—that makes four—and a discreet little swallow of beer.

He throws the shredded suicide note into the garbage pail under the sink and realizes he needs to piss. He does not want to be found with a wet lap but in order to empty his bladder one last time he must steal into the bedroom and pass by Tori in bed on his way to the toilet. She came in about three this morning and refused to talk to him about where she had been or about anything else. Her face was streaked with tears; she was carrying one of her shoes, broken at the heel. He forced her to kiss him—it was like drinking beer out of an ashtray. Then she pushed him away and threw herself into bed and was asleep in five seconds, still wearing her little lilac cardigan with the pearlized buttons.

Now it is nine in the morning and she sleeps still. He stands in front of her. Her lips are parted. Her greedy little hands clasp the satin border of the blanket, as if she were worried that someone was going to try and take it away from her.

"Hello, Tori," he says, standing close to her side of the bed.

She sleeps.

"You're a murdering whore," he says, his voice at the decibel level of normal conversation. He doesn't want to cater to her deep, drunken snooze, but he doesn't want to awaken her, either. "And that's too bad," he continues. "It's really a shame."

The urgency to urinate increases, and Butler unzips his fly and takes a couple of steps closer to Tori. Standing there on the thin line between living and dying is like being on a mountain peak. He can see farther than ever before. He can see the lay of the land, its emptiness, and how it's been trashed, and he is certain as never before of how alone he is. *Above us only sky.*

Imagine all the people . . . The keening, pleading lyric, and the memory of Lennon's voice . . . *Imagine all the pee-pee*, and suddenly he hears a stunned laugh that turns out to be his own. *Imagine all the pee-pee.* And then he realizes what he is going to do and he unzips his pants and hurriedly takes out his dick. Maybe he should make a real effort to wake Tori up. A big, slow, hazy No, dark orange and veined with blue, dissolving at the edges.

Actually this could work. This will be better than the note.

He goes back to the kitchen and sweeps the sleeping pills into his hand, and grabs the beer with his other hand. He stumbles. His mind has taken its first nibble of its own demise.

Back in the bedroom, the air like dirty velvet, he silently sets the beer bottle on her night table, alongside *The Celestine Prophecy*, a sleep mask, a little bottle of Visine. His fly is still unzipped, his penis half-exposed. He pulls it forward, but in all the movement back and forth his desire to urinate has become elusive.

Swing low, sweet chariot. Comin' for to carry me home.

Ah, good, that's doing it. He hears Eric Clapton's voice singing the words along with him, a beautiful duet, with the guitar lines wrapping them both in bright silver. And he can feel his urine, silver, too, rising like mercury in a thermometer. *What women don't understand about men,* Butler thinks, *is how often we defy gravity. We must go up up in a world where everything is pushing down.*

Swinglowsweetchariotcomin' fortocarrymehome.

Fucking Clapton, man. That guitar. Even messed up he was God.

Butler moves stealthily, ever closer, until the slit of his penis is three inches from Tori's sleeping face, with its worried brow and hawk nose. He picks up the beer, takes another swig, and then looks up at the low ceiling, blue and wavy as water. *I looked over Jordan and what did I see? A band of angels coming after me.*

Thomas spreads his arms. Beer pours out of the bottle's open mouth, fizzing and hissing onto the carpet. His legs tremble and he thinks for a moment he will fall to his knees. He hears voices. Something is happening. When you walk to the border of life, things occur. You have entered a secret place.

"What's going on?" Tori asks, lifting herself up on her elbows. Her eyes are creases. She kicks the covers a little to one side, to free one bare foot. "What are you doing?"

Butler staggers to the window, zipping himself up. A black-and-white from the LAPD has pulled in front of the house. An old lady he's never noticed before is standing in her bathrobe on her front porch, waiting to see what will happen. The mailman has been stopped by one of the cops, and he is nodding agreeably and stepping back and then completely turning around.

The cop who turned the letter carrier around is joined by another cop, even younger. In their contoured britches and gleaming knee-high boots—or were they in plain clothes? *Coming for to carry me home.* Butler will never quite be able to keep this life-saving moment clear in his own mind, this fucked-up miracle, this fully armed band of angels sent for him and him alone. The two cops have a few words with each other and one of them points to Butler's house and the other one rests the heel of his left hand on the butt of his revolver and they make their way to Butler's front door.

Now that they have a positive ID on him they can proceed with placing him under arrest for the murder of William Claff, in the town of Tarrytown, New York.

CHAPTER
TWENTY

Usually the dreams Paul remembers are the morning dreams, the often nonsensical neural narratives he creates to keep himself asleep. This morning, with Kate already out of bed and Shep trying to bark a squirrel down from a tree, he is dreaming that Annabelle is telling him that they are going to dig up their father so that he may be buried next to their mother's grave in Kent. As he objects to this plan, Shep's barking becomes more insistent, pulling Paul halfway out of sleep, and when he returns to his dream he is walking behind his sister as they mount the steps to their father's First Avenue apartment and Paul is saying to Annabelle, "He's still here?" but she does not answer. *My sister has a nice ass,* he dreamthinks and then they are on the third floor where droopy, bedraggled-looking people are milling about the landing in undershirts, smoking cigarettes, drinking strong-smelling coffee. "Are you here to see your father?" one of them asks, a skinny, unshaved guy, with something ingratiating and evil about him. Paul follows Annabelle inside but she's no longer there and as he walks through the rooms in his father's apartment there are paintings lined up on the floor, leaning against the walls, and he hears some dog barking, a dog he cannot see, and he stops and looks for Annabelle and now she's back in the dream but as a younger self, maybe twenty years old, and he says to her, "He's still here?" to which she answers with such intensity that she is practically *hissing* at him, "He's always here," at which point Paul awakens, and lies quietly on his back in the warm bed, surprised to find that his heart is squirming with anxiety and that he is near tears.

He slides out of bed and goes to the window. The sky is pale blue, the sun already scorching. *Thank you Father for another day.* He says the words tentatively to himself, and feels shaken by them. Kate, in jeans and a sleeveless shirt, uses a leash to lead Shep away from the tree and the squirrel and into the house—she still doesn't feel confident enough to take him by the collar.

She notices Paul at the window; her face lights at the sight of him and she calls up, "Sorry, I couldn't stop him from barking. Are you going to watch that thing with me?" Shep noses against her hand, trying to eat the biscuit he has been following, and the touch of his wet nose startles Kate. She makes a little yelp and then laughs nervously.

"I'll be right there."

A television program called *First Thing Sunday Morning* is interested in taping a segment about Kate and the ongoing phenomenon of her book. *First Thing* is not a religious show, but Rebecca Adachi, the show's cohost, a woman in her late twenties, a cancer survivor and the daughter of a man who went to prison after a well-publicized trial for embezzlement, has read *Prays Well with Others* at least three times, listens every week to Kate's broadcast, and has attended a couple of Kate's events in New York, and getting *First Thing*'s producers and the network to agree to air a piece about Kate is as exciting to Rebecca as it was to book Maxwell, who was riding his hit song "Fortunate." It came close to not working out. The publicist at Kate's book publisher and the publicist for Heartland Radio, having struck an uneasy alliance, had almost convinced two of the producers at *60 Minutes* to do a piece about Kate and her book, and it was only at the last minute when someone at CBS decided that a segment about a forty-one-year-old recently sober convert to Christianity might not have a broad enough appeal for *60 Minutes* that Kate's publicists began casting around for other venues, at which point Adachi personally stepped in, quickly vaulting over the publisher and the radio station and contacting Kate herself, which was surprisingly easy to do.

Kate hasn't ever seen Rebecca Adachi's show—Paul's presence in the house makes turning on the television feel odd and embarrassing; if he finds her watching it he will stop and look at the set as if it were a crack in the wall that needs to be repaired. However, people at Heartland Radio and at Kate's publishing house assure her that Adachi is a friendly, decent reporter and that her show will be both a dignified and highly effective showcase for Kate and her book.

The program plays at nine a.m. and Kate and Paul bring their coffee and bowls of melon to the front of the house and watch it while they have breakfast. The show is a mix of hard news, sports, weather, and human interest stories, and in its second half-hour, two segments with something spiritually encouraging in them. Today, the first story, reported by Adachi's cohost, is about the men in presidential candidate George W. Bush's Texas prayer group, and the second, reported by Adachi herself, is about a woman in St. Louis who lost her son in a construction accident and now prepares bag lunches for about a hundred schoolchildren in her economically distressed neighborhood.

"What do you think of her?" Kate asks Paul, pointing to the TV set with her spoon.

"What do *you* think of her?" Paul asks.

"She looks about twelve," Kate says.

"What difference does that make?"

"Only a man could say that."

Paul leans forward. "Hey, you know what? I was sitting next to her once. At one of your events. In the city. She was sitting right next to me. She had a tote bag from CBS and she was taking notes."

He's not sure why, but recognizing Adachi fills Paul with happiness. Anything that connects one thing to another is a source of reassurance to him. Maybe Adachi was fated to ask Kate on her show. And if that is the case there is something in the universe—something ineffable, a force, an intelligence, *something*—that makes sense of us, that sees us, that knows us, that punishes and rewards us, or that at the very least and in some way, shape, or fashion cares.

When Rebecca Adachi looked over at Paul in that church on the Upper West Side last November, the night before Paul's path crossed with the man in the woods, he was struck by how much she looked like Mary Jones, a woman he worked for five years ago, who was also half-Japanese, and seeing her now on TV it seems all the more uncanny. Both Rebecca and Mary have a gamine quality, boyish but delicate, as well as a swimmer's haircut and a taste for large jewelry in somewhat the cubist style. They both have a kindergarten-teacher sweetness, a sort of encouraging brightness that doesn't always seem quite real.

Mary Jones, a young, well-provided-for widow, had hired Paul to make a display case in her apartment on Gramercy Park, in which she planned to show her small collection of Joseph Cornell boxes. One evening she hired a car to take them both to Queens, to Utopia Parkway, where Cornell had lived with such ravishing sorrow with his mother and his disabled brother and where he had scavenged for the knobs and spools and assorted junk that constituted his art. The old frame house was nowhere to be found, but looking for it drew Paul and Mary Jones closer and that night they became lovers. How long had it lasted? Certainly for the duration of the project, and, it seems to him, for a couple of months after. Now, thinking of Mary as he watches Adachi talking to the Lunch Bag Lady, he finds he cannot remember their relationship coming to an end. When had it happened? Where was the break point? He remembers the sharp, flowery smell of her perfume, the flatness of her ass, the extraordinary ivory color of her skin, the natural Mohawk of her secret hair. He remembers her voice, her cough of mysterious origins, her distrust of doctors. But why had they stopped seeing each other? He can think of nothing, no quarrel, no moment. But he can remember the beginning, he can recall it in exquisite detail: looking together at the houses on Utopia, salmon-colored brick on the ground floor, white vinyl (where there used to be white wood) on top, each with a bath mat's worth of lawn in front, and then there were the people on the street: Indians, Koreans, recently immigrated Jews.

Adachi is asking the Lunch Bag Lady how much money she spends every week on preparing lunches for the children in her community, and the Lunch Bag Lady says, "Gee, Rebecca, the money comes from all over, people hear about us and want to be involved. Maybe they've had to miss a meal or two themselves, one time or another. Or maybe they're just looking for a way of saying thank-you to the Heavenly Father."

Paul's eyes fill with tears, and he clears his throat, lowers his head, but not before Kate has noticed.

"What's wrong?" she asks him.

"That's what I want," he says.

"Lunch in a brown paper bag?"

"A heavenly father. A father to talk to. A father who sees me."

"Really?" Her smile is tentative.

"Yes. Someone to look up to."

"Most fathers are pretty run-of-the-mill," Kate says.

"Mine lives in Santa Barbara," Ruby says.

They look up, surprised to see her. Her nights have not been as tumultuous as before, but nevertheless she has continued to sleep late, until this morning, and she now stands before them in her underwear, with beads of perspiration in her hair and her bangs plastered to her forehead, holding a bowl overflowing with cereal. Shep, who has been uninterested in the honeydew melon and coffee, is brought to his feet by the scent of Cheerios.

"Hey there," Kate says.

"Hi there," answers Ruby. "What are you guys watching?"

"Ho there," Kate says.

"This lady wants your mom to be on her TV show," Paul says. He slides away from Kate on the sofa to make room for Ruby.

Ruby moves with extreme caution, as if once a floor had collapsed beneath her feet and forever compromised her faith in the durability of the physical world. Even at her slow pace, she has sloshed some Cheerios onto the floor, and Shep laps them up quickly.

"Thank you, Sheppy," she says, placing the bowl on the table and climbing between Paul and Kate. Mosquitoes have had their way with her; her bare legs are a mass of red stars in a milky way of white scratch marks.

"Look at you," Kate cries. "You've been eaten alive."

"I don't care," Ruby says. "Bites are funny. That we're food?" Ruby reaches for her cereal bowl and rests it in her lap and begins to eat.

The sound of an approaching car—the shudder of an engine, the nervous chewing sound of tires over gravel—captures Ruby's attention. She places her cereal bowl on the floor—Shep is eating it before Paul or Kate can stop him—and runs to the window to look out. "It's Evangeline," Ruby announces.

Kate looks at Paul questioningly and he shrugs.

"But it's Sunday," Kate persists.

"She's going to the shop," Ruby says.

"You've turned her into a workaholic," Kate says. "She never stops."

"She likes her job," Paul says.

"Now she sees me," Ruby says, waving to Evangeline. "And now she's coming to the house!"

Kate has a notion to tell Ruby to get some clothes on, but decides she has another year or two before lessons in bodily shame need to begin. Ruby, however, is stung by a dart of modesty and hurries up the stairs. A different sort of modesty compels Kate to turn off the TV—there seems something spongy and unclean about watching television in the morning, or watching it at all in front of anyone except your most intimate companion.

"Do you think I ought to let this person do a segment about me?" Kate asks, picking up the remote and speaking quickly to encourage a fast answer.

"She seems okay to me," says Paul.

The answer is so casual and ill-considered it strikes Kate as cavalier, almost contemptuous, and she feels herself falling through some internal emptiness she hadn't before realized was there, a sudden aloneness that makes her gasp. Instead of turning the set off, she mutes the sound, and a moment later Evangeline is knocking at the door and Kate calls for her to come in.

"I brought you that coffee you like," Evangeline says to Paul. Her exuberance and good cheer grace her with an aura of overflowing good health. She looks as if she is restraining herself from doing cartwheels across the room. Glancing uneasily at Kate, she adds, "There's actually enough for two. In fact this is triple-roasted Ethiopian and if you drink it all you probably won't close your eyes until Tuesday." She crouches down, placing the black-and-silver thermal cup on the table, and then pets Shep, stroking his ears. Shep moans affectionately.

"His energy seems down," Evangeline says.

"I was thinking that, too," says Paul.

"You think he might have a little Lyme disease?"

"Oh fuck," says Paul. "That's all we need."

"He seems fine to me," Kate offers.

"He's sort of gimpy, don't you think?" Paul says.

"He seems like his old self," says Kate. "We don't even know how old he is. Or what his medical past has been."

"I can't let anything happen to this dog," Paul says, and then, hearing himself, he adds, "Or any of us."

"His energies are definitely a little on the down side," Evangeline says, rising up again. "And you've got all those deer out there, each one of them infected with Lyme."

She watches the TV for a moment as the Lunch Bag Lady, her long, creased face a portrait of sorrow and contemplation, bows her head in a church. "Wow," Evangeline says, "I think I'd never get anything done if I had a TV. I could never turn it off."

"Oh it's not that difficult to turn off," Kate says.

"This show wants Kate to be on it," Paul says.

"Really? That's awesome," Evangeline says.

"Hey Evangeline," Ruby calls from upstairs. "Do you want to see what I got?"

"Okay," Evangeline calls back. "I'll be right up." Then she asks, in a whisper, "How's she doing?"

Kate doesn't think that Evangeline is in a position to be whispering inquiries about Ruby, but she answers nevertheless. "Actually, she seems great."

"Terrific. I'll run up there, and then I'm going to go out to the shop and work on dovetailing those mahogany drawers. God, let's keep away from mahogany."

"I know," Paul says. "It can be stubborn. But that's sort of what I love about it, too."

"Too stubborn for me," says Evangeline. "Pine's more my speed, you don't need to seduce it or force it."

"Like me!" Kate says, smiling brightly. She switches off the TV and tosses the remote control to the other end of the sofa.

The phone rings, and Paul, who generally seems deaf to its beseechments, moves quickly toward it and answers. After he says hello he is plunged into a frozen yet clearly agitated state of listening to someone's bad news. At last he says, "We're just hanging out. Come whenever."

"Who was that?" Kate asks.

"Annabelle. Bernard got a bad letter from the IMS."

"You mean the INS?"

"I guess. She wants to come over, they don't have anyone else to talk to."

"Should she be moving around?"

"I don't know. I guess she knows best." In a delayed reaction, Paul feels the affront of Kate's correcting his error about the INS, and suddenly it seems as if she is continually tidying up after his little verbal spills and he doesn't want her to do that anymore, not even one more time.

Kate takes a deep breath, but before she can speak the phone rings again. "My turn," she says, and takes the handset, presses the green button. "Sunday morning," she says.

"Hello, Kate, it's Sonny." There's a pause. The sound of traffic fills the silence. "Sonny B.," he adds. And then, lest there be any lingering doubt, "Sonny Briggs."

Kate feels a little jump of nerves: is there some place she is meant to be today? Is Sonny on his way to pick her up?

"Hello, Sonny. Where are you?"

"I don't know," he says. His breath catches in his throat and by the sound of it he is crying now. "I slipped, Kate. I slipped and fell."

For a moment she thinks he has actually fallen and hurt himself, and then she realizes this is someone trying to live sober, and even as pity goes through her like the slash of a knife, she is wondering: *Why is he calling me?*

"Have you called your sponsor?" she asks him, walking into the dining room.

"I don't want to," Sonny says. "You, I want to talk to you." Now, suddenly, he sounds so impaired, it reminds her of a bad actor playing a drunk, the kind that makes you think: that's not how it is, that's totally over the top. He seems to be talking while virtually unable to move his lips, and there is barely a rise or fall in the pitch of his voice, it's just a sliding, unhappy slur. If this voice had a hat it would be cockeyed, if it had a chin it would be dark with stubble. Yet it reminds her of something it's good for her to remember: being drunk makes you sound like an idiot. Why do they call it lit, or high, or flying, or even buzzed? Stoned, maybe, blasted, stumbling drunk, hammered. That's it. Hammered.

"Can you tell me where you are, Sonny?" she says. She continues walking through the dining room and into the kitchen. She sits at the table. Ruby has left the box of Cheerios open and left the milk out, too. There's a kidney-shaped puddle of milk on the floor. Where's the brown dog when you need him?

"I'm just driving around," Sonny says.

"You're going to hurt someone, Sonny. I want you to pull over right now."

"I can't go home."

"I don't want you to go home, Sonny. You're not in a condition to go anywhere. I want you to pull over and tell me where you are and I'll come and get you."

"You'd do that?"

"Of course I would. It's what we do."

"Fuck," Sonny says through tears.

"Have you done it?" Kate asks.

"What?"

"Have you pulled your car over someplace safe?"

"No."

"I'm hanging up. I don't want to be on the phone with you when you run somebody over, or kill yourself."

"Wait," he says.

"Why? What am I waiting for?"

"I'm at the top of your driveway. I'm sorry, I'm sorry. Oh, shit, somebody's following me." The connection goes dead.

Kate goes to the sink. The window there gives her a view of the courtyard in the back of the house as well as the driveway. All is serene for a moment or two until she hears the familiar sound of Sonny's blue Ford Taurus, with its suddenly well-deserved bumper sticker. Close behind is an unfamiliar car, a white sedan. At the wheel of the second car is Bernard, with his bare left arm hanging out the window, and his rising and falling fingertips tapping out a complicated rhythm on the door.

Kate goes back to the living room to tell Paul his sister and Bernard have arrived and that Sonny has come over, as well. He is sitting with Shep on the sofa—on the sofa!—with his arm around the dog's shoulders, while the dog pants. Paul presses his forehead against the side of the dog's head.

"Are you okay?" Kate asks.

"Not really," Paul answers.

"Your sister and Bernard just pulled in. And Sonny Briggs is here, too."

"Why is he here? Are you going somewhere?"

"He just wants to talk for a few minutes."

As Kate turns to leave, Evangeline comes into the room, carrying Ruby on her back.

"Is it okay with you guys if Ruby comes out to the shop with me?" Evangeline asks.

"Perfect," Kate says with a wave, brushing past them on her way to Sonny, joined by Paul who is on his way to greet Annabelle and Bernard.

For a few moments they are all gathered at the base of the circular drive. The confluence of chrome bumpers reflects the hot summer sun, sending out bursts of blinding light. Sonny, perhaps wondering if his appearance and manner are going to be sufficient to convince Kate of the gravity of his situation, is holding a nearly empty vodka bottle in one hand and in the other hand a bottle on which the seal has not been broken yet. Choosing at the last moment to try to act charming, Sonny addresses his initial remarks to Ruby, who is peering at him over Evangeline's shoulder. "Well look at you up there," he says. "You've got a chauffeur just like your mom!"

"Come on in, Sonny," Kate says. "You can help me make some coffee." She cups her hand on his elbow to guide him in and with her free hand she relieves him of one of the vodka bottles.

Paul catches Kate's glance and relieves Sonny of bottle number two, giving him a pat of greeting and acceptance with his other hand and saying hello to his sister and brother-in-law.

Annabelle, dressed in pale orange pajamas and a white cotton robe, moves with difficulty over the pea stone driveway and watches her slippered feet, as if they might suddenly do something rash. Bernard keeps his hands just beyond the outlines of her body, hovering and practically vibrating, as if creating a force field of support for her.

"Oh, Annabelle," Evangeline says, "it's so great you're already out."

"Yeah, thanks. I'm not so sure this was the best idea in the world."

As she leads Sonny into the kitchen, Kate hears Evangeline saying, "No, no, it's always better to move around if you can," and Kate wonders on what medical authority a carpenter's apprentice makes this statement.

Paul turns to watch Kate bringing Sonny into the house, and seeing her helping someone is compelling, almost erotic. This is the woman who loves him. This is the woman who has opened her home to him, given her body to him, shared her child, her money, her mind. She is the person whom Sonny seeks in his desperation, the woman whom people wait in line to see, buying her books and listening to her show on the radio—how could this creature, through whom people find their way to goodness and God, look at him and say: let's eat, let's talk, let's make love, let's make a life together?

That this would happen to *him* is not a miracle like the parting of the waters or the raising of Lazarus, it is a sort of slow-motion miracle, an incremental, daily wonder, full of sleeping and silence and not even realizing your own good fortune. From November on Paul experienced Kate's love with amazement and gratitude—had he ever given anyone a better reason to turn away from him? Yet just as there are moments when he forgets he has taken a life, there are moments when he is no more grateful for Kate than he is for his own breathing. But she has seen the darkness and she not only decided not to turn away but she has followed him into it, and now the darkness belongs to both of them, and they belong to it.

Kate opens the door to the kitchen, dislodging the sun's reflection, and then she is gone, the door is shut, the sun returns in its bluish pool of old glass, and with a lurch Paul realizes they were not able to really talk about *First Thing Sunday Morning*. What had happened? What had he said? The day and all that needed to be said is being hijacked by all these people.

"I don't want any coffee," Sonny is saying to Kate.

"You have to have coffee," she says. "It'll make you feel better."

"I don't want to feel better."

Kate is at the sink. She lets the water pound into the teakettle, in whose silvery curvature her face swells. She puts the kettle on the burner grate, turns on the gas, and the flame blooms yellow and blue.

"Listen, Sonny. I didn't invite you here for a pity party. I got you off the road because you blew it and you were a danger to others out there."

"I was being careful."

"Not really. You're lucky nothing happened. You could have killed someone."

"I want to kill myself."

"Really? Maybe that's what you should do. Not putting other people's lives in jeopardy. Do you have any idea what it would be like to take a life, to actually kill another human being? You guys . . ." Her voice trails off as she takes a seat at the table, directly across from Sonny.

"I'm not like other guys," he says.

"Really? Are you sure?" She hears Paul's voice in the other room, but she can't make out what he's saying. *We can't always protect you? We can always connect you? Detect you? Inspect you?* And then there comes Annabelle's voice, nearly as slurred as Sonny's—Vicodin, surely, but who knows what else is going on? the brain is such a hot-house flower and hers has been bounced around—making grateful-sounding murmurs.

"All it takes is one second, Sonny," Kate says. "Someone's injured, killed. Lives are ruined."

"I drove *here*," he says, jabbing his finger against the table. "This is where I wanted to be."

"Do you know why?"

"Yeah, I sure do." His voice trembles and to compensate for this he draws himself up, looks at her defiantly, almost glaring. "Because this is where you are. And I just fucking love you, Kate."

She reaches across the table and gently touches his wrist with her fingertip and then withdraws her hand. "Sonny, you are so in love with Chantal, there's not really room in your heart for some-body else. Remember? How she massages your back when you come home from work? How she doesn't let you drive when you go out together? Chantal! Anyhow that's not why you came here. That may be what you're telling yourself, but it's really not the reason. You came here because you knew I was going to be really mad at you for drinking."

"You're the most special person I've ever known," Sonny says miserably. He forces himself to keep his eyes on her.

"Oh please, will you stop this bullshit. You're going to make up this entire saga about the things we do for love, but it's really about the things we do for alcohol. It's like a demon, Sonny, and it's furious with you for turning your back on it. It will do anything and say anything to get you to put it inside of you. How many days do you have?"

"I don't know."

"Let's figure it out. I remember it was winter when you came to your first meeting. Right?"

"You had a cold," Sonny says. "You were holding your coffee cup with both hands and the tip of your nose was red."

"Shut the fuck up. Okay? And help me figure this out. What month was it?"

"February."

"That's right. I remember. February what?"

"February 15."

"So you remember. That's interesting." Kate pauses, thinks. "That's the day after Valentine's Day."

"Yeah."

"So let me ask you something. This is just a shot in the dark—but was deciding to get sober your Valentine's present to Chantal?" She doesn't wait for Sonny's reply; there's little doubt in her mind that she's right. "And now you've decided to take it back? Is that what's happening?"

"I'm not taking anything back. I just had a drink."

"You've got about six months in, Sonny. That's a tough time for all of us. I really struggled around this time, too. It's like the first few months it's such a novelty being sober and everything seems so bright and hopeful, and it's just life, day after day, ups and downs, and then a little voice starts to tell you *Well, we've accomplished that, we've proven we're not alcoholic, because you can't be alcoholic and not drink for six months, so now that that's been put to rest let's celebrate with a drink.* Right?"

Sonny shrugs.

"I know I'm right. Look, Sonny, we all struggle, day by day." The teakettle begins to whistle, first a low note and as the water's turmoil increases the whistle winds toward a shriek. "See?" Kate says, getting up. "Even the teakettle agrees with me."

"I drank because I wanted to see you," Sonny says, rather loudly, even though Kate has only walked to the stove. She extinguishes the flame and the kettle swallows its cry.

"No, Sonny. It's just not true. You wanted to see me because you drank." She pulls a couple of cups out of the cupboard and puts a plastic cone over the coffeepot, and, advancing on all fronts, she puts enough coffee in the paper filter to make the coffee very, very strong: what reason cannot do, caffeine may well accomplish.

"I feel sick," he says.

"Good, the less pleasure the better."

"Yeah, I guess. It's my higher power making me nauseous."

"Maybe. Or it could be the vodka."

He looks at her quizzically.

"Look, Sonny, what the fuck do I know? I'm out there beating the drum for Jesus but I don't know anything you don't know. Higher power." She says the words as if they were *pixie dust*. "Maybe we're really just here on our own, like all the other animals, and maybe there's no one looking down and no one ordering events in any way, and the universe isn't keeping score, and there's no karma and no balance and good deeds aren't rewarded and the wicked aren't punished—it doesn't matter. We still can't drink."

The coffee is made. Kate remembers that Sonny likes his with no sugar but a lot of milk and as she goes to the refrigerator this knowledge of what this man likes and doesn't like gives her a strange, peaceful feeling of happiness.

"I can't believe you remembered all that stuff about Chantal," Sonny says, taking the cup from her.

"It's my job. I was going to ask you if I could use it sometime."

"I think she's got Lyme disease. She's achy and tired. You know she's always in the garden and at night the deer come to feed there, too. There's a lot of Lyme around."

"So I hear," Kate says.

Sonny takes a long drink of coffee, and then with exaggerated caution sets the cup down. "I better go," he says.

"You're still pretty hammered, Sonny."

"I'm mostly just tired."

"Why not call home? Tell Chantal where you are and take a little nap. When was your last drink?"

"Top of your driveway."

Kate laughs, surprising them both. "Okay. Well maybe a big nap."

"I thought maybe we could pray together."

His eyes, once drowning in vodka-infused anguish, take on a sudden keenness, and it seems to Kate that he has an instinct that something has changed in her.

"Sonny, I'm sorry. I can't help you there. Let's just find you a place to crash for a couple of hours. You want me to call Chantal for you?"

"I better do it. She's not going to want to hear your voice."

"Oh no."

"I had to tell her."

"Oh Sonny. That was really not nice."

Sonny lifts his chin, purses his lips, like a captain deciding to go down with his ship, though in his case the ship is someone else's heartbreak and actually he is not really on board.

In the front of the house, Paul sits with his sister and Bernard, listening, with his hands folded between his knees and his head down. Bernard is telling him about what the INS seems to be focusing on in their investigation.

"They are now saying Cessez-Feu was a meeting place for Phalangists," Bernard says, his normally careful, tranquil voice now curdled with contempt.

"What is Cessez-Feu again?" Paul asks.

"My club in Beirut."

"It means cease-fire," Annabelle says, as if that alone should exonerate her husband.

"And what's a Phalangist?" Paul asks. "I'm sorry, but I'm just a simple carpenter."

"They're a Christian party in Lebanon, with its share of bad elements," Bernard says. "I had nothing to do with them. They call themselves Social Democrats, they call themselves Kataeb, in the end they stay true to their origins, which is with the fascists of Spain and Italy. The man who brought these ideas to Lebanon was Pierre Gemayel, who was a family friend, though not a close one, and now that's being used against me."

"They were all Maronites," says Annabelle. "So of course they knew each other. All the well-off Christian families knew each other. It's so ridiculous. Listen, Paul. I don't know what to tell you. They're talking about kicking Bernard out of the country."

"I don't excuse the behavior of the Phalangists," Bernard says. The sun pours through the windows behind him and the thick old glass bends the light so that it touches the back of Bernard's head pinkishly and pale greenishly. He sits next to Annabelle and he pats her hand with the steadiness of a metronome as he speaks. "They committed unforgivable atrocities in the name of the Blessed Virgin. During the Civil War they were very bad."

"Wow, religious fanatics doing bad things," Annabelle says. "Stop the presses."

"But why is the government bothering you right now?"

"We don't know," says Bernard. "It seems to be coming out of nowhere."

"Bernard," Annabelle says, giving his name a cautionary curl.

"Well perhaps you would prefer to make the explanations," Bernard says.

"His wife," Annabelle says. "We think she contacted someone at State or some other agency. The Beauty Queen's in and out of the U.S. all the time."

"You must not call her that," Bernard says.

"Wait a second," Paul says. "You're Bernard's wife."

Annabelle waggles her hand back and forth. "It seems Bernard forgot to get divorced from his first wife, the well-named Reem. But, yes, I am his wife and yes we did get married—but now there's a question of its validity. So we're fucked."

"I have not seen Reem for thirteen years," Bernard says. "That we are still married is a fantasia."

Paul has not noticed before how delicate Bernard is—or perhaps fear has shrunk him in some way. His bright yellow short-sleeved shirt is three sizes too big; when he shrugs his shoulders they seem no larger than tennis balls. He wears white linen slacks and gray slippers without socks, revealing slender ankles.

"The point is what are we going to do about it?" Annabelle says. "We need a lawyer."

"Oh, that's too bad," says Paul.

"Bernard has been given the name of a very good immigration

attorney," Annabelle says. "Most of the people practicing immigration law are just a bunch of kids or old lefties. But this guy—his name is Hodding Wainwright—has had years of State Department experience and he's supposed to know everyone you need to know to get this horrible mess straightened out."

"It's strange how the law seems to be completely asleep," Paul says, "and then suddenly one day it just opens its eyes and grabs you."

"It was not my intention to be here under false pretenses," Bernard says. "Now they are going to be making a picture of me as a religious extremist, when all I am is a simple man who owned a bar in a troubled city. How was I to conduct myself? To refuse service to my Maronite clients? At Cessez-Feu when you walked in the door you were welcome."

"They're going to come after me at the post office, too, I can guarantee you," Annabelle says. "A federal employee implicated in a green card marriage? That will really be something."

"So this lawyer," Paul says. He clears his throat and the sound of it rouses Shep, who has been relaxing on the cool, roast beef–colored bricks in front of the hearth. The dog picks himself up rather carefully and hobbles over to Paul and collapses onto the floor again with a long, low groan.

"Yes," Annabelle says. "He can help. At least we think he can."

"Is he expensive?" Paul asks, because in this instant he has realized that is why Annabelle and Bernard are here: they need to borrow money.

"Very," says Annabelle. "We might find a lawyer to do it out of the goodness of his heart, but it won't be Hodding Wainwright."

"The dog is looking at me with unusual interest," Bernard says.

"I think he knows your family ate someone from his family," Annabelle says.

"We did nothing of the kind. It was discussed and rejected."

"I can pony up," Paul says. "I want you two to stay."

"Oh Paul," Annabelle says. "I love you, I really do." She stops, considers what she has said, and decides to amend it. "Not for the money, but I just do. I always have."

"How much do you need?" Paul asks.

"We're not sure," Annabelle says. "Maybe ten thousand dollars. For the retainer. We have some of it, but frankly our savings are depleted. How much can you spare?"

"I can spare whatever I have," Paul says. He feels a rush of joy and it is so alive and so energizing that it is all he can do to remain seated and not rush upstairs and bring down the two shoe boxes in the back of his clothes closet, both of which are filled with fifty- and hundred-dollar bills. He remembers counting the cash before closing the boxes; there was three thousand dollars in each box, rubber-banded and then covered with pigeon-pink-and-gray slate roofing tiles rescued from a demolished Lutheran church, not to conceal the money but merely to keep it flat.

Sunday continues to be a day of unexpected visitors. Cheryl arrives to have words with Evangeline, and ends up staying, playing with Ruby while Evangeline runs the lathe. The painter Hunter DeMille, whose lighthouse Paul has been working on, arrives in his Aston-Martin spontaneously stopping by after a visit to the Sunday farmer's market in Leyden, though the later he stays the more clear it becomes he has not completely given up on the idea of buying Shep and presenting the dog to his seven-year-old son, Cooper. The last time DeMille attempted to buy Shep off of Paul he had begun by offering five hundred dollars and finally worked himself up to the incomprehensible sum of ten thousand, and the coincidence of that being what Bernard's lawyer needs drones like a honey-drunk bee around and around Paul's mind as DeMille wanders nonchalantly through Paul's workshop.

Hunter is unaware that Evangeline has not said one word to him, nor does the tall, brooding painter notice her scornful glances. After having spent years admiring his work and studying him in her art history classes at the college, she has not forgiven him for disillusioning her with his presumptuous behavior regarding Paul's dog, though Cheryl seems not to have heard anything about this little skirmish of wills and, no stranger to art history herself, cannot take her eyes off of DeMille. Shep is hobbling along with them but barely lifting his head, not even when Ruby tempts him with little pieces of cookie, which she has brought out to the workshop despite the rule not to. Paul is showing DeMille some long curls of charcoal-gray bark stripped from a plum-cherry tree, bark which Paul plans to dry, lacquer, and cut into small squares to use as inlay, which he will work into the edge of a countertop, along with the greenish nubby bark of a possum wood. Suddenly, DeMille whirls on Evangeline and looks frankly at her, in an openly appraising way, up and down, his eyes resting on this feature or that. "I'd like to paint you," he announces. "I'm doing a series called 'Ten Triptychs in a Semiclassical Mode,' and I want you in them."

Bernard and Kate are on the patio, reading the Sunday papers, while Annabelle rests on the sofa, gathering her strength before the ride home. Sonny Briggs's wife, Chantal, arrives, dressed as if for a beauty contest at a county fair, in cut-off jeans and the tails of her checkered shirt tied off at the navel, wearing high-heeled sandals and plenty of lipstick. For moral support, she has arrived with her friend Wendy Moots, who has two coincidental connections to the people already gathered at Kate's house—she is a nurse at Windsor County, working the same floor that Annabelle was on after the accident, and she is the sister of Liza Moots, the housekeeper-astrologist-potter whose paralyzing fear of dogs Paul and Shep have helped her to conquer. Chantal seems uncertain as to what attitude to strike in the odd situation in which she finds herself, and her demeanor veers unpredictably from iciness to abashment. She asks where she might find her *husband*, giving the word a weightiness it can barely support, and then she goes upstairs to the guest room where Sonny sleeps. Wendy Moots, in the meanwhile, is treating Shep, about whom she has apparently heard a great deal, as if he were a long-lost relative or perhaps a celebrity. "It's you, I can't believe it's you," she says, squatting down on her powerful haunches and getting face to face with the dog, who seems to have perked up considerably, stimulated by the promising rush of human activity.

As the afternoon arrives, they are all eleven of them seated at a long table on the patio in the full, glorious sunlight with the deep, spicy smell of someone's newly mowed field perfuming the light breeze and no sounds except those of human voices and the mysterious telegraphy of the few birds and squirrels who continue to forage despite the midday heat. Paul has chosen a dozen Brandywine tomatoes from the little garden he maintains behind his workshop, along with several stalks of purple basil, and he's made a salad of it with the mozzarella Hunter DeMille had in his car along with his other groceries—the cheese has practically liquefied in the heat but its near ruination has brought out its hidden milky and nutty flavors, and in combination with the moist, warm tomatoes and the wild astringency of the basil, olive oil, salt, pepper, and a few chopped cloves of garlic, the salad is devoured by everyone with exclamations of amazement.

A languid sort of merriness prevails as the meal is consumed in the August heat. Toasts are proposed to summer and to the tomatoes and Sonny stands with tears streaming down his face and raises his cup of sparkling water and makes a toast to Chantal, who looks at her husband with adoration and the supreme human kindness of forgiveness. All through the lunch, Paul and Kate exchange helpless but happy looks, and Paul tries to communicate with his eyes alone that he is anxious to return to the conversation they were having before their Sunday took its unexpected turn.

But that time doesn't come until nearly evening, with the sky still blue but seeming to wither and the heat suddenly inescapable. Their visitors have at long last left and Kate has taken a nap, falling into unconsciousness as if she has spent the afternoon drinking wine. Paul and Ruby have put the dishes in the dishwasher and done their usual half-assed job of straightening up, and now they sit on the sofa in the front of the house while Ruby reads aloud from the newest install-ment of the Harry Potter saga, and Paul does his best to stay engaged. Somewhere along the way, Paul succumbs to Shep's imploring stare and pats the cushion, inviting Shep to sit next to him. As he drifts in and out of listening to Ruby, Paul is overcome by a wave of melan-choly. *Someday*, he thinks, *this will all be gone.* Ruby's childhood, for all its troubles, seems so delicate and fleeting, and that will be gone, as will the velvet nights of August and the summer itself. This house that he has arrived in as if purely by chance—what law of the universe will keep him here? These bricks, the wood, the glass in the windows, the smell of the air, the deep, snoozing breaths of the great brown dog, the love he has been given, everything feels impermanent, and everything *is* impermanent. It is the mute, sorrowing knowledge of summer's end, the knowledge that comes when you are listening to the guileless piping of a child's voice, the knowledge of a man who knows that everything changes without warning, a man who some-times looks at his own hands and shudders at the sight of them.

It is dark by eight-thirty. The coyotes, who normally don't begin their revels until midnight, are already yipping and yodeling and howling. The owls are hooting and the bullfrogs have begun their chorus of moans. The cicadas have arrived and their innumerable cries fill the air like a vast electrical disturbance. Ruby falls asleep on the sofa and Paul carries her up to her bed. When he comes down, Kate is in front of the empty hearth, wrapped in a blanket, her hair chaotic from what must have been a fitful nap.

"You're up," Paul says.

"You should have wakened me. I slept for two and a half hours."

"You must have needed it."

Kate pats the sofa, hoping that Paul will sit next to her, and the force of her hand launches a small cloud of dog hairs left by Shep earlier in the evening. "Goddamit," she says.

When Paul has gotten close, she presses herself against him, wraps her arms around him. "Brrr."

"It's actually a little warm," Paul says.

"Does it seem ridiculous, me going on that TV show?"

"No. I don't even know what you're worrying about. You're good at your job. You're good at everything."

"I'm just tired of being this person. The person who has all the answers. Ms. Grace and Spirituality. I'm sort of sick of it, to tell you the truth."

They hear Shep's claws as he walks down the stairs. With Ruby asleep he has been released and now he clicks into the front room and makes eye contact with neither of them, as if there is some chance he won't be noticed, and slowly lies down on the hooked rug.

"Maybe you're tired," Paul says. "You work all the time."

"Maybe." She leans forward, peers at the dog. "He does seem a little under the weather."

"Yeah. I think Annabelle was right. I'm going to take him to Julian tomorrow."

Julian? Is that a place? And then she remembers: Julian Atkins, the vet.

"I know this sounds a little crazy," Paul says.

"Feel free. This is the house that craziness built."

"I don't believe God is going to let anything too bad happen to Shep."

"I don't know what to think," Kate says.

"I just think," Paul says, "that whatever happened, you know, back then, me finding him and taking him away from that man, it was all just somehow meant to be. And now this silence, this long big nothing that followed it?" His voice drops to a whisper and he moves his lips closer to her. "It just seems that as far as the universe is concerned, what I did was basically okay. And I'll tell you another thing. I'm so glad we went back there that time. Now at least I know that he's still not just lying there waiting for someone to find him. Now it's really between me and God."

"Paul," Kate says, moving away, just to turn and look at him. "I got a FedEx the other day from my agent, and inside it was a huge check. Royalties for my book."

"Great. I actually gave away a bunch of money today. It seems sort of fitting."

Kate blinks, deciding not to make any inquiries about this. "It was for about a million dollars."

"Are you serious?"

"And there's at least one more coming that will be at least that much, or maybe more. And the way I figure it if I do this little TV show there will be another big check after that. I really think I need to maximize this thing. Just keep it going while it's going because I'll tell you this—I am never going to write another book like this again. I'm not going to keep going with Heartland and I'm not doing any more appearances. I've reached the end."

"I don't blame you. It's exhausting."

"It's more than that. I don't even want to say. But I'm going to let it run its course and then there's something I want to do."

"You're amazing."

"I want to take all the money, every penny of it, and I want to sell the house—this area is hopping and I'm sure I can get a lot of dough for it—and I want us to move."

"Move? Where would we go?"

"I don't know. I was thinking about Greece. I don't mean now. Maybe in six months? After that the book will stop selling anyhow, that's how books are."

"Are you serious?"

"Or Italy. Someplace beautiful. What you do, you can do anywhere. Same with me. And it's not as if Ruby is exactly thriving here. She can have one of those international childhoods. And we'll have enough money, we won't have to worry. We can be these very cool and mysterious expatriates no one can quite figure out. We'll walk into our favorite little seaside café and people will say *I wonder what their story is.* It'll be good. And we'll have each other. If you are half as into me as I am into you that will be more than enough. I could light up a city with how much I love you. We'll be fine."

"I'm fine here. Anywhere with you." He feels the sting of tears. Who knew such a love was possible?

"You know where I would love to go? Mykonos. My ex and I were on our terrible little honeymoon, skipping around Greece as if we were on a scavenger hunt looking for happiness. Everything was off, every museum was closed, every meal was a disaster, Joe sprained his ankle in Crete, I was stung by a bee right above my eye and my eye was as closed as the museums—but Mykonos was magical. I've always wanted to return."

"It's beautiful there," Paul says. "I once stayed in this amazing house surrounded by palm trees. We cooked octopus on an open fire."

"You were there? Cooking *octopi*? Sounds romantic in a sort of grotesque way. Who were you with?"

"It was a while ago," Paul says. "But Kate? I'm not going to let you tear down your whole life."

"I'm scared all the time, Paul."

"You don't need to be."

"Paul! There's no magic spell. There's no karma, there's no making a special deal between you and fate, there's nothing but what happened and what might happen next and I think we need to get out of the way. We need to be away. We need to be out of here. Things can happen, things we can't foresee. God, maybe six months is too long to wait. Maybe we can get out of here in four. You might say something to someone, or I might. Just by accident. And Ruby. Fuck! You can see what this is doing to her. She knows something's wrong. And I do, too. We're too close to where it happened. What if something happens to you? What if you're taken away? I'm scared."

She's allowed her voice to rise, and hearing it startles her into silence. Instinctively, she claps her hand over her mouth. "You see what I mean?" She whispers the question, and even in the darkness that has gathered Paul can see her eyes are wide with fright.

The September sky seems uncommonly blue and a bit farther from the earth than any sky Paul remembers seeing ever before, as if the old sky has been torn away like wrapping paper to reveal a sky beyond that, a sky that in the bright blue daylight is luminous and uncreased.

Paul is scheduled to meet with a couple new to Leyden, a man named Wolf Damberg, who is a private dealer in Renaissance art, and his boyfriend Leonard Harris, who was a violinist for the New York Philharmonic until an early onset of arthritis ended his career. Damberg and Harris have recently purchased Rose Hall, a small cottage locally famous for its spectacular plantings—over eighty varieties of rose, some in colors almost unheard of in roses: shades of brown and blue. The house, however, holds moisture in its old timbers and the humidity is creating havoc with Damberg's cache of ancient drawings and paintings. The two men want to turn their home's largest room into a temperature- and humidity-controlled archive, in which Damberg's stock will be safe. They want the walls paneled in oak, they want the ceiling lowered, and they want wide, deep archival drawers in which the hundreds of valuable works of art can be stored indefinitely without risk of discoloration, fading, or curling. Paul has sent Evangeline to Rose Hall to go over the plans for the upcoming project, along with a basket of pale orange French tomatoes, picking the last off his best plant, hoping to convey that his absence from today's meeting does not suggest a lack of interest.

Now, alone in the workshop, he looks down at Shep and tries to remember if he gave the dog an antibiotic tablet at the morning meal. "Hey, Shep," he says, "no kidding around this time. Did you get your pill at breakfast?" The dog, who Paul often thinks is his closest confidant, even though they do not speak the same language, wags his tail energetically. Paul has come to realize this wagging is not necessarily a sign of happiness. More often it means Shep is confused and does not know what is expected of him. If the wagging means anything that could be put into simple English it is a request for clarification. "Come here," and when the dog is next to him Paul lifts his muzzle and sniffs at his mouth—sometimes there's a rank reverb of the pill on the dog's breath. But all he can smell is kibble and tongue. Shep, having no idea why Paul is sniffing him, places his forepaws on Paul's shoe tops, and when Paul lifts his shirt and covers the dog's head Shep stiffens his legs and presses his profile onto his belly.

With Shep contentedly breathing beneath his shirt, Paul looks around at all that he will leave behind him in a few months—this perfect work space, this silvery light he has come to know so well, the exact unevenness of the floor, board after board of precious woods, the tools swapped for, worked for, and purchased over two decades, the peeling frames and mullions, the old glass, the hooks and hinges, bin pulls and latches of another time, another world. It's overwhelming to think of the work involved in bringing any of it with him, and he thinks the easiest thing to do is to transfer it all to Evangeline.

She can pay for it whenever she's got the business running smoothly again.

He uncovers Shep's head and the dog looks up at him with a kind of wild goofiness and prods him with his snout, perhaps asking for more time under the shirt. "I don't believe you had your pill this morning," Paul says.

Paul walks with Shep into the house, passing Kate's writing studio on the way. Two weeks ago, the crew who was here to tape Kate's segment on *First Thing Sunday Morning* knocked down the rock border Paul himself once built along the edges of the driveway, and he reminds himself to repair the damage, though knowing he and Kate and Ruby are not long for this place saps his will to keep up with the repairs. Every time Shep passes the wrecked spots on the driveway he sniffs at the ground and the dislodged stones with almost absurd avidity, as if they contained the answer to some great mystery. When the crew was here, he was in turn ill-tempered and gregarious, and though Paul tried to keep the dog out of the way, Shep several times bounded into the shot with his signature seesaw motion.

"No, that's fine, we like the dog," the assistant director had called to Paul, as he pulled Shep out of the way.

Parallel now with Kate's windows, Paul keeps his head down so she will know he isn't going to disturb her while she's at work; he sees her, glancingly, pacing back and forth; the whoosh of the oscillating fan lifts her hair when she crosses its path. She holds the phone to her ear, but he can't tell if she's talking or listening. Since last Sunday's appearance on TV, Kate has been on the phone for hours—with her agent, with her publisher, with her growing list of foreign publishers, with the agency that books her appearances, and with those reporters not too proud to pursue a story begun by another journalist.

The house remains cool in the summer if they keep the shades and curtains drawn, but neither Paul nor Kate has the heart for it in these fleeting days before the autumn chill and so it feels close everywhere in the house, especially in the kitchen. Paul lodges a doxycycline pill in a small chunk of brie and tosses it to Shep, who swallows it instantly, his tail slapping a tom-tom beat of approval on the warm wooden floor. Rather than closing the refrigerator, Paul looks for things he might make for lunch and in short order he has made what might be the last tomato and basil salad of the year, and cut up some apples he got from the Martin orchard, which is between Kate's house and town, and which specializes in disappearing varieties and has some early ripening Boikens and Henry Clays. Paul arranges the apples on the platter and pours some balsamic vinegar on his hands and flicks the vinegar onto the apples, freckling them with it. Finally, he squeezes some lemons into a pitcher and puts in a little bit of cane syrup and a bottle of sparkling water and a few mint leaves and stirs it all together.

At lunch, Paul and Kate talk about the dietary recommendations that Ruby's therapist, Dr. Montgomery, has made—as little sugar as possible, avoid packaged foods with their high-fructose corn syrup, dyes, and preservatives, no caffeine.

"It makes sense," Paul says. "Everything in nature reacts to what it ingests. Birds, bees, trees. You can tell the state of the soil by looking at the leaves of the trees, their bark."

"First of all: caffeine? What does Dr. Montgomery think? We're sending Ruby to school with a cappuccino?"

"She's probably thinking about sodas," Paul says.

"Well wouldn't that be covered in the no-sweets rule?"

"Some people give their kids diet colas."

"That wouldn't be covered in the no-additives rule?"

"I feel sorry for anyone who has to argue with you."

"You mean you feel sorry for yourself?"

"No, I don't have to argue with you. I just sit back and amaze."

"I know I'm a pain in the ass," Kate says. "But at least I . . ." She is about to say *at least I never killed anyone.* But the joke is impossible, insane, cruel, and she chooses instead the awkwardness and perhaps even the obviousness of a sudden silence.

"I think Dr. Montgomery's doing a pretty good job," Paul says. "I'm not much for therapy and all that, but you have to admit Ruby seems a little happier."

"She does, she really does. Maybe we can take Montgomery to Mykonos with us. Can I have the last . . ." She counts the remaining slices of apple on the platter. "Eleven slices of apple?"

"Take eight."

As Kate picks up the vinegar-flecked apples, the sound of an auto closes in on the house.

"Remember when this place was sort of tucked away and cozy?" Kate asks.

"I do."

"When people come to see us in Mykonos they'll be in little sailboats and by the time they've got them all tied up and they've shivered their timbers and hoisted up their hoisters we'll be halfway up the stony little goat path behind our house, and when they come in all they'll find are two abandoned little cups of espresso and an unmade bed." Kate has slid out of her chair and goes to the window in a sideways fashion, hoping not to be seen. A van with something written on the side—she sees the word ELKINS and that's all Kate can make out—has pulled in front of the house. The van has Pennsylvania plates.

"Here's the good news," she says to Paul. "It's not Joyce Drazen wanting me to help her get Nina into the Sorbonne."

Whoever is in the van is slow to get out. Kate can vaguely make out a woman's silhouette behind the wheel, but she seems motionless. Paul places his glass of lemonade onto the kitchen table and it thunks against the wood, a sound that will resonate in his memory for years, the sound that marks the ending of one part of his life and the beginning of another.

At last, the van's door opens, and a woman slowly emerges, looking so bony and light that a decent pair of wings might make her airborne. Her pixie-cut hair is russet, the color the leaves will be next month. She is wearing skinny blue jeans and a yellow cotton sweater, and she is holding something in her hand, a photograph.

"I'll get it," Paul says, when they hear the knocks at the door, four knocks in four/four time, *largo*. "You can go upstairs, or just stay here."

"Under the table might be nice. I haven't been under a table since my old Pinot Grigio days."

"I'll meet you there after I send whoever this is away."

In the foyer, Paul glances up at the ceiling a little crack has presented itself in the plaster. Another thing he probably won't be able to get to . . . He opens the door and because this door doesn't have a screen he and the visitor stand with barely three feet between them. She looks extremely nervous. Her breathing is rapid and shallow; her eyes are so glassy that for a moment Paul wonders if she's blind.

"Hey," he says. "I don't want to be a bad guy here, but we're not really into people just dropping by. I see you've come a long way, and I hate to do this to you, but I'm going to have to ask you to leave." He lowers his eyes, not wanting to intimidate this woman with direct eye contact, and he sees a few flakes of white plaster on the floor, and then he looks up at the ceiling and sees that the crack is a bit worse than the last time he looked.

"My name is Dinah Maloney," the woman says, "and I think you have my dog." She holds up the photograph; it shows her and Shep at what looks like a birthday party in a wainscoted parlor, with a white marble hearth and a Persian rug. She has one hand on young Shep's shoulder as she leans over a blazing birthday cake; they are both wearing orange-and-silver party hats. "I've got hundreds of pictures of Woody, but I brought this one because it's both of us together," Dinah says.

"Oh my God," Paul says, before it occurs to him that right now it might be better to say nothing at all. But it cannot be unsaid.

No longer able to resist his instinct to follow Paul, or perhaps hearing Dinah Maloney's voice, Shep has come to the entrance foyer, preceded by the click of his claws against the wooden floors.

"Woody!" Dinah cries. Her face contorts as if she is in pain and she drops the photograph, which does not fall to the ground right away but is suspended in midair for a moment, drifting left and right, like a boat rocking in a lagoon. "Woody, Woody, I knew it."

Shep stops in his tracks, still some ten feet away. He cocks his head, repositioning his ears to hear the woman's half-familiar and half-forgotten voice. A moment before, his mouth was open and his tongue was out, giving him an insouciant appearance; now he draws his tongue back and his mouth is shut.

"Come on," Paul says to Shep, "let's go out." And then, to Dinah, "We can talk out here."

But Dinah has fallen to her knees and her arms are outstretched. "Woody, Woody," she calls. Slowly, the dog approaches her, his tail making its helicopter spin at an ever-quickening rate. He takes a couple more tentative steps toward Dinah, until finally her fingers can touch him. Since coming home and finding he had been stolen, Dinah has posted thousands of Lost Dog notices on lampposts and bulletin boards, farther and farther from her home. She has put notices in the newspapers, called innumerable animal rescue organizations, pounds, and veterinarians. She has offered such a handsome reward that she has had to deal with dozens of false leads. She has gotten calls from people who have spotted stray poodles and beagles; even a one-eyed disoriented cat was enough to trigger a call from one slurring, gravel-voiced fortune hunter. Every failure had the perverse power of increasing desire and mocking hope, until the longing for her dog became almost unendurable, and the undying hope of ever finding him began to seem like madness.

Yet here he is! And when she buries her fingers in his brown, red, and black fur, the touch transmits joy from her fingertips to her mind, to her heart, to every receptor of sensation in her body, and though no one who knows Dinah has ever described her as overly emotional, she is full of heedless passion, moaning, crooning, and weeping, and though she is in some ways quite out of her mind right now, this is a moment she will never forget, a moment she will always say is the happiest of her life.

Kate, having heard the cries, comes to the door and sees Dinah with her face buried in the thick, variegated fur on the back of Shep's neck.

"Oh hi," Dinah says.

"Are you all right?" Kate asks. At this moment, her guess is this is somehow AA-related and she needs to help this person.

"We're okay out here, Kate," Paul says. "It'll be a few minutes."

"But . . ."

"Please," Paul says. His voice is as startling as a slammed door; she has never heard such insistence and irritation in it before. The nerve! It's a revelation of the wrong sort. He glares at her until she retreats.

"That was Kate Ellis," Dinah says. "I saw her on Becky Adachi. Becky and I went to school together. And I never miss her show—unless I'm doing a brunch. I have a small catering company. And so there I was"—she struggles to her feet, using the dog to find her balance—"watching the show and there *he* was."

Paul has made a gesture to help her to her feet but thinks better of it. With his hand half-extended, he introduces himself instead. "I'm Paul Phillips."

Her hand is cold to the touch and seems almost without weight.

Her breath smells of recently drunk coffee. There is a faint dusting of powdered sugar on the fly of her jeans. "Hello, Paul. May I ask you how is it you have my dog?"

"What makes you so sure this is your dog?"

"Are you going to try and tell me Woody's your dog?"

"I'm saying that Shep's been here for a while and before that I don't know where he was."

"How long has he been living here?"

"Since November," Paul says, and wishes he had said October, or August—anything but the truth. But the truth shall set you free. Yes, he thinks, the truth: but tell it to God, not to some woman who appears out of nowhere.

"How did he get here?" Dinah asks.

Paul breathes in and exhales, letting the air out with reluctance, as if turning the page in a book whose ending he doesn't want to know. "Let's walk," he says. "We can go to my workshop and I'll tell you what I know."

They walk side by side, with the dog between them, laboriously trotting along, looking at neither of them. His attentions are on the low, suspenseful buzzing of a bee that is nearby—a few weeks ago he was stung in his hindquarters and since then he has been vigilant about flying pests.

"He seems to be dragging his back leg," Dinah says.

"He has Lyme disease. He's getting better though."

"Lyme disease?"

"The deer bring it in. The ticks that feed on them carry it. The deer don't ever get Lyme but they spread it around."

"I saw so many deer driving up here. They're so graceful. I always thought deer were good."

"Nothing's good," Paul says, opening the door for her. Shep steps over the threshold. But rather than trot over to his dog bed, with its plaid covering thoroughly furred in long hairs and snowy tufts of undercoat, he stands next to Dinah. He looks up at her and his tail is rotating with ever-increasing enthusiasm.

"Oh Woody, I was starting to give up hope."

Paul cannot help himself. "Come here, Shep," he says, and he puts his hand at his side, even going so far as to hold his fingers in a way that suggests he is holding a tidbit. Shep steps closer to Paul and touches his fingers with his nose, but without the energy he would normally expend if he truly believed there was a treat in Paul's hand, and it is all Paul can do to not grab Shep's collar and keep him close.

There are a couple of chairs on the far end of the workshop, near where most of the old windows are stored, and Paul with a gesture invites Dinah to sit with him there. With every step they make toward the chairs, the dog gravitates an inch or two closer to Dinah, though when they are seated he curls up directly in front of Paul.

"He's really not on top of his game," Dinah says. "Have you been feeding him commercial dog food?"

"It's the antibiotics," Paul says. "He does pretty well for himself, believe me."

"You're not going to give me a hard time about this, are you?"

"No, I don't want to give you any trouble. I just don't know how to tell if this is really your dog. There are a lot of dogs who look like Shep."

"I think you can tell. He obviously is excited to see me."

"You seem more excited than him."

"I wish I had chipped him," Dinah says.

"You mean with a microchip? Oh, I'd never do that to an animal."

"He was stolen from me. Last October. I've been looking for him ever since." Her eyes fill with tears and she lowers them; as she composes herself, she notices the powdered sugar in her lap and brushes it off.

As casually as he can, Paul asks, "Who stole him?" Just being this close to learning more about the man whose life he ended overwhelms Paul. His heart leaps within him.

"I met this man. I was walking with Woody and . . . it's really hard to explain, mostly because I've never done anything like that before. And obviously I never will again. We ended up together for a really short time until I sort of snapped out of it and came to my senses. I told him it was over and he seemed fine with it. A little later I had to go to a job and when I got back my place was trashed and Woody was gone. I blamed myself. I don't know what I was doing. I guess I just didn't want to be there while he packed his little bag and got out. Big mistake."

"Where is he now?" Paul asks.

"He's here. And you know it."

"No, sorry. I mean the guy who stole your dog."

Dinah narrows her eyes, and for a moment she seems to move in slow motion. "Why do you ask?" she finally says.

"Some guy steals your dog? What sort of guy? I mean what was he like?"

"You seem very curious about him," Dinah says. "His name was Robert. Bob," she adds, with a shudder, as if even this common bit of nicknaming was an intimacy she would rather forget.

"Bob," Paul says. He feels himself sinking. He places his hands on his knees, sits straighter.

"There was something sort of sweet about him," Dinah says. "I have to remind myself of that, because it all ended so horribly. But there was something about him, some lost little boy quality . . ." She sees the look of dismay on Paul's face, and stops right there.

"I just love this dog, to tell you the truth," Paul says, though even to say the word *truth* further undoes him.

"And you found Woody how?" She folds one leg over the other, crosses her arms, like tightly folding the flaps of a cardboard box.

Tell her, Paul thinks. *You saved her dog's life. She'll thank you.* But he remains silent.

"I guess you know someone killed Robert," Dinah says. "Actually, Robert wasn't really his name. He never told me anything but lies. I was really stupid. His name was William?" The interrogative lilt, the raised eyebrows.

"How would I know that?" Paul says. He wonders if his voice is barely audible, or if it just seems so because blood is pounding in his ears.

"The police called me. A week after the fact. They found one of my business cards with his stuff. They knew I didn't have anything to do with it and I couldn't help him, this detective from Tarrytown. It was so strange, I mean really. I had a friend who died in a plane crash, but this was worse, even though by the time I heard about it I sort of hated him. But you haven't told me—how'd you find Woody?" She lowers her voice. "Or maybe you don't remember."

"I remember, of course I remember."

She looks at him.

"I found him running along the side of the Taconic Parkway," Paul says.

There's a knock at the door, and after a brief moment's hesitation Kate lets herself in. "Is everything okay here?" she says to Paul. "I thought you were coming right back."

"Hey, Kate," he says, "this is Dinah Maloney. From Philadelphia. Shep's her dog."

Kate's face whitens, as if with one catastrophic contraction of the heart every drop of blood has drained from it. "Oh," she manages to say, reaching back for the door. "I'll be in the house."

As soon as Kate closes the door, Dinah uncrosses her legs, unfolds her arms. "I really need to be going," she says. "I've got a long drive and I'd like to get back home before it's the middle of the night."

"It feels like the middle of the night right now," Paul says.

"I know it must. You're probably very attached to him."

"Very."

"That's Woody for you."

"It's hard to talk about," Paul says. He looks down at the dog; it's impossible to imagine losing him.

"I hope you're not angry," Dinah says. When she gets out of her chair, Woody struggles to stand, too. He seems committed to following her.

"He's really hurting with this Lyme thing," Dinah says.

"He's already getting better. I'll give you the rest of his pills."

"I appreciate it."

But Paul makes no move to get up. He stares at the floor, with his hands on his knees.

"Do you want a moment alone, to say good-bye?" Dinah asks.

Paul shakes his head. "What am I going to do? Cry on him? He won't know what's going on."

Dinah purses her lips and nods her head. The dog is sitting next to her now and she is scratching the top of his head with one finger.

"I really should be going."

"I'll get those pills for you," Paul says.

"Great. I'll just wait outside."

As Paul walks toward the door, he gives Shep a final ear-tug. "Bye Shep," he says, his voice breaking.

He notices that Dinah has sidestepped a few extra feet away from him, giving him a wide berth.

Kate finds Paul in the kitchen, crying openly and looking in the cabinet over the sink for Shep's antibiotics, even though they are on the windowsill. There are bottles of aspirin, Advil, vitamin C and other supplements, and in his frustration he swats them all away, sending some deeper into the cabinet and sweeping others into the sink.

"She saw him on TV?" Kate asks.

Paul nods. He is holding on to the sink now with both hands because his legs feel useless.

"What are you doing?"

"I'm giving her his pills. I'll give her the rest of his food, too. She's driving back to Philadelphia and when five o'clock comes around he'll wonder where his food is."

"Paul . . ."

"Food, safety, and comfort. It's what he thinks about."

"The pills are on the windowsill," Kate says, but Paul hears only half of what she's said. His attentions are seized by the sound of running and when he looks out the old glass of the window he sees Dinah, wavy and prismatically tinted by the mouth-blown glass, racing for the Elkins Park Gourmet van with Shep at her side. She opens the door for him and he clumsily clambers in and then, with one panicked glance toward the house, she runs to the driver's side.

"Hey," Paul manages to shout, but she certainly can't hear him—her van starts with a roar—and even if she did she wouldn't stop. She throws the car into gear and swerves around Paul's truck, Kate's car, with gravel spitting out from her spinning wheels. And Paul, still holding on to the sink, cranes his neck and follows the van's flight with his eyes for as long as he can, wondering if he will perhaps see Shep turning back toward the house for one last farewell glance.

Three hours later, Paul, Kate, and Ruby sit at the dining table over a meal of bow-tie pasta—multicolored to amuse Ruby—sauced with pesto Paul made from the last of the basil. He is bereft and would rather not speak and so it has fallen to Kate to explain Shep's absence to Ruby, and she tells the story of the dog's miraculous reunion with his owner in such a way that Ruby is actually happy.

"This house needs a dog," Kate says. "This family needs a dog. I never thought I'd hear myself saying that, but it's true."

"We could get another dog," Paul manages to say.

Ruby looks at them, her eyes bright with gratitude. "I want one like Shep, though," she says.

"They're all a little bit like Shep," Paul says.

"Maybe a smaller version," Kate says. She is already thinking about shipping the poor beast to Europe—and doing it soon.

"Oh, I forgot," Ruby says, her voice rising. A bit of her old theatricality is returning. "Mr. Wexler wants to know if you can come to our class and talk to everyone."

"Who's Mr. Wexler?" Kate asks. "Your new teacher?"

"Only for social studies. Our fall unit is religions of the world. We don't just do the regular ones. And after class he told me you can come to talk to the whole class."

"Oh, sweetie," Kate says, "I don't know. I'm not an expert. It was just that one book."

Paul looks up from his food. "We could go to the Windsor SPCA and find a nice dog who needs a home."

"That's a good idea, baby," Kate says, reaching across the table and grazing his arm with her fingers. "We can drive over there tomorrow."

"One that doesn't look like Shep," Paul says.

"But I have school," Ruby says.

"Maybe after school," Paul says. He thinks of those dogs in their cages and the idea of saving one of them lifts his spirits for a moment.

"We'll make a nice home for him," Kate says.

Home. Paul looks around the room, at the grain of the plaster on their ceiling, the lingering light in their windows, the pale paint on the walls, the faces before him, Ruby, Kate, and his hands on the table. "I don't think I ever believed that something like this was even possible," he says.

"Oh, Paul," Kate says, her voice catching.

"Uh-oh," Ruby says.

"What is it, sweetie?" Kate asks.

"There's a birdy fairy angel on the wall."

"Oh no, Ruby," Kate says. "Not this again."

Ruby doesn't bother to defend herself. She simply points at the mirror on the wall, and both Kate and Paul obligingly turn around. Colored lights blue and red dance in the beveled glass around the mirror's border. Amazed, and believing for one moment that an angel really is on its way, Paul says, "Will you look at that?" He stands up and touches the flickering glass, red and blue, red and blue, until the mirror itself fills with the reflection of a squad car rolling up to the house, its emergency lights urgently spinning, though the car itself is moving slowly, in no particular rush.

ACKNOWLEDGMENTS

A novelist is essentially a lone wolf, and every working hour is spent in solitude. However, experience has taught me when and where to look for help, and now it's time to thank four people who have given me comfort and aid: my agent, Lynn Nesbit; my editor/publisher, Dan Halpern; Tom McDonough; and Jo Ann Beard.

About the author

About the book

Read on

Insights,
Interviews
& More ...

Meet Scott Spencer

WENDY EWALD

Scott Spencer is the author of nine previous novels, including *A Ship Made of Paper*, *Waking the Dead*, *Willing*, and the international bestseller *Endless Love*. He has been a Guggenheim Fellow and has twice been nominated for the National Book Award for fiction. Two of his novels have been the basis for major motion pictures. He has written extensively about music, primarily for *Rolling Stone*, and has profiled such artists as Sonny Rollins, Mark Knopfler, and Al Green. He has also written for many publications, such as the *New York Times*, *Harper's*, *O, the Oprah Magazine*, *Travel + Leisure*, the *New Yorker*, and *First of the Month*. He has taught writing at the Iowa Writers' Workshop, Columbia University, Williams College, and for the Bard Prison Initiative. He lives in Rhinebeck, New York, and New York City.

"I Believe in Dog"
Scott Spencer's *Fresh Air* Interview

FRESH AIR with Terry Gross, *the Peabody Award–winning weekday magazine of contemporary arts and issues, is one of public radio's most popular programs. Each week, nearly 4.5 million people listen to the show's intimate conversations broadcast on more than 525 National Public Radio (NPR) stations across the country. The program is also heard in Europe on NPR Worldwide and Radio Berlin.*

On September 15, 2010, Terry Gross interviewed Scott Spencer. They talked at length about Spencer's novel Man in the Woods. *What follows is a slightly condensed version of their conversation.*

TG: This is *Fresh Air.* I'm Terry Gross.

I always hope that I'll find something really special to read during my summer vacation, and I lucked out this year because I got an advance copy of the new novel by one of my favorite writers, Scott Spencer.

The novel was published yesterday, and Scott Spencer is my guest today. The book is called *Man in the Woods.* The main character, Paul Phillips, accidentally kills someone in the woods and has to decide whether to confess to the police or just continue his life.

He finds himself wishing there was a god he can turn to, a god that would understand what went wrong, but he doesn't believe. The woman he lives with does. She's a recovering alcoholic who's written a bestseller about recently finding Jesus and realizing "that most of my old friends think I'm ready for the funny farm, especially my liberal progressive friends who fear that I've gone all Pat Robertson on them."

Scott Spencer is the author of the bestselling books *Endless Love* and *A Ship Made of Paper.* He's taught fiction writing at Columbia University and in prison.

Scott Spencer, welcome back to *Fresh Air.* I really love the book.

SS: Oh, thank you, Terry, it's great to be here.

TG: Let's set the book up a bit. Paul is a carpenter who is driving and takes a detour from the highway to go into the woods to be alone. But soon he's not alone. A man joins him, a man who owes a gambling debt he can't repay. This man is paranoid because he thinks the guys he owes the money to are trying to hunt him down and that when they find him, they'll break his legs or kill him. This man also has a dog that he stole from his now-ex-girlfriend, and he treats the dog abusively. Would you explain what happens in the woods when he meets the main character, Paul?

SS: Paul sees this man yanking his dog around and hitting the dog. And it just is so deeply offensive to him that he wants to intervene. It starts off with him saying: Hey, stop doing that. But one thing leads to another. The man is so fearful that he feels that the only way to protect himself is to actually become even more violent toward the dog. And that enrages Paul, and they have an altercation, an altercation that really is the kind of pushing and shoving and futile hitting that people who don't really know how to fight engage in. But it does become very violent, and the man is accidentally killed.

TG: Your novels often have a turning point, a dividing line in which some dreadful, often unplanned and unintended horrible act has been committed, after which nothing will be the same. This time, it's this accidental, totally unintended murder. Why did you choose murder this time to be the turning point?

SS: I think that you're right that I am very interested in lives being changed very suddenly. I'm interested in how close our orderly lives are to utter chaos. We certainly have seen the way savagery can break out in societies that a year before were orderly.

In my novels, I've had people change their life by setting a fire, and I've had people changing their lives by failing to prevent someone from leaving. But this act of—and I don't really call it murder; I really call it manslaughter because there was no intention—this act of violence, this expression of some inner rage and some inner beastliness is compelling to me partly because I can identify with it. I think our capacity for violence is something that we all wonder about. I think we all wonder if we're capable of an act of violence, and under what circumstances we would be capable of it and what the aftermath would be.

I'm also very interested in writing about conscience. And I wanted to test somebody's conscience. I wanted to really push somebody to the very edge of what they could accept about themselves.

TG: Do you think of this as your cerebral version of a crime novel, a crime novel about someone who isn't a criminal type, someone who hasn't been in a fight since he was a teenager, someone who never intended to commit a crime?

SS: Well, I'm not sure that I think of it that way. You know, it might be that without my having intended it to be. I was really moved by something I read; I think it was one of Camus' notebooks or diaries when he says a guilty conscience needs to confess. To which he adds: A work of art is a confession. I thought that was so beautiful, and it reminded me of something that I wanted to deal with in my own writing. I also wanted to deal with dogs because I live with so many dogs. So, all these things sort of converged and I found myself with a book on my hands.

TG: How many dogs do you have?

SS: I have three dogs.

TG: Okay. Let's get to dogs. We've seen Paul commit manslaughter. He accidentally kills a man who has been abusing his dog. After the murder, Paul wishes he could believe in a god. He wishes he could believe in a god that is watching us and that understands our intentions, understands what we are really thinking and the reasons behind our actions. But he doesn't believe in that god.

So let's get to the question of the dog. Paul has to decide what to do with the dog. Does he keep the dog? Does he get rid of the dog? Because the dog is the witness and the dog is the evidence. Dog is God spelled backwards. Do you believe in dog more than you believe in God?

SS: I definitely believe in dog. There's no question, you can't have as much dog hair in your house as I do and not believe in dog. And God was one of the things I was most interested in figuring out while writing this book. At one point, I thought, I'm really writing a religious book here. Then at another point, I said, I'm really writing a very irreligious book or anti-religious book. When I finally finished the book, I realized what I had written was something that was   this is not a contradiction in terms—passionately agnostic, really as passionate about agnosticism as Graham Greene is passionate about his Catholicism, because I could feel the otherworldly intentions of fate hovering over my characters. Yet I could not ever quite come to a true narrative understanding that this fate was really some sort of otherworldly intelligence that made sense enough that we could call it God.

TG: Is being passionate about agnosticism a position that you only recently arrived at?

SS: Yes. I've bounced between atheism and a desire to have some sort of religious meaning to my life. You know, I was just talking to my mother last week and she talked to me about when I was a little kid. Sometimes she'd have to bring me to a church, not that we went to church because my parents were militantly atheistic, but she'd go to a church for some community meeting and then turn around and I'd be gone. And she'd find me in one of the pews praying fervently. And I always had this feeling that I wished that I had religion and a belief in God, and that the ritual and the living metaphor in which I could explain my life was available to me. And there would be times when I would feel such withering contempt for the whole thing that I was sort of glad that I hadn't entered into that system of thought.

But, you know, novelists think a lot about God. They say doctors play God, and they do to an extent because they're always monkeying around or trying to change the body's fate. But they're dealing with what's already there. We novelists take that God thing one step further. We create whole worlds and then we people them. And then we tell the people what to do: we make them fall in love or jump out of windows. So there is that curiosity about God that I think all novelists have.

TG: Were you brought up with a religion?

SS: No, I was brought up militantly without a religion.

TG: What was the religion you were not brought up with, if you know what I mean?

SS: Let me list all the religions I wasn't brought up with. But my parents' parents were Jews.

TG: But you mentioned going to church.

SS: Well, it was a church, but my mother wasn't there for religious reasons. She was there for a community meeting. My parents were civic-minded. They were always going to meetings. And this one happened to be in a church.

I was raised on the south side of Chicago in a working-class neighborhood. My father worked in a steel mill. And our neighbors were, by and large, either Polish or Irish Catholics. And from time to time, one of their older sisters would get married or confirmed. I would go to church, and I would be filled with not only awe but longing. Really, it was only out of some sort of great love and respect for my parents that I kept it to myself because my feeling was that they would be absolutely heartbroken and mortified if I ever confessed to them that I would like to give that churchgoing thing a crack. So much so that I would lie on our little lawn and stare up at the sky and wait and wait and wait for some sort of definitive sign that would give me the courage to go in and tell my parents that I'd had it with being an atheist, that it was time for me to go to church.

TG: But it had to be church, not a synagogue?

SS: I didn't even know about synagogues yet. This might have been before synagogues came to America. A few years later, some new houses were built in our area. The houses that we lived in were $11,000, and these new houses were kind of posh, $14,000 houses. And some Jewish families moved in, and suddenly, there was a temple in the area. So that became another place where I would have liked to have gone, although maybe it's because my first taste of religion was in the Catholic Church, nothing really that I've ever seen since has had that kind of visceral impact on me.

TG: Because there are so often crimes that are usually unintentional, or acts of passion gone wrong in your novels,

I find it especially interesting that you've been teaching writing in prison as part of the Bard Prison Initiative, in which prisoners can actually earn a degree.

You're spending time teaching people who have been convicted of a crime and who are living in that place in which you are put away to pay for your crime and theoretically to reflect on what you've done. I'm curious what that experience is like for you—as somebody who's written about people who have transgressed, who've crossed the line.

SS: It's the most amazing teaching experience I've ever had. The prison population I worked with were all guys, all men in a maximum security prison. They had all done really severely wrong things. I had one man in my class who was there for armed robbery, and he was the only nonviolent, I mean relatively nonviolent, criminal I was teaching.

It was inspiring in so many ways because you couldn't find fifteen men who read more carefully and more passionately and with more eagerness and hunger than the guys in that class. They read everything from Robert Stone to Edgar Allan Poe to Alice Munro, and they always had the most complex and interesting and engaged response to the work.

A lot of them were men whose formal schooling outside of the prison was patchy at best. One of the things that you sort of despair about when you're teaching in MFA programs is you have writers who actually have a lot of talent and have chops and who have a great deal of desire to write, but they just haven't had that much happen to them yet in life. So their stories tend to either be notional or too youthfully observed or just about things that are basically about their families.

But in the case of the people in the prison writing program, they had a lot to write about. They had a lot of stuff that you sort of eagerly go to writers to find out because they've seen something of the world that you haven't seen. Just the way people would read Melville's early novels to find out what life was like in the South Seas, you would want to read these guys' stories to find out what life was like in some of their communities.

TG: Did you feel like you were getting insights into the kind of life, the kind of mind and the kind of conscience—or lack of conscience—that you want to understand more about as a novelist?

SS: One of the things that I learned from working with these guys is how alike we all are. Most of these men, if I had met them somehow under different circumstances, I would probably not have been able to guess that they had killed anybody or had been part of some vast criminal undertaking. The commonality that we have just as human beings is, for me, the most moving and the most instructive part of working with them.

TG: What's it like for you the moment you walk into the prison, and what's the moment like when you leave the prison? It must feel pretty overwhelming.

SS: Yeah. It is overwhelming. Between my car, when I pull into the prison parking lot, and the classroom where I meet with the students, I go through at least twelve locked gates, all of them big thick cast-iron gates with these gigantic jailhouse keys. And it's a maze. You're always escorted. You can never go anywhere alone, of course. Although, in the classroom I am alone; there's not a guard there. It's just me and the students. And so you are going deeper and deeper and deeper into the cavern of this prison and you're passing guys, some of them being marched by guards with their hands handcuffed behind their back and some of them are pushing mops and some of them are getting ready to work in the cafeteria, some of them looking at you, most of them not looking at you, everyone's sort of locked in their own personal space, and you do feel this tremendous despair.

Whatever you think about criminal justice, whether you think these guys have gotten the right deal, whether you think their lives could've been different if they'd been given different breaks in life, whether you think their sentences could've been different if they'd had better representation, whatever your feeling is about crime and punishment, you'd have to be deeply anesthetized not to feel this great sinking sense of sadness to be in an environment where there are hundreds and hundreds and hundreds of men locked up in cages. It's really nightmarish and overwhelming. It's a terrible thing to see but it does make you very, very appreciative of your own life.

You asked me what it was like going in and going deeper and deeper into this environment where everybody is in a cage. The opposite is when you walk out and suddenly there's the sky and there's your car and you're going to get in your car and you're going to drive home and in forty-five minutes you're going to be in your own house and your girlfriend's going to be there and you're going to eat whatever you want and drink whatever you want and do whatever you want. It's stuff that we take for granted, but it feels absolutely like you've won the lottery every time you leave that place.

TG: Your novel is called *Man in the Woods* and in it, one of the characters says, "Guys get into the woods. We go back to our elemental selves and stuff happens." And then he says, "Men do what men do. We're just part of the scheme of things. We're just nature." After reading that, I read a piece that you wrote for *O* magazine, in which you wrote: "The simple truth is that men are somewhat violent, even those of us who abhor violence. Even if we are cerebral, out of shape, blind in one eye, many of us expect of ourselves levels of daring and aggression that would quite frankly horrify most women, if it didn't reduce them to helpless laughter." Do you believe that somewhere deep inside most men there's a violent instinct, and that it can be unleashed in the woods?

SS: I do believe that. I do also want to say that I'm not terribly out of shape or blind in one eye.

TG: Okay.

SS: But I think that men have an acceptance of the validity of violence. I believe that if a man is walking down the street and some stranger comes up and smacks him in the back of the head, and if the man who is smacked in the back of the head just says "Oow," and continues to walk on and doesn't do something about it, his greatest grudge will be against himself at that point. He won't say, "What was wrong with that crazy guy who just came up to me for no reason and smacked me in the back of the head?" He'll ask, "What was wrong with me that I didn't respond in kind?" And I do think that that is gender specific.

TG: In the same article you wrote, "From the beginning of organized society, boys have been raised to accept the idea that one day they might be called upon to either kill or be killed, to be ready to defend their home, their villages, their tribes against harm." Have you ever felt that pressure to physically defend somebody or a home against harm?

SS: I've always felt that that is a responsibility that I was born to because I'm male. When I was ten years old, my father told me men don't sleep as deeply as women because we need to be ready if somebody comes. . . . I haven't been in some situation like Dustin Hoffman's character in *Straw Dogs* who's there with his little wire-rimmed glasses and his sort of porn-star-looking wife while all these cretinish locals pound on the windows and try to get in, but there have been a couple of instances when I've had to sort of man up, as we say, and step between someone whom I felt was mine to protect somehow and someone who was going to do them some harm.

TG: Would you share one of those instances?

SS: I'll share a funny and somewhat banal one: my mother got out of a taxicab and she was having this huge argument with the cab driver because, in her view, he had taken her way out of her way as a way of running up the fare. And I'm not sure that that was really true, but she was very, very irritated at the idea that this guy was cheating her. And when she got out of the cab, she said this guy cheated me on my fare. And the cab driver, who was a guy about my size, maybe a few years younger than me at the time, you know, got out and wagged his finger in my mother's face and called her a name, a pretty bad name. And I thought to myself, oh no. Now I have to do something. This guy is probably, in the full scheme of things, he's probably in the right, because I was looking at the fare on the meter. It didn't seem unreasonable. She had come in from La Guardia; it was all the way to the Village. It seemed like a normal fare. But on the other hand, he had crossed the line. He had called my mother a name. So I hit him.

TG: Wow.

SS: I hit him. Not that hard.

TG: On the face?

SS: No. I hit him in the stomach.

TG: Oh, you punched him.

SS: Yeah. I punched him.

TG: What did he do?

SS: He called me a name and he just looked at us like, "You two deserve each other. I'm getting out of here."

"I Believe in Dog" *(continued)*

TG: This idea that deep inside men is an almost genetic impulse to be prepared to defend friends, family, home, cities, villages against harm—I'm wondering if you think that's a philosophy you created to explain these occasional impulses that you have.

SS: You know, it's very hard to say what anyone is genetically because you can never see anybody outside of society, because people don't exist outside of society. You can't find a person who isn't culturally determined to one extent or another.

TG: True.

SS: We all are. So I don't know. I mean until we start making people in test tubes. . . .

TG: I thought we were doing that.

SS: But then we send them off someplace and then we have to keep them in the lab and study them. But even then, they'll be victims of some sort of depravation. So it's very hard to say what people are in essence. I think it's one of the jobs that novels have, really. I mean it's one of the things that keep people reading, that we are endlessly sort of amazed and curious and perplexed about what is our nature.

TG: Your biggest hit, in terms of your books, is *Endless Love,* which was a bestseller and was adapted into a film that had little to do with the book that it's based on. It's a wonderful, wonderful book.

SS: Thank you, Terry.

TG: The title song was a hit for Diana Ross. Who did she duet with on that? Lionel Richie?

SS: Lionel Richie. Who I think wrote it.

TG: I've just been thinking about how the title of your new book is *Man in the Woods*. It's not *A* Man in the Woods. It's not *The* Man in the Woods. It's about Man in the woods. The lack of an *a* or *the* in the title is significant. So I was thinking of the title song from the movie adaptation of your book *Endless Love*. The lyrics are something like "And your eyes, your eyes, your eyes, they tell me how much you care. Oh yes, you will always be my endless love." No. A person isn't your endless love—the endless love in your title is about the kind of love that won't stop. The kind of obsessive, dangerous love that forces a person to transgress all ethical boundaries and become a horrible stalker and commit horrible acts. How did you feel about the word *my* in "my endless love"?

SS: Well, it was actually the least of my worries. And who knows what's going to happen next, because I just learned a couple of months ago that Universal Pictures, which owns the rights to that book, is planning now to do a remake.

TG: No. Really?

SS: Yeah. It makes you want to quote William Burroughs.

TG: Who said?

"I Believe in Dog" *(continued)*

SS: "Pack your ermines, Mary. We're getting out of here right now."

TG: Scott Spencer, it's always great to talk with you. Thank you so much.

SS: Thank you, Terry. It was wonderful to talk to you.

A Reading Group Guide for *Man in the Woods*

1. *Man in the Woods* begins in the last two months of the twentieth century. Why do you think the author chose that time? What do you think the lead-up to what was then called Y2K (Year 2000) has to do with the themes of this novel?

2. The novel is divided into two parts, and each begins with a line from a country song. Why do you think the author chose those quotations, and what bearing do you think they have on the story and the underlying themes of the book?

3. At one point in the novel, Paul Phillips and his friend are walking through the woods, and his friend recalls that early settlers in America used to believe that the American woods were a kind of church, and, in fact, some preachers used to say, "No Jesus in the parlor." How does this idea play itself out in *Man in the Woods*?

4. Though secular in tone, *Man in the Woods* seems to be imbued with religious imagery and religious concerns—there are angels, serpents, etc. Can you identify the ones that seemed most meaningful to you and discuss how they work their way through the novel?

5. What happens to Kate's belief in a Higher Power and what happens to Paul's?

6. Shep is, for some readers, a character in this novel as fully realized as the human characters. What do you think of Shep? What is his function within the novel? How is he different from other dogs in other novels?

7. If Shep were given a voice, would his account of the events cast a different light on the story? What is Shep feeling by the story's end?

8. From time to time, the novel cuts away to a police investigation, in which logic and a belief in the law lead a detective through a step-by-step search for the person who has killed the man found in Martingham State Park. How do this character and his actions lend themselves to the book's overall story and meaning? Who else in this novel is trying to bring the killer to justice?

9. Paul Phillips is a classic American type—the loner who communes with nature and makes his living with his hands. *Man in the Woods* examines the conflict between the individual and the community. Did you think Paul needed to be punished for his act of violence? Can a person be his own judge and jury, or does he need to stand trial in a court of law? Are there laws that go beyond earthly law? Can a person be pure of heart and still deserve to be punished for wrongdoing?